PENGUIN MODERN CLASSICS

Aranyak: Of the Forest

Bibhutibhushan Bandyopadhyay (1894-1950) was one of the greatest Bengali writers. His best known work is the autobiographical novel *Pather Panchali*, now published in Penguin Modern Classics in a new translation. This novel and its sequel, *Aparajito*, have been translated into several languages and also inspired Satyajit Ray's iconic and award-winning cinematic trilogy. Badyopadhyay was posthumously awarded the Rabindra Puruskar in 1951, the most prestigious literary award in West Bengal, for his novel *Ichamati*.

Bhaskar Chattopadhyay is an author and translator. His novels include *Patang* and his translations include *14 Stories That Inspired Satyajit Ray*.

BIBHUTIBHUSHAN BANDYOPADHYAY

Aranyak: Of the Forest

Translated by Bhaskar Chattopadhyay

PENGUIN BOOKS

An imprint of Penguin Random House

PENGUIN BOOKS

USA | Canada | UK | Ireland | Australia
New Zealand | India | South Africa | China

Penguin Books is part of the Penguin Random House group of companies
whose addresses can be found at global.penguinrandomhouse.com

Published by Penguin Random House India Pvt. Ltd
4th Floor, Capital Tower 1, MG Road,
Gurugram 122 002, Haryana, India

Penguin
Random House
India

First published in Penguin Books by Penguin Random House India 2022

ISBN 9780143426011

Typeset in Adobe Garamond Pro by Manipal Technologies Limited, Manipal
Printed at Replika Press Pvt. Ltd, India

www.penguin.co.in

CHAPTER 1

[1]

It was a long time ago—must have been fifteen or sixteen years earlier. I was sitting idle after completing my graduation. There was hardly a prospective door in the commercial district of Kolkata that I hadn't knocked on. But no one had offered me a job.

I remember it was the day of the Saraswati Puja. My long tenure was the only reason why they hadn't thrown me out of the hostel yet, but that didn't stop the manager from sending me one notice after another, requesting payment of rent. I felt suffocated, miserable and helpless. There was a puja ceremony going on downstairs with much fanfare that morning, complete with a large idol of the goddess. When I woke up in the morning and realized that the few offices that had shown me a gleam of hope would all be closed for business today, I decided to make the most of the day by roaming in the streets from one *pandal*, a marquee, to another, trying my best—if at least for a change—not to think of the frightening future that lay ahead of me.

I was just about to pick myself up and step out, when Jagannath, one of the servants in the hostel, walked into my room and handed over a small piece of paper to me. A quick glance made me realize that the manager had sent one more notice. Apparently, an elaborate feast had been arranged after the puja, and everyone in the hostel had contributed, over and above their usual monthly rent. I, on the other hand, had not even paid last two months' rent, and had been instructed—in a manner as curt as written words could convey—to send at least Rs 10 through the servant, failing which, I would have to look for someplace else to have my meals from the following day.

A very valid demand, I thought, but a thorough rummaging of my pockets yielded only a couple of rupees and a few hapless annas. Avoiding eye contact with the servant and without saying anything by way of response to the missive he had so hopefully carried to me, I stepped out of the hostel. Loud music was being played in various pandals in the neighbourhood, young boys and girls were busy playing and clamouring in the lanes, an irresistible aroma was wafting out of the sweet-seller's shop around the corner, four men were playing *shehnais*—an Indian musical instrument played during auspicious occasions—on a raised platform above the gates of Hindu College on the other side of the main road, and several groups of men and women were returning from the market with a varied range of items peeping out of their bags—items that would all be used in the puja ceremonies at their respective homes.

As I walked, I wondered where I could go. It had been more than a year now that I had been sitting idle after quitting the job at the Jorashanko Primary School. Well, it would be a mistake to say that I was sitting idle. There was not a single merchant office, school, newspaper or rich man's residence that I had not visited—several times at that. But everywhere I went, I met with the same response—no vacancy.

As such hopeless thoughts trailed through my mind, I chanced upon Satish all of a sudden. He and I used to be roommates at the Hindu Hostel, he was now a lawyer in Alipore Court. By the looks of it, he didn't seem to make much. Apparently, a side-job of tutoring the child of an affluent man in Ballygunge was destined to act as a puny raft that kept his family afloat on the raging waves of the ocean of life. Satish had a raft, at least. I, on the other hand, didn't even have a straw of hope that I could clutch on to, in order to keep myself from drowning. I often shuddered to think of what the future held for me, but that morning, on meeting Satish, I was able to ignore such ominous thoughts for some time, primarily because he patted my back and said,

'Where are you headed, Satyacharan? Let's go and watch the Puja ceremony at the Hindu Hostel—that old den of ours. And yes, there will be a concert in the evening—you must come. Remember Avinash? From Ward 6? The son of the zamindars from Mymensingh? Yes, he is a famous singer now. He will sing tonight. I take care of a few small jobs for their estate every now and then, so he sent me a card. Do come, he will be very happy to see you.'

My mind went back five or six years, during the days of college, when festivities and entertainment used to feature right at the top of our existential needs. Standing in the middle of the road that day, on hearing Satish's words, it occurred to me that things were no different even now. My heart danced in joy! And to add to it all, on reaching the Hindu Hostel, I received an invitation to lunch from the resident students, several of whom turned out to be from my own village.

'The concert is in the evening, isn't it?' I said, by way of a courteous formality, 'There's still a lot of time. I'll go back to my hostel and come back after lunch.'

My weak-spirited protest fell on deaf ears. Had it not, I would have had to spend the day of the Saraswati Puja on an empty stomach. Because no matter what, I would not have brought myself to gorge on the fancy dishes back at the hostel shamelessly. No, not after such a strong letter from the manager, and certainly not when I had not contributed a single rupee to the event. But providence/destiny had different plans for me that day, to my convenience for a change. After a hearty lunch, I accompanied Satish and settled down in a comfortable seat at the concert. Albeit for a few hours, I found myself submerged in the joy and cheer of the good old college days. Did it really matter, after all—whether I got a job or not, whether the manager was waiting for me with a grim face back at the hostel or not? I pushed all those thoughts aside and let my mind drown in the sweet melodies of thumris and kirtans. By the time the concert ended, it was 11 p.m. Avinash and I caught up and spoke briefly. In college, he and I used to be the heads of the debating club. I remembered, on one occasion, Sir Gurudas Bandyopadhyay had been invited to preside over a session. The topic in motion was—'Religion studies should be made compulsory in educational institutions'. Avinash spoke for, and I against. After several rounds of spirited arguments and counter arguments, the judge ruled in my favour. Since then, Avinash and I became very good friends, although this was the first time that we were meeting each other after college.

Avinash said, 'Come, I'll drop you in my car. Where do you live?'

When we reached the gate of my hostel, he said, 'Listen, why don't you come home for tea tomorrow? Let's say around 4 p.m.? I live in Harrington Street. Make a note of it in that little diary of yours—33/2. Don't forget.'

The next day, I asked around and made my way to Harrington Street. Soon, I found my friend's house. It wasn't a very large building, but there were beautiful gardens both in the front and behind the house. There were wisteria vines on the gates, and a Nepali chowkidar was wiping a brass plate that proudly announced Aavinash's father's name. A pathway covered with brick-dust meandered through the verdant lawns and made its way to the house. The lawns themselves were skirted by *champa*, mango and *muchakunda* trees. A large car waited patiently under the portico. There was a sure yet muted sign of abundance everywhere. A short flight of stairs took me to a drawing room. Avinash came down from his room upstairs and welcomed me with open arms. We settled down in the comfortable chairs and almost immediately found ourselves lost in nostalgic reminiscences of our college days. Avinash's father was a renowned zamindar in Mymensingh, but presently, none of the members of the family were present at their Kolkata home. The entire family had visited their ancestral home last month to attend a family wedding, and hadn't returned yet.

After a long conversation, Avinash asked me, 'What are you doing these days, Satya?'

I said, 'I used to teach at a school in Jorashanko, but now-a-days I'm quite idle. I don't think I'll go back to teaching again. I'm trying to see if something works out somewhere else . . . there have been some assurances from one or two places . . . let's see . . . .'

I had no option but to lie about the assurances. Avinash belonged to a rich family, owners of a huge estate, but he was also my friend. Under no circumstances could I give him the impression that I was begging him for a job.

Avinash thought for a few seconds and said, 'A deserving person like you won't have any problems finding a job. You have studied law as well, haven't you?'

'Yes, I cleared the exams too. But I don't want to practise.'

Avinash said, 'Well then, I have a proposal. You see, we have a forest estate in the district of Purnia. Almost twenty–thirty thousand acres of forest land. We have someone in the position of Collector there, who is in charge of general administration and rent collection. But we are looking for someone trustworthy to take care of the region, and to manage the affairs of the estate. Would you be interested?'

Human ears have often been known to be deceptive. I was sure I had misheard Avinash! I had been roaming the streets of this city for more than a year in search of a job. And today, just like that, over a cup of tea, a job was being offered to me?

But I had to maintain my dignity. Making an epic effort to suppress my excitement, I said, quite casually, 'Let me think about it. You will be at home tomorrow, I presume?'

I had known Avinash for several years; he was quite an open-minded and straightforward person. He said, 'What's there to think about, Satya? I'll write to my father today. We're looking for someone we can trust. We certainly don't want someone from the extended family as an employee there—because most of these people are utterly dishonest. That estate needs an educated and intelligent man like you. Thirty thousand acres of land; so many subjects and tenants.

We don't want to leave such a mammoth responsibility to just about anyone. You are my friend, I know you personally. Just nod, and I'll write to my father and ask him to send the appointment letter right away.'

[2]

The details of how I secured the job are quite redundant here, and independent of the objective of this story. It would suffice to say that two weeks after having tea at Avinash's place, I found myself stepping off a train at a small BNW railway station, with luggage in hand.

It was a wintry evening. Vast expansive fields lay all around me, with a faint shadow slowly descending upon them. A thin veil of fog hung over the head of the trees lining the horizon. Pea-plants lined both sides of the train tracks, and the cool dusk breeze, laden with the soft and sweet smell of peas, somehow gave the impression that the life that I was about to begin would be a very lonely one—as lonely as this wintry evening, as empty as the vast undulating fields that surrounded me, and as desolate as the indigo forest in the distance.

I spent the whole night travelling more than thirty miles in a bullock cart; the rags and blankets that I had so confidently brought along from Kolkata soon turned wet and ice cold under the straw shed of the cart, and I realized that I had grossly underestimated the weather. When the sun rose in the morning, I noticed that we were still on the move. The sights around me had completely changed though, nature seemed to have donned a whole new attire. No more farms were to be seen, no habitation either; only woods and jungles of varying kinds—small and big, thin and dense—often interspersed with bleak open fields, with hardly any vegetation on them.

I reached the *cutcherry*, the estate's administrative office, around ten in the morning. Around four to five acres of land had been cleared off in the middle of the jungle and a few huts had been erected with the help of bamboos, thatch and what seemed like timber from the jungle itself. The walls were made of dry grass and the narrow trunks of wild pines, cemented off with mud.

As soon as I entered the cutcherry, a strong smell of freshly cut straw, half-dried grass and sliced bamboos reached my nose, and I realized that the rooms themselves must have been built quite recently. I was then told that the cutcherry used to be somewhere on the other side of the woods earlier, and that there having been a scarcity of water in the winters at the erstwhile location, these new rooms had to be built. Apparently, there was a stream nearby, which made this spot quite suitable for habitation.

[3]

I had spent almost all my life in Kolkata, never having to think of a life without the company of friends, or one sans libraries, theatres, cinemas, clubs and evening soirees. Let alone live in one, I had never even imagined in my wildest dreams that a place so desolate could even exist. And then, one fine day, I suddenly found myself in one such nightmarish place, for merely the love of a few rupees. Days went by, I watched the sun rise every morning in the eastern sky over the distant hills and the tall trees, and then witnessed the reddish hues of vermilion all around me as the same sun kissed the tips of the palm trees to the west and dove behind them at dusk. How I would fill the time between these two events—that remained my primary concern for the first few days. Doing some work would help, of course, but I was too new a stranger in the land to comprehend the local tongue, and too inexperienced to delegate work. All I could do was to sit in my room all day and read the books that I had brought along from the city. And so I did. The handful of people working in the cutcherry could be best described as utterly uncivilized barbarians. Neither did they understand what I had to say, nor could I make out what they tried to tell me. The first ten–fifteen days were terrible! Every now and then, I resolved to quit my job and go back to the city; after all, it was better to survive on half a meal a day in the city than to die a stifling death in this godforsaken place. I realized I had made a big mistake by accepting Avinash's offer; this lonely life was simply not for me.

Night had fallen, I was sitting in my chair with such thoughts going through my mind, when the door parted and Goshtho Chakraborty, an elderly clerk of the cutcherry, entered the room. This was the only gentleman with whom I could have a conversation in Bengali. Goshtho Babu had been here for a long time—at least seventeen or eighteen years. He originally hailed from some village near Bonpash station in Burdwan district.

'Come sit, Goshtho Babu,' I said.

Goshtho Babu occupied the other chair in the room and said, 'I stopped by to tell you something, in private, of course. Don't trust anyone in this place. This is not Bengal. Most of the people here aren't very good.'

'I imagine you could say that about most people back in Bengal as well, don't you think?'

'That's true, Manager Babu. What do you think made me come here, in the first place? That, and malaria. The first few days were pathetic, absolutely stifling. And now? Let alone going back home, even if I go to Purnia or Patna for work, I can't stay away for more than a couple of days.'

I looked at Goshtho Babu's face with amusement—what on earth was the old man saying?

I asked, 'Why can't you stay away? Do you find the forest appealing?'

The old man stared at me for some time and smiled a little—'You could say that, Manager Babu; yes, you could say that. You'll see for yourself. You've been here only for a few days, and your heart must still be back in the city. Moreover, you're young, less than half my age. But give it a few days, and then you'll see.'

'See what?'

'The forest will get to you, Manager Babu. Gradually, you'll stop liking any kind of din or clamour, you'll abhor crowds, and you'll embrace the solitude. That's exactly what happened to me too. Why, just last month I had been to Munger with some court papers. All I could think of was how to get out of there.'

I thought to myself—God willing, I wouldn't have to know what that felt like. I would be gone far before that.

Goshtho Babu said, 'Keep the gun next to your pillow when you sleep. You never know. Sometime ago, dacoits had looted the cutcherry. But don't worry, since then we don't keep any cash here anymore.'

I asked out of curiosity, 'Is that so? When did this happen?'

'Not very long ago—let me see—must have been eight or nine years ago. You'll get to know a lot about this place gradually; it's not one of the safest places to be in, certainly not as safe as the city. There are dense forests all around, you know—if someone robs you and kills you, no one will even come to know.'

As Goshto Babu left, I rose from my chair and stepped up to the open window. Far away, the moon was rising above the heads of the trees. And with its silvery disc in the background, a wild tamarisk had spread its branches, painting such a pretty picture that it instantly reminded me of the inkworks by the Japanese painter, Hokusai.

Of all places, *this* was where I had to find a job! Had I known how dangerous this place was, I would have never said yes to Avinash.

Despite my concerns, though, one thing was undeniably true. I couldn't help but marvel at the beauty of the rising moon.

[4]

Not very far from the cutcherry, there was a small hillock, and on it, stood an ancient and mammoth banyan tree. The locals called it Grant Sahib's banyan tree. How it came to acquire such a name, I did not know. One lazy afternoon, as I went out for a little stroll, I climbed my way to the top of the hillock with the intention of watching the sun set in the western horizon.

Standing in the shade of Grant Sahib's banyan tree, I looked out towards the horizon and was immediately taken aback by how far and wide my eyes could see—my hostel in Kolutola, the club near the Kapalitola bridge where my friends and I would spend hours chatting away, my favourite bench near the Goldighi Lake—on which I used to sit every day at roughly this hour of the day and watch the steady stream of people and traffic on College Street. They were so far away. My heart suddenly seemed so empty! What was I doing? What was I thinking? What end of the world had I come to, for the sake of a job? How can anyone live here? There wasn't a soul to be seen anywhere around, no matter where I looked—not a single person with whom I could hold a conversation. These uneducated, uncivilized natives, who stared at my face blankly when I spoke to them—how could I spend the rest of my days in their company? Standing there under the shade of that tree that evening and staring into the horizon, my heart ached, and I felt somewhat scared. I made up my mind that very moment—there were just a few days to go till the end of that month, I would somehow make it to the end of the next and then write a detailed letter of resignation to Avinash, get back to Kolkata, receive a warm welcome by my civilized friends, eat civilized food, listen to the civilized notes of civilized music, interact with my civilized fellowmen and fill my ears and mind with the daily din, clamour and commotion of a civilized society.

Little did I know that I loved living amidst human beings so much. Or that I loved human beings so much, for that matter! Perhaps I couldn't always do unto them what I expected them to do unto me, but I did love them. Why else would I be so aggrieved to be stripped of their company?

The old Muslim bookseller, who set up his shop on the footpath against the railing of Presidency College every day, whose second hand books and magazines I browsed through oh so often—perhaps, I should have bought a few from him, but I never did. Even he seemed like a dear friend today, and I seemed to miss him sorely.

I returned to the cutcherry, entered my room, lit the lantern and sat in my chair with a book in my hand, when Sepoy Muneshwar Singh walked in and greeted me with a salute. I had managed to pick up a few isolated words of the native dialect by now, and I put them to good use.

'What is it, Muneshwar?'

'Huzoor, if you could kindly ask Goshtho Babu to give me some money to buy a small iron pot, it would be a great help.'

'A pot?' I asked, 'Why?'

Muneshwar's face lit up in the anticipation of receipt. In a polite voice, he said, 'A small pot would be very useful for me, Huzoor. I could carry it along with me, I could cook my food in it, and it would be quite hard, so I could even use it to store some of my things. I don't have any utensil to eat my food in, Huzoor. I've been thinking about it for several months now—but as you know, a thing like that would cost around six annas, and a poor man like me can't afford it. So, I thought, let me go and speak to Huzoor sahib, Huzoor is most kind, he will understand my plight.'

That an insignificant item like a pot could be an aspiration for someone, that its possession could be something that someone could desire so passionately—that was what surprised me the most. Were there really such poor people in this world who could dream of an iron pot worth six annas when they slept? I had only heard of the poverty in these regions. But not once had I imagined that the natives were *so* poor. I felt quite bad for the man.

The next day, thanks to a chit with my signature on it, Muneshwar Singh went to the market of Naugacchia, procured a number-five-size iron pot, entered my room, placed his prized possession on the floor, struck a smart salute and said, 'That's it, Huzoor. Thanks to your kind heart, I have a pot now!'

As I stared at the sparkling smile on his face, for the first time in the one month that I had spent in the forest, I said to myself, 'Such nice people! They're so poor and sad!'

CHAPTER 2

[1]

No matter how hard I tried, I just couldn't bring myself to adjust with my surroundings here. I'd arrived from Bengal, lived all my life in Kolkata, the loneliness of the forest seemed to weigh in like a heavy rock on my chest.

On some days, I would go out on long walks in the evening. As long as I would remain in the periphery of the cutcherry, I could still hear one or two voices, but even those died down once I took a turn around the bend of the path and looked back to find that the cutcherry compound was now hidden behind rows of wild tamarisks and tall catkins. And it was during those times that it seemed to me that I was completely alone in this world. And then, as far as my legs could carry me, all I could see around me were dense forests on both sides of the path. Jungles and shrubs, *gajari* trees, thorny babuls, groves of wild bamboo, bushes of cane. Thanks to the setting sun, the heads of the trees would seem like someone had smeared them with vermillion—the sweet smell of wild flowers and plump vines would waft around in the cool evening breeze, a sweet din of bird-calls would emanate from the bushes, and I would often find Himalayan wild parrots perched on the branches around me. Verdant fields ran far and wide, without any constraint whatsoever, green trees swayed in joy without a care in the world.

It was during these times that it often occurred to me that I had never seen this image of nature anywhere else. As far as I my eyes could see, all of this was mine, and mine alone. I was the only human here, no one would ever disturb my solitude—and if I so desired, I could spread my mind and my imagination as far as I wanted under this clear blue sky.

A couple of miles from the cutcherry, there was a low-lying area, where a thin brook flowed through the woods. On its shores was a dense bed of water lilies—in Kolkata, they called these flowers spider lilies. I had never seen wild spider lilies before, nor did I know that they could look so pretty and smell so fragrant on the pebble-strewn shores of an unnamed brook in the middle of the woods. I would often go and sit amidst those flowers, watching the stream run by, and enjoying the solitude of the dusk.

I would also go horse-riding every now and then. In the beginning, I didn't know how to ride. But gradually, I picked it up quite well. And as soon as I did, I realized that there was nothing quite as fulfilling in life as riding a horse. He who has never galloped through lush green open fields under an azure sky without a care in the world would never be able to understand the joy it gives to the heart! Around ten or fifteen miles from the cutcherry, there was a spot where a survey party was busy with their work, and I would often have to go and visit them. I would have a cup of tea in the morning, load the saddle on my horse's back, mount it and take off. On some days, I would come back to the cutcherry at sundown, and on others, on the way back, I could see the stars twinkling in the clear sky, the Vesper shining bright in all its glory, the sweet aroma of wild flowers mixed with the mysterious moonlight caressing my face, crickets chirped in unison and foxes announced the hour with their eerie yelps.

[2]

I had been trying my best to focus on the job that had brought me here. But taking care of several thousand acres of land was neither going to be easy nor would it be accomplished in a hurry. Moreover, there was one more problem that I had to take care of, and I had learnt of it only after I'd come here. Apparently, around thirty or so years ago, there was a devastating flood in the region, and this entire tract of land had disappeared under the river. The people who had originally leased the land from the zamindar had lost all their possessions to the deluge and had migrated to other places, including far-flung towns and cities. There, they had somehow managed to start their life anew, but could never save enough to lead a decent one. Around twenty years ago, as the waters receded, the land had emerged out of the river once again, and the original tenants had returned to the place they were once forced to abandon, in the hope that they would now get their land back. But the zamindar was now reluctant to lease the land to these people anymore. New tenants would mean increased rent and large money deposits. The poor, displaced and homeless original tenants would hardly be able to pay anything, and were hence denied their rightful claim. The plight and tears of these people failed to get them their land back.

Many of them often came to me too. I felt bad for them, but the zamindar had issued strict orders—no old tenant was to be allotted any land. The zamindar was rich and powerful. The tenants had been roaming around from one place to another for the last twenty years, working as bonded labour, earning meagre wages, barely managing to get two square meals a day, some of them had passed away, leaving young helpless children behind—even if they would try and raise their voices against the zamindar, they would be washed away like a twig in the torrents.

On the other hand, where would one find so many new tenants? Folks from places like Munger, Purnia, Bhagalpur, Chhapra and other nearby districts would often come enquiring, but would step back on learning of the lease rates. A handful of them had agreed to take up the leases, no doubt. But at this rate, it would take more than twenty years to lease out all of the thirty thousand acres of land.

We had a sub-cutcherry in the estate, around nineteen miles from here, surrounded by dense forests. The name of the place was Labtulia, and the terrain wasn't much different from the one here. The only reason for setting up a cutcherry there was that every year, the jungle land used to be let out to milkmen and cowherds for them to use it as a grazing ground for their cattle. Apart from this, wild berries grew over a vast area of almost six hundred acres in this forest. These forests were infested with lac bugs, which secreted a resin from which shellac was produced and sold. The entire affair of cattle grazing and resin picking fetched a pretty handsome amount of rent—the collection of which was the sole responsibility of a deputy collector, who had been posted there with a small cutcherry and a monthly salary of ten rupees.

The berries were seasonal; they would bloom soon and the bugs would come to eat them, and the lac-traders would come looking for the bugs. In other words, it was time for me to pay a visit to the place. One fine morning, I saddled my horse and set out for Labtulia. On the way, I crossed what was known in the region as the Fulkiya Baihar—a slightly raised plateau of flat land, seven or eight miles long, with more than a hundred varieties of flowering plants, trees and colourful bushes growing on red soil all along its length. At places, the vegetation was so thick that branches and leaves would touch the sides of my horse. At the spot where the plateau descended to meet the plains below, a beautiful mountain rivulet named Channan could be seen flowing over a shining bed of smooth pebbles. In the monsoons, the river would be quite deep, but thanks to the winter setting in, it was merely a trickle now.

This was my first visit to Labtulia. The cutcherry was a tiny hut, with a roof made of straw and walls made of dry catkins and the twigs and branches of wild tamarisks. By the time I reached, dusk had begun to fall. I had no idea that it could get so cold around here and I was hopelessly unprepared for what was to come as the night grew darker. Had the sepoys not gathered dry branches and made a fire outside the hut, I'd have surely frozen to death that night. I sat down on a camp-chair beside the fire, the rest of the staff sat down on the ground around me.

Since I was coming, the deputy collector had arranged for a huge Rohu fish from somewhere, and it was now presented before me. But the question was—who would cook it? I had come alone, the thought of bringing my cook along had never occurred to me. Nor did I myself know how to cook. There were seven or eight people gathered there, waiting to meet me, and one of them—a Maithili Brahmin named Kontu Mishra—was appointed by the collector to cook the fish.

I asked the collector, 'So, these are the lessees?'

He said, 'No, Huzoor, they've all come for the food. They've been waiting here for two days now. There are more on the way.'

I had never heard of something so strange. I said, 'But . . . I never invited them! Did you?'

'No, Huzoor, no one invited them. These people are very poor, you see? Rice is a luxury to them. Husk and grist of pulses is what they usually get to eat. When they heard that you're coming, they knew there would be rice, and to them having rice is almost like a feast. So, they have all flocked here. Tomorrow, you'll see more of them.'

For some strange reason, such a simplistic gesture of these men seemed perfectly logical to me—as if they were right, and all the people in the city, who would never dream of doing something so outlandish, had been wrong all along. I immediately became fond of all of them, and seeing that they had sat at a respectful distance from me outside the warmth of the fire, I asked them to come and sit closer to the flames. The men seemed warm and happy, and I listened to them as they chatted amongst themselves. Kontu Mishra was sitting near me and cooking the fish over a slow fire, sending a mouth-watering aroma wafting through the air. I had stepped away for a short while, and I realized that the ground had frozen stiff.

By the time we finished our dinner, it was quite late. Everyone present at the cutchery had a hearty meal. Then I sat near the fire once again, because as soon as I stepped away from its periphery, it seemed even the blood in my veins would freeze. I reckoned it was the open spaces that made the cold so severe. Or perhaps, the proximity to the Himalayas.

Seven or eight people were gathered around the fire, two tiny huts stood in front of us. I was to spend the night in one, and the rest of the people, in the other. Spread all around us were dense forests and hanging over our heads was the dark sky bejewelled with glittering stars. A strange feeling suddenly seemed to come over me. It seemed to me that I had left my old life behind and had landed in some faraway planet of the galaxy, and was now beginning to enjoy the mysterious ways of its inhabitants' lives.

A man in his early thirties, sitting amidst these group, had particularly caught my attention. His name was Ganori Tewari, his skin was dark, his build massive and strong, his hair long, two long smears of vermilion adorned his forehead, and even in this unearthly cold, he had nothing but a flimsy sheet of cloth wrapped around his body—not even the customary local waistcoat that the natives usually wore. I had been noticing him for quite some time; he was staring at everyone's faces with a certain sense of hesitation, never protesting anything being said and always nodding in affirmation. Every time I spoke, he would nod his head softly and utter a single word—'Huzoor'.

When the people of this region spoke to someone and agreed to what they had to say or agreed to their command, they would simply nod their head softly and say with great respect—'Huzoor'.

I asked Ganori, 'Where do you live, Tewari-ji?'

Startled by my sudden question, and vividly overwhelmed with the undeserving honour I had so generously and so unexpectedly bestowed upon him by addressing him directly, he stared at me with an expression of gratitude and said, 'Bheemdas Tola, Huzoor.'

And then Ganori Tewari told me all about himself and his life, not of his own accord, but in response to the several questions I asked him—

When he was twelve, Ganori lost his father. An old aunt raised him, and when she too died within five years of his father's demise, young Ganori set out to try his luck in the world. But his world was limited to the town of Purnia in the east, the borders of Bhagalpur district in the west, the Fulkiya Baihar in the south and the Kushi river in the north—he knew nothing outside this. He roamed from one village to another, from one house to another, sometimes working as a priest in small household ceremonies, sometimes teaching students in village schools and sometimes toiling day and night to arrange for a fistful of pea-grist or a flake of bread made from the seeds of China grass to fill his stomach. For the last two months, however, he was unemployed, because the local school in the village of Parbata had been shut down due to poor attendance. Population was scarce near the plateau and there were no households or families where he could earn his bread; so, he was left with no other option but to go from one pasture to another and beg for food from the wandering milkmen and cowherds of the region. He had heard that Manager Babu was coming to the cutcherry, and like many others, he had come with the hope of getting to eat some rice.

I asked him, 'Don't these people get to eat rice?'

'No, Huzoor. The Marwaris in Naugachhia eat rice. I myself had rice after several months tonight. Rashbehari

Singh Rajput is a very rich man, he had thrown a feast last monsoon. It was at his feast where I had rice last.'

Not one of the people who had come had any warm clothes on. As the night began to grow colder, they began to huddle around closer and closer to the fire.

I don't know why, but I really liked those men. Their abject poverty, their simplicity and their honesty had never allowed them any kind of luxury. But the dense and dark forest, the ice-cold air and the unforgiving vast skies had chiselled them into real men. Men who could walk nine miles from as far as Bheemdas Tola and Parbata, just to have a fistful of rice, that too without worrying about whether they had been invited or not. A man like me could only marvel at the immense capacity of their hearts to embrace the joy of survival and the fervent zeal to relish that joy.

It must have been very late that night when a strange noise woke me up. It was painful to even peep out from within my blanket, which anyways had turned ice-cold by now. There was no way I could turn from one side to another in the bed. The other side would be freezing. Turning towards that side would seem like taking a dip in the icy waters of a pond at midnight in the month of February. But I still bore the pain and turned around, because just outside the wall, in the jungle, someone was running, there were heavy footsteps all around. I soon realized that it was not someone, but something, and that there were several, and not one set of footsteps that I could hear around me. A group, a very large group of something, was running breathlessly, trampling dry tamarisks and small bamboo shoots under their feet.

I listened for some time and then called out to sepoy Vishnuram Pandey and schoolmaster Ganori Tewari. The two men sat up, rubbing their eyes, a strange mix of sleepiness and reverence floating on their faces in the dim light emanating from the last remaining cinders of the fire that had been lit to keep us warm through the night. Ganori Tewari raised his ears and immediately said, 'That's nothing, Huzoor, just a herd of nilgais running through the forest.'

Having said these words, Ganori was just about to turn to his side and promptly return to his much-coveted slumber when I asked him, 'What's making them run like that in the middle of the night?'

With the air of giving assurances, Vishnuram Pandey said, 'Perhaps they are being chased, Huzoor; there's nothing to worry.'

'Chased by who?'

'Chased by some wild animal, Huzoor. Who else will chase them in the middle of the jungle at this hour? Perhaps a tiger, or a bear.'

Quite involuntarily, my eyes turned towards the catkin-stem door of the room. The 'door'—if one could even dare to call it by that name—was so flimsy, that even if a dog would place a paw on it, the entire thing would keel over and fall inside the room. Needless to say, the news of a herd of wild nilgais being chased by a tiger or a bear in the forest just outside the walls of the hut failed to assure me or put me back to sleep.

A few hours later, I realized that dawn had broken.

[3]

As the days went by, the beauty of the forest seemed to overpower me. What mystical attraction lay amidst its dense woods and in what hypnotic voice its silent trees, plants and rivers called out to me, I could never tell. But I gradually began to realize that it would not be possible for me to leave these open spaces, these aromas of the sunburnt earth and this freedom, and return to the pandemonium of the city.

One must understand that I hadn't reached this conclusion overnight. Oh, the glimpses that nature showed my bewitched and unaccustomed eyes over the days and nights! If the evenings came prancing over twilight clouds like a free-spirited doe, then the blazing rays of the afternoon sun came dancing amok like a woman possessed. And the cold nights came like the mythical goddess—a dark-skinned beauty bathed in silvery moonlight, holding the glowing sword of the Milky Way in her hand, wearing the crown of the skies with a hundred diamonds sparkling on it, seeped in the fragrance of some unknown wild flower that had just begun to drip with dew.

[4]

I shall never forget the events of one day in particular. I remember it was the day of the Dol. The sepoys of the cutcherry had taken leave to play Holi to the beats of drums and dhols all day. Even as dusk fell, they showed no signs of stopping, and I lit the lamp on my table and sat down to write a series of letters to the head office. By the time I had finished writing the last letter, it was almost 1 a.m., and I was almost freezing to death. A cigarette would help, I thought. I lit one, peeped out of the window and was instantly captivated by what I saw outside. It was a full-moon night, and the whole place was bathed in a soft and mysterious moonlight—the likes of which I had never seen in my life, one which mere words couldn't hope to describe.

Perhaps because I had never ventured out so late in the wintry night so far, or perhaps because of some other reason, this was the first time I had experienced the complete, unrestrained beauty of a night so replete with moonlight in the forest.

I opened the door and stepped out. There was no one around, the sepoys had danced and made merry all day and fallen asleep. There were silent woods all around me, as I stood alone in the dead of the night. There were no words to describe that night. There weren't too many large trees around me, only wild tamarisks and half-dry catkins. The shadows they cast on the shining white sand-covered ground could barely diminish the illumination that the silvery disk in the sky had so generously offered. I felt a strange fear as I looked at the ethereal beauty around me; my heart sank and I felt hollow inside, a sense of sadness numbed me from head to toe, and it seemed to me that this place was a faraway land of fairies, that no rule of man would apply here and that I had disturbed its sanctity with my inadvertent intrusion.

I had experienced the beauty of the full moon several times after that night—for instance when, towards the end of March, the *dudhli* flowers would bloom and make the entire land seem like a colourful carpet, I would often step out into the moonlit night and fill my lungs with the sweet fragrance floating around in the cool air—and every single time, I had wondered why such strange emotions of fear mixed with sorrowful emptiness had never occurred to me during my life in the city. It would be futile on my part to make any attempts whatsoever at describing that moonlit night in the forest. If one has not experienced something so other-worldly by oneself, it is not possible to get a sense of its sheer beauty by simply hearing or reading about it. It is only under such free skies, in such solitude and silence, amidst such lush green forests running away towards the horizon that such hidden worlds can exist. For at least once in one's life, one must experience such a moonlit night. And if one has not had the good fortune of doing so, one must accept the fact that one has been forever rendered unacquainted with a unique and unparalleled creation of God.

[5]

One day, while returning from the Azamabad survey camp in the evening, I lost my way in the woods. The forest land was not plain everywhere; there were green hillocks rising here and there, with small valleys between them. But the forest was everywhere, there was no end to it. I climbed on top of a hillock to see if the light atop the flag of Mahaveer in the middle of the cutcherry compound could be seen anywhere. Not a sign of it. Only forests of pine, tamarisks and catkins, with the occasional grove of sal and *asan* here and there. After roaming two hours in the jungle, when my situation did not improve, I suddenly asked myself, why not use the stars to guide myself? It was summer, I looked up to find the Orion right above my head. But I couldn't make out from which direction it had climbed up there, nor could I trace the Great Bear. Hence, I abandoned all plans to use the stars for navigation and decided to go where my horse took me.

After a couple of miles or so, I saw a light in the middle of the forest. I steered my horse towards the source of the light to find myself in front of a very low-roofed hut, made of grass and thatch, on a land approximately twenty square feet in size. It was obvious that the hut had been built by clearing off a part of the jungle, and even on this summer evening, a fire was burning in front of it. A man sat at a distance from the fire and seemed busy with something.

The sound of my horse's trot startled the man. He rose to his feet and said, 'Who goes there?'

And then, on recognizing me, he immediately ran up to my horse and helped me down with great reverence. I was exhausted, to say the least, I had been riding for more than six hours after all, because even in the camp, I had to ride along the surveyor as he inspected the jungles. So I sat down on a grass mat laid down by the man, and asked him, 'What is your name?'

The man said that his name was Gonu Mahato, and added that he was from the Gangota caste. I had come to know by then that the Gangotas depended on agriculture and cattle rearing for their livelihood in the region, but what was this man doing all by himself in the middle of this dense forest?

I asked him, 'What are you doing here? Where are you from?'

'Huzoor, I rear buffaloes. My home is more than twenty miles from here, towards the north, in Dharampur, Lakshmantolia.'

'Your own buffaloes? How many of them?'

The man said with an air of pride – 'Five of them, Huzoor.'

Five buffaloes! I was quite shocked!

With only five buffaloes in tow, this man had come from his home more than twenty miles away, leased the land for grazing, built a shanty hut and was now living here in the middle of this forest, with not a soul to be seen anywhere – day after day, month after month? How did he live here all by himself? How did he spend his time? The young city-bred man in me, entertained by cinema and theatre, sustained by the company of friends and acquaintances, failed to understand how this man had survived so long.

It was only later, when I had gained more experiences of this land, that I had realized why Gonu Mahato lived like that. I realized that such was his notion of life. If he had five buffaloes, then he would have to rear them, and if he had to rear them, then he would have to live in the jungle all by himself. It took me quite a bit of time to realize the simplicity of this perfectly normal and natural equation of life.

Gonu rolled a tender sal leaf into some sort of a crude cigar and offered it to me with great reverence. In the light from the fire, I watched him closely—a broad raised forehead, a sharp nose, dark skin—a face filled with simplicity and calmness. He must have been more than sixty, not a single strand of hair on his head was black anymore. And yet, his body was so strong and so well built that one could call out each muscle from the other.

Gonu shoved in some more wood into the fire and rolled a sal leaf cigar for himself. In the glow of the fire, I could see a couple of brass utensils shining inside the shanty. Outside the periphery of the fire, the woods were dark and deep.

I said, 'You live here all by yourself, Gonu, aren't you scared of wild animals?'

Gonu said, 'How can I afford to be scared, Huzoor? This is my livelihood. Why, just the other night, I heard a tiger growling right behind my hut. There are two buffalo calves in the shed, the beast has had its eyes on them for some time.

I immediately woke up and did everything I could—beating the tin canister, waving a torch of fire, screaming at the top of my voice. It walked away, but I couldn't sleep anymore that night. The winters are worse, every night I can hear jackals howling and chasing tigers through the forest.'

'What do you eat? I'm sure there are no shops around here, where do you get your food from—rice, pulses, grains?'

'Huzoor, even if there would have been a shop right here, who has the money to buy such things? We are not so fortunate as Bengali babus, we don't get to eat rice or pulses, Huzoor. Behind this hut, there's a small piece of land where I grow horse gram. And in the jungle, there're some weeds of *bathuwa*. I boil the gram and the weed, add a bit of salt—that's all I eat. In spring, I pluck some *gurmi* fruits from the forest. I eat them raw, with a bit of salt—they're very delicious, Huzoor. Stunted, vine-like plants, the fruits look like berries. Dozens of young boys and girls come every day to pluck gurmi fruits in spring. That becomes our only food for those few months.'

I said, 'You eat boiled gram and weeds every day? Don't you get bored of it?'

'What can I do, huzoor? Who will give me rice? In this region, only Rashbehari Singh and Nandalal Pandey can afford to eat rice twice a day. I toil after the buffaloes from dawn till dusk, Huzoor. When I come home at the end of the day, I feel so hungry that I enjoy whatever I get to eat.'

I said, 'Have you ever been to Kolkata, Gonu?'

'No, Huzoor. But I've heard about it. Once I had been to Bhagalpur, several years ago. What an amazing city! I remember I saw a new kind of cart there; it was very strange.

There was no cow, no bullock, nothing tied to it—and it was running along the road, all by itself!'

The solitary source of Gonu's livelihood were five buffaloes. But who would buy their milk in the middle of this jungle? So, he would churn the milk to make ghee out of them. He would accumulate two-three months' worth of ghee at a time and then walk twenty miles north to the market in Dharampur to sell his ghee to the Marwari traders there. All he had for food was a farm of horse gram—which, by the way, was the staple diet for almost every poor man in the region. That night, Gonu led me back to the cutchery through the dense forest. But I had taken such a liking to this simple man that I was to spent several evenings sitting with him near the fire outside his shanty hut in the days to come. Gonu would tell me several interesting stories about life in the forest, and there was no one in the land who could tell stories like Gonu Mahato.

He used to tell me such strange tales—of flying snakes, breathing stones, and day-old newborns walking around. Sitting in the middle of that dense forest, Gonu's tales seemed particularly mysterious and fascinating to me. I was aware that perhaps if I had listened to the same stories sitting in Kolkata, they would seem nothing short of hyperbole to me. But ask anyone who loves listening to stories and he would tell you that the credibility of a story depends, to an extent beyond imagination, on the environment and circumstances in which it is being told. Of all the experiences that Gonu had shared with me, the one which had seemed the strangest to me was that of the deity of the wild buffaloes, otherwise known in the region as the Tyandbaro.

But in as much as the story of Tyandbaro has a strange conclusion, I would therefore tell the captivating tale at the right place and the right time. I must also haste to add that the stories that Gonu used to tell me could under no circumstances be branded as myths or legends, because he had personally experienced each of them himself. Gonu had watched both life and nature from very close quarters, and with an entirely different set of eyes than what might seem normal to you and me. His close encounters with the forest had made him an expert on it. I could never dismiss anything he said, nor did it ever seem to me that a simple man such as he could summon up the imagination required to fabricate any of his tales.

CHAPTER 3

[1]

With the advent of summer, a large flock of cranes came flying from the direction of the Peerpoiti Hills and settled down on top of Grant Sahib's banyan tree, giving the impression of the tree blooming with thick bunches of white flowers.

One morning, I had had my desk set up near the half-dry jungles of catkins, and as I sat there working, sepoy Muneshwar Singh arrived at the spot and said,—'Huzoor, Nandalal Ojha has come to see you.'

After some time, a man in his early fifties walked up to me, bowed in greeting and as directed by me, sat down on a small stool. The first thing he did after taking his seat was to bring out a silk purse, from which he pulled out a tiny nut-cracker and a couple of betel nuts. Once he had diced the nuts to smaller pieces, he placed them on the flat of his palms, offered them to me with great reverence and said, 'Some supari for Huzoor.'

Although I was not in the habit of having betel nuts in that form, I took some to avoid being impolite and asked him, 'Where are you from? How can I help you?'

The man responded by saying that his name was Nandalal Ojha and that he was a Maithili Brahmin. He hailed from a village called Shungthiya, eleven miles beyond the north-eastern cutchery of the forest. He owned several farms, and also ran a moneylending business. He had come to invite me to his home for lunch on the day of the next full moon— would I be so kind as to set foot in his humble abode; would he be so fortunate as to count on my presence?

I had no intentions of traveling eleven miles under the strong sun to have lunch with someone I was unacquainted to, but when Nandalal Ojha continued to insist and didn't show any signs of relenting, I was forced to say yes. More than the food, I was interested in the ways of life of the people of this region, and considered this as an excellent opportunity to learn more about them.

On the day of the full moon, a massive elephant was seen emerging from within the tall blades of catkins near the compound. As the elephant came near the cutchery, the mahout announced that Nandalal Ojha had sent his personal vehicle to take me to his home. This was completely unnecessary, because I would have reached his home much faster on horseback.

Anyway, I mounted the elephant and set off for Nandalal Ojha's house. The green treetops were now beneath my feet, the sky above seemed within my reach, the blue outlines of faraway mountains seemed enchanting—as if I was the inhabitant of some magical land, a god amidst the high heavens. And as if unknown to mankind, it was my daily routine to soar high in the azure skies and look down at all the verdant forests of the world through the ever-shifting gaps in the clouds.

We crossed the Chamta Lake on the way. Although winter had passed, flocks of geese and cranes were seen crowding the place. I figured they were here just for a few more days, and they would fly away as soon as it started to get a little warmer. We passed by a couple of hamlets of poor farmers and a few tobacco farms bounded on all sides by perilous and uninviting fences of cacti.

When the elephant entered the Shungthiya village, I saw scores of villagers lined up on both sides of the path, they had been patiently waiting all morning to welcome me. After some time, I reached Nandalal's house.

Nine or ten thatch-roofed mud huts stood quite separately from each other across a large compound. As soon as I entered the house, two loud gunshots startled me, and before I could find my bearings, Nandalal Ojha emerged from within the house with an ear-to-ear grin on his face, welcomed me into a large courtyard and offered a chair. The chair was made from local rosewood and bore evidence of being crafted by local rustic carpenters. When I had settled down in it, a ten- or twelve-year-old girl walked up to me shyly and held out a plate in front of my face. A few leaves of betel, uncut betel nuts, a little otto-of-rose in a small shallow dish and a couple of dates constituted the contents of the plate, and I had absolutely no idea what to do with them. So, I smiled ignorantly, immersed the tip of my little finger in the extract of rose-oil and said a sweet word or two to the little girl. The girl placed the plate next to me and disappeared within the interiors of the house.

And then came the food. Little did I know that Nandalal had made such an elaborate arrangement. A large massive sitting stool was laid out for me, and before it was placed a large plate, the like and size of which I had never seen before. On the plate was a strange combination of edible items— pooris the size of the ears of the elephant I rode in on, fried leafy vegetables, a raita made of ripe cucumbers, a curry with raw tamarind, curd made by souring buffalo milk and sweetmeat made by solidifying the same milk. The courtyard was teeming with people, all eager to catch a glimpse of me. I learnt that all of them were Nandalal's tenants.

Just before dusk, as I bid him farewell, Nandalal handed a small pouch to me and said, 'A small gift for Huzoor.'

I opened the mouth of the pouch to find a lot of money inside—must have been at least fifty rupees. I couldn't possibly take such a large sum of money as a gift, moreover Nandalal was not even a subject of the estate. But since refusal to accept a gift would be tantamount to insulting the host, I took a rupee out of the pouch, handed the rest back to Nandalal and said, 'Get some sweets for your children on my behalf.'

Nandalal began to insist, but I turned a deaf ear to his requests and mounted the elephant for my journey back.

The very next day, Nandalal came and saw me at the cutcherry—this time, with his elder son in tow. I welcomed them and showed them due courtesy, but they politely refused to have any food. Apparently, Maithili Brahmins would not have food prepared by anyone else, not even Brahmins of another clan. After several minutes of small talk, Nandalal stated the principal purpose of his visit—he had come to request me to appoint his elder son as the Tehsildar of Fulkiya Baihar. I was quite taken aback by the strange demand, and said, 'But that post is not vacant, there is already someone working there.'

In response, Nandalal winked at me and said, 'You are the king of the land, Huzoor. If you wish, everything is possible.'

This surprised me even more, and I said, 'What are you saying? The tehsildar in the region is doing his job just fine. Why would I throw him out?'

Nandalal said, 'How much does Huzoor want for his *paan*, please tell me? The money will reach you before sundown. But you simply have to give my son that job. Tell me Huzoor, how much? Would five hundred suffice?'

By then I had realized the true motives behind the previous day's invitation. If I knew that he was such a scheming man, I would never have accepted his invite. This was too much!

Without mincing my words, I told Nandalal exactly what was on my mind before sending him away. But I also had a feeling that he would not give up so easily.

A few days later, I saw Nandalal waiting for me just outside the densest part of the forest. Oh, what a mistake it had been to set foot into this man's house! If only I knew that he would feed me a couple of pooris only to make my life so miserable!

As soon as he saw me, Nandalal smiled politely and said, 'Namaskar, Huzoor!'

'Hmm . . . where to?'

'Huzoor knows everything. Huzoor is too kind. I'm offering you twelve hundred rupees, cash. Please give that job to my son.'

'Are you crazy, Nandalal? It is not in my power to appoint anyone to that position. You can always write a letter to the zamindar with your appeal. Moreover, how can I throw the current tehsildar out? What is his fault?'

Having said these words, and without wasting a single moment anymore, I rode away towards my destination.

As the days passed by, Nandalal continued to insist, and my responses to his pleas continued to become harsher and sterner. With my curt behaviour and sharp words, I made Nandalal Ojha a bitter enemy of the estate. But even by then, I had not realized what a dangerous man he was. I had learnt that much later, and in a very hard way.

[2]

One of the essential activities here was to fetch the mail from the post office, which was situated nineteen miles away. Since it was not possible to travel such a great distance and back on a daily basis, I used to send my man to bring the mail twice a week. I could have sworn that sitting in his tent in the desolate, impassable and unforgiving Taklamakan desert in Central Asia, famous explorer Sven Hedin too might have waited as eagerly for his mail as I waited for mine in the heart of this forest. Over the last eight to nine months, thanks to the enchanting experiences of watching the sun set, the moon rise, the stars twinkle across the vast expanse of the skies and herds of nilgais run freely through the jungle, day after day, night after night, I had left my urban roots behind—and it was through those few letters that I could sometimes try and find a connect with that life once again.

On the specified date, Jawahirlal Singh had gone out to fetch the mail. He would return in the afternoon, today. The Bengali treasurer gentleman and I were throwing frequent glances towards the forest every now and then. The path meandered through the forest, rising on top of a hillock around a mile and a half away from the cutcherry. Once

Jawahirlal would reach the top of the mound, we would be able to see him clearly from where we were.

The afternoon was rolling away lazily. No sign of Jawahirlal yet. I was pacing in and out of my room restlessly. There was quite a bit of workload here. Reading the reports of all the surveyors, signing the daily cash registers, writing correspondences with headquarters, checking the collections of rents and taxes, reading and responding to various kinds of applications, issuing decrees, going through the reports of the lawyers and solicitors of the multiple cases that were being heard and argued in the courts of Purnia, Munger, Bhagalpur and others, and then writing letters to these solicitors—such activities constituted my day to day work, and if not carried out meticulously on a daily basis, they would pile up rapidly and make my life miserable. With the mail would come more work, with specific instructions to meet various people and go to various places.

Around 3 p.m., Jawahirlal's white pagri was seen atop the mound, shining in the bright afternoon sun. The treasurer called out to me—'Look Manager Babu, there comes the mail . . .'

I stepped out of the office. In the meantime, Jawahirlal had descended down the mound and entered the jungle once again. I had my opera glasses brought to me, and when I looked through them, I indeed saw Jawahirlal walking towards the cutcherry through the faraway forests of tamarisks. That was it! I couldn't concentrate on the office work anymore. What a long and restless wait that was! I had a realization that day— the rarer a thing was, the more value our mind attached to it. It was true that this value was a make-believe one, a product of the mind's imagination, and that it had almost nothing to do with the true merit of the item in question, but it was also true that such was human nature—it was quick to attach an artificial worth to everything that it came across, if only to determine what was important and what was not.

Jawahirlal was now seen traversing a low-lying and narrow tract of sand-covered land in front of the cutchery. I rose from my chair. The treasurer walked up to Jawahirlal, who struck a weary salute, pulled a bundle of letters out of his pouch and handed it over to the former.

There were a couple of personal letters addressed to me too—the handwritings were so familiar. As I was reading the letters, my eyes suddenly fell on the surrounding forests and I was immediately taken aback. What on earth was I doing here? Not even in my dreams had I imagined that I would live in a place like this ever in my life, away from my friends, away from the city. I had subscribed to a British magazine; its recent issue had come by the mail today. Printed on the cover, in bold were the words—'The Wondrous Flying Machine'. Had I been sitting in a densely populated city like Kolkata and reading about this fascinating invention of the twentieth century, would it have seemed so wondrous to me? Perhaps not. But in the middle of this forest, where time was in ample abundance, where all one could see around oneself was the pristine beauty of nature and the simple lives of the natives, one could experience the sheer bliss of being awed by even the most insignificant achievements of mankind. There was something in the air here that made one vulnerable to such admirations.

Truth be told, this place had taught me how to think. So many thoughts crossed my mind, so many questions arose, so many fond memories came visiting; I had never enjoyed my own existence in this manner ever before. Among hundreds of inconveniences that marked this place, it was the simple joy of being alive that had gradually begun to intoxicate me day by day.

However, it wasn't like I was marooned in some desolate and forgotten island in the Pacific. The railway station must have been hardly thirty miles away. A train from there would take me to Purnia in less than an hour, Munger in three. But then, the journey to the station itself was a huge pain, and even if I were to endure that, who would I meet in Purnia or Munger? There was no one there whom I knew, or who knew me.

Sometimes, the thought of visiting Kolkata would cross my mind. That's where I had left my entire life behind after all. But I couldn't go to Kolkata without permission from the headquarters, and moreover, a visit to Kolkata would cost me quite a bit of money, which would not be able to justify a trip of four-five days.

[3]

The days passed by, and by the end of April, a serious problem began to raise its ugly head. It had rained a bit towards the end of the previous year, but there wasn't a single drop of rain over the next few months. The summers rolled in, the scorching sun began to burn our skins and there was an acute shortage of water.

Such ordinary and commonplace terms as 'summer' and 'scarcity of water' are grossly insufficient to describe the terrifying picture of mother nature's fury that I had the misfortune of witnessing. Right from Azamabad in the north to Kishanpur in the south, from Fulkiya Baihar and Labtulia in the east all the way up to the borders of Munger district in the west, every single pond, canal, swamp or lake, both outside and within the jungle, dried up. Wells were dug, but no water was found. Even if a tiny trickle would be seen on the bed of the sand, it would take more than an hour to fill the smallest of pails. Needless to say, this posed a serious problem. Our only hope lay to the east, in the form of the Kushi river, which was a good seven or eight miles beyond the easternmost border of our estate, on the other side of the famous Mohanpura Reserve Forest. A small rivulet originated from the Terai region of Nepal and flowed through the area between our estate and the Mohanpura Forest, but presently, its only remaining signs were a sandy tract of land with polished pebbles strewn across it. Dozens of girls and women came walking from far-flung lands in the hope of digging out whatever little water they could from the sandy bed of the rivulet, and after straining the sand out of the water for the entire day, walked back to their village with less than half a pot of murky water each.

But the mountain river—its local name being Michhi—that lay beyond Mohanpura was of no use to us, because of its great distance from where we were. There was only one small well in the cutcherry compound, but it hardly had any drinking water. It took an entire afternoon to gather three small buckets of water.

Standing outside my room and staring at the coppery fire-spewing sky scorching the dry catkins and tall blades of grass, it seemed like a scary sight to see—as if the entire area would burst into flames any moment. Strong bursts of loo blew past me, scathing my exposed skin; never had I seen or imagined such a fiery look of the sun, such a fiery image of a summer afternoon. Every other day, a dust storm would come raging in from the west—these regions were notorious for such storms in the months of May and June—and everything beyond hundred yards from the cutcherry would lie hidden behind an impenetrable wall of dust and sand.

I had appointed a sepoy named Ramdhania as the local water scout. Most of the days, after roaming around the jungle all day, he would come and report to me by saying— 'There's no water anywhere, Huzoor.' On other days, he and a few others would dig the bed of the well for an hour, strain the water for another hour and manage to produce barely half a bucket of liquid mud for me to take my bath in. Under such severe circumstances, even that dirty bucket seemed priceless to me.

One afternoon, as I stood under the faint shade of a black myrobalan tree behind the cutcherry and looked around, it seemed to me that not only had I never experienced such a frightful picture of nature's fury, but that I would never see something like this if I were to leave this place. Ever since I was born, I had seen the cruel summer afternoons of Bengal, but such cruelty seemed like a big boon or a comforting relief in comparison to what I was witnessing now. And for some inexplicable reason, I felt a strange sort of attraction to the sights around me. I looked up at the sky with great difficulty, and managed to catch a quick glimpse of the sun, which was a massive ball of fire. Calcium burning, hydrogen burning, iron burning, nickel burning, cobalt burning and hundred and thousands of known and unknown metals and gases—all burning together in a fiery and dazzling furnace a million miles wide—and it was the heat from this orb of fire that had travelled through the infinite emptiness of space, torn through the layers of ether, fallen on the forests and grasslands of Fulkiya Baihar and Lodhai Tola, sucked the last drop of moisture out of the very veins of every single leaf and twig it touched and scorched the earth in an eerie dance of destruction. I looked out towards the open fields and saw the air above the ground shimmer. The horizon itself was shrouded in a thin film of fog created by the burning earth. Not a day of summer passed when the sky was blue. Puce, coppery, tawny, brown—these were the usual colours of the sky, one in which not a single bird was to be seen, because they had all managed to escape to distant and more bearable skies. How strange and beautiful the afternoon looked! I stood there under that tree, ignoring the heat. I have never seen the Sahara or the Gobi, nor had I had the opportunity to witness the ethereal beauty of the Taklamakan as described by Sven Hedin, but it seemed to me that the barren beauty of those faraway places would not be too different from what my eyes were seeing right now.

Around three miles from the cutchery, there was a pond in the middle of the forest, and a bit of water in this pond had miraculously managed to survive the drought somehow—perhaps because the pond itself was very deep. But this water had not been of any use to anyone—for three reasons. First, there was hardly any human habitat around it. Second, it was almost impossible to get to the waterbed, thanks to the soft muck that separated it from the banks of the pond. Even if one were to reach the water somehow, the chances of getting back to shore with a pot full of water were virtually none. And finally, the water itself was not at all suitable for drinking or other daily purposes. I never quite figured out what was mixed in it, but there was a strong and unpleasant metallic malodour in it.

One evening, I rode out to this pond after the heat from the sky had come down a bit. I stood over a tiny mound of sand by its banks; the sun was slowly setting, but was still visible beyond Grant Sahib's banyan tree behind me. With the intention of saving a bit of the cutcherry's precious water, I decided to take my horse down to the bed of the pond, so that the poor animal could quench its thirst. I figured no matter how much mud there would be on the way, the horse would still be able to wriggle its way out. But as I neared the pond, my eyes fell on one of the strangest of sights that I had ever seen. All around the pond, at least nine or ten snakes of varying sizes and at a little distance from them, as many as three massive buffaloes were drinking from the tiny puddles of water in the middle. The snakes were all venomous—kraits and cobras, in fact—commonly seen in these regions.

But it was the buffaloes that surprised me, because I had never seen such strange looking buffaloes. A massive pair of horns, long furry hair all over their hide, and a humongous body. As I said before, there was no human habitat anywhere nearby—so, no question of a buffalo shed either; so, where had these three buffaloes come from? Had some cattle-rearers surreptitiously built a shed or two somewhere deep within the forest in order to evade rent and taxes? Possibly. Anyway, I abandoned any hope of quenching my steed's thirst and turned around to get back home. As I neared the cutcherry, I met Muneshwar Singh and told him what I saw. He shuddered a little and said, 'Oh, what are you saying, Huzoor! Hanumanji has saved your life tonight. Those are not tamed buffaloes, those are wild bisons! They must have wandered out of Mohanpura Forest in search of water. There's no water in those parts; so, they may have been forced to leave their territory and come to the pond.'

Within a matter of minutes, the news spread within the cutcherry. Everyone walked up to me and said, – 'Oh, Huzoor! You have no idea how lucky you have been to survive. If a tiger were to catch you, you can still evade him and come out unscathed, but if a bison gives a chase, there's no escape. And if even one of them would have come after you, not even your horse would have been able to outrun them.'

From that day onwards, the small pond in the middle of the forest came to be known as a common waterhole for all thirsty wild animals of the region. As the summer weather began to worsen and the heat continued to become more and more unbearable, news began to flow in from various quarters that people had seen tigers, bison, deer, nilgais and wild boars drinking from that pond. I myself had ridden to the pond one more time, although this time, I was accompanied with as many as four armed guards, and the principal purpose of our visit was hunting. The scene that I had witnessed that night was something that I would never forget till I live and breathe. Imagine a desolate moonlit night in the middle of a vast forest. Also imagine, if you can, a strange and still shroud of silence hanging over the forest, although, I must say, it would be impossible to imagine something like that if you have never experienced it first-hand.

The warm air was rife with the smell of the stems of dry catkins, we had wandered too far out, and I had pretty much lost my sense of direction, and under such circumstances, I saw the pond.

Without making the faintest of sound, two nilgais were drinking water from the bed of the pond on one side, and two hyenas were doing the same on the other side, and both sets of animals were looking at the other in turns, silently, cautiously—and right in the middle of the two groups, a two-to three-month-old nilgai calf played happily and without a care in the world. I had never seen a more tragic sight ever in all my life, and I refused to fire at the thirsty animals, asked my men to turn around and headed back to the cutcherry.

Meanwhile, even the month of June went by, but not a drop of water rained from the merciless sky. Moreover, one more problem began to crop up. Even under normal circumstances, it was not uncommon for people travelling through the plateau and the woods to lose their way, but now with such acute water crisis, there seemed to be a distinct possibility of such lost travellers dying of thirst and dehydration. There were one or two rapidly disappearing pools of water deep within the forest, but it was impossible for inexperienced, lost and weary travellers to get to them. That is exactly what happened one day.

[4]

That day, at around 4 p.m. in the evening, I gave up all hope of concentrating on my work—thanks to the unbearable heat—picked up a book and had just begun to turn its pages, when Rambirij Singh stepped into my room and announced that a strange looking man had been seen on top of the mound towards the west of the cutcherry; apparently, the man was waving his hands around from a distance and trying to say something. I walked out to find that, indeed, there was a man on top of the mound—he seemed to be swaying and staggering like a drunk as he tried to climb down and walk towards us. Everyone in the cutcherry was standing and staring at the man with their mouths open. I sent two sepoys to go and fetch the man.

When the man was brought to me, I found him without a shirt—he only had a plain white dhoti on, he had a strong build and fair skin. But it was his face that shocked me, because he was frothing from the corners of his mouth, his eyes had turned blood red and his gaze made it seem that he had lost his sanity. There was a little water in a bucket in the corner of the veranda outside my room. On seeing the bucket, the man dashed past me and pounced towards it, but before he could reach it, Muneshwar Singh swiftly whisked the bucket away. The stranger was not being able to talk, so he was made to sit, and his lips were pried open to reveal that his tongue had swollen up to fill his entire mouth. It was a horrible sight to see. After a lot of effort, his tongue was pushed to one side of his mouth, and small trickles of water were poured down his throat little by little for over half an hour to make him feel a little better. We had lemon in the cutcherry, the man was made to drink a glass of warm water and lemon juice, and after an hour or so, he was able to state, in a trembling voice, that he was feeling much better. It was learnt that he was from Patna. He had come to this region in search of berry bushes, and had apparently started his journey from Purnia two days ago, entering our forests in the afternoon, only to lose his way in less than an hour—which was quite possible, because it was very difficult to find your way through the woods in the region, where everything looked the same no matter which direction you went, especially to inexperienced foreigners. Having spent an entire day roaming the forests in the middle of strong and scorching loos flowing in from the west, and having failed to find a single drop of water anywhere, or to meet a single human being in the woods, he had collapsed under a tree from thirst and exhaustion as night had fallen. When the morning came, he had picked himself up and started roaming again. Had he kept his nerves and tried to get a sense of the directions from the rising and setting of the sun, he could have perhaps found his way out of the forest and made his way back to Purnia, but he had become so overwrought and incapacitated with fear that all he had managed to do all day was to run around in circles like a madman, crying out for help at the top of his voice, trying to draw the attention of people.

People? If only the man knew that over a good ten to twelve square miles ranging from the berry forests near Fulkiya Baihar all the way up to Labtulia, there was not a single soul to be seen anywhere, and that the forest was absolutely desolate and without any human habitation whatsoever, he would have perhaps spared himself the agony of his miserably fruitless attempts. Instead, the man had been convinced that the djinns and fairies of the forest had spotted him, and that they were sure to hunt him down by nightfall. He had a shirt on, but by noon, thanks to the intense heat and to his unbearable thirst, when his skin started developing rashes and burns, he had gotten rid of it somewhere. Under such horrifying circumstances, had he not seen the red flag of Hanuman fluttering over the cutcherry at a distance, the man would have surely died in the forest that very night.

On another such hot and dry day, sometime in the afternoon, I was informed that a massive fire had broken out in the middle of the forest a couple of miles towards the south-easterly corner of the cutchery, and that it was headed right towards us. I rushed out of my room to find large coils of smoke and reddish flames of fire rise high up in the sky in the distance. The strong westerly loos were making matters worse, as were the tall and dry blades of grass and bushes of wild catkins all around us, which, for all practical purposes, had turned into deadly mounds of gunpowder, for even a single spark riding the winds and falling on them would send vast tracts of land up in flames in a matter of seconds. As far as my eyes could see towards these open fields, there were thick blue coils of smoke, along with fiery red flames, accompanied by crackling sounds. Thanks to the winds from the west, the swaying flames over the forest had turned towards us, and were now rushing towards the puny thatch huts of the cutchery at breakneck speeds. Our faces turned pale in an instant, and we realized that if we stayed here any longer, we would be in grave trouble.

There was no time to think. All the important papers of the cutchery, money from the treasury, government documents and maps, cash reserves—plus our respective personal belongings—everything was under threat. The sepoys were terrified too, they turned to me and said, 'The fire is almost upon us, Huzoor! What do we do?' I said, 'Get everything out—government papers and documents first.'

A few men rushed towards the fire to try and clear out the jungle between the flames and the cutchery compound. A few cattle-herders from the other side of the forest had seen the fire from a distance, they too came running to help and save the cutchery.

What a strange sight it was! Thrashing, trampling, tearing their way out of the jungle, herds of nilgais were running for their lives. Foxes were running, rabbits were running; a bunch of wild boars ran right through the front yard of the cutcherry with their little ones and disappeared around the back. The cattle-herds had freed their buffaloes by now and the poor animals ran away from the swelling flames. A bunch of wild parrots rushed over our heads to escape the rapidly increasing heat in the air, a flock of red geese followed them. Rambirij Singh widened his eyes in surprise and said, 'There's not a drop of water anywhere in the forest. Where do you think these red geese came from, eh Ramlagan?' The aged treasurer Goshtho Babu said in an irritated voice, 'We are all dying here, and all you can think of is where the red geese came from?'

In less than twenty minutes, the fire was almost upon us, and for the next one hour or so, ten–fifteen people put up a brave fight with it. There was no water, all we had as weapons in this unfair battle was some sand and a few green twigs and branches. Thanks to the heat from the flames and from the merciless sun, the faces of everyone around me had turned fiery red—like those of monsters, their bodies were covered in ash and soot, the veins on their arms had swollen up and most of them had boils on their hands and bodies; meanwhile, all the almirahs, chests, trunks, desks, cupboards, beds were still being heaved out of the cutcherry and thrown in the courtyard in a haphazard manner. Amidst all this confusion, there was no way to keep a track of what went where! I called the treasurer and said, 'Keep the cash with you, and the deeds too.'

Soon, the fire arrived right at our doorstep, but on finding nothing to burn in the front yard and in the cleared-out land just beyond it, it flanked towards the left and the right, raced on towards the east in an instant, sparing us in a stroke of luck that could only be described as a miracle. We took some time to catch our breath, and then everything was taken back into the huts once again. But throughout that night, we could see the devastating fire wagging its tongue and devouring everything it met on its way as it continued to spread towards the east, until dawn broke, and it reached the borders of the Mohanpura Reserve Forest.

After two or three days, we learnt that as many as ten bisons, two leopards and several nilgais had been found buried and dead in the mud on the banks of the Karo and Kushi rivers. Apparently, the poor animals had been trying to escape the fire and had jumped into the mud in a bid to save themselves. What surprised us the most was that both the rivers were a good eight to nine miles away from the reserve forest.

CHAPTER 4

[1]

Gradually, April and May went by. In the beginning of June, came the day of the annual festival of the cutchery. In as much as I hardly had a chance to meet anyone in the middle of this forest, I had decided to invite a large number of people to a feast on the day of the festival. There was no habitation nearby, so I made arrangements for Ganori Tewari to go to far-flung villages and invite people to the feast. A day before the festival, the sky was overcast, and it began to drizzle, and on the day of the festival, it started raining cats and dogs. Meanwhile, ignoring the heavy rains in anticipation of a hearty meal, a steady stream of people started flowing in, in large groups, just after noon. Soon, it came to a situation where there was no place for them to sit. Some of these groups had women and children among them, I somehow managed to have them sit inside the cutchery's office room, the men sat outside.

In these parts of the country, if you wished to invite people to a feast, there wasn't much you had to do, really. I had never imagined that human beings could be so poor. I had seen poverty in Bengal, but it was nothing like this;

even an average poor man back home had the good fortune
of leading a better life than a middle-class man of this region.
With the thunderstorm raging over their heads, these people
had walked miles through the forest just to have seeds of
China grass, sour curd, molasses and laddoo—for that was
the customary menu of a feast around these parts.

A ten- to twelve-year-old boy—whom I had never seen
before—was running around since the crack of dawn, helping
with the arrangements of the feast. His name was Bishua; he
came from a very poor family; he must have come from some
faraway slum. At around ten in the morning, he asked for
some food. The storekeeper of the cutchery brought him a
fistful of China grass seeds and a pinch of salt.

I was standing nearby. The boy had ebony-dark skin,
and with a pretty little face, he looked just like a stone idol
of Krishna. When he hurriedly spread the end of his yard-
length dhoti and accepted the meagre food offered to him
with utmost gratitude, all I could do was wonder at the
beaming smile on his face! I can say this with confidence
that even the poorest Bengali boy wouldn't bother to put a
single seed of China grass in his mouth, let alone enjoy it.
And I know this for a fact, because just out of curiosity, I had
myself tried to eat a few seeds of China grass one day, and
promptly written it off my list of acceptable edible items on
the face of the earth.

Despite the heavy rains, the feast had been quite successful
and all the poor Brahmins had blessed us and headed back
home. But just before evening, I noticed three women sitting
in the front yard in the middle of the incessant rains, along
with two little children—all drenched to the bone. The sal-
leaf plates before them had China grass seeds on them, but

no one had bothered to give them curd or molasses, and the women were sitting still in the rain, staring at the cutcherry with their mouths open. I called the storekeeper and asked, 'Who is serving them food? Why haven't they been served curd and molasses? And who has made them sit out there in the rain?'

The storekeeper said, 'Huzoor, those women are Dosads by caste, untouchables. If we bring them into the building, no Brahmin, Kshatriya or Gangota will touch the food, let alone eat them, we will have to throw everything away. And where else will we let them sit, Huzoor?'

As soon as I stepped out into the rain and stood in front of those poor low-caste women, everyone in the cutcherry rushed to the spot and began serving them food. If I had not seen it with my own eyes that day, I wouldn't have believed that human beings could consume so much curd, molasses and the inedible China grass seeds, and that too with such looks of contentment and gratitude on their faces. Standing there, seeing those eager and happy faces, I decided to invite just those Dosad women and their children to another feast a few days later, where I would be able to feed them civilized food in a more civilized manner. That feast did happen, and it was the storekeeper who was sent to the village of the untouchables to invite the women and their children. The food that they had that day—poori, fishes, meat, sweet curd, chutney and sweets—perhaps they had never imagined that they would have the good fortune of having such food ever in their lives. Their surprised and smiling faces stayed with me for several days to come! Even the vagabond Gangota fellow, Bishua, had been invited to the feast that day.

[2]

I was riding back from the survey camp one day, when I saw a man sitting in the middle of the forest, next to a bush of catkins, and eating a mixture of gram grist. He did not have a bowl, so he was using one corner of his faded and dirty dhoti to knead the mound of grist—a mound so large, that my common knowledge failed to make me believe that a human stomach could consume it all. When he saw me coming, the man quickly rose from the ground, bowed reverentially and said, 'Manager sahib! Please pardon me, Huzoor, I was having a bit of food.'

I failed to understand why I would need to pardon a man who was sitting all by himself, having his food in the middle of a desolate forest. I said, 'Yes, yes, please continue, you don't have to get up. What is your name?'

The man was still standing; he said with great respect, 'Your humble servant's name is Dhaotal Sahu, Huzoor.'

I looked at the man with some interest. It seemed like he was in his sixties. A tall, lanky build, dark skin, and he was wearing a faded dhoti and a dirty vest, with no footwear.

That was the first time I met Dhaotal Sahu.

On reaching the cutcherry, I asked the collector Ramjyot, 'Do you know this man—Dhaotal Sahu?'

Ramjyot said, 'Yes, of course, Huzoor. Everyone around here knows Dhaotal Sahu. He is the biggest money lender in the province, a millionaire himself; almost every single person in the region has borrowed money from him at some point of time or the other. He lives in Naugachhia.'

I was quite surprised to hear what Ramjyot was saying. That a millionaire could sit in the middle of a forest and knead an ugly mound of grist in one corner of his dress in order to have his meal—this seemed quite unbelievable to me. In my mind, I tried to assign the picture that I had seen in the forest to a millionaire from Bengal, but failed to do so. Which led me to think that perhaps Ramjyot was exaggerating. But on asking everyone else at the cutcherry, I got the same response. Dhaotal Sahu? Oh, there was no telling how rich he was.

After that day, Dhaotal Sahu had come to see me at the cutcherry's office several times, and the more I spoke to him and got to know him better, the more I realized that I had made the acquaintance of one of the most remarkable men I have ever come across, and that it was difficult to believe that such a man lived and breathed in the twentieth century.

My guess about Dhaotal's age had been quite right. He was sixty-four years old. He lived in the village of Naugachhia, around twelve or thirteen miles from the forest beyond the south-eastern corner of the cutcherry. Everyone in the region had borrowed money from him—right from the peasants to subjects to traders and even the zamindars. But there was something strange about Dhaotal Sahu. His problem was that he would lend money, but would not know how to get it back. As a result, everyone would borrow money from him, and very few would actually pay him back. A simple, mild mannered and good-natured man like him should never have become a money lender, but he could not refuse requests from people to borrow money. In fact, he believed that when everyone had promised him a high rate of interest, it would be foolish not to lend them money. One day, Dhaotal came to see me with a bundle of documents in his hand. He said, 'Huzoor, would you be so kind as to take a look at these?'

A quick glance through the papers made me realize that more than ten thousand rupees worth of loan agreements had lapsed, simply because Dhaotal Sahu had not sent a legal notice.

The man pulled out another old and worn-out bunch of papers and said, 'And what about these, Huzoor? Sometimes, I think I should go to town and show these to a lawyer. But then, I have never been to court, can't afford the hassles. I send reminders, ask people to pay, they say they will, but most of them never pay back.'

I said, 'Not everyone can be in the business of lending money, Sahu-ji. In this region, a tough and aggressive man like Rashbehari Singh Rajput can afford to be a money lender; he has a small army of stick-wielding goons, he himself rides into his borrowers' farms and seizes their crop to get his money back. Everyone will take advantage of a good man like you. Don't give money to anyone anymore.'

But Dhaotal shook his head and said, 'Not everyone is like that, Huzoor. The world hasn't gone to the dogs yet, there's still someone up there running things. How can I simply let my money lie around idle, tell me? I have to make it grow. That's our business.'

I could not see his logic, because I failed to comprehend what kind of business allows you to lose your principal in the hope of earning interest. Right in front of my eyes, Dhaotal Sahu tore at least fifteen-sixteen thousand rupees worth of papers to pieces, all with a straight face. As if the papers weren't worth a penny, although that wouldn't be too far from the truth. Neither his hands, nor his voice trembled even a little bit. He said, 'I had made all my money by selling mustard and castor seeds, Huzoor, my father hadn't left me a single penny. I earned it, and now I am the one losing it. What can I do? Profit and loss are part of any business.'

While that may be true, I was wondering how many people would have had the guts to face such huge losses in so calm and detached a manner. The only thing on which the old man didn't seem to mind splurging his money was his betel nuts. Every now and then, he would bring out a nut-cracker from his waistcoat's pocket, cut a betel nut with it and put the small piece in his mouth. When he noticed that I was watching him clip the nuts, he smiled and said, 'I have to have these every day, Huzoor. I end up spending all my money on these nuts.'

If apathy towards wealth and neglect towards larger losses can be thought of making a man philosophical by nature, than I have never seen a bigger philosopher than Dhaotal Sahu.

[3]

Every time I passed through Fulkiya, I went past the corn-leaves-roofed shanty of Jaipal Kumar. Kumar, not to be confused with the potters' caste, was a landless Brahmin.

Jaipal's hut was right under a massive fig tree. He was an old man, didn't have a family, had a tall and thin build, with long, white hair. Every time I went past his hut, I found him sitting silently just outside his door. He never smoked, I had never seen him do any kind of work, nor had I ever heard him sing—how a human being can sit still in complete silence without doing any work, day after day, was beyond me. He never failed to amaze me and make me curious. Every time, I couldn't help but pull up my horse in front of his hut and exchange a few words with him before moving on.

One day, I asked, 'What are you doing, Jaipal?'

'Just sitting here, Huzoor.'

'How old are you now?'

'I don't know, Huzoor, but the year they built the bridge over the Kushi river, I could still take the buffaloes out for grazing.'

'Were you married? Did you have children?'

'The wife died a long time ago, must be twenty or twenty-five years ago. I had two daughters—they died too, around thirteen or fourteen years ago. Now, I live here by myself.'

'Tell me something: you live here all alone, you never speak to anyone, you never go anywhere, nor do you do any work—do you like this life? Don't you get bored?'

Jaipal stared at me with a surprised look on his face and said, 'Why won't I like it, Huzoor? I like it just fine.'

Jaipal's words seemed strange to me. I have studied in a college in Kolkata. I cannot imagine life without any kind of occupation or work, or chatting with friends, or reading a book or watching a bioscope, or going on a trip. The world had moved so far ahead in the last twenty years, but Jaipal Kumar sat still outside his door, day after day, in all these years. When I was in primary school, Jaipal used to sit outside his door, when I graduated from college, Jaipal was still sitting outside his door in the same manner. When I compared all the exciting and fascinating things that I had done in my life to Jaipal Kumar's monotonous and desolate existence, I couldn't help but wonder what a strange man he was.

Although Jaipal's home was right in the middle of the village, there was no human habitation around the hut, thanks to the coarse and undulating nature of the surrounding land. Fulkiya was a very tiny hamlet. There must have been merely a dozen huts or so there. Everyone reared buffaloes to earn their living. They toiled likes donkeys all day, and in the night, they made a fire by lighting straws and thatch and sat around it, chatting and smoking. But not even once had I seen any of them have a chat with Jaipal Kumar.

Cranes and egrets gathered on the branches of the fig tree, giving the impression of thousands of pristine white flowers blooming on it. There was a dense shade under the tree, quite desolate, and in every direction you looked, the blue hills stood against the horizon in the shape of an arc—like a row of little children holding each other's hands. When I stood under the fig tree and spoke to Jaipal Kumar, the impenetrable serenity under the tree and the quiet, unruffled and unhurried lifestyle of the man seemed to overpower my mind, slowly yet surely. What was the use of running around, really? How cool the shade was under this tree, how still life stood here, how comforting the pace of time!

Jaipal's indifferent outlook towards life and his carefree ways gradually began to make me feel the same way about my own life. I was beginning to see things that I had never seen before, I had begun to think thoughts that had never crossed my mind. And very slowly, I was falling in love with these vast open fields, these dense dark forests and the inherent beauty of nature all around me—so much so that even if I had to go to Purnia or Munger for work, my mind ached to return to the greens once again. I yearned to leave everything behind and rush back to the dark woods, the silver-shine moonlight, the breathtaking sunset, the dark monsoon clouds and the open and unhindered star-studded jet black firmament.

On my way back to the cutchery after finishing my work in town, as soon as I crossed the babul-wood posts erected by Mukunda Chakladar and stepped into the territory of my jungle, it seemed to me that I was once again amidst the vast woods that had spread all the way to the horizon, the rocky hillocks, the sun moving along the arc over my head, the bunch of wild parrots, the herds of nilgais—and I would shut my eyes in absolute contentment and realize that I had finally come home.

CHAPTER 5

[1]

January was almost on its way out, wintry chills were sending shivers down my spine. I had gone out on inspection from the main cutcherry to the sub-cutcherry in Labtulia. While I was there, I could get to my dinner only by around 11 p.m. One night, I had just finished my dinner and stepped out of the kitchen, when I saw a young girl standing outside the compound of the cutcherry under a freezing, dew-dripping moonlit sky. I called the cutcherry's collector and asked, 'Who is that girl standing over there?'

He said, 'She's Kunta. She must have heard that you were coming, so she told me yesterday—"Manager Babu is coming, could I take away the leftovers from his plate? I'll be able to feed my children"—so I told her, yes, she could.'

Right in the middle of my conversation with the collector, I noticed the cutcherry's guard, Baloa, carry whatever little leftovers I had discarded in my plate and pour it in a brass vessel that the young girl was carrying. The girl walked away and disappeared behind the trees.

I had stayed in Labtulia for over a week that winter, and on all the nights, I saw the girl standing outside the cutcherry in that bitter cold, with nothing but a thin piece of cloth to cover herself, waiting patiently to take my leftovers home. After I had seen her a few days, I asked the collector one night, out of curiosity, 'That girl—Kunta—the one who takes my leftovers away every night, who is she? And where does she live in this dense forest? How come I've never seen her during the day?'

He simply said, 'I'll tell you, Huzoor.'

There was a fire burning inside the room since dusk. I had set up my desk near the fire and was busy looking through the accounts of collections. I now felt that I had done enough for the day, kept my papers aside and turned my chair around to listen to the collector's story.

'Huzoor, around ten years ago, an influential man used to live in this region. His name was Debi Singh Rajput. All the peasants and the herders around here used to fear him. His business was to lend money at very high rates, and then to recover the principal and the interest by using gangs of armed men. Just like Rashbehari Singh Rajput is the moneylender in the province now, back in the day, it used to be Debi Singh.

Debi Singh was originally from Jaunpur, he migrated to Purnia and immediately started lending money to the gullible and needy people of the province. Once the Gangota subjects borrowed money from him, he had them under his control. He wielded his power over the people of the region and became one of the most notorious and feared men around. Within a year or two of his arrival here, he went to Kashi, where he visited a courtesan for an evening of music. There, he struck up a friendship with the courtesan's fourteen- or fifteen-year-old daughter. The two ran away from Kashi and came here, to get married. Debi Singh must have been around twenty-six or twenty-seven by then. But when his own kin, the Rajputs, somehow found out that his wife was a courtesan's daughter, they criticized him severely and boycotted him. Debi Singh couldn't care less, for he had all the money in the world. But good times don't last forever. Thanks to his extravagant lifestyle and a bitter legal battle with this Rashbehari Singh, Debi Singh lost every single penny he had. It's been four years since he passed away.

The girl you saw—Kunta—she is none other than Debi Singh's widow. There was a time, Huzoor, when she used to travel from Labtulia all the way to the confluence of the Kushi and the Kalbalia rivers—daily—riding her beautiful regal palanquin, peeping from behind those stately Kinkhwab curtains, just to take her bath. There was a time when she wouldn't drink a glass of water without having a few grains of sugar crystals from Bikaner first. And look at her now! Since people know that she is the daughter of a courtesan, nobody wants to be friends with her, neither the high-caste Rajputs, nor the local Gangotas. You may be aware that after a crop of maize is reaped, the husks and dusts are left behind—they are of no use to anyone. It is these husks that Kunta collects every day, wandering from one farm to another, just so she can give her children something to fill their hungry stomach with. But one thing must be said—in all these years, none of us have ever seen her beg for alms, Huzoor. You are the manager of the estate, no less than a king; so perhaps, she didn't consider eating your leftovers as an insult.'

I was listening all this while, now I said, 'Her mother, the courtesan—did she never look for her in all these years?'

The collector said, 'I don't think so, Huzoor; we've never seen her. Kunta, too, never bothered to go back to her mother.

Her only concern seems to be feeding her children. When you see her now, you'll never realize how pretty she used to be! No one in this region had seen anyone as ethereally beautiful as her. But now, she is just a poor widow, and life has been very cruel to her. She is a very nice girl, though—very calm and polite. But no one seems to be kind to her, the shadow of her past seems to be haunting her forever.'

I said, 'But is it safe for her to walk all the way to her village in Labtulia through the woods all by herself, that too so late in the night? It must be more than three miles away, isn't it?'

'What else can she do, Huzoor? Fear is a luxury she simply can't afford to have. She walks around the woods all the time, entirely by herself. Or else, how would she feed her children?'

That was the end of January, I had finished my work in Labtulia and returned to the main cutcherry. But the very next month, I had to travel back to the sub-cutcherry, with the objective of putting a tract of grassland on lease.

The place hadn't had any relief from the cold yet. On the contrary, thanks to the freezing westerlies blowing all throughout the day, the chill turned twice as bad by the time night fell. One day, I had ridden out a bit too far out towards the northern borders of the estate. As far as my eyes could see, there were only shrubs of berries all around. Merchants from as far as Chhapra and Muzzafarpur would lease these woods to grow lac bugs and make a fortune. I was almost beginning to wonder if I had lost my way in the woods once again, when suddenly, the wails of a woman, the whimpers of children and the rough, ruthless voices of masculine rebuke reached my ears. On advancing towards the source of the clamour, I saw two men employed with the lac merchants dragging a poor and nearly disrobed woman by her hair, and three little children weeping and begging them to let go of her. One of the men had a basket in his hand; I saw a few freshly picked berries in the basket. On seeing me, the two guards narrated to me with great enthusiasm how they had caught the wretched woman red-handed as she was trying to steal berries from the leased land, and how they were taking her to the cutcherry to be tried and punished, neither of which would be necessary, now that Huzoor was here.

My first reaction was to reprimand the guards and asking them to let go of the woman. The poor woman—her clothes torn to bits, her hair dishevelled and streams of tears incessantly rolling down her cheeks—was in such a distraught condition of fear, agony and shame, that she immediately took shelter with her children behind a tree. I felt decidedly sorry for her.

But the two men were not willing to let her go so easily. I had to explain to them, 'Look around you, my man. There are so many trees out here. If a poor woman were to pick half-a-basket of berries from your trees to feed her starving child, would that be too big a loss for you to bear? Why don't you let her go home?'

One of them said, 'You don't know this blasted woman, Huzoor, her name is Kunta. She lives in Labtulia, and wanders into the forest to steal berries every now and then. We had caught her stealing last year as well; if we don't teach her a lesson this time—'

I was startled to hear the name. Kunta! How come I hadn't recognized her? And then it occurred to me that whenever I had seen her, it was in the middle of the night, and that too from a distance. Now that I was seeing her in daylight, in such a distraught condition, it was impossible to recognize her. I threatened the guards and asked them to let her go. Kunta drew her children close to herself, wiped her tears in visible embarrassment and walked away towards her home. There was a long pole with a hook fastened to its end lying on the ground at a distance—she must have been using that to pluck the berries. She was so shaken up that she didn't even dare to take the pole and the basket with her. I asked the guards to take the two to the cutcherry, which they gladly did, perhaps assuming that said equipment were being seized. On reaching the cutcherry, I summoned my rent-collector Banwarilal and said, 'How can the people of this place be so heartless, Banwarilal?'

On hearing everything, Banwarilal felt sorry about the entire affair. He was a good man, and had a kind heart. He immediately asked one of his men to take Kunta's basket and the pole she had left behind all the way to her hut in Labtulia.

But ever since that night, Kunta never came to the cutcherry to take away my leftovers ever again.

[2]

Finally, the winter ended, and spring set in.

Around fifteen–sixteen miles from the south-easterly borders of our forest estate, or in other words, around thirty miles from the cutcherry headquarters, there would be a very famous fair in the month of March every year, just after the Holi celebrations. I had only heard about it so far. This time around, I too had planned to go to the fair. I hadn't seen a crowd in ages, and I was curious to see what a local fair looked and felt like. But the men at the cutcherry discouraged me from going, saying over and over again that the road to the fair was treacherous and full of dense woods infested with tigers and wild buffaloes, and that the little clusters of habitations that did fall on the way were so scant as to be of no use to me in the grim possibility of my ending up in the clutches of a carnivore.

In all my life, I had never had the opportunity to do anything daring, and I was keen on making the best use of my time here. Once I returned to the city, where on earth was I to find dense woods, tigers or wild buffaloes? As the faces of my future grandchildren—listening to the stories of my adventures with rapt attention and profound awe—started hovering in my mind, I waved off the many protests of Muneshwar Mahato, collector Banwarilal and treasurer Nabeen Babu, woke up at the crack of dawn on the day of the fair, and set out for my destination on horseback. It took me more than two hours just to cross the boundary of our estate, for it was towards the south-easterly direction that the forest was the densest. There were hardly any roads in the conventional sense of the term. It would be impossible for any vehicle other than a horse to navigate the path. There were rocky boulders of various sizes strewn here and there. There were dense jungles of sal, and impenetrable bushes of catkins and wild tamarisks. The path would rise to an elevation every now and then, and suddenly end in a sharp slope. Dunes of sand here and there, plateaus of red soil, hillocks crested with thick shrubs of unknown thorny plants that I had never seen before. Thanks to such an unwelcoming terrain, I was not being able to maintain a steady speed. My horse was being forced to break his pace—galloping, trotting and even coming to a complete standstill once too often.

Not that any of these was bothering me in the least bit. On the contrary, I was enjoying myself to the hilt. Ever since I had come to this region, its wide-open spaces and green forests had gradually made me forget what civilization meant, what urban conveniences and habits felt like and even what my friends back home looked like. So what if my horse was going slow? As long as the flaming blossoms of palash adorned the sides of the hills, as long as the branches of the plants around me almost succumbed to the weights of the first blooms of spring, and as long as those unknown flowers that resembled sunflowers—but were certainly not—were making the afternoon sun cast a sleepy and somewhat hypnotic spell on me, who cared how much distance I had travelled, and in what direction?

But even before I had crossed the outer limits of our estate, I realized that care I must—for if I didn't, I was bound to lose my way. My mind must have been somewhere else, and I must have been lost in my own thoughts, when I suddenly noticed a large forest in the distance, directly ahead of me, and spreading as far as my eyes could see, right from one horizon to the other. Where on earth had such a large forest popped up from? No one back at the cutcherry had told me about such a forest on my route to the Moishondi fair. It didn't take me long to realize what had happened. I had lost my way, and what I saw ahead of me was nothing but the Mohanpura Reserve Forest, which lay directly across the north-eastern border of our estate. There were no pathways in these parts of the land, and there was no telling one direction from the other; even the terrain looked the same all around. It was no surprise that a novice such as me had completely lost his bearings.

I turned my horse around. Carefully surveying the terrain around me, I was able to determine the direction in which I would have to go in order to reach my destination. Riding a horse in such vast pathless open fields was no different from navigating a ship on the high seas, or from flying an aeroplane in the open skies. Anyone who has had the experience would vouch for this fact.

For several hours, I had to go back the same way I had come. The same sunburnt flora, the same intoxicating fragrance of unknown forest flowers wafting in the mild breeze, the same hillocks, the same blood-red blooms of palash. The sun had been climbing the firmament steadily, the thought of wetting my parched throat occurred to me, and as soon as it did, I suddenly recalled that other than the Karo river, there was no other body of water around here that I could drink from. I had not even crossed the borders of our own forests, the Karo was still several miles away from those borders. The more I thought about this, the more I seemed to feel thirsty.

I had instructed Mukunda Chakladar to put up a sign of some sort to demarcate the border of the estate—either a wooden post or a flag or something similar. I now realized that the man had never bothered to execute my orders. He must have thought the very idea of the Manager Babu from Kolkata coming all the way here to have a look to be utterly improbable. I rode on.

After crossing what I had mentally estimated to be the border of the estate, I saw smoke. I reached the spot to find a band of men burning wood to make charcoal—they would sell this charcoal to the villagers in the winter. The people of this land lit the coal to protect themselves from the winter.

Despite the fact that the charcoal was dirt cheap, very few people could afford them, and I often wondered if it was worth all the hard work of gathering the wood from the trees, burning them, making charcoal out of them and then carrying them such large distances to earn so meagre a profit, if at all. Ever since I had come here, I had come to realize that money was far more valuable in this region than it was back in Bengal.

On looking around, I saw a tiny canopy made of leaves and dry grass in the middle of a gooseberry grove, a few men were huddled under it, eating boiled corn out of green leaves. Other than salt, they had nothing else to eat the corn with. A few large holes had been dug around the shed, dozens of branches and twigs were being burnt in these makeshift kilns, a young lad was sitting next to these holes and turning the burning branches over with a long slender stick in his hand.

I asked, 'What is that inside those holes? What are you burning?'

The men immediately left their food behind and stood in a single file with their hands folded, their eyes lined with fear. One of them somehow managed to say between frightened stutters, 'Charcoal, Huzoor.'

I realized they must have seen me on horseback and mistaken me for an officer of the forest department. These regions were part of the core area of the forest and it was illegal to chop trees or burn wood without permission.

Once I had assured them that I was not who they had assumed I was, and that they could make as much coal as they wanted to, I asked if I could get some water to drink? One of them ran and fetched me a clean vessel of clear water.

incline of its banks, I could sense how deep the water must have been during the monsoons. Now, of course, there was very little water in it. I began my descent on horseback, and it almost seemed like I was climbing down the steep side of a hill. As I crossed the river, the water began to rise on the side of my horse's body, till a time came when it reached the stirrup. After some time, as it rose even more, I had to raise my feet above the saddle to keep myself dry, and manoeuvre the waters carefully to reach the other side. This bank was covered with the fiery red blossoms of wild palash as far as my eyes could see, so much so that even the ground on which the branches of the trees had cast their shadows had acquired a reddish hue. And then I saw a wild buffalo emerge from within the forest in the distance, it came out in the open and started digging the soil with its hooves. I reined in the horse to a halt and watched the animal with bated breath. There was not a single human being around here for miles. What if the beast charged at me? But fortunately, it turned around and disappeared within the same forest it had stepped out of.

I rode on. After crossing the river, the scenery had turned captivatingly beautiful, despite the scorching sun burning right over my head. In that blistering afternoon, I saw rows and rows of hills far towards my left, and to my right were long undulating strips of land strewn with pyrite, with woods of red and white flowers just beside them. I had never seen such barren and yet so beautiful a scene. How deep the blue of the sky was! Not a single bird in the sky, not a soul on land other than me and my horse. Only a seemingly unending hush had descended upon the land—stark, unforgiving and dangerously desolate. I looked around in silent admiration. Who would have thought that there was such a place in

India? As if I was witnessing a scene straight out of the book of Hodson, describing the basins of the Gila river. Or a picture of the South American deserts of Arizona or Navajo.

By the time I reached the fair, it was well past 1 p.m. in the afternoon. It was a massive affair, set up in the middle of the woods that skirted a village on the southernmost fringe of the same hills that had been accompanying me to my left all this while. The visitors to the fair were mostly women—young women, at that—all the way from such near and distant villages as Mahishardi, Tintanga Karari, Laxmaniatola, Bheemdastola, Mahalikharup and others. Also present were young forest-dwelling women, white buds of piyal or red *dhatup* flowers adorning their hair. Some of them had wooden combs holding their buns in place just over the shining nape of their shapely necks. Their forms and figures were quite full and attractive, and some of them looked rather lovely. They grinned and bantered among themselves, and were busy buying beaded necklaces, cheap Japanese and German soap-boxes, flutes, mirrors and essences of extremely poor quality. Ten Kali brand cigarettes were being sold for a paisa, and the men had huddled around to buy them. Little boys and girls were counting their pennies to budget for frozen sugar syrups, colourful sweets and fried bars of sesame.

A sudden piercing cry in a shrill feminine voice nearly threw me off horseback. A bunch of men and women were standing on top of a small hillock and chatting away gleefully amidst giggles and cuddles—it was from this crowd that the cry had emerged. What on earth was going on? Had same poor soul departed this mortal earth? On asking someone, I learnt that there was nothing to worry about, and that some married woman had accidentally met a distant relative from her father's village. Such was the custom of the land, apparently—if a married woman were to chance upon a friend or kin or even a former neighbour that she had not had the opportunity of meeting in several years, the two of them would inevitably embrace each other and start wailing their hearts out. Anyone unaware of this custom would naturally assume that someone acquainted to either of the two women must have passed away. But no, this was an expected form of greeting. If they didn't cry, they would be harshly judged and criticized in their villages. That a married woman may not weep on seeing the kin from her father's house—such unexpected and dishonourable behaviour was an indicator that she did not miss her paternal family and was therefore happy and content in her husband's house. This—I was told—was as unthinkable as it was severely frowned upon in this land.

In one corner, a man had spread a gunny bag on the ground and set up a bookshop—the fable of Gulabkavli, the immortal love story of Laila and Majnu, the tales of King Vikram and the spectre Betal, and other books, such as *Premsagar*, were the fairs on display. A few aged men were seen turning the pages of the books—on seeing them, it occurred to me that the book browsers described by Anatole France in Paris are no different than those in this spring fair in the jungle village of Tintanga Karari. If they get to read books for free at the shop itself, no one really bothered to buy them—and this was true anywhere in the world. The present bookseller turned out to be a man of acute commercial acumen though. Without a trace of hesitation in his voice, he asked every engrossed local reader if they were planning to buy the book in hand, for if not, they were to put the book down without any further delay and be on their way.

A little distance from the fair, a few people were engrossed in a little picnic of sorts in the middle of a sal grove. They were procuring the vegetables fresh from the fair market, and some of them were even busy buying dried fish, scrunchy prawns and red-ant eggs to take back to the makeshift kitchen. Red-ant eggs were a delicacy around these parts. Other than these, I also noticed raw papaya, dried berries, Kend fruits, guavas and wild beans on sale.

Suddenly, I heard someone calling out—'Manager Babu!'

I turned around to find Brahma Mahato making his way towards me through the crowd—he was my Labtulia collector's brother.

'When did you come, Huzoor? Who's come with you?'

I said, 'How are you, Brahma? Come to see the fair?'

'No, Huzoor, I am in charge of the fair. This land is mine. Please come with me to my tent, please come Huzoor.'

On one side of the fairgrounds was the tent of the lessor. Brahma welcomed me inside and offered me a Bentwood chair with great reverence. There, I saw a man, the like of which I doubt I will ever see again in this world. I was not quite sure who the man was, perhaps an employee of Brahma. Fifty or sixty years of age, with dark skin, bare chest and a head full of black and grey hair. He was carrying a large bag of coins in his hand and an old notebook under his armpit. I figured that he was walking around the fair, collecting rent from the shopkeepers and vendors, and was about to explain the accounts to Brahma Mahato.

The man exuded a strange mix of courtesy and modesty— perhaps a hint of respectful fear as well. Brahma Mahato was no king, no magistrate, not even a public servant. He was merely a senior subject of the estate; so what if he granted the lease of the fair here—why did this man seem so obliged to him? He was not even being able to gather the courage to make eye contact with me. Was he very poor? There was something in the man's face, I could not help myself staring at him from time to time. *Blessed are the meek for theirs is the kingdom of heaven*—said the holy book. I had never ever seen a face like that in my life.

I asked Brahma Mahato about the man and learnt that he lived in Tintanga Karari, the same village where Mahato lived. His name was Giridharilal, he was from the Gangota caste. A young son was all he had by way of a family. I was right about the man's financial condition—he used to live in abject poverty, until recently, when Brahma Mahato had employed him to collect rent from the vendors of the fair, with the promise of a daily wage of twenty-five paise and two meals a day.

That was not to be the last time I was meeting Giridharilal. In fact, the circumstances of our last meeting were rather tragic. But more of that later. I have met a lot of people in my life, but never before and never since have I met a man as honest as Giridharilal. So many years have passed, so many people have come and gone, but there are some people whose memories are to remain etched in some corner of my mind forever. Giridharilal was one of them.

[3]

It was getting quite late, I had to set off now. When I said as much to Brahma Mahato, he was visibly shocked. And not just him, everyone else present in the tent stared at me with wide eyes and open mouths. Impossible! Thirty miles and more, that too at such an hour! Huzoor was from Kolkata, and totally unaware of the norms of traveling in these parts. Huzoor wouldn't even be able to cover ten miles before sundown, and so what if it was a moonlit night, the forest was far too dense, there was not a single human soul for miles, there were tigers and wild buffaloes in the woods, and with all the wild berries ripening all around, even bears could be expected to come out of their hibernation and frequent the jungle. Why, just the other day, in the forests of Mahalikharup on the other side of the Karo, a tiger had dragged a bullock-cart driver into the woods; the poor old man was driving his cart through the forest all by himself in the middle of the night. Impossible, Huzoor. Please stay the night here, and dare we say, please grace us by dining with us, and when the day breaks, you can have a relaxed start to your long ride back home.

A full moon night in the peak of spring. And me galloping through the woods and hills with the wind on my face. How was I to expected to resist that? And perhaps I would never get such a wonderful opportunity ever again in my life. And all the scenery that had enchanted me on my way here—wouldn't I witness their ethereal beauty getting enhanced a thousand times in the soft glow of the full moon? Impossible!

Ignoring the pleas and requests of everyone present there, I set off on my journey back. Brahma Mahato's estimate had been on point. Even before I could reach the Karo river, the deep red disc of the sun began to sink behind a low range of hills on the western horizon. I had just reached the banks of the Karo and was just about to embark upon the cautious descent down to the river bed, when suddenly, I looked up to see the last remaining arc of the sun drop behind the hills, and as if on cue, a small silvery ball jump up over the dark and distant head of the lines of trees in the Mohanpura Forest Reserve. The phenomenon that I had just witnessed—the perfectly naturally synchronized setting of one celestial body with the rising of another—was as unreal as it was bewitching.

On the way, I found scattered woods at some spots, and dense jungles at others. At times, the trees and branches seemed to suddenly close in on me, and at times, they would again spread out to give my horse some room to manoeuvre. How dangerously desolate these places were! In daylight, they had presented a certain form of natural beauty, and now, by night, it almost seemed like I was riding through an enchanted land of fairies. At the same time, the threat of tigers was something that I was not being able to ignore. It wasn't just Brahma Mahato, everyone back at the cutcherry had repeatedly prohibited me from entering the forest at night. I recalled how, two or three months ago, a subject of the estate—his name was Nandakishor Gosain—had recounted the tale of a man being eaten alive by a tiger in the jungles of Mahalikharup. Moreover, there was the problem of the bears, thanks to the ripe berries. And although wild buffaloes did not live in these jungles, I would not be surprised if one of them lost its out of the Mohanpura Forest Reserve and wandered around here. I had seen one of them earlier today, after all! And I still had fifteen more miles to cover through the densest part of the forest.

It was then that I experienced for the first time that fear enhances the beauty of the surroundings. The path was not straight, it would bend to the left now and to the right minutes later. To my right, a short range of hills was my constant companion. Its slopes were covered with the shining bloom of *golgoli* and palash, with trees of sal and long blades of grass covering its crest. The moon was shining brightly, the shadows of the trees were shortening rapidly, an unknown aroma was wafting through the night air, and amidst all this, far away in the distance, there were flames dazzling on the side of the hills—dozens of them—lit by the Santhal villagers to clear land for their annual cultivation. I had never watched anything like this before, nor have I ever since.

Had I not come to these places, I wouldn't have believed that such desolate forests and hills existed so near to Bengal, nor that they could be compared to the deserts of Arizona or the Bushveld of Rhodesia—as much in beauty as in terms of dangers posed by its fauna.

As I rode on, I began to wonder what a strange life I was living right now! For those who do not like the notion of being confined to their homes, for those who do not care to settle down and start a family, it was for those off-beat, slightly eccentric wanderers that such a life was most suitable. The more I thought about it, the more I began to feel convinced that I was now an integral part of this land, and this land of me. Would I ever be able to return to Kolkata and remain caged in the humdrum of urban affairs? No, I wouldn't trade this freedom with even the most precious treasures of the world.

And then came a time when the moon began to shine so bright that the stars began to disappear. I looked around, only to be awed and amazed by this sublime beauty of nature. As if this was not the same planet that I had inhabited all my life. As if this was some strange extra-terrestrial world, where supernatural beings descended from time to time.

This image, this very notion of mother nature needs to be worshipped, needs to be dreamt of, needs to be paid tributes to, over and over and over again. To those who don't see beauty in a jungle flower, to those who have never felt the irrepressible desire to heed to the call of the horizon, they would never know the true meaning of living, and this planet that they call home would forever remain alien to them.

At about four miles after crossing the forests of Mahalikharup, I entered the borders of our estate. I reached the cutchery well past 9 p.m.

[4]

One day, a loud, repeated sound within the cutchery compound made me look out of the window of my cabin. A bunch of unknown men had gathered outside, playing dhols. The sepoys and staff of the cutchery had come out by now, and were watching the spectacle. I was wondering if I should call someone to ask what was going on, when head constable Muktinath Singh came and stood at the door, struck a salute and said, 'Would you please step out for a moment, Huzoor?'

'What's the matter, Muktinath?'

'The crops have failed in the southern provinces this year, Huzoor. There's been a famine. The people of the region have no food left, so they're wandering from place to place in small groups, dancing and singing. They are keen to perform for you. If Huzoor so permits, that is.'

The troupe came and stood outside my office room.

Muktinath Singh asked them what kind of dance they could perform. In response, the sexagenarian leader of the group gave a courteous bow and said, 'Huzoor, we will show you the *ho-ho* dance, and the *chhakar-bazi* dance too.'

I took a moment to survey the troupe, and it seemed to me that none of these men knew the first thing about dance, and that they were merely driven by the merciless pangs of hunger. They danced and sang for a long time. They had come when the sun had begun its descent from the zenith. Gradually, dusk fell, and the moon rose, bathing the compound with its light. The men were still dancing and singing. It was a strange recital, and the tune was something I had never heard the likes of before. But such strange melodies and stranger words seemed apt compositions under a starry sky, amid such vast open spaces. One of the songs went something like this—

> *I was a happy child*
> *Out there in the forest hills behind my village,*
> *Where I foraged for ripe fruits and*
> *Plucked sweet-smelling flowers of piyal*
> *My days were happy and carefree*
> *For I knew not what love is*
> *And then came the day when*
> *Armed with my wooden blowpipe and sharp darts*
> *I went snipe-hunting beside the five-streamed springs*
> *And clad in a plain yellow sari*
> *You came to fill your pots with sweet water*
> *You said to me—Shame on you!*
> *For no man in the land would do such a thing*
> *As to kill an innocent bird of the forest*
> *I threw away my pipe, I threw away my wooden darts too*
> *And away flew the forest bird, but*
> *You caged my heart in yours—forever!*

Tell me then, my love,
Who is the better hunter—you or me?

I understood some words, while the others seemed cryptic to me. Which is perhaps why I loved the songs even more. Words strung on the back of tunes. Tunes created in the shades and fragrances of the wild piyal trees from the southern hills.

As it turned out, their fee was a mere twenty-five paise. On seeing the look of surprise on my face, my staff began to tell me, 'Huzoor, this is more than enough; they don't expect anything more that this. Please do not give them more; it will only make them greedy. Moreover, it will also do the irreparable harm of ruining the chances of others who might want to hire them at reasonable rates.

I was quite taken aback. Seventeen-eighteen men of varying ages had danced tirelessly for over three hours. And all they were asking for was twenty-five paise! Twenty-five! They had walked miles through the forest, just to come to my cutcherry, so that they could show me their recital. Which also meant that they would not be able to perform anywhere else tonight.

I made up my mind. I made arrangements so that they could have their dinner at the cutcherry and spend the night here. In the morning, on handing over two rupees to the leader of the troupe, the old man was so surprised, that he could not say a word and kept staring at my face. Perhaps he was not expecting either such a hefty reward for their performance, or the previous night's food.

There was a young lad in the troupe, barely into his teens. His name was Dhaturia. The boy looked as pretty as an idol of Krishna. A headful of curly hair, manes flowing down his shoulders, pitch-dark skin, a calm pair of eyes. This was the boy who had stood right in front of the group last night. When he started singing and stomping on the ground with his anklet-clad feet, I had noticed a faint smile of innocence and devotion on his lips. How sweetly he sang, his hands swaying in the air—

Do accept my greetings
O Lord,
Do accept the greetings from this stranger

I looked at him and thought—here was a young boy, wandering with this group of men, only for a meal a day? And what meal, after all? A few seeds of China grass, and a bit of salt to go with it. On a lucky day, he would perhaps get a bit of curry with that. Not of potatoes or cauliflowers or such other delicacies. Of wild berries, jungle weeds, strange fruits. And with such bleak promises in mind, he had such a divine smile on his face when he sang! And not just a pretty smile, the boy had a strong build and elegant manners too.

I told the leader of the group, 'Why don't you leave that Dhaturia boy with us here? Let him work for the cutcherry, we will take care of his food and shelter.'

The old man was no less strange—quite childlike, even at the age of sixty-two.

He said, 'He won't be able to live here, Huzoor. He is with his own people from the village, that's what makes him happy. He is a young boy, he will feel bad if we leave him behind. I promise you, Huzoor, we will return to perform before you again, and when we do, we will bring him along.'

CHAPTER 6

[1]

Extensive surveys were being carried out in various parts of the forest. In this regard, one of our supervisors named Ramchandra Singh was stationed in the jungles of Bomaiburu, approximately six miles away from the cutchery. One morning, a strange news was brought to me—three days ago, Ramchandra Singh had suddenly gone mad.

On hearing this, I immediately reached the spot with a small posse of sepoys. The jungles of Bomaiburu weren't too dense. It comprised merely of a few scattered groves of wild bushes on an undulating plain. A few tall trees stood here and there, with thick vines hanging from their branches, bearing a strong resemblance to the masts of a ship rising high into the open skies, with ancient and weathered ropes hanging from them. The jungles of Bomaiburu were entirely devoid of any form of human habitation whatsoever.

Far from the bushlands, in the middle of an open field, there stood a couple of shanty huts. One was slightly larger— Ramchandra Singh lived here. His *tindal* (assistant), a man named Asrafi, lived in the other. When I arrived at the spot, I found Ramchandra lying quietly on a wooden charpoy inside his hut. On seeing us, he gave a start and sat upright. I asked him, 'What's the matter, Ramchandra? How are you?'

Ramchandra folded his hands and remained silent.

The response came from Asrafi instead. He said, 'It's a strange story, Huzoor. You'll probably refuse to believe what I'm about to tell you. I wanted to come to the cutcherry and report the matter to you myself, but how could I have left Supervisor Babu here all by himself? Especially after everything that has happened? Here is the crux of the matter, Huzoor—

For a few days now, Supervisor Babu has been complaining about a dog entering his hut in the night and disturbing his sleep. I sleep in the other hut, Babu sleeps here. Two–three days passed by, Babu had the same thing to say everyday, "Oh, there is this blasted white dog that comes every night, hides under my bed, makes soft whimpering noises, tries to snuggle up to me." I listened to him, but never bothered to care. Four days ago, he suddenly called out to me in the middle of the night, "Asrafi, come quickly, the dog is here. I've grabbed its tail, bring your stick."

By the time I sprung up from my bed, picked up the stick and the lantern and stepped out of my cabin, I saw—perhaps you wouldn't believe me, but I don't have the audacity to lie to you, Huzoor—a girl come out of this hut and run away towards the jungle. I was stumped for a moment or two. And then I entered the hut to find Babu sitting upright on his bed and looking for his matches in the dark. He said, "Did you see the dog?"

I said, "What dog, Babu? I saw a girl running out of the hut."

He said, "Idiot, are you trying to act smart with me? What girl do you think will come here in the middle of the forest, that too in the dead of the night? It was a dog, I had it by its tail, its long ears had brushed my arms. It was sitting under my bed and weeping in soft whimpers. What have you been smoking, eh? You want me to report you to the headquarters?"

The next night, I was on alert. I was planning to be up all night, but late after midnight, I must have dozed off a little, when I suddenly heard Babu crying out my name. I quickly rushed out, but just as I had reached my doorway, I saw a girl running along the northern wall of Babu's hut and going towards the jungle. It was then that I decided to enter the jungle myself, Huzoor. How far could she go, after all, and where would she hide? And we have surveyed the land, we know every little nook, every little hiding place like the back of our hands. I combed the woods, Huzoor, looked throughout the night, but I didn't find the girl. In the end, I had a doubt. I held the lantern close to the ground, and all I could see were my own footprints. Hers were nowhere to be seen.

I decided not to speak to Babu that night about any of these. It's just the two of us living all by ourselves in the middle of these jungles. What happened that night gave me a deathly scare. And I had heard these ominous stories about the woods of Bomaiburu too. My grandfather had told me. You see that huge banyan tree up on the hill over there, Huzoor? Many years ago, he was on his way back from Purnia after selling a crop of legumes, he was on his horseback, with a wad of cash in his pocket; night had fallen and the full moon had risen to the skies. As he was passing by the banyan tree, he saw a group of young girls holding hands and dancing in the moonlight. The people of nearby villages call them the 'damabanu', bewitching fairies who live deep within the desolate forest.

If they find an unsuspecting traveller stumbling upon them, they grab him and kill him.

The next night, I decided to stay in Babu's hut myself. I sat in one corner and stayed up all night, going over the calculations from the day's survey. I must have dozed off towards the end of the night, when I suddenly heard a soft sound. I opened my eyes and looked this way to find Supervisor Babu fast asleep in his bed. But it seemed to me that something was hiding under his bed. I lowered my head to take a look under the bed, and as soon as I did, my heart stopped. In the half-light, half-dark, I saw a girl sitting under the bed, all curled up, and smiling eerily at me. I saw her with my own eyes, Huzoor—I can swear by the touch of your feet. I still remember the look in her eyes, and her head full of curly black hair. I came back to fetch the lantern from the spot where I was doing my calculations, when I heard a sound behind me. I turned around to find something crawling out of the bed and going towards the door of the hut. The light from the lantern had fallen on the door, Huzoor, and I saw a dog—a large, sparkling white dog—run out of the door.

Babu had woken up by now, and he said, "What's the matter, what are you looking at?"

I said, "Nothing, Babu. Must have been a fox or a dog. It had entered the hut, it's gone now."

He said, "Dog? What kind of dog?"

I said, "It was a large, white dog, Babu."

He frowned and said, "White dog? Are you sure it was a white dog? Not a black one?"

I said, "No, Babu, it was a white dog."

On hearing this, he seemed a little disappointed for some strange reason. In the light of the lantern, I saw him let out a deep sigh, lie back on his bed, turn around and promptly go back to sleep! I was so scared that I couldn't sleep for the rest of the night, Huzoor. I couldn't understand why Babu was expecting it to be a black dog, and not a white one. Early next morning, while Babu was still fast asleep, surprising as it may seem, I decided to check under the bed. I crawled under his bed to find a lock of curly black hair. Here it is, Huzoor, a lock of hair from a woman's head. Where did this hair come from? How did it get under the bed? A beautiful, soft, lock of jet-black hair. Such a long strand of hair couldn't have come from the body of a dog, and certainly not from the body of a white dog. This was last Sunday, it's been three days now. Over these three days, Babu has slowly gone mad, Huzoor. And, I'm scared, because I know it's my turn now.'

It did seem like a tall tale to me. The lock of hair didn't mean much either. It had undoubtedly come from the head of a girl. But Asrafi was a young man, and everyone in my staff vouched for the fact that he neither drank nor touched opium or anything of that sort.

The supervisor's tent was the only sign of human habitation in the middle of this desolate forest. The nearest village was Labtulia, and that was six miles away. Why would a young girl wander around every night in these woods, especially when there were tigers and wild boards around?

If I were to believe Asrafi's story, there would be no doubt that the matter was utterly baffling. Or perhaps, neither the twentieth century, nor the nineteenth, had found a way to enter this godforsaken land yet, and perhaps the region was still shrouded in the inexplicable mysteries of the dark past. Everything was possible here.

I decided to disband the station at Bomaiburu, and to have Ramchandra Singh and his tindal brought back to the cutchery. As the days passed, Ramchandra's condition began to worsen. In the end, he turned completely insane. He slept during the day and stayed up all night—screaming, singing or simply blabbering nonsense. I summoned a doctor to have him looked at, but nothing seemed to work. After a few days, a cousin of his came to the cutchery and took him away.

There was a conclusion to this strange incident, and although it happened a good seven or eight months after Ramchandra left us, it would not harm to talk about it here.

Around six months after this incident, in the month of April, two men came to see me at the cutchery. One of them was old—must have been sixty or sixty-five, and the other was his son, who seemed to be in his early twenties. They had come from the Balia district, with the intention of leasing a piece of forest land so that they could graze their cattle.

I had already distributed all other grazing grounds by then; only the woods near Domaiburu was still available, and that's what I arranged for them. The old man even paid a visit to the woods along with his son. He seemed quite happy upon his return, and said, 'Such tall blades of grass, Huzoor, such a lovely jungle! If you wouldn't have been so kind to us, we'd never have found such a nice piece of grazing ground for our cattle.'

The matter of Ramchandra and his tindal Asrafi was completely out of my mind by then. And even if I would have remembered, perhaps I would not have told the old man about it. Because it was a large piece of land, and if the story would have scared the man away, the estate would have suffered a considerable loss. Ever since the incident with Ramchandra Singh, no one dared to go near those woods anymore.

A couple of months later, in the beginning of June, the old man made a rather furious appearance in the cutcherry, with his somewhat frightened young son in tow.

I asked, 'What's the matter?'

The old man was trembling in rage, he said, 'I had to bring this rascal to you, Huzoor. He deserves a hundred smacks of Huzoor's shoes—perhaps that would drive some sense and shame into his ungrateful mind.'

'Why, what happened?'

'I'm ashamed to say this to you, Huzoor. Ever since this idiot has come here, he's completely lost his mind. I have been noticing for the last seven or eight days, Huzoor—how do I even utter such scandalous words in your presence—every night, a girl runs out of the hut, before I can nab her. We have a single hut out there, Huzoor, just a few feet across, the roof covered with thatch and dry grass—he and I both sleep there. And I'm not the kind of man who is easily duped. On two consecutive nights, I noticed the girl leaving, so on the third day morning, I confronted my son and asked him what was going on. He feigned such a shock, it would have put even the best of stage-actors to shame! He said, "What girl? What on earth are you talking about?" So I thought I must have made a mistake, perhaps I saw something else with these sleepy eyes of mine. But when I saw the girl that very night once again, I pulled up my boy and gave him a nice beating. I wasn't going to let him turn into one of those wayward little brutes, was I? But would you believe it, Huzoor? He did it again! The girl came back the next night too, and the night after that. And then I said to myself, if I have to save my boy,

I will have to take him to Huzoor. If only Huzoor would be so kind as to give him the hardest of spankings . . . '

The incident with Ramchandra Singh came back to me, I said, 'When exactly do you see this girl?'

'Almost towards the end of the night, Huzoor. Just an hour or so before the crack of dawn.'

'And you are absolutely sure it was a girl?'

'My eyes have still not lost their sight, Huzoor. It was a girl alright, a young girl. Clad in a white sari some nights, red or black on others. One night, as she was running out, I jumped out of my bed and followed her into the tall bushes of catkins. But I lost her, couldn't find her anywhere. So I returned to the hut, only to find this blasted imbecile lying in his bed, acting as if he was fast asleep. When I roared at him, he woke up with a start, as if he had woken up from a deep sleep. I tell you, Huzoor, this is not the job of a doctor, oh no. Only Huzoor's rebukes can cure this shameless bugger.'

I took the boy aside and said, 'What's all this I'm hearing about you?'

The boy instantly fell at my feet and said, 'Trust me, Huzoor, I don't know a thing about any girl. I graze my buffaloes in the woods all day, and sleep like a log at night. I wake up right at the crack of dawn. Even if the hut were on fire, I wouldn't know anything about it.'

I said, 'You've never seen anything enter the hut?'

'No, Huzoor. Once I'm asleep, I'm completely out of my senses.'

I thought for a few moments and realized that there was nothing else to say. The old man seemed quite happy, though. He must have thought I had taken his boy aside and gave him a bit of talking-to. A fortnight or so later, the boy came back to me and said, 'Huzoor, I wanted to ask you something, if you permit me. The other day, when I had come to the cutcherry with my father, why did you ask me if I had seen anything enter the hut?'

'Why, what's the matter?'

'Huzoor, ever since that day, I haven't been able to sleep properly, perhaps because of my father's scolding, or perhaps because you asked me that strange question. Most of the nights, I tend to fleet in and out of sleep every now and then. For the last few nights, I have been noticing a white dog inside the hut, I don't know where it comes from. It comes past the dead of the night, an hour or so before dawn. The strange thing is, the moment I wake up, it runs away, and it does this even if I've simply opened my eyes without making even the faintest of sounds. How does it get to know that I have woken up? I noticed this for a few nights. But something has happened last night, Huzoor, my father doesn't know, I haven't told him yet—I figured I should speak to you first. Late last night, I woke up to realize that the dog had entered the room once again, and was slowly making its way out of the door. There was a window on the wall, next to the door. In the time that it takes to blink an eye, I jumped up and looked out of the window. But there was no dog there, Huzoor. All I could see was a young girl running away towards the woods behind the hut. I immediately ran out and looked around, but there was no one to be seen anywhere. I didn't tell my old man about this. I don't understand what's going on.'

I said a few words of assurance and told him that he must have had a dream or something. I also told him that if he and his father were scared to stay in the hut at night, then they could come and sleep here in the cutcherry. Somewhat embarrassed at this offer, and at the doubts that were being cast on his courage, the boy went away. But I began to feel uncomfortable. I decided that if I heard about this even one more time, I would send a couple of guards to sleep in their hut with them.

Even then, I had not realized the seriousness of the situation. And by the time I did, it was too late. The accident had already happened, and in the most sudden and unexpected manner possible.

Three days later, I had just risen from bed in the morning, when news came that in the jungles of Bomaiburu, the old man's son had been found dead. I immediately rode to the spot, to find the poor boy's corpse still lying on the ground in the groves of wild catkins behind his hut. There was a look of horror on his face, as if he had seen something terrifying and his heart had stopped in an instant. The boy's father said that he had woken up late at night to find his son absent from bed. He had come out of the hut to look for his boy, but it was not until dawn that his corpse was discovered. From the stick and the shattered lantern that lay near him, it seemed that the boy must have seen something late in the night, and then followed it into the jungle. What was it that he was pursuing? There was no way to tell, for other than his own footprints, there were no other prints on the soft ground— neither human, nor of any animal. Even his corpse had no wound or bruise of any kind. This mysterious incident in the jungles of Bomaiburu remained unsolved forever, and even though the police came and carried out their investigation, it was never found why or how the young boy had met such a macabre end. The incident created such an unprecedented terror in the minds of the locals that everyone stopped going out after dark. It came to a point, where for a few days, I myself was scared to death as I lay alone in bed in my cabin at the cutchery, and I was frightened to open my eyes and look out of the window at the moonlit night, and at the vast open spaces and dense woods that had once seemed so enchantingly beautiful to me. My heart would be aflutter, and my mouth would turn dry, and I would wonder if I should run away to Kolkata, to escape this unearthly and bewitching nocturnal beauty of nature. It seemed to me as if this image of nature was nothing but a beautiful illusion to trap me and then ruthlessly suck the life out of me. As if these lands were never meant for the habitation of humans, as if it was those unnamed ancient mysterious beings who had always lived here, and as if they were riled to see us humans take over their land. I was convinced that they would avenge this unwanted trespass at the first opportunity they found.

[2]

I still remember the day I met Raju Pandey for the first time. I was busy with my work one morning at the cutchery, when a fair, good-looking Brahmin stood in front of me and offered a namaskar. He must have been at least fifty-five or fifty-six, but he couldn't be called an old man by any stretch of imagination, for back in Bengal, even the most masculine young men wouldn't have so toned and so well-built a physique as him. He had a small smear of vermilion on his forehead, a white chuddar on his body and a small cloth bundle in his hands.

On being questioned about the purpose of his visit, the man said that he had travelled a great distance to come here, and that he wanted to lease some land to grow crops. He added that he was very poor, didn't have any money to pay the lease and asked if I could arrange a small piece of land at half the regular amount.

There is a certain kind of people who hardly say anything about themselves or let their feelings show, but even a cursory glance at their faces reveal a lot about them. I felt the same way about Raju Pandey. The man had come all the way from Dharampur pargana with the hope of getting some land, and I knew that if I were to turn him away, he would go back without saying a word alright, but would be left heartbroken and dejected.

I gave half an acre of land to Raju near the dense forests of Labtulia Baihar, almost free of cost. I told him that he would have to clear the land before he could start cultivating, and that for the first two years, he would not have to pay anything. From the third year onwards, he would have to pay half a rupee as tax for his land. Raju went away happily, and even then, I had not realized what a strange man I had helped settle down in the estate!

Raju must have come in the month of September or October, and soon, amidst a flurry of work and activities, I completely forgot about him. The next winter, I was returning from the cutcherry in Labtulia one day, when I suddenly saw someone sitting under a tree and reading a book. On seeing me, the man quickly hid his book behind his back and rose to his feet. I recognized the man, it was Raju Pandey. But ever since he had leased the land last year, he had never come to the cutcherry, not even once. What could be the meaning of this? I said, 'I didn't know you were still here, Raju? I thought you must have left the land and gone back home. Didn't you grow your crop?'

Raju's face had turned pale and white by now. He stammered, 'Yes, Huzoor. I did . . . manage to . . . but . . . '

I suddenly felt quite angry with the man. These kinds of people had the habit of sweet-talking their way through to get their job done. I said, 'Well, I haven't seen a hair on your head in the last year and a half. You've done a fine job of tricking the estate and keeping all the crop for yourself, I'll give you that. The thought of bringing the cutcherry its share of crop never crossed your mind, I suppose?'

Raju raised his shocked and frightened eyes towards me and said, 'Crop, Huzoor? I never thought I'd have to give a share . . . it's just China grass seeds . . . '

I did not quite feel like trusting those words. I said, 'You've been eating China grass seeds all these days? There's no other crop? Why, haven't you grown maize?'

'No, Huzoor. The jungles are too dense and thorny. I am here all by myself, I couldn't clear it all. After a lot of effort, all I could prepare for tilling were a few square yards of land. Would Huzoor be so kind as to grace my land with his visit?'

I followed Raju. His land was in the middle of such dense jungles, that even my horse was finding it difficult to make its way through. After traveling for some distance, I came across a clearing in the heart of the forest, with a circular piece of land right in the middle of it. Two small shanties stood in one corner, they were made of wild grass and dead leaves. One was for Raju. The other for his crop. I peeked inside—indeed, there was a heap of China grass seeds stored in the granary, no other crop. I said, 'I didn't realize you were so lazy, Raju! You couldn't clear out half an acre of forest in eighteen months?'

Raju said in a trembling voice, 'I . . . I hardly get any time, Huzoor.'

'Why, what do you do all day?'

Raju didn't say anything, he stood in shy silence, hanging his head. I peeked into his hut now, there was hardly anything in his possession. Except a large metallic pot. I figured he must have been cooking his rice in this pot. But then I remembered, he had only been having China seeds all these months. Why need such a large metallic pot then? Grass seeds are best had off the green sal leaves. And as for water, there's a small pond nearby. What was the pot doing in Raju's hut then?

And then I saw the idol. It was a small idol, made of black stone, and smeared with vermilion. It had been placed in one corner of the hut, on a stone slab. Radha and Krishna, side by side. It was then that I realized that Raju Pandey was a devout and religious man! There were a few wild flowers placed in front of the idol, and a couple of books and handwritten manuscripts kept next to the stone slab. In other words, Raju spent most of his time in prayer and other customs of devotion, and hardly found time for his cultivation.

Such was Raju Pandey. He was quite fluent in reading and writing Hindi, and even knew a bit of Sanskrit. It wasn't like he read all the time. Often, he would simply sit under his favourite tree and quietly stare at the distant hills and the blue sky. On another day, as I was passing by his hut, I saw that he had made a quill from the stem of a reed and was busy writing something with it on a piece of paper. I was curious! Did Pandey write poetry too? But he was so shy, and spoke so little about himself, that it was virtually impossible for me to get him to say anything.

One day, I asked him, 'Do you have a family, Raju?'

'I do, Huzoor. Three boys, two girls, a widowed sister.'

'How do they manage?'

Raju raised his hands in the air, looked at the sky and said, 'God almighty takes care of them. I've come all this way from home in the shelter of Huzoor, only to feed my family. Once I am able to clear out the land . . . '

'But how will the crop from a mere half-an-acre land feed so many mouths? And you don't seem to be trying too hard either?'

Raju did not respond for some time. Then he said, 'Life is very short, Huzoor. When I begin to clear the jungle, so many thoughts cross my mind, I sit down and start thinking. You see all these woods around you? They are so beautiful! These flowers—they have been blooming since eternity. Those birds—forever chirping, forever happy. The gods ride the chariot of winds and step onto this land. In a place where people only talk about money, about give and take, about buying and selling—the air in those places have turned into venom, Huzoor. The gods avoid those places. But here . . . I raise my axe to clear the jungle, and they come and snatch my axe away from my hand. Then they whisper such wonderful things in my ears that I don't feel like thinking about money and such other worldly matters anymore.'

I realized Raju may or may not be a poet, but he was certainly a philosopher.

I said, 'But Raju, the gods will never tell you not to send money home, or to let your children go without a meal, would they? I think you should get back to work. Or else, I will be forced to take the land away from you.'

A few more months passed by. I visited Raju every now and then. Truth be told, I quite liked the man and his simple ways and thoughts. How he lived in the middle of that dense jungle all by himself, I will never know.

The more I saw of him, the more I began to realize what a simple, pious and austere man Raju was! He had not been able to grow any other crop, so he had been eating seeds of China grass year after year—that too with a smile of contentment on his face. He never got to meet anyone, never chattted with anyone. But that did not seem to bother him at all. On the contrary, he seemed to enjoy the solitude. When I passed by his land in the afternoon, I found him toiling away. In the evenings, I often saw him sitting under that myrobalan tree of his, staring into the void quietly. On some days, he had a sheet of paper in his hands; on other days, he did not.

One day, I told him, 'I'm giving you some more land, Raju. Make sure you work harder and grow more crops, or else your family is going to starve to death!' Raju was as calm as ever. He did take the land, but in the next six months, he never managed to clear the jungle and start growing another crop. By the time he finished his morning prayers and chants of the Geeta, it would be 10 a.m. He would set out for work after that. After working for a couple of hours, it would be time for him to cook his meal. He resumed his work after lunch and toiled the whole afternoon, all the way till 5 p.m. in the evening. After this, he sat under his tree in silence till the stars came up.

That year, on my insistence, Raju grew a crop of maize. He didn't even keep a single cob for himself, and sent the entire crop home. His eldest son came and took the crop away. When the young fellow had come to pay me a visit at the cutcherry, I gave him a bit of chiding, 'You've left your old man all by himself in the middle of this forest, aren't you ashamed of yourself? Why don't you and your brothers earn your own living?'

[3]

That year, there was a serious outbreak of cholera in the village of Shuormari, I heard the news in the cutcherry itself. Shuormari was not part of our estate, it was located near the confluence of the Kushi and Kalbolia rivers, around twenty miles from here. Dozens of people were dying every day, corpses were seen flowing down the Kushi river, there were no provisions to cremate them. One day, news came that Raju Pandey had left for Shuormari to treat the patients. I never knew that Raju Pandey had any medical knowledge, but I myself had dabbled with homeopathy for some time, and I was wondering if I could be of any assistance to those poor people in Shuormari. A large group of men from the cutcherry travelled with me to the village. On reaching there, I met Raju Pandey. He was running around from one household to another with a few barks and roots in a small purse. On seeing me, he offered a respectful namaskar and said, 'Now that Huzoor is here, these poor people will be saved from their doom.' As if I was the district civil surgeon, or Doctor Goodeve Chuckerbutty himself. Raju took me from door to door.

Raju gave all his medicine away on credit. Apparently, it had been decided that the patients would pay him once they had been cured. Oh, what brutal and fearsome images of poverty I saw in every hut that day! Tiny little shanties made of thatch and leaves, impossibly low roofs, no windows, no light or air in the rooms. Almost every household had a victim or two; they were all lying on soiled beds placed on the ground. There were no doctors, no medicine and not even a proper diet for anyone. Raju was trying his best, of course, running from one hut to another, feeding his medicine to the patients, even if they did not call him. I even heard that he had spent the whole of the previous night trying to nurse a dying child back to health. But despite all his efforts, the epidemic did not show the slightest sign of slowing down. On the contrary, it seemed to spread and turn deadlier than ever.

Raju took me to a household. A single room, with signs of abject poverty everywhere. The patient was lying on a tattered mat on the ground. A man in his early fifties. A seventeen to eighteen-year-old girl was sitting at the doorway and crying her heart out. Raju consoled her and said, 'Don't cry, my child. Now that Huzoor has come, everything will be fine.'

Those words made me ashamed of my inability to help these people. I asked, 'Is she the man's daughter?'

Raju said, 'No, Huzoor. She is his wife. She has no one else in the whole wide world. She had a widowed mother, who died soon after her wedding to this man. Please save him, Huzoor, or else the girl will have nowhere else to go.'

I was about to say something in response, when all of a sudden, a wooden shelf on the wall just behind the man's head caught my attention. In one corner of this shelf was an uncovered bowl of stone, and in the bowl was a small mound of rice, with at least a dozen flies sitting on it. Dear God! The man was dying from Asiatic Cholera, one of the most deadly diseases in the world, and within three feet of his head, there was an uncovered vessel with rice in it!

Having nursed her husband throughout the day, the young girl would perhaps sit down with the rice at sundown and gobble it up hungrily with some salt and a couple of chillies! Poisoned food, with ruthless, certain and unforgiving death written on every single grain! I looked at the simple tearful eyes of the young girl and shivered in fear. I told Raju, 'Ask her to throw away this rice. Whose idea was it to keep food in this room?'

The girl stared at me with a blank expression on her face. Why was she to throw away the rice? What would she eat, then? Why, the good folks of the Ojha family had very kindly left the bowl of rice for her this morning.

I recalled how rice was considered a delicacy in this land, just as mutton or pulao was in ours. I summoned a stern voice and said, 'Get up and throw this rice away first.'

The frightened girl did what she had been asked.

But her husband could not be saved. Soon after dusk fell, the man breathed his last. The girl began to wail, and even Raju could not hold back his tears.

After this, Raju took me to another household. This was the house of a distant kin of his. When he had first come to the region, it was this family that had sheltered him. Now, mother and son both were suffering from cholera. Two rooms, side by side, the mother had been kept in one, the seven- or eight-year-old son in the other. The woman was eager to see her son, the boy was crying for his mother.

It was the boy who died first. We did not let the mother know. My homeopathy slowly began to bring her back from the clutches of death. As she began to come back to her senses, she began to ask for her son every now and then. Why was there no sound coming from the other room? How was her child doing?

We assured her, 'He has been given a sedative, he's fast asleep.'

With a great deal of effort, the tiny little corpse was secretly brought out of the other room and taken away.

These poor, illiterate villagers knew nothing about health and hygiene. There was all but one pond in the village, and it was used for bathing and washing clothes. Despite my best attempts, I failed to explain to them a simple fact, that under no circumstances could they even think of drinking the same water that they were using to wash themselves and their clothes.

Several men, women and children had been abandoned by their families. I saw a patient lying inside a hut, all by himself. There was no one in the household anymore. After the outbreak, his family had left him behind and run away. Thanks to my medicine, the man survived. But he was left so weak and helpless, that I realized his troubles had only begun.

Raju and I were taking a break, when I saw him counting his earnings from the fees. I asked him, 'How much did you earn, Raju?'

Raju finished his counting and said, 'Nearly a couple of rupees, Huzoor.'

It was quite obvious that he was quite content with whatever he had earned. Not without good reason, I thought. People of this land hardly saw the face of a paisa without toiling blood and sweat, two rupees were a big amount for them. For over a fortnight, Raju had to work incessantly, day and night—as a doctor, and as a nurse—to earn two rupees.

It was quite late in the night. A shrill sound of wailing pierced the silence. One more dead. I could not sleep. Most people in the village were wide awake. They had made fires out in the open and were burning sulphur to cover the stench of death. Everyone was huddled around the fire, talking in low, frightened whispers, terror plastered over their face. Whose turn would it be next?

Late in the night, news came—the young girl who had been widowed that very morning was now down with cholera herself. Raju and I rushed to the household once again. She was nowhere to be seen. We discovered her in a cowshed, next to her home. On being asked, she said that she was too afraid to sleep in the same hut where her husband had died so gruesome a death earlier today. When she had gone from door to door looking for some shelter, no one had opened their doors to her, just because she had touched her husband's corpse. Finally, exhausted and diseased, she had collapsed in one corner of this cowshed. We saw her tossing and turning in pain in the dark. Raju and I tried our best. Not a single lantern, nor a single drop of drinking water was to be found anywhere. No one came offering their help. Everyone was scared to death, even before the disease could kill them.

Dawn began to break.

Raju was good at reading pulse. He grabbed the girl's wrist for some time and said with a grave face, 'This doesn't look good, Huzoor.'

What could I do? I wasn't a doctor myself. Perhaps, she needed saline; a qualified doctor could have helped her.

The girl died at nine in the morning.

Had we not been there, her corpse would have been left right there in the cowshed. On our ardent pleas, a couple of

cattle-grazers came with thick, long sticks, and began pushing
and rolling the corpse with the sticks along the dirt-covered
road that led to the river, till I turned around and shut my
eyes to such an inhuman sight.

Raju Pandey said, 'That takes care of her, Huzoor. It's
better this way, you know? A young widow, penniless, with
nowhere to go. Who would have taken care of her?'

I opened my eyes and said, 'How cruel your land is, Raju!'

Raju sighed and hung his head. And I began to wonder
if I would ever be able to forgive myself for denying a hungry
young girl a tiny mound of rice that she had so eagerly set
aside for herself.

[4]

In the dead calm of the afternoon, the hills of Mahalikharup
and the adjoining forests seemed so enchanting! I had made
countless plans to scale those hills, but had never found
the time to act upon them. I had heard that the hills were
impassable, covered with impenetrable forests—ones that
were home to hundreds of slithering king cobras, gigantic
bears and the rare wild *chandramallika* flowers. Perhaps
because there was no water at the top of the hills, or perhaps
because of all the snakes, even the woodcutters never dared to
venture into those forests.

Spread across the horizon like a blue streak of light, the
hills had a rather hypnotic and dreamlike quality to them.
The more I began to witness the beauty of the region, the
more it began to seem to me like some mythical playground
for frolicking fairies. Its deep forests, its never-ending
desolation, its grave silence, its mysteries, its people, the

sweet chirping of its birds, its colourful flora—everything seemed strange to me, and lent such an inexplicably peaceful sensation to my mind—one that I had never experienced ever before in my life. Even more inviting were those distant hills of Mahalikharup, and the borders of the Mohanpura Reserve Forest. Together, they offered images of such incomparable beauty to my eyes and raised such melancholic thoughts in my mind at the same time!

One day, I set out for the hills. After riding nine miles on my horse, I found myself navigating a narrow pass between two hills towering over me to my left and to my right. The slopes of the hills on both sides were covered with dense and strange-looking forests, the path ahead meandered through wild bushes and thorny shrubs, sloping up at times, then down again, intersecting tiny streams trickling along beds of smooth pebbles and shiny boulders. I had not come across any chandramallikas yet, for autumn was almost around the corner, and this was not the time for chandramallikas to bloom. But I did witness the wild beauty of *shefali* flowers—hundreds of them had fallen on the ground, turning it into a white carpet. Many other flowers had bloomed after the monsoons—strange bunches of bloom that seemed to scatter the seven hues of the rainbow all around, *arjun* and piyal, vines of varied kinds and colours, beautiful orchids—they had all come together to scatter such an intoxicating aroma in the air!

I had been around for so many years, how come I had not known anything about the beauty of these hills? From a distance, the jungles of Mahalikharup had always been a fearsome place for me—infested with snakes, tigers, large sleuths of bears. Why, I had not seen even a single bear yet!

forests, these hills—they must have stood here in this manner
for hundreds of years now. In the distant past, when the
Aryans had crossed the Khyber Pass and entered the land of
the five rivers, these forests and these hills had been standing
here in the same manner. When Gautam Buddha had
secretly walked out on his newlywed young wife, that night
too, the peaks of Mahalikharup must have been smiling in
the same manner in the moonlight as they do now. Sitting
in his hut by the banks of the Tamasa, when Valmiki must
have been lost in his composition of the great epic, and the
gentle bleating of the does returning to his ashram at the end
of the day must have startled him, he must have looked up to
find the setting sun slowly disappearing behind the horizon,
and the reddish tinge on the clouds of the sky must have been
reflected on the still waters of the Tamasa. Even that evening,
the same sun must have reddened the peaks of Mahalikharup
in the same way as it was about to do right in front of my
eyes today. All those years ago, when Emperor Chandragupta
ascended the throne for the first time, when the Greek
ambassador Heliodorus constructed the famous pillar with
the statue of Garuda as its crest, the day Princess Sanyukta
chose to garland the statue of King Prithviraj in a hallroom
full of suitors, the night a doomed Dara secretly escaped from
Agra to Delhi after being defeated in the Battle of Samugarh,
the night Chaitanya Dev performed kirtan at Sreebas' house,
or the day when the Battle of Plassey began—those mighty
peaks of Mahalikharup, these forests all around me were just
the same. Who must have lived in these forests at that time?
I had passed through a village in the foothills on my way
here, with merely a few thatch-roofed huts and shanties. Just
a couple of makeshift foot-driven wooden husking pedals,

now being used to smash seeds of mahua to extract oil. And an old woman, at least ninety years old, if not more—her hair as grey as a sheaf of flax, tiny chips of wood flying off her wrinkled and wizened skin—the old hag was sitting calmly in the sun and looking for lice in her own hair. Sitting here, I remembered that decrepit old woman, who reminded me of the description of the disguised goddess, Annapurna, from Bharatchandra Ray's eulogy. She was the symbol of an ancient civilization, one that was born deep within these forests. Her ancestors had been dwelling in these forests for hundreds of years now. And early this morning, the descendants of those very men and women had crushed the seeds of mahua and extracted oil, just like they had done the day when a young man was being crucified outside the city of Jerusalem. A million memories of the past had vanished forever in the dense fogs of time, and these people were still hunting birds and rabbits with their wooden blowpipes and hand-sharpened darts. Neither their knowledge, nor their understanding of God, or of the rest of the world, had seen any progress in the last hundred years. I was willing to give away a year's worth of my earnings to know what went through the mind of that woman day and night.

I don't know what seeds of civilization are sown deep into the hearts and minds of certain races, whereas there are others, who—despite prolonged passages of time—remain frozen where they are. Within a span of four or five thousand years, the barbaric Aryans wrote the Vedas, the Upanishads, the Puranas and the epics—not to mention the great treatises of astronomy and geometry—along with the much-followed compendia of Charak and Sushruta. They planned and executed great conquests, established empires, created such exquisite artwork as the Venus de Milo, built the Parthenon, the Taj Mahal and the Cathedral of Cologne, composed the Darbari Kanada and the Fifth Symphony, invented ships, trains, aeroplanes, wireless and electricity—whereas the primitive inhabitants of Papua New Guinea and Australia, along with our own Mundas, Kols, Nagas and Kukis, had not progressed at all in these five thousand years.

Eons ago, there must have been a great ocean at the spot where I was sitting now; its raging waves must have crashed and broken on the sandy shores during the Cambrian period—the same shores that have now been turned into these mighty hills. Sitting here on one of the rocks of the same hills, I imagined the deep blue waters of that ancient ocean.

Where there once flowed a mighty river
Now lay only the sandy silt of time.

It was on these mountain peaks made of sand and stone that the great oceans of the forgotten past had left the signs of their rage and fury; those signs were very clear and were easily visible to the discerning eyes of a geologist. Mankind had still not appeared on the face of this planet, nor had the trees or the plants that we see around us today. The crust of the earth now bore signs that the flora and fauna of those times had left behind. These signs were visible to anyone who would care to visit a museum.

The evening sun had bathed the peaks of Mahalikharup in a golden hue. In the air laden with the sweet aroma of shefali, I also felt the slight nip of the autumn chill. It would not be prudent to stay back here any longer, I thought, for as per my calculations, the night that was about to fall upon me very soon would be black and moonless. A pack of foxes yelped from within the forest to announce the hour, and I hoped and prayed that I would not chance upon any other beasts on my way back.

I did encounter wild peacocks on the way, though. There were two of them, sitting on a low perch of rocks. As I approached on horseback, one of them flew away, but the other remained motionless. With the thought of tigers still lurking at the back of my head, I took a moment to halt right in front of the bird and admire its beauty. This was the first time I was seeing a peacock in the wild. I had heard rumours that they inhabited the forests of Mahalikharup, but I had never really seen one of them before. But I did not dare to linger on too long, for I had heard other rumours too, those that involved the big cat, and I had no intention to find out first-hand if those were true as well.

CHAPTER 7

[1]

Homesickness is a strange feeling. Its myriad emotions are alien to those who have spent all their lives in one place, to those who have never had to stay away from their native country at all. When one has stayed long enough in a land far from home, stripped of the company of dear friends and near kin, one knows how empty, how barren one's heart feels every now and then. Even the most insignificant incidents of the past turn themselves into fond memories, and one wonders if one would ever be able to have the good fortune of such sweet experiences ever again. There is a perpetual feeling of depression, and the mind seems to crave for every little thing that belongs to home.

Having spent so many years here, those were the exact feelings that I had. Several times, I had thought of writing to the headquarters, applying for leave, but the pressure of work was so high that a strong feeling of hesitation and guilt had stopped me from doing so every time. But then again, spending day after day, month after month, year after year in these desolate forests and hills all by myself was gradually becoming more and more difficult. It felt as if I had forgotten everything about Bengal. I had not seen the festival of Durga Puja in so many years, nor had I listened to the traditional beating of the drums that were so inseparable a part of the Charak festival. I had not filled my lungs with the sweet aroma of incenses burning before the altar of deities in the temples back home. Or lain in my bed and enjoyed the sweet and familiar chirpings of birds on summer mornings. Or seen the domestic interiors of a Bengali household with my own eyes—that calm, sanctified and oh-so familiar place—a kitchen full of utensils made of brass and bell metal, the elegant decorations of a prayer room and the inconsequential little belongings of a homemaker that she had carefully stowed away like a priceless treasure in a tiny little alcove on the wall of her bedchamber. All of these seemed like a dream that I had once seen, but had forgotten all about upon awaking.

When the winters went by and spring came along, this barren emptiness of my heart seemed to get the better of me.

Under such yearning circumstances, I went out for a ride towards Saraswati Kundi one day; it was a large lake surrounded by forests on all sides. On my way, I got off my horse in a low-lying valley and stood there for some time in absolute silence. All around me were raised plateaus of red soil, and on top of them were the dense and wind-swept jungles of tall white catkins and wild tamarisks. Over my head was the clear blue sky. Bunches of purple flowers had bloomed in a thorny bush, they looked somewhat like European cornflowers. A single flower wasn't so remarkable, but with hundreds of them swaying in bunches, they gave the impression of a purple sari blowing in the wind. Under the dull grey jungles of catkins, these little flowers seemed to be celebrating the festival of spring in their own colourful ways,

Nadha on his way back to the cutcherry after finishing his day's survey of the western borders of the Baihar. Alighting from his horse, he asked me with concern, 'What are you doing here, Huzoor?' I said, 'Just wandering around, Puranchand.'

He said, 'You shouldn't be here all by yourself, Huzoor; it isn't safe. Let's go back to the cutcherry, please. My tindal has seen a massive tiger in those catkin jungles with his own eyes. Please come with me, Huzoor.'

From somewhere far behind him, the melodious voice of Puranchand's tindal came floating in the twilight breeze in the form of an evening prayer:

Bless me with your mercy, o Lord—

From that day onwards, my heart used to pine for home every time I saw those purple thorn-flowers, and every time I heard Puranchand's tindal, Chhottulal, sitting in his little hut and singing to his heart's content as he baked his bread in his earthen kiln:

Bless me with your mercy, o Lord—

As I used to stare at the jungles of tamarisks near my cabin, or at the distant horizon mingling with the forests and hills, I used to say to myself—never again in this lifetime would I be able to stand on the sandy shores of the river in my village and fill my lungs with the fragrance of spring, for I would perhaps end up giving my life to some ferocious carnivore right here in these wilds. But no matter how many of such ominous thoughts crossed my mind, the jungles, the hills and the horizon stood just as they are—unfazed, insouciant and visually bountiful as ever.

On one such morning of abject homesickness, I received an invitation to Holi from the household of Rashbehari Singh. He was a well-renowned money lender in the province, an influential man, Rajput by birth, and had leased a vast tract of land from the government on the banks of the Karo. His village was a good thirteen-fourteen miles away from the cutchery, just outside the borders of the Mohanpura Reserve Forest.

Declining the invite would be the most discourteous thing to do. On the other hand, I was not at all keen to enjoy Rashbehari Singh's hospitality. His primary business comprised of lending money at high interest to the poor and downtrodden members of the Gangota caste, and then to collect it all back—almost always by force. The man had built his fortune on the corpses of the poor. He ruled the entire province with an iron hand, and no one dared to say a word against his oppression. He had an entire army of henchmen on his rolls, and they muscled their way to get him what he wanted. If, at any time, Rashbehari Singh felt that such and such person had not showed him enough respect, then that person was done for. Rashbehari Singh would go after the man with everything he had, and either through the full force of his might, or through an intricate and prolonged series of carefully planned deceptions and trickery, he would end up teaching him a lesson.

Ever since I had come here, I was told that for all practical purposes, Rashbehari Singh was the king of the land. Young and old, poor or comparatively well-to-do—no one dared to say anything against him. His army of men ran amok through the region, swiftly silencing any feeble voices of protest. Even the police were rumoured to be living off his purse. Senior government officials and circle managers would accept his hospitality every now and then. Why would he care for anyone in the middle of this jungle?

When Rashbehari Singh tried his antics on my subjects, I protested. I firmly let him know that he was free to do anything that he pleased in his own area, for I was not the law of the land, but if he or his men were to even think of touching a strand of hair on any of my subject's heads, then he would regret it for the rest of his life. It reached to a point where early last year, there was a brief battle of arms between Rashbehari Singh's men and the sepoys of my staff Mukundi Chakladar and Ganpat Tehsildar. A few months later, when another episode of trouble started brewing, a senior officer of the police came and mitigated the matter. Ever since then, the subjects of my estate had not had to face any trouble from Rashbehari Singh.

Naturally, on receiving an invitation from the same man, I was quite taken aback.

I summoned Ganpat Tehsildar and sought his advice. Ganpat said, 'I don't know, Huzoor, I don't trust that man at all. He can do anything and everything, God knows what ulterior motive he has behind inviting you into his home? My advice would be not to go.'

I somehow couldn't concur. The festival of Holi was of utmost importance to the Rajputs, if I were to decline his invite to celebrate such a big festival, he would feel seriously insulted. What was worse, he might take my reluctance to attend as a sign of fear—and that, in turn, would be a matter of great personal insult to me. No, come hell or high water, I had to go.

Almost everyone in the cutcherry tried to dissuade me in various ways. Good old Muneshwar Singh came to my cabin and said, 'I know you've made up your mind, Huzoor, but you don't know the wayward ways of these people. They don't bat an eyelid before taking someone's life. Uncultured, illiterate people—they don't have a care in the world for consequences and repercussions. Moreover, Rashbehari Singh is a dangerous man. He has committed countless murders with his own hands, Huzoor. There's nothing he's not capable of doing—murder, arson, false legal cases, he has been doing all these for years now.'

Paying no heed to all such warnings, I set out for Rashbehari Singh's house. It was a large house, with brick walls and pantile roof—as the more well-to-do people of the region often had the luxury of affording. There was a wide veranda in front of the house, with tar-painted posts. A couple of charpoys had been laid out, and a few people were sitting there and smoking tobacco out of hookahs.

As soon as my horse reached a neighing halt in the courtyard of the house, the loud and sudden sound of a couple of gunshots reached my ears. This did not take me by surprise though. Rashbehari Singh's men were expecting me, and I was aware of this gesture of welcome. But where was the man of the house? It was not customary to dismount till the man of the house had come out himself to usher me in personally.

A minute or so later, Rashbehari Singh's elder brother Rashullas Singh stepped out of the house, extended his arms forward and said in a courteous voice, 'Welcome, welcome. A hearty welcome to our humble home.' The slightly uncomfortable feeling in my mind disappeared in an instant.

If no one would have come out to greet me, I would have turned around and left.

The yard was full of people, mostly subjects from the Gangota caste, dressed in unclean, tattered clothes, colours smeared on their faces, busy playing Holi in the house of the richest man in the land.

After almost half an hour later, Rashbehari Singh came, and seemed rather surprised. Perhaps he had not expected me to accept his invitation. He took great care of me, though.

The adjacent room that he took me to had all but two or three large thick-legged and thick-armed chairs made of Sheesham wood, obviously crafted by local carpenters. There was a small bench in one corner and a vermilion and sandal smeared idol of Ganesh in an alcove on the wall.

A few minutes later, a young boy came and placed a large tray in front of me. I looked down at the tray and saw a small heap of coloured powder, several flowers, some money, a few crystals of sugar, a few seeds of cardamom and a small garland. Rashbehari Singh smeared some of the colour on my forehead, and I returned the gesture. Having picked up the garland from the tray, I kept staring at the tray, wondering what else was I supposed to do, when Rashbehari Singh pointed towards the money and said, 'This is a humble tribute to Huzoor, you have to accept it.' I brought some money out of my own pocket, placed it on the tray and said, 'Have some sweets distributed among everyone.'

Rashbehari Singh spent the next hour or so showing me around his house and giving me a glimpse of his prosperity. The number of cows in the shed wouldn't have been any less than sixty or sixty-five. Seven or eight horses in the stable—two of them could apparently dance so well that he expressed his desire to have them put up an exclusive show for me some day. He didn't have any elephants yet, but he was planning to buy one soon, for that was the one true hallmark of being wealthy, prosperous and respectful in this land. His farm produced more than 300 quintals of wheat, which fed more than eighty people every day. He himself claimed to have a litre and a half of milk for breakfast every morning, along with specially made sugar crystals from Bikaner, not the cheap ones that were found in the local markets here. That, apparently, was another sign of prosperity in this region.

After this, Rashbehari Singh took me to a room, where I saw at least two thousand unpeeled corn cobs hanging from the ceiling. These, as he told me, were seeds of corn—being prepared for next year's crop. He showed me a large vessel, made by riveting sheets of iron together, in which 40 litres of milk were supposedly boiled every morning, for that was the daily consumption of his household. In another room, there were so many spears, shields, knives, swords and sticks stacked, that it looked like a fully functional and often-accessed armoury in itself.

Rashbehari Singh was father to six sons. The eldest must have been thirty years old at least. The first four sons were just like their father—strongly built, and a face full of dark twirling moustaches and beards. Looking at his sons and his armoury, I realized why the poor, feeble and unfed Gangotas feared them so much.

Rashbehari was a grave man of few words, and I soon realized that he was rather sensitive about his honour as well. The fact that he was the most influential man in the region seemed quite important to him, and he always made it a point to have a regal air about him. Those around him were always on their toes, and spoke to him only when asked to, choosing their words and tones with great care.

If anyone were to ask me to describe a symbol of unrefined prosperity, I would point them towards Rashbehari Singh's house. In all the abundance I witnessed in his household—in the granary full of grains, in the sheds full of milch cows, in the armoury full of deadly weapons and a kitchen full of rice, wheat, fish, meat and sugar crystals from Bikaner, there was a clear sign of coarseness and lack of good taste. There was not a single photograph or painting on any of the walls, no sign of a book or a written word, and let alone a comfortable couch or an armchair, there was not even a decent bed in the house. The walls were covered with the red stains of betel-leaf juice and even the white ones of lime to go with them. There was a filthy open drain behind the house, a perfect breeding ground of all the flies buzzing around. There was no sign of elegance or domestic décor. The children never went to school, their own clothes and shoes were rather cheap and extremely shabby. Last year, as many as four children of the household had succumbed to smallpox. To what end was all this wealth for, then? Of what use was all the money earned by beating those poor Gangotas black and blue every day? What was the purpose of all this prosperity? Other than to feed the ego of one man?

But there was an unquestionable abundance in the food I had been served. How on earth was it possible for one man to have so much? Fifteen or sixteen large pooris—as big as an elephant's ears. Dozens of bowls filled to their brims with curries of various kinds. Sweetmeats, condiments, curds and papads. I never had this much food in four meals of mine put together. On being told so, Rashbehari Singh said that he himself consumed twice as much in each meal.

By the time I finished my meal and stepped out onto the courtyard, the sun had begun to set. Hordes of Gangota subjects were huddled outside, happily gorging on the curd and fried seeds of China that were being served to them. Everyone's clothes had turned red after the day's celebrations, everyone had a smile on their faces. Rashbehari Singh's brother was strolling around, supervising the entire affair. Although the food being served to those poor souls was rather petty and practically inedible, they seemed quite happy and content, as evident from the smiles on their faces.

It was there at Rashbehari's house that I met Dhaturia after all these years. The boy had grown up into a fine young man by now, and his dance had improved too. He had been hired to perform at the Holi celebrations.

I called him closer and said, 'Do you remember me, Dhaturia?'

Dhaturia greeted me with a smile and said, 'Yes, Huzoor. You are Manager Babu. How are you, Huzoor?'

I looked at the honest, innocent smile of the boy and felt sorry for him. A poor orphan, left with no other choice, but to dance at festivals and ceremonies in order to earn his living—that too in front of vain, uncultured brutes such as Rashbehari Singh.

I asked him, 'You'll have to dance all the way till midnight here, won't you? What would you get paid?'

Dhaturia said, 'Twenty-five paise, Huzoor. And all I can eat.'

'You mean, rice?'

'No, Huzoor. The water they boil their rice in—that water. And curd. And sugar. They might even give a sweet if I'm lucky; they'd given one last year.'

Dhaturia's face lit up in the anticipation of the upcoming meal. I said, 'Is this what you get everywhere you dance?'

Dhaturia said, 'No, Huzoor. Rashbehari Singh is a rich man; so, he will give twenty-five paise, and the food. Others pay only half of that, and there's no food. But sometimes, they give a small mound of gram grist. That tastes quite nice.'

'Are you able to manage with this?'

'Dance doesn't pay, Babu. It used to, in the past, but not anymore. These days, most people are trying to make ends meet somehow. Where will they get the money to pay for a dance show? When they don't hire me, I end up working in the farms and fields as labour. Last year, for instance, I had survived somehow by reaping the maize crops for a local farmer. What can I do, Huzoor? I have to eat, after all. I'd learnt this Chhakkarbazi dance from Gaya with a lot of interest. But no one wants to see it anymore. It's a lot of hard work too.'

I invited Dhaturia for a recital at the cutcherry. He was an artist—a talented young man with the usual nonchalance of a true practitioner of the arts.

With the moon high up in the sky, I set out for the cutcherry back from Rashbehari Singh's home. As I raced my horse away from the courtyard, I once again heard two gunshots in my honour, ringing through the air.

It was the night of the Dol or Holi festival, the perfectly circular disc of the full moon was shining down upon me, lending a shimmer to the silica in the path that ran through the open fields ahead of me. Somewhere far away, an unknown night bird was calling out from its nest, as if a wandering traveller was pleading for help after losing his way in the vast and desolate terrain.

Someone called out to me from behind, 'Huzoor! Manager Babu!'

I looked back to find Dhaturia running behind my horse.

I stopped and asked him, 'What's the matter, Dhaturia?'

Dhaturia took a moment to catch his breath, and after a bit of hesitation, said in a shy voice, 'I wanted to ask you a question, Huzoor—'

I said in an assuring tone, 'Sure, what is it?'

'Would you please take me to your city, Huzoor? To Kolkata?'

'Why, what would you do there?'

'I've never been there, Huzoor. But I've heard that they really value their artists there—singers, musicians and dancers. I'd learnt so many dance forms, Huzoor. But there's no one here to understand or admire my dance. I . . . I feel very sad sometimes. Moreover, I'm beginning to forget everything I had learnt. I'd taken a lot of pain to learn them all. Huzoor will be surprised to hear my story.'

The village was far behind us now; we were standing in the middle of moonlit plains that rolled away all the way to the horizon. I realized that Dhaturia wanted to speak to me in private, because if Rashbehari Singh were to come to know, he would be in trouble. I looked around to find a lone flowering tree of *simul* standing nearby. I got off my horse under the tree, sat down on a rock and said to Dhaturia, 'Go ahead, tell me your story.'

After a moment's pause, Dhaturia began—

'I had heard about a man named Vittaldas, who lived in the district of Gaya. He was a great master of the Chhakkarbazi dance. I had always wanted to learn the dance; so, I went to Gaya. I wandered around from one village to another, looking for Vittaldas. No one could tell me where he lived. Finally, one night, I had taken shelter under a shed of buffaloes that belonged to a group of cattle herders, when I suddenly heard them talking among themselves about Chhakkarbazi dance. It was quite late at night, and it was freezing. I was lying on the hay in one corner of the shed, but as soon as I heard them talking about the Chhakkarbazi dance, I jumped up and ran up to them. I sat amidst them and heard them talking about the dance. I can't tell you how happy I was that night, Huzoor! It seemed to me as if I had found a connection with those strangers—as if they were my own men, my own blood. It was from them that I learnt where Vittaldas lived. Thirty miles from there, in a village called Teentanga.'

I was listening with rapt attention to the fascinating story of a young artist's tutelage. I said, 'So, you went there?'

'Yes, Huzoor. On foot. Vittaldas turned out to be an old man. A face full of silver white beard, on seeing me, he asked, "What do you want?" I said, "I've come to learn the Chhakkarbazi dance." He seemed surprised to hear that, and said, "Do young men like these things these days? People have all but forgotten about such things." I touched his feet and said, "You have to teach me. I've come looking for you from a long, long way." The old man's eyes filled up with tears. He said, "This dance has been there in my family for the last seven generations. But I don't have a son; so, I had given up all hope of passing on my knowledge to the next generation. Nor has anyone ever come to me and asked me to teach them in all these years. You are the first. Very well, I'll teach you." That's how I started, Huzoor. It's taken me a lot of effort to learn the dance. But it's a waste performing before the Gangotas. They don't understand head or tail of it. But

CHAPTER 8

[1]

Nature has the habit of bestowing the most precious of gifts upon those who worship her. But the devotion she seeks in return must be sincere, everlasting and excruciatingly arduous. And like any other woman, jealousy is an ornament that always adorns her beauty, for she demands one's unwavering and undivided attention at all times. Anything short of that, and she will summarily refuse to be wooed into unveiling her priceless charm.

On the other hand, if you were to devote all your thoughts and considerations to her and her alone, she would grace you with such amazing boons of bliss and ecstasy, that you are bound to be enamoured by her radiance and benevolence. Night and day, she would open new windows in your mind, through which, she would show you such sights that you would have never seen before. She would keep your mind fresh and youthful, and be your faithful companion as you walk down the coveted and elusive path of immortality.

Let me tell you about a few such experiences of mine. Although I could write pages after pages of such futile descriptions and would still be unable to convey what I mean.

Moreover, I scarcely find people who would have the ear and the patience to listen to me, or the imagination to understand what I am trying to say. How many people truly love nature, after all?

At the edge of the forest, in the grasslands of Labtulia, the blooming of the *dudhli* flower would announce the advent of spring. It was a pretty flower, which looked just like a star, yellow in colour, with a long slender stem disappearing amidst the blades of grass to grab the heart of the earth with its strong roots. At dawn, it could be found in all its glory, and in full bloom, in the fields and by the side of pathways. But as the sun's rays would grow stronger, the flowers would begin to curl up, back into the buds. The next morning, I would see the same buds in full bloom once again.

Blood red flowers of palash were abundant in the reserve forest of Mohanpura and in the foothills of the Mahalikharup. These places were far away from our estate, a four to five-hour-long ride at the minimum. In these places, the spring air was laden with the fragrance of freshly sprouted shoots of the sal tree, the scarlet flowers of simul would light up the horizon with their hue, but neither the koel, nor any other singing bird could be heard—perhaps they did not quite like the perches in these parts of the forest.

Once in a while, I would crave to pay a visit to Bengal. The familiar rural imagery of my own land would ache my heart, and I would wonder how I ended up truly knowing my motherland only when I had left it behind. I had never pined for my land when I used to live there, but here I was now, yearning for a glimpse. It was a strange, quaint feeling—it could only be felt, it could never be described in words.

But what I have been trying to explain over and over again, in so many ways, and perhaps failing to do so each time, is the mysterious limitlessness of the forest, its inaccessibility, its vastness and its inexplicable fear-inducing beauty that is sure to leave the curious onlooker in goosebumps. It is impossible for me to explain this in something so futile as words.

As the sun went down and I sat on the back of my horse in the middle of the rolling fields of wild tamarisks and swaying catkins of Labtulia, my mind seemed to be veiled in the deepest mysteries of the forest. On some days, it came to me in the form of unadulterated fear. On others, it took on the form of a dull, hopeless and grave emotion. Sometimes, it seemed like a sweet dream, and sometimes, it left me with a searing pain—the same pain that men and women all over the world must feel when they lose something that is dear to them. As if it was some silent music of the highest order, rising and falling with the faint twinkling of the stars, sustaining in the stillness of the full moon nights, throbbing with the rhythmic calls of the pintail and sweeping past me like the tail of a comet in the sparkling October sky.

If you were a family man, bound by the duties and responsibilities of day-to-day life, then perhaps, you were better off not witnessing this aspect of nature. For if you did, you were certain to leave everything behind and become a roving wanderer—just like Harry Johnston, or Marco Polo, or Hudson, or Shackleton. Once you have heard the call of the forest and made the mistake of heeding to it, you would never be able to return home, no matter how much you tried, and no matter how much your heart craved for it. Such had been my condition too.

Once in a while, I would step out of my cabin in the middle of the night and stand outside, staring into the dark plains that lay before me, or admiring the beauty of the full moon in the sky. It would not be even the slightest exaggeration to say that such moments were perilous, for they were perfectly capable of driving the more fainthearted among us to insanity. Such were their profound beauty.

But it must also be said that such unearthly glimpses of nature were rather rare. If such vast forests, such blue hills, such rare flora were to be easily available everywhere, then would the entire country not have been infested with poets and madmen?

Let me tell you how I had once witnessed this unusual beauty of nature.

I received a telegram from our lawyer in Purnia one afternoon. It said that I was to present myself in court the very next day, or else we were sure to lose an important litigation of the estate.

Purnia was at a distance of fifty-five miles from the cutcherry. There was only one nightly train that could take me there. The nearest station was in Kataria, which was seventeen miles away. Which meant that even if I were to start right away, I would still miss that train. I saw no other option but to make the entire journey on horseback.

It was to be a long journey, and the path went through the middle of the forest. Dusk was about to fall. So, it was decided that Tehsildar Sajjan Singh would accompany me.

The two of us set out in the evening. By the time we had entered the forest, the moon was already up in the sky. In the faint moonlight, the forest around us began to look strange and mysterious. We were riding side by side—Sujan Singh and myself. The path was sloping up and down, the sand on the ground was shining in the moonlight. A shrub here, a bush there, and forests of catkins and tamarisks all around us. Sujan Singh was talking away and I was listening. The shine of the moon began to grow brighter by the hour, and everything around us seemed to come alive. To our left were the plains of catkins, reaching far out to the horizon. To our right was the forest. There was no sign of human habitation as far as the eyes could see. A dead calm had descended over the forest. It seemed like we were two inhabitants of some alien planet, riding along in the middle of the night.

Suddenly, Sujan Singh stopped his horse and gestured towards me to stop too. What was the matter? I looked ahead to see a large wild boar coming out of the jungle and crossing our path, leading its litter from one side of the woods to the other. Sujan Singh said, 'Oh, thank God! For a moment there, I had thought it was a wild buffalo. We are almost at the edge of the Mohanpura Forest, these places are full of wild buffaloes. Just the other day, a man was viciously attacked and killed by one.'

We moved on. After some time, in the bright light, we saw something black standing on the side of the path up ahead.

Sujan said, 'Stop your horse, Huzoor, it will get scared.'

In the deathly silence of the night, we waited with bated breath. But the black mass didn't seem to move at all. In the end, on being approached with tense caution, it turned out to be an abandoned shanty, made of thatch and leaves. Much relieved, we set our horses to a gallop, to make up for the lost time. Trees, shrubs and fields—all rushing past us. I turned around to find a huge cloud of dust that the hooves of our horses were leaving behind in the forest. Somewhere in the night sky, a lonely bird must have lost her companion and was crying out in acute shock and fear. We raced through the woods and the plains at breakneck speed.

Several hours passed by, my back had begun to hurt by now, the seat of the saddle had become too warm to bear and the horses had broken pace and were now trotting along. My horse was a rather skittish animal; so I had to watch the path ahead quite keenly. If it saw something in the dark and came to an abrupt halt, I would be thrown clean off its back.

Those who had been on this path before had been kind enough to tie the heads of the catkins into a knot. This was the only way for us to tell the route, as there were no signposts or such other in the middle of the jungle. After some time, Sujan Singh said, 'Stop, Huzoor. We seem to have come the wrong way.'

I looked up at the Great Bear and found the north. Purnia was straight towards the north from our cutchery. So, we were on the right path, after all. I explained the same to Sujan Singh.

Sujan said, 'No, Huzoor. We have to cross the Kushi river at a particular spot and have to go north-east from here. Once we are on the other side, we can keep riding north.'

As it turned out, Sujan was right. After some time, we found the correct path.

The moon was shining in all its glory now, bathing the sand-covered pathway, the fields of catkins and the trees of the forest with its light. The two horses were galloping at the top of their speed. They had begun to tire out now, as were Sujan and I. Even in this wintry night, we were drenched in sweat.

We stopped our horses under a large shimul tree on the edge of the forest, and decided to take a short ten-minute break. Up ahead, at a distance, a small rivulet was flowing, I knew it would flow right into the Kushi towards the east. The shimul tree had flowered, it was the tallest tree in the vicinity, the rest were all stunted shrubs and bushes. There was no sign of a path anywhere in the jungle. Both Sujan and I were feeling thirsty.

The light around us had become quite faint by now, as the moon had almost descended behind the hills in the horizon. There were long, dark shadows all around. I looked at my watch, it was almost four. The end-of-the-night air had become quite chilly. I was afraid we would stumble upon a herd of wild elephants. I had heard that there was one such herd on the run in the forests of Madhubani nearby.

We started off once again. Gradually, tiny hillocks and boulders began to appear around us, our path meandering around them. The night had become pitch dark now, the hills and the forests looked strange and scary. After some time, the eastern sky started showing early signs of fair light. The wet air of dawn began to cool our faces. The two horses were dripping with sweat. Both the animals were quite strong, we had left the cutchery at dusk, and they were galloping straight into dawn. But up ahead, the path just did not seem to end. Miles and miles of forest still lay ahead of us.

From behind the hills of the north, the red disc of the sun had begun to peep out—just like the circular smear of vermilion on a woman's forehead. We stopped in a village on the way and bought some milk. After gulping it all down and finding our strength, we started off yet again. After two more hours of riding, we reached the town of Purnia.

I finished my work in Purnia, but only in a partially attentive state. My mind was still on the moonlit path that

I had traversed, and the possibility of witnessing it all over again on the way back. My companion expressed his desire to set off immediately after finishing our work—while there was abundant daylight all around, but I turned a deaf ear to his requests.

We started at dusk once again. Moonrise was slightly delayed that night, but the shine on it remained all the way till the crack of dawn. And what a pretty shine it was! Everything around us looked so calm and serene in that charming light. The same hillocks, the same plains, the same flowers and the same forests seemed even more beautiful to our exhausted eyes this time. As if we were two lone souls loitering the world that Buddha had described as one where the moon did not rise and yet there was no darkness.

Many years later, as I sat in my own house in the lanes of Kolkata after leaving the freedom of the forest behind, as I heard the wheels of my wife's sewing machine turn in a steady din, as I let myself drown in the warm reminiscences of a forgotten life, I had recalled those two nights of galloping through the windswept forests and moonlit fields with great fondness, and I had dreamt that I was on horseback once again, riding back from Purnia.

[2]

Towards the end of April, one fine day, news came that there was a Bengali doctor named Rakhal Babu in the village of Sitapur; he had passed away quite unexpectedly the previous night.

I had never heard of the gentleman before. Nor did I know that there was a doctor in Sitapur. As it turned out, the

man had been living in Sitapur for over two decades now.
I also learnt that he practised his trade in the region, which
had helped him build a house in the village, and that he was
survived by his wife and sons.

A Bengali gentleman had passed away in an alien land,
that too quite suddenly, what condition were his wife and
son in, who was looking after them, what arrangements had
been made for the man's last rites—such questions began to
haunt me. After giving the matter some thought, I came to
the conclusion that my first and foremost duty was to go and
pay the family my condolences.

On inquiring with my staff, I found that the village
of Sitapur was around twenty miles from the cutcherry,
within the estate of Karari. I reached the place that very
evening. I asked around on the roads to find the late
Rakhal Babu's house. Two large rooms on one side, a few
smaller ones on the other and a sitting room modelled after
local architecture, which essentially meant that the room
had no walls on three sides. There was no way to single
this out as a Bengali household. From the charpoy in the
sitting room to the flag of Hanuman in the courtyard—
everything was local.

A twelve–thirteen-year-old came out of the house and
asked me in coarse Hindi, 'Who are you looking for?'

The lad didn't look like a Bengali boy at all. He had a
typical tuft of hair on his head, tied into a knot, just like
the Hindustani locals, and although he was dressed in the
customary attire of bereavement, he looked decidedly native
to the region.

Having introduced myself, I said, 'If there is an elder in
your home right now, I would like to have a few words.'

The boy said that he was the eldest of the sons, and that he had two younger brothers. There was no other guardian in the house.

I said, 'Go and tell your mother that I would like to speak to her.'

After some time, the boy returned and ushered me into the house. Rakhal Babu's wife was quite young, perhaps under thirty; she was dressed in the whites of a widow and her eyes were swollen from all the weeping. There were signs of poverty all around the house. A couple of broken charpoys, tattered quilts, shabby pillows, a trunk made of tin, a few utensils here and there. I said, 'I am a Bengali, I live nearby. I heard about Rakhal Babu, so I came. I feel I have a certain duty towards you and your family. If you need any kind of help, please do not hesitate to tell me.'

Rakhal Babu's widow stood behind the door and wept silently. I did my best to consoler her and expressed my willingness to help in any way I could. The lady now stepped out in front of me. She said, 'You are like a brother to me, a godsend in these difficult times.'

Over the next hour or so, I learnt that the demise of the man of the house had left this family in grave and helpless circumstances. Rakhal Babu had apparently been bed-ridden for more than a year now. With the primary source of income gone, the family had been left with no choice but to dip into their savings for Rakhal Babu's treatment and the running of the household. They were now left with no money for his last rites.

I asked, 'I'm told that Rakhal Babu had been in the village for several years now. Did he not have a good trade?'

The poor lady's hesitation had subsided to some extent by now—perhaps, on having the unexpectedly good fortune of being able to talk to someone in her own tongue in the middle of this alien land. In fact, she seemed somewhat relieved to speak to me.

She said, 'I don't know about his income in the past. We had been married for fifteen years now; he had a wife before I came. When she passed away, he married me. Ever since I have come, we have hardly been able to make ends meet. No one has any money in this place, you see. They can't pay any fees. They usually give wheat or maize. It was the month of February last year when he took to bed, and ever since then, I have not seen the face of a penny. But the people of this land helped in whatever little ways they could. They cleared their dues and brought in wheat, maize and pulses. Otherwise, we would have starved to death.'

I asked, 'Where do your parents live? Have they been informed?'

Rakhal Babu's wife remained silent for some time. Then she said, 'I have never seen my parents; I have only heard that they were somewhere from Murshidabad. Ever since I was a child, I had been living with my sister and her husband in Sahebganj. My parents were long dead. A few years after my wedding, my sister passed away. Her husband has married again. How can I go back to him anymore?'

'Didn't Rakhal Babu have any relatives anywhere?'

'He used to say that his cousins lived in his native place, but they were never in touch with him, nor he with them. I don't think they were on good terms; so, there's no point in giving them the news. My husband had an uncle from his mother's side—I had heard he lived in Kashi. But I don't know his address.'

It was a dangerously helpless situation. The poor woman had no one to care for her in this friendless, kinless land far away from home, which was clearly not her home anymore. On imagining what her condition would be in the face of such extreme poverty—that too with three children to feed—I felt extremely hopeless. I did whatever little I could for the time being and returned to the cutchery. I wrote to the headquarters and got a sanction of hundred rupees from the estate towards Rakhal Babu's last rites.

After this, I used to go to Rakhal Babu's house from time to time. I had managed to get a monthly sanction of ten rupees from the estate towards the family that the deceased man had left behind. I had visited his widow personally to hand over the first month's allowance. I had begun addressing her as sister by then. She used to treat me very warmly and was immensely grateful for what I had done for her and her children. Soon, her kindness and hospitality became a relief for the times when my own heart wept for home, and I never missed an opportunity to visit her.

[3]

Beyond the northern borders of Labtulia lay the Saraswati Lake, which the locals referred to as the Saraswati Kundi. And on the banks of the lake was a dense forest. Such a strange forest was not to be found in Labtulia or anywhere else in our estate. Everywhere you looked, there would be large trees all around, with the ground covered thick with strange vines and wildflowers—perhaps because of the proximity to the water.

This forest had covered the shore of the blue lake on three sides. The fourth was open, offering an unrestricted view of the distant hills and the blue skies. So, if one were to sit on the shore that ran from the east to the west, one would be able to truly appreciate the beauty of the place. A glance to the left would offer a glimpse of the dense green foliage of the nearly impenetrable forest. And looking towards the right, one could witness the calm and clear waters of the lake reflecting the hues of the azure sky—a view that was bound to have a distinctly serene and cooling effect on a restless mind.

I would often go and sit atop a large boulder on the shore every now and then. Sometimes, I would spend a lazy afternoon wandering around in the forest. I would sit under one of those large trees and listen to the chirping of the birds. Sometimes, I would collect flowers and saplings and gather fruits. Our estate didn't have as many birds as I got to see in those forests. Perhaps because of the abundance of fruits, or perhaps because they could build their nests high up above the ground on top of those tall, massive trees, the forests of the Saraswati Kundi were thronging with birds. There were a wide variety of strange looking wildflowers too.

The forests ran more three miles in length, and were almost a mile and a half wide. There was a narrow pathway that ran from the edge of the lake deep into the heart of the forest—I used to walk along the path and explore the woods. Sometimes, when I used to turn around and look back, I could see the shining blue waters of the lake, along with bits and pieces of the sky hanging over it, and the grave, dignified hills in the distance. There would be a soft breeze blowing, birds chirping over my head, and the sweet smell of some unknown wildflower wafting around in the air.

One day, I climbed my way up to the branch of a tree. It was a sense of joy that I had never felt before. Over my head, there was a green canopy of leaves, offering the occasional glimpse of the blue of the sky. Just beside me, within my arm's reach, was a large thick vine covered with bunches of flowers gently swaying in the breeze. Several feet below me, I could see the massive mushrooms that had sprouted from the damp ground. All I felt like doing in a place like this was think. New thoughts, new ideas, new feelings and emotions—all gathered around in my mind. A strange sensation of desire and glee made its way from the deepest core of my being all the way to my heart. And with every throb of my pulse, with every beating of my heart, I could sense that all the vines swaying around me, all the trees and all the flowers were alive, just like I was.

As I said before, there were hardly any birds around in our estate. That part of the province had its own distinct flora and fauna. Even when spring came, one would never hear the sweet call of a koel, or see a flower that one commonly associated with the season. The entire place donned a crude, barren look—gentle and elegant in its serenity, but devoid of any sweetness and charm. Like the constant humming of a single, unwavering note that dare not be disturbed by the gaiety of a joyous and colourful melody. Such a sight of nature lent a certain kind of deep stillness to the mind, but failed to cheer one up.

The forests of Saraswati Kundi, on the other hand, had the power to infuse mirth in every pore of my body, just like a lively tune would. They took me to a languid, dreamlike state. I had spent countless afternoons sitting in silence in the shade of a tree by the calm waters of the lake, and my mind would to wander away from the chirping of the birds, the fragrance of the freshly bloomed flowers of wild neem and the bounty of water lilies right in front of me. Having spent hours lost in my own thoughts, I would suddenly realize that night was falling, and that it was time to head back home.

Land was being surveyed for distribution among subjects in the Narha Baihar, I had to go there quite often to explain everything to the supervisors. On my way back, I would take a detour of a mile or two towards the south-easterly direction, just so I could wander around in the shade of the forests of Saraswati Kundi.

One day, I was returning from the survey; it was almost three in the afternoon. The sun was blazing in all its glory, its ruthless rays scorching everything in sight, far and wide. Sweating and out of breath, I entered the narrow pathway of the forest and rode all the way up to the lakeshore. I tied my horse to the branch of a tree, stretched out an oilcloth on the ground under a thick outgrowth of bushes and lay down. I was surrounded by trees and branches from all sides in such a manner that no one would be able to see me from outside. There were leaves and twigs and branches hovering at arm's length or so over my face, with a canopy of thick vines hanging over them. A bunch of long, flat, strange-looking green fruit of some kind was swaying almost near my chest. Another plant was almost touching my forehead—its twigs laden with thick bunches of flowers that I had never seen before. The flowers were so tiny that you wouldn't be able to see them unless you were standing up close. But what a sweet scent they had!

So many birds all around! Sparrows, mynas, wild parrots, the white-rumped thrush, pheasant crows, jungle babblers, doves, green pigeons and more. Eagles, kites and curlews were found on the high perches. Cranes, snipes, ducks, egrets and swans were to be seen in the blue waters of the lake. Their incessant calls, chirps and tweets could be soothing at times and irritating at others, but not even for a single moment would these pretty feathered fellows be bothered by the fact that merely a few yards away, a human being was lying on the ground and watching them.

I enjoyed the absolute absence of hesitation in their manner. Even if I sat upright, they would not care. One or two of them might fly away to a nearby branch, but would come hopping moments later, till I could almost reach out and touch them.

It was in the forests of Saraswati Kundi that I saw a wild deer for the first time. I knew that there were deer in these forests, but I had never one seen one till then. I was lying under the shade one day, when I heard footsteps on the dried leaves on the ground and sat upright. When I turned around to look over my shoulder, I saw a wild one standing at a distance, almost invisible in the camouflage of vines and shrubs and bushes. It was a fawn, not a grown deer. It has seen me too by now and was staring at me, wondering what on earth this strange looking animal was!

The minutes were passing by, both creatures were staring at each other in complete silence.

The deer now took a few steps towards me, perhaps to take a closer look. I was looking at its eyes—they had the same eager curiosity that one could see in the eyes of a human child. There was no way to tell if it would have come closer, because my horse chose that exact moment to let out a grunt. The fawn gave a frightened start and bounded away deep into the forest, perhaps to convey the news of the most surprising encounter of the day to its mother.

I turned around to face the lake again. The waters of the lake were gently lapping along the shore. The sky was blue and cloudless. A flock of water birds were quarrelling among themselves, and an old and sagely egret was sitting on top of a nearby tree and casting occasional glances at the proceedings with acute disdain. The slenderer of the trees along the shoreline were almost stooping over the surface of the water, thanks to the large flocks of pristine white cranes that were crowding on top of them.

The rays of the sun had started turning red. The tip of the hills on the other side were bathed in a bronze hue. The cranes began to fly away in flocks. The chirping of birds gradually increased in intensity, as did that intoxicating fragrance in the air. In the rapidly lengthening shadows of the afternoon, that scent seemed sweeter than ever before. A couple of yards away, a mongoose had popped out of the woods and was now staring at me.

It was so quiet and lonely! So peaceful! I had been here for over three and a half hours now, and hadn't heard anything other than the chirping of the wild birds. Or the soft creaking of the branches as the birds crowded on them, with the occasional sound of dry leaves or vines dropping to the ground. For as far as my eyes could see, there was not a single sign of humankind anywhere.

All around me, the treetops came in various shapes and sizes. Their beauty was now enhanced manifold by the golden hues of the setting sun. So many vines and creepers had spread over them. There was a specific kind of creeper—the locals called it the *bhionra* vine and I called it the 'bee' vine;

it had the habit of climbing to the topmost branches of the trees and embracing them in stifling grips. Around this time of the year, tiny white flowers would bloom along the bodies of these vines. They had a nice, sweet smell—somewhat like the scent of the flowers of mustard, but not as strong.

The forests of Saraswati Kundi were full of shiuli plants. In some places, there were so many of these plants that it seemed like a mini forest of shiulis. In one spot, I could see a pile of rocks on the ground, with tall blades of coarse wild grass surrounding them. A few thorny bushes grew right next to them. A rather crude and harsh scene—I thought—made pretty and elegant by the layers of pristine white shiuli flowers that had fallen on them from the plants above. The flowers must have fallen in the early morn, but thanks to the dew-soaked ground and the cool shade all around, they had still not withered away.

I had the invaluable experience of seeing the Saraswati Kundi in its many different forms. I had heard that there were tigers in the forests of Saraswati Kundi, but I had never seen one. I was more interested in seeing the calm waters of the lake on a moonlit night; so, on one such night, I snuck out of the Labtulia cutcherry, gave the watchful eyes of collector Banwarilal the slip and rode all the way to the lake.

I may not have seen a tiger that night, but I had indeed witnessed something far more precious. The forest was calm and peaceful. The surface of the water was mirror-still. Only a pack of foxes would yelp once in a while from deep within the woods of the eastern shore. Far away, I could see the faint outline of the hills and the forests in the night sky. The damp air of the night was laden with the sweet fragrance of the bee vine flowers. The tops of the trees were covered with these white flowers as they dropped down from the vines above. It made the treetops look as if they had been sheathed with the white robes of night fairies, who would descend from up there any moment and wade into the waters of the lake to bathe each other.

A dull, constant sound came to my ears, somewhat like that of a cricket, but it must have been some other unknown insect. One or two leaves would drop to the ground, and sometimes, I could hear the soft rustling of dry leaves on the ground as nocturnal wild animals ran over them.

I waited to see if the myth of the water fairies were true. Did they really come by the side of the lake on full moon nights in the months of autumn? I waited for over an hour or so, but when I couldn't bear the chill of the night anymore, I decided to go back.

I had heard the myth of the night fairies over a campfire. Many months ago, I had had to spend a night in the survey camp of the Northern borders of the estate. For company, I had surveyor Raghuvar Singh. The man had been employed with the government in the past. He had known the Mohanpura Reserve Forest and other forests in the vicinity like the back of his hand for over thirty years.

When I told him about my little jaunts to the Saraswati Kundi, he said, 'That's a dangerous place, Huzoor. In the night, djinns and fairies descend upon those woods. You must have seen those boulders by the side of the water. The fairies take off their robes and place them on those boulders before getting into the water. And there was no escape for any man who would see them there at that time; those fairies would then lure him into the water and drown him in the deeps. On moonlit nights, if you stare at the surface of the water long enough, you would see the faces of the fairies rising up above the water; they almost seem like lotuses in full bloom. I have never seen it with my own eyes, but Chief Surveyor Fateh Singh had. He had seen it and had somehow managed to run away from the spot. A couple of nights later, he was travelling through the forest towards the survey camp, but he never reached the camp. The next morning, his corpse was found floating in the waters of the Kundi. One of his ears had been completely bitten off, Huzoor—some say that it must have been one of those large fishes in the lake. I wouldn't go there if I were you.'

It was by the side of the Saraswati Kundi that I met a strange man one afternoon.

On my way back from the survey camp, I was coming through the forest near the lake when I suddenly saw a man digging the ground in the middle of the woods. At first, I thought he was digging for *loam* pumpkin. This is a vine-like plant, with large pumpkin-like outgrowths for roots. The pumpkins themselves have some medicinal value, and fetch quite a bit of money. Out of curiosity, I got off my horse and walked up to the man, to find that he wasn't digging to get anything out of the ground. He was merely sowing seeds of some kind.

On seeing me, the man stood up, with a somewhat frightened expression of not knowing what to say. It seemed to me that he was in his middle ages, his hair had started turning grey. He had a sack with him, and the blade of a spade was peeping out of it. A crowbar was lying next to it, and there were tiny crumpled balls of paper strewn all around him.

I asked the man, 'Who are you? And what are you doing here?'

He said, 'You must be Manager Babu, Huzoor?'

'Yes, I am. Who are you?'

'Namaskar, Huzoor. My name is Jugalprasad, I am the paternal cousin of Banwarilal—he is one of your collectors in Labtulia.'

I recalled how Banwarilal had indeed spoken of a cousin brother from his father's side. The position of accountant at the main cutcherry, the one where I lived, had been lying vacant for some time; I was looking for a good man. On asking Banwarilal if he knew someone who would be suitable, he had said that no one in the region could be more suited to the position than his own cousin, because he was quite educated, rather bright and had the gift of understanding numbers. But—he had added, with great dismay nonetheless—the man had a peculiar nature, and could be quite whimsical at times.

I had asked, 'Why, what do you mean?'

Banwarilal had said, 'He has a number of weird habits, Huzoor. One of them is to wander around from place to place. He doesn't do anything to earn a living, and although he has a wife at home, he is not the homely kind at all. He roams around forests and jungles all day, although he is not a monk or a hermit. A very strange man, Huzoor.'

So, this was Banwarilal's cousin?

I was quite curious by now; so, I asked, 'What are you sowing over there?'

With the air of a man who had been caught doing something secret, the man turned red in shame and fear. He somehow managed to say, 'Nothing much, Huzoor. Just . . . a seed . . . '

I was quite surprised. What seed was he talking about? He didn't own this land. What seed could he be possibly sowing in the middle of this dense forest? And what would come out of such an odd effort? Why was he doing it? I asked him.

He said, 'I have quite a few different kinds of seeds with me, Huzoor. In the town of Purnia, for instance, I had seen a pretty vine-like plant. It wasn't from around here, must have been brought from abroad. Pretty little reddish flowers. There are seeds of that plant, and several others too, mostly wildflowers and plants. Our forests do not have such plants and flowers, so I had to collect them from far-flung places. I was sowing those seeds. In a couple of years, they would bloom, and this place would look so lovely!'

On discovering his intent, I could not help but feel a sense of respect and admiration for the man. Simply in order to enhance the natural beauty of a vast forest—no part of which he personally owned, and none of which will ever be visited by another human being – the man was spending his own time and money? What a selfless man he was!

I asked Jugalprasad to come and join me under the shade of a tree. He told me more about himself, and I was fascinated by what I heard.

'I have been doing this for years now, Huzoor. All the flowers, plants and vines that you see in Labtulia—I had brought them from the forests outside Purnia or from the Laxmipur estate in south Bhagalpur. I planted all of them ten-twelve years ago. They have all grown up now.'

'Do you like doing this?'

'The jungles of Labtulia are very beautiful. I have always wanted to grow new plants, new flowers in those jungles, or in these jungles by the lake.'

'What kind of flowers do you usually get?'

'With your permission, let me first tell you how I started doing this. I live in the Dharampur province. I used to take my buffaloes out for grazing on the banks of the Kushi—around ten-twelve miles from my village. There, in the forests and the fields, I used to see a new kind of flower called *bhandi*, which I had never seen in my village. They looked very pretty. So, I took a few seeds of bhandi to my village and planted them. Within a few years, my village got a complete makeover. Everywhere you saw—in vacant lands or by the side of the road, on the banks of the village pond or in the gardens, there were lovely blooms of bhandi all around. Since then, I got hooked on to this. It became my habit to take flowers that are local to a specific region and grow them in other places too. I have been doing this all my life.'

On speaking to Jugalprasad, I quickly realized that he knew a lot about the flora of this region. There was no doubt in my mind that he was a specialist in the subject. I asked him, 'Have you ever seen the Aristolochia vine?'

On my describing the structure of the flower, Jugalprasad immediately said – 'Oh, the swan flower? The one in which the flowers look just like a pair of swans? Yes, I had seen it in a British sahib's garden in Patna. That flower is not from around here, Huzoor.'

I kept staring at him in disbelief. How many such men had I met in my life? Men who lived and breathed only to worship the beauty of nature? He roamed around from one forest to another, toiled day and night, sowing seeds and planting flowers and plants, with one and only one selfless objective—to make the forests look more beautiful. He didn't have any income, nor did he have any worries or fears.

He said, 'I have travelled to a lot of places, Huzoor, but I have never seen a forest as beautiful and rich as the one here on the banks of the Saraswati Kundi. And such calm, still waters! Tell me, Huzoor, do you think I could grow lotuses in those waters? The ponds in and around Dharampur are rife with lotuses. I could get a few stalks and plant them here.'

I made up my mind to help him in this rare and noble endeavour. From that day onwards, I was addicted to a new hobby—that together with Jugalprasad, I would fill up these forests with new varieties of flowers, vines and plants. I gradually came to know that Jugalprasad's family was in dire financial straits. So, I wrote to the headquarters and got him the job of an accountant at the cutcherry, with a monthly salary of ten rupees.

That year, I ordered several different kinds of foreign wildflower seeds from the catalogues of Sutton and procured cuttings of various wild jasmines from the Dooars region and planted them in the forests of Saraswati Kundi. Needless to say, Jugalprasad was elated! So much so that I had to pull him aside and explain to him that he was not to reveal his joy and excitement to anyone in the cutcherry. Because if people came to know what we were up to, it would not be merely him that people would laugh at, serious doubts would be cast upon my sanity too. Thanks to a generous monsoon next year, the plants and vines we had sown started growing bigger and greener. The banks of the lake turned out to be extremely fertile, the seeds and plants were also suitable for this land. We did face some trouble with some of the seeds from Sutton though. Every packet of seed had the name of the flower and a brief one-line description printed on it. I had carefully selected the seeds myself, and among the ones we sowed, the whitebeams, the red campions and the stitchworts showed remarkable growth. Even the foxgloves and the wood anemones turned out quite decent. But despite our best attempts, not a single sapling of dog rose or honeysuckle could be saved.

I had sown some seeds of a yellow datura-like flower along the shoreline. They bloomed quite quickly. Jugalprasad had got some seeds of the boyra vine from the jungles of Purnia, and within seven months of sowing them, I found one day that the vines had reached the tops of several bushes and trees. I had heard that the flowers of boyra looked very pretty and had a sweet smell. Oh, when would they bloom? I could not wait to see them!

Towards the beginning of autumn, I was passing through the forest, when I saw that the vines were covered with tiny white buds. On sending word to Jugalprasad, he dropped everything and ran seven miles from the cutcherry to the woods by the lake.

In a voice choking with emotion, he said, 'People used to tell me—you're planting boyra, but don't expect flowers. The vines will spread, but it is extremely rare for the flowers to bloom. Look at them, Huzoor; there are hundreds of them!'

I had planted the roots of an aquatic plant called water croft in the shallows of the lake. These started growing and spreading so rapidly that Jugalprasad began to fear that they might throw the lotuses out of business!

I had thought of planting bougainvilleas too, but the vines and flowers of bougainvillea were so deeply associated with the fancy gardens and parks of the city that I feared they would look rather out of place in the wilds out here. As it turned out, Jugalprasad's thoughts were exactly the same and he advised me against the idea too.

I had ended up spending quite a bit too. One day, Ganori Tewari told me that on the other side of the Karo River, in the forests of the Jayanti Hills, a strange wildflower bloomed. Locals called it the *dudhia* flower. The tree itself was quite large, with large leaves. The flower pushed its way upwards from a thick stalk, and rose by at least three or four feet above the stalk. Each tree had four or five such stalks and each stalk had exactly four bright yellow flowers blooming on it. Not only did the flowers look very pretty, they smelled nice too. Apparently, one of its specialities was that at night, its smell reached vast distances. The plants grew quite rapidly and more plants cropped up when the seeds dropped on the ground.

Ever since I heard this, my mind became restless. I wanted that flower in my forest. Ganori said that we would have to wait for the monsoons. The roots had to be planted and they needed generous doses of water in order to survive.

When the rains came, I called Jugalprasad one day, gave him some money and sent him to the dense jungles of Jayanti Hills. After a few days, he returned—exhausted but overjoyed—with as many as a dozen bundles of dudhia roots.

CHAPTER 9

[1]

Almost three years had passed by.

In these three years, I had undergone a significant number of changes. The wilds of Labtulia and Azamabad must have cast a spell on me, for I had stopped thinking about the city altogether. The pull of desolation, the draw of the starry night sky had become so strong that on a recent visit to Patna, I became uncontrollably restless, craving to leave everything behind, and return to the terrain I was so familiar with—where the vast, unending forests and grasslands stood under the blue sky, where there were no highways, or concrete buildings, nor the deafening noises of motor vehicles, where the only sound one could hear in one's sleep were the distant yelps of foxes announcing the deepest, darkest hours of the night, or the sound of a herd of nilgais stampeding through the misty woods, or the grave grunt of wild buffaloes outside one's window.

The authorities at the headquarters had been sending me one letter after another, asking me to explain why I had not begun the distribution of land leases so far. I was aware that leasing of the estate's land to the subjects was one of

my principal duties, but somehow, I had not been able
to bring myself to giving away such glorious treasures of
natural beauty to subjects and lessees. I could not possibly
expect the subjects who paid good money for the land to
keep them adorned with trees, plants, vines and flowers.
No, the first thing they would do after securing the land
would be to clear off the trees and make the land cultivable.
They would then start farming and build houses. With
so many people pouring in, the desolate jungles, the
virgin forests, the lush plains and the untouched beauty
of nature would all disappear or be turned into human
habitat. There would be very little natural beauty left in
these forests anymore.

In fact, I could very well imagine what such a habitat
would look like.

Every time I went to Patna, Purnia or Munger, I saw such
neighbourhoods. Shoddy, ugly looking houses built here and
there, slums and shanties, unwelcoming bushes of cactus
everywhere, mountains of dirt and dung, shabbily dressed
men and women walking around like grief-struck ghosts,
drawing water from dirty wells and naked children rolling in
the dust on busy roads.

This was a change that I was simply not prepared for.

Such a vast and rich tract of priceless forest land was
nothing short of a national treasure; had this been any other
country, there would have been laws passed to turn this land
into a protected national park. Wearied and exhausted from
their day-to-day lives, men and women from the cities would
have come here to spend a few quiet days in contact with
nature. But that was not to be. Why would the owners of the
land throw their property away?

I had come here to dole out leases of the land, but ever since I had seen the unsurpassable beauty of the forest, I had fallen in love with it. And now, all I could do was to keep postponing the day when I would have to succumb to the pressure from my employer. Whenever I rode out into the forest in the middle of the night, I looked around to find my heart weeping in apprehension of the inevitable disaster. Of all people in this whole wide world, why did it have to be me to spell the doom for this forest?

But a job was a job. Towards the end of March, a Rajput named Chhattu Singh came from Patna and submitted an application to lease more than three hundred acres of land. I found myself in big trouble. Three hundred acres of land was not a matter of joke! A significant portion of the forest would be lost forever, and thousands of trees, plants and flowers would be destroyed!

Chhattu Singh kept breathing down my neck. I directed his application to the headquarters in a bid to delay the beginning of the destruction.

[2]

One day, I was riding back to the cutchery through an open field in the Narha Baihar on the northern edge of Labtulia, when I saw someone sitting by the side of the road.

I stopped my horse next to the man. He was at least sixty, was shabbily dressed and had a tattered chaddar thrown around his body.

What was he doing here in the middle of nowhere?

The man asked, 'Who are you, Babu?'

I said, 'I'm from the cutchery here.'

'Are you the Manager Babu?'

'Yes, I am. Who are you?'

The man rose to his feet and raised his hands in the gesture of blessing me. Then he said, 'Huzoor, my name is Matuknath Pandey, I'm a Brahmin. I was on my way to meet you.'

'Why?'

'I'm a poor man, Huzoor, I've come from a village far away. I had heard about you, so I wanted to meet you. I've been walking for the last three days. If Huzoor would kindly keep me in his employment, then—'

I asked him curiously, 'Three days through the forest? What have you been eating all these days?'

Matuknath showed me a corner of his chaddar and said, 'I had left home with a mound of grist tied to this, Huzoor. That's what I have been surviving on. But now, as you can see, it's almost over. But God is kind, he will find a way.'

I looked at the man and wondered, with what hopes had he set off from his home with a mere lump of grist in the corner of his chaddar? What employment did he hope to secure in the middle of this forest? I said, 'You should have gone to the big cities, Pandey-ji—Bhagalpur, Munger, Purnia or Patna. There's hardly anyone here. Who would give you a job?'

Matuknath stared at my face with a look of hopelessness. He said, 'Can't I find anything here, Babu? Where would I go then? I don't know anyone in those big cities, and I'm scared of those busy streets. That is why, I was on my way to—'

Matuknath seemed like a good man, poor and helpless. I brought him along to the cutcherry.

A few days passed by. I could not arrange a job for Matuknath, because he was not skilled at doing anything.

But he had learnt Sanskrit, he used to teach in a local school. Every now and then, he would sit next to me and chant one indecipherable Sanskrit sloka after another, perhaps in a bid to impress me.

One day, he said, 'Please give me a small piece of land next to the cutcherry, Huzoor. I'll set up a school there.'

I waved it off by saying—'Who would study in your school, Pundit-ji? Wild buffaloes and nilgais? I doubt if they will understand the poems of Bhatti and Raghuvansh.'

Matuknath was a simple man. He must have offered to set up the school without a proper plan in place. I figured he would forget about the matter. But after a few days, he came to me again.

He said, 'Please consider setting up the school, Huzoor. Let me give it a try? What else would I do otherwise?'

The man must be mad, I thought. And quite adamant at that. I couldn't look at his face without feeling sorry for him. A simple, naïve man who had pinned his hopes on heaven knows what or who.

I tried to explain to him, saying that I was willing to give him a piece of land where he could do his farming, just like Raju Pandey was doing. Matuknath pleaded with me and said that for generations, his forefathers had been in the profession of imparting education and since he did not know the first thing about farming, the land would be of no use to him.

I could have asked him what a traditional and orthodox educator such as him was doing in my cutcherry, but somehow, I could not say anything to him too strongly. All said and done, it was true that he was a good, simple and harmless man. Finally, giving in to his importunity, I had a small cottage built for him in one corner and said, 'This is your school; now see if you can find a student.'

Matuknath did a little ceremony before founding his school, which was completed with feeding a few Brahmins. I was invited too.

After he opened the school, Matuknath began acting in a weird manner.

What a strange man he turned out to be!

In the morning, he would take his bath, have his meal and sit in his school on a mat that he had woven out of the leaves of a date palm. Then he would open the pages of an old and tattered copy of the *Mugdhabodh* grammar and start chanting sutras to an imaginary audience of students! And he would do this at the top of his voice—so much so that I could hear him loud and clear from my office on the other side of the cutchery.

Tehsildar Sajjan Singh came to me one day and said, 'That man is insane, Huzoor! Have you seen what he has been doing?'

A couple of months passed by in this manner. Sitting comfortably in the empty cottage, Matuknath continued to teach his imaginary students with enviable excitement and vigour—once in the morning, once in the evening. Meanwhile, the day of the Saraswati Puja was almost upon us. Every year, we would do a small ceremony in the office room, but without an idol of the deity. Where would we find an idol in the middle of the forest? This year, there was a rumour that Matuknath would do a ceremony in his school, and that he would build an idol himself.

One had to see it to believe the excitement of the sixty-year-old!

With his own hands, he built a small idol out of clay. Then he held a separate ceremony in his cottage.

With an expression of pride and contentment on his face, the old man smiled and said, 'This is a ceremony that my ancestors have been doing year after year, Babu. My father used to do this ceremony in his school, and now I do it in mine.'

But where was the school?

Of course, I held myself back from asking the question to Matuknath.

[3]

Ten or twelve days after the Saraswati Puja, Matuknath Pandit came and informed me that a student had come to enrol himself in his school. Apparently, he had reached the cutcherry that very day.

Matuknath brought the student to me. A young lad, fourteen-fifteen years old, dark skin, reed thin, Maithili Brahmin by caste, extremely poor—other than the shabby dress that he was wearing, he didn't have any other possession of any kind.

Matuknath's excitement knew no bounds, of course! Without sparing a thought to the fact that he had no means to feed himself, he immediately took full responsibility of the boy. Such, apparently, was the custom in his ancestral profession—a student who had come to his doors and expressed his desire to learn could not be sent away, no matter how impoverished a life he himself had led before. All memories of such hardships were to be cast outside the doors of the school, and a new life would begin for the ward.

In a couple of months, a few more students enrolled themselves in Matuknath's school. These boys could manage only one square meal a day. The sepoys put some money together to give them pulses, grist, wheat and china grass seeds; I too helped to some extent. The students went out to the jungle and brought back odd leafy vegetables now and then, boiled them and had them for a meal. Matuknath too ate the same food as his pupils.

I could hear Matuknath teaching his students till 10 or 11 p.m. in the night. They would sit under the myrobalan tree outside his school—sometimes in moonlight, sometimes in the dark, because they didn't have oil to burn a lamp.

But there was one thing that had struck me as rather surprising. Other than his initial prayer for some land and the setting up of his school, Matuknath had never asked for any financial help. He had never come to me and said—'I'm not being able to run the school, please give me some money'—or anything of that sort. In fact, he had never told anyone about any of his hardships; whatever the sepoys did for him and his students, they did it of their own free will.

From April to September, there was a significant increase in the number of students. Almost a dozen boys—most of them chased out of their homes by an irresponsible father or an irate mother—came from various places and gathered in Matuknath's school with the hope of getting food in return of minimum effort. Because in this region, word spread like wildfire. When I saw the boys, it seemed to me that they used to rear buffaloes. Not a single one of them showed any signs of intelligence, and I had my doubts if they could be taught even a fraction of all the poetry and grammar that Matuknath was trying to teach them. He was a simple man, and the boys were here merely to take advantage of his innocence. Matuknath, on the other hand, didn't seem to have a care in the world, he was visibly excited to have so many students in his school.

One day, I heard that the students had not been able to manage any food, and were fasting. Matuknath was fasting with them too.

The contributions that the sepoys had made were all over. And some of the students had fallen ill after consuming the leaves and vegetables that had been picked from the forest. In other words, there was nothing left to eat for the dozen or so students and their teacher.

'What are you planning to do now, Panditji?' I asked.

'I can't see a way out, Huzoor. Those little boys are all hungry . . . '

I called my staff and made the necessary arrangements. Rice, pulses, ghee and wheat—enough for a dozen people for two or three days. Then I said – 'What's the use of going on like this, Pandit-ji? Why don't you shut down the school? How are you going to feed all these boys?'

Matuknath was visibly hurt by my words. He said, 'How can I do that, Huzoor? How can I shut down an entire school? This is the profession of my forefathers, after all.'

I realized Matuknath was content and carefree by nature, and that there was no point explaining all this to him. He was happy with his band of students.

But trouble began when the students started stealing vegetables from the cutcherry's farm, picking flowers from the garden and even stealing one or two items of value from other people. The sepoys and other members of the staff began to whisper among themselves, and some of these whispers reached my ears too.

One day, the treasurer had left his cash box open in his office. Someone stole some of the cash and the treasurer's own gold ring from the box. The sepoys raised a big hue and cry about it. After a few days, one of the students from Matuknath's school was caught red-handed with the ring; apparently the boy had hidden it in the folds of his dress.

I sent for Matuknath. He was indeed a naïve, honest man. And a few incorrigible students were taking advantage of his simplicity to do whatever they liked. There was no need to shut down the school, but some of the notorious students would have to be thrown out. The rest of them could stay, I would give them a small portion of land—let them work hard and grow their own food.

Matuknath presented my suggestion to his students. Eight of the twelve students immediately dropped out of his school when they heard that they would have to grow their own food. Even the other four that remained did not seem the least bit interested in receiving any education. Perhaps, they had realized that they had no other place to go, and that farming was still better than rearing buffaloes. Ever since then, Matuknath's school had been running just fine.

[4]

Chhattu Singh and a few others had been granted the land they had requested for. More than three hundred acres of land. Narha Baihar had the most fertile land in the region; hence, I had had to give them a vast tract of land there. The forests on the borders of the Narha Baihar were very pretty.

On several occasions, while passing through the woods on my way back to the cutchery, I had looked around and thought of the place as a beauty spot on the face of the earth. Gone were those woods!

From far away, I could see the flames rising in the skies—the dense woods had been set on fire to clear the land for cultivation. The wind carried the crackling sound of the fire destroying hundreds and thousands of priceless flowers, trees and vines forever. I sat in my room and heard the sound of devastation; my heart wept for the irreparable loss of an irreplaceable national treasure—all for a fistful of wheat.

In the beginning of October, I paid a visit to the place. The entire forest had disappeared, leaving behind a vast open field. Mustard had been sowed in the field. The farmers had set up their huts and dwellings here and there. When winter came, the mustard flowers began to bloom, and what a sight it was to behold! A rich sapphire sky, hanging over an endless carpet of yellow.

One day, I went on an inspection of the new villages that had come up. Other than Chhattu Singh, most of the subjects were quite poor. Dozens of children were running around the edges of the mustard farms all day; on seeing them, I planned to set up a night school in the village.

But soon, the new subjects started causing a lot of trouble. As it turned out, these people were not peace-loving at all. I was sitting in the cutchery one day, when news came that a big fight had broken out between the subjects of the Narha Baihar. Apparently, the farmers had not taken care to set up proper demarcations and boundaries for their lands, and as a result, ownership had become a matter of contention. Those who had two acres of land were now trying to seize the crop from five. I further learnt that just a few days ago, Chhattu Singh had brought in a large number of armed goons from his homeland—the true purpose of such a move was now apparent. Over and above the hundred acres of land that I had given him, the man was now scheming to seize the entire crop of Narha Baihar by force.

I spoke to the surveyors from the cutcherry and they all said the same thing—such was the law of the land. The one who wielded the greatest power owned the crops too.

The ones who were powerless came to meet me in the cutcherry and broke down. These were weak, poor and innocent peasants. All they had were one or two acres of land. They had brought their wives and children and set up their homes here. They had mouths to feed. And now, thanks to the might and cunning of a man like Chhattu Singh, the outcome of their year-long toil and hardship was about to be taken away from them.

I sent a couple of sepoys to inspect the scene of the dispute. They ran back to me and reported in a breathless manner that the situation was not good. Trouble was brewing on the northern borders of Bhimdastola.

I immediately took Tehsildar Sajjan Singh along with all the sepoys of the cutcherry and set out for Bhimdastola. Even before we reached the spot, we could hear a ruckus. A small mountain river flowed through the middle of the Narha Baihar—apparently, that was where the sound was coming from.

As we approached the river, I saw large crowds gathered on both sides of the river—almost sixty-seven people on this side, and on the other side, there were at least thirty–forty men of Chhattu Singh, armed with sticks and spears. The men on the other side were trying to cross the river and come over to this side. The men on this side were trying to stop them. Two men had already been injured in the scuffle; both were from this side of the river. They were lying on the riverbed for some time, when suddenly, Chhattu Singh's men had attempted to get into the river and cut off their heads. The men from this side had foiled their attempts and dragged the injured men out of the river. There was very little water in the river, it being more of a brook, and this being the end of winter.

On seeing the staff and officials of the cutcherry, both parties stopped screaming and stood before me. Both sides tried to show themselves as good and innocent, while describing the other as vile and treacherous. I realized it would be impossible for me to mediate between the two in the midst of this riot. So, I asked both parties to come and meet me in the cutcherry. The two injured men needed medical attention; so, I asked my men to bring them along too.

Chhattu Singh's men discussed among themselves and said that they would come and see me at the cutcherry in the afternoon. I thought that the matter had been diffused for now. But little did I know how evil these men could be. In the afternoon, news came to the cutcherry that the riot had broken out in Narha Baihar yet again, and this time, things were worse than before. I once again gathered all my men and set out. Meanwhile, I had sent one of my men on horseback to the police outpost in Naugachhia, fifteen miles away. When I reached the river, I realized that the situation had not improved. In fact, more of Chhattu Singh's men had gathered at the spot. I was soon told that Rashbehari Singh and Nandalal Ojha were helping Chhattu Singh in the matter. Chhattu Singh himself was not present at the spot; his brother, Gajadhar Singh, was sitting on his horse at a little distance. As soon as he saw me coming, he turned around and left the spot. I looked around to find that as many as two Rajput men had guns in their hands.

The Rajputs yelled out from the other side, 'We strongly advise you to leave this place right now, Huzoor. We have a score to settle with these bastard Gangotas.'

On my command, my men went and stood between the two warring factions. I let everyone know that word has been sent to the Naugachhia outpost, and the police were on their way. I warned them that even if a single shot was fired, I would personally see to it that the culprits were jailed for life.

On hearing this, the two gunmen lowered their guns and took a few steps back.

Then I spoke to the Gangota farmers and asked them to go back. I assured them that my men were there to protect them, and that I would be responsible for the safety of their crop.

The chief of the Gangotas put his faith in my words and asked his men to leave the spot. They gathered under a large chinaberry tree, waiting to see what would happen next. I called the chief once again and told him that I would not be able to help them if they stayed there, and instructed him to ask his men to go home. The police would arrive soon.

The Rajputs were not ones to give up so easily. They huddled around on the other side, talking among themselves. I called my tehsildar and said, 'What's the matter, Sajjan Singh? Would they attack us?'

The tehsildar said, 'It's that blasted Nandalal Ojha, Huzoor. He's the main culprit. The man can't be trusted at all.'

'In that case, ask your men to be prepared. Don't let anyone cross the river. We need to block them for a couple of hours. The police will be here by then.'

A posse of Rajputs stepped forward and said, 'Huzoor, we want to come over.'

I asked, 'Why?'

'What do you mean "why"? Don't we have land on the other side?'

'If you do, then speak to the police about it. They will be here any minute. I can't let you cross the river.'

'Have we paid a ton of money to the cutcherry as lease in order to let our hard-earned crops be looted by those wretched Gangotas? You are being very unfair, Huzoor.'

'Say that to the police.'

'So, you won't let us go over to the other side?'

'No. I won't allow bloodshed in my estate.'

Meanwhile, a few more people had come from the cutcherry. As soon as they came, they began shouting that the police had come. In twos and threes, Chhattu Singh's men began to disperse from the spot. The riot was stopped that day, but this was only the beginning of murders, arsons, brawls and police-cases in what was once a calm, peaceful and beautiful forest. As the days passed, the vile acts of men became more and more frequent. And my worst fears became true as I realized that the estate had made a mistake in giving away such a vast amount of land to a man like Chhattu Singh. One day, I sent word to Chhattu Singh and asked him to come and see me in the cutcherry. The man calmly denied any knowledge of everything that was going on in Narha Baihar. He claimed that he spent most of his time in Chhapra and was therefore not responsible for what happened in his land out here.

I realized the man was as sly and shrewd as a fox. It would not be easy to straighten him out by merely talking to him. I would have to think of another way.

Ever since then, I completely stopped giving land to anyone other than the Gangotas. But what was done was done. Peace and quiet was never to return to Narha Baihar ever again.

[5]

On the northern borders of our twelve-mile long estate, more than six hundred acres of land had been given away on lease by now. Towards the end of February, I had had to visit the place once, and I was surprised to see that the new subjects had completely changed the terrain.

As soon as I had come out of the jungles of Fulkiya, my eyes were met with a sprawling farmland of mustard flowers, a yellow carpet of sorts rolling away all the way to the blue hills in the distant horizon. In any direction I looked—left, right or ahead of me—all I could see was this unhindered, patchless rug of yellow. Hovering over it was the clear, cloudless and deep blue winter sky. Here and there, the farmers had built their tiny huts, mostly with dried catkins. How these people lived here in the vast open fields in the middle of such harsh winters, that too with their wives and little children, I would never understand.

The crops were about to ripen and reaping season would begin soon. Labourers had started pouring in from various places. These people led strange lives; they came from Purnia, North Bhagalpur, the Jayanti Hills and even the Terai regions, their wives and children in tow, setting up shanties in the farmland and reaping the crop. As wages, they received a certain portion of the crops they reaped. And when the reaping was over, they would leave their huts behind and move on to other places, only to return next year. They belonged to various castes; most of them were Gangotas, but one could even find Kshatriyas, landless Brahmins and even Maithili Brahmins among them.

As was the custom of this region, we had to be physically present in the farm in order to collect the tax from the lease, because the peasants were so poor that once they left the land, they would be in no position to pay the taxes. In order to supervise the collection of the taxes, I had to stay in the vast mustard farms outside Fulkiya Baihar for a few days that year.

The tehsildar asked me, 'Shall I pitch the small tent over there, Huzoor?'

'Why don't you have a small hut built instead? With dried catkins, just like the ones the farmers live in?'

'Would you be able to live in such a hut, Huzoor? That too in the peak of winter?'

'I'll be fine, you see to it that the huts are built before night falls.'

Three small huts were erected, side by side—one was for me to sleep in, the other would act as a kitchen and the final one was where the sepoys and the collector would sleep. These kinds of huts were called *khupri*s in this region. The walls and the roof were made of dried catkins, and the windows were cut out to enable ventilation. But at night, the same windows let in the unbearable chill too, for there was no way to shut them. The roofs were so low that one had to crawl on all fours in order to get into the khupris. A thick layer of dried catkins and wild tamarisks were placed on the ground to form a mat of sorts. On this, a mattress was placed, with bedding. This was where I would have to sleep. My hut was eight feet in length and four feet in width. It was impossible to stand up straight, for the roof was a mere four feet from the ground.

But I rather enjoyed living in these khupris. I found them far more comfortable than the three- or four-storeyed buildings in Kolkata. Perhaps, my long stay in the region was slowly having an impact on my mind; perhaps, the vast open fields and the dense forests were slowly turning me truly wild. Perhaps, that explained why I would prefer living in a shanty dwelling to the pleasures of a lavish building.

The first thing that struck me upon entering the khupri was the distinct smell of the freshly cut stems of catkins—the ones used to build the walls of the hut. The next thing that absolutely took me by pleasant surprise was the rectangular window that had been cut out on the wall nearest to my head. As I half lay on my bed, and peered out of the window, I could see—right in front of my face, and at the same level as my eyes—a vast yellow carpet of mustard flowers. To top it all, there was a strong smell of mustard in the cold breeze.

And what a winter it was! There was not a single day's respite from the chilly westerly winds, which had the power to turn even the strongest rays of the sun into meek streaks of light. Riding by the jungles of wild berries outside the Fulkiya Baihar, I would often witness the ethereal sight of the winter sunset. Far away towards the west, over the hills of the Tirashi-Chouka, the dipping sun seemed to bathe the skies with liquid fire. When I stared at the horizon for a long time, the skies seemed to offer an illusion—as if it was not the sun that was setting behind the hills; it was as if the hills themselves were rising in the sky to engulf the sun instead.

As soon as the last remaining rays of the sun vanished, there came the chill. And worn out from our day-long running around from here to there on horseback, we would retire in front of a fire outside our huts.

As we sat there and looked up at the sky, we could see the constellations – dazzling in front of our eyes. Never had I seen the Great Bear or the Seven Sisters so clearly in the Kolkata night sky. Night after night, I would stare at them, so much so that it almost seemed like I had struck an acquaintance with them, and they with me. I stared at them for hours and wondered what secrets they must hold and what cosmic events they must have witnessed! Dense, desolate forests below, and the oh-so-familiar celestial bodies up there in the sky. On some nights, the crescent of the moon kept company to the twinkling stars, resembling the beacon from the top of a faraway lighthouse, as seen by a lone sailor lost in the vast openness of a calm ocean. On other nights, the dark bejewelled expanse of the sky would be sliced by the arrow of shooting stars, one after the other. To the south, to the north, to the east, to the west, over there, and there, there went another one, and then another—every minute, every second.

On some days, Ganori Tewari and several others would come visiting. We would sit and chat by the fire in the evening. On one such night, I heard a strange story. That night, the discussion had veered towards hunting. We started talking about the wild buffaloes of the Mohanpura Forest. A Rajput man named Dashrath Singh Jhandawala had come to the Labtulia cutchery that night, in order to pay his taxes. The man had been a frequent visitor to the forests in the past and had the reputation of being a seasoned hunter. Dashrath

Singh said, 'Huzoor, once when I was out hunting wild buffaloes in the jungles of Mohanpura, I saw the Tyandbaro.'

I remembered how Gonu Mahato had once told me about the Tyandbaro. I asked, 'What did you see?'

'It was a long time ago, Huzoor. They hadn't built the bridge over the Kushi yet. There was a ferry in Kataria instead, a double ferry that went both ways. The buses would stop there, and the passengers would have to take the ferry to the other side, along with their goods and luggage. During those days, we were very excited about dancing horses, me and Chhattu Singh of Chapra. He would buy horses from the fair at Hariharchhatra, and the two of us would train those horses to dance. Once the horses learnt how to dance, we would sell them off at a premium and make some money. There are two kinds of horse-dances, *Jamaity* and *Fanaity* The horses trained in Jamaity always sold at higher prices. Chhattu Singh was an expert Jamaity trainer. For three long years, the two of us made quite a bit of money.

One day, Chhattu Singh came up with a new idea— we would take out a licence to hunt wild buffaloes in the Dholbaja forest. We made all the necessary arrangements. Dholbaja was a reserve forest owned by the Maharaja of Darbhanga. We bribed the forest officials and took out a permit. And then, for several weeks, we kept wandering in the forest, looking for the tracks and footprints of wild buffaloes. It was such a huge forest, Huzoor, but we couldn't trace a single buffalo. Finally, we gave up and hired a wild Santhal to track the animals down for us. He took us to a bamboo grove deep within the forest and pointed to the ground beneath it. The buffaloes would go this way at night to a waterhole, he said. We immediately set out to work. We dug a deep pit on the ground and covered it with bamboo and loose soil. The buffaloes would fall into the pit and we would have what we came for.

The Santhal looked at the arrangement and remarked, "Set as many traps as you like. You won't be able to hunt a single buffalo in these woods. Tyandbaro won't let you."

We were taken aback to hear this. Who or what on earth was this Tyandbaro?

The old Santhal said, "Tyandbaro is the god of wild buffaloes. He protects the beasts."

Chhattu Singh said, "Those are silly old fables, old man. We don't believe them. We are Rajputs, not Santhals."

You'll be surprised to hear what happened next, Huzoor. The very thought of it gives me goosebumps even today. Late in the night, we were hiding inside the bamboo grove, waiting for the animals to come. We heard the footsteps approaching—a whole herd was headed our way. They came very near—less than 20 yards from the pit. Suddenly, we saw a tall, dark-skinned man standing in silence a few feet away from the pit with his hands raised. He was so tall, Huzoor, his head was almost touching the tip of the bamboo grove. The buffaloes saw him and stopped on their tracks. Then they turned around and ran away into the jungle. Not even a single buffalo came near the trap. Believe it or not, I saw the entire thing with my own eyes.

After that night, we spoke to a few other hunters who knew the forest. They advised us to forget about hunting wild buffaloes in that forest. Tyandbaro wouldn't let us hunt his animals, they said. All that money to get the permit, Huzoor—all gone down the drain. We couldn't catch a single buffalo in those woods that year.'

Once Dashrath Singh had finished his story, even the collector from Labtulia said, 'We've been hearing the tales of Tyandbaro too, Huzoor, ever since we were little children. Tyandbaro is the god of the wild buffaloes. He wouldn't let any harm come upon them.'

I did not know whether there was any truth in the story; nor did I need to know. But as I listened to the story, I would look up at the fiery sword-wielding Orion in the sky. The black sky hunched over the dense woods and vast fields. The crowing of a wild rooster was echoing from somewhere deep inside the jungle. The dark and silent sky was meeting the dark and silent earth in the horizon, taking turns to whisper sweet nothings into each other's ears. And far away in the distance, watching the dark outline of the Mohanpura Forest Reserve, I shivered to think if the huge, dark-skinned mysterious god of the beasts was indeed watching us silently from behind the numerous rows of trees. It was only in the middle of such a dense forest, sitting by the fire and enjoying the chill in the wintry night wind that one enjoyed such stories the most.

CHAPTER 10

[1]

I had spent fifteen days living in the wilds here and during this period, I had had to live just like the Gangotas or the landless Brahmins did. Not that I had a choice though, the circumstances were such. Where would I find milk and ghee and fish in the middle of these jungles? All I had to live on were rice and curries made of sponge gourd. Sometimes, the sepoys would pick wild *kantola*s, spiny gourds, or dig up sweet potatoes in the forest—and I had to eat them, either in boiled or fried form.

Not that there was any dearth of pheasants and peacocks in the forest though. But somehow, I did not feel like killing those birds; so, despite all the guns with us, I preferred having vegetarian meals.

There was a fear of tigers in Fulkiya Baihar though. Let me tell you what happened one night.

It was freezing that night. After a long and exhausting day, I had finished my dinner and gone to bed by ten in the night. Sometime late in the night—I didn't know when exactly—a loud and tumultuous uproar woke me up from my deep slumber. Several men had gathered by the edge of the forest and were yelling at the top of their voices. I got off my bed and quickly lit the lantern. My sepoys had come out of the adjacent khupri by now. We were wondering what to do next when suddenly, a man came running to me and said, 'Manager Babu, please bring your gun. A tiger has dragged a little boy into the forest.'

Less than a hundred yards from the edge of the forest, in the middle of the farm, a Gangota farmer named Domon had built a small khupri. His wife was sleeping in the khupri, along with their six-month old baby boy. To save themselves from the bone-chilling cold, they had lit a small fire inside the hut itself, and in order to let the smoke out, they had kept the door slightly ajar. The tiger must have entered the hut through this open door and taken the baby away.

But how did they know it was a tiger? Could have been a fox too. When we reached the spot though, there was no more confusion regarding the matter. On the soft ground at the base of the crop, we could clearly see the pugmarks of a fully-grown tiger.

My surveyors and sepoys were keen to avoid any rumours from being spread about our estate. They immediately began to say, 'This animal can't be from around here, Huzoor. It must have come from the Mohanpura jungles. Look how big the pugmarks are!'

I had to explain to them that the origin of the tiger was a point that we could debate later, and that the baby had to be found. I asked them to gather all their men and light up a few torches—we were going into the jungle. On seeing such massive and fresh pugmarks in the middle of the night, most of the men had started trembling in horror. I rebuked a few of them, yelled at a few others and brought them to their senses. A dozen or so of us entered the forest, wielding burning torches and beating tin canisters, but found nothing.

The next morning, at around 10 a.m., the bloodied remains of the baby were found in the middle of the south-east part of the jungle, almost two miles from where we were.

A seemingly never-ending series of long, dark and frightening nights followed that incident.

I summoned constable Banke Singh from the main cutcherry. Banke Singh was a seasoned hunter, he knew a lot about tigers as well. He said, 'Huzoor, there's nothing as cunning as a man-eating tiger. You can expect a few more deaths. We have to be alert at all times.'

Exactly three days later, in the dim twilight of dusk, a young cowherd was taken away by the tiger from the edge of the forest. People started having sleepless nights. When night would fall, it would be a strange sight to see! In various huts across the vast expanse of the Baihar, people would beat tin canisters all night, or burn the stems of catkins to light a fire. Banke Singh and I would sit up all night, firing our guns in the air every hour. And as it turned out, it was not just the tiger that we were dealing with. Because just the other day, a large herd of wild buffaloes had wandered out of the Mohanpura Forest and destroyed a significant portion of the crops.

The sepoys had lit a large fire near the door of my hut. I would wake up in the night sometimes to throw a log or two in the fire. Lying in my bed, I could hear the sepoys talking among themselves in the adjacent khupri. Looking out of the window near my head, I could see the vast rolling field steeped in darkness, and in the distance—visible in the faint light of the stars—the shadowy outline of the forest.

I looked up at the sky and it seemed to me as if wave after wave of freezing cold air were gushing towards me from the lifeless skies, turning my bed into a slab of ice and slowly dousing the fire that had promised some respite. Oh, I almost froze to death! And how fast the wind blew—unpaused, unhindered—through the open fields.

I lay in my bed shivering and wondering how could people live in this place? Under such inhospitable living conditions, sleeping night after night on cold beds, with constant fear of wild boars, buffaloes and even tigers? And with all the pains that these poor peasants have to take in order to guard their crops? Would our farmers from Bengal be able to endure such harsh conditions? If only they knew how fortunate they were to have such fertile land to till and such trouble-free, conducive circumstances to grow their crops in, they would stop cursing their luck and be grateful for what they had.

Around a hundred yards from my hut, there was a small habitation of reapers who had come with their wives and children from the north of Bhagalpur. One evening, while walking by their huts, I found them sitting huddled around a fire.

I was entirely unacquainted with their world; so, curiosity got the better of me and I walked up to them.

'Well, what are you all up to, old man?'

My question was directed to what seemed like the senior-most member of the gang. The man rose to strike me a salute, and welcomed me to share the warmth of the fire with them. This was the custom of this land. In the winters, an invitation to sit by the fire was considered a gesture of courtesy.

I went and joined them. A quick glance inside their huts revealed that there was nothing even remotely resembling a bed in there—merely a few layers of grass laid out on the floor. As for utensils, each hut seemed to have one large pot and a small tumbler of sorts. Other than the ragged attire each of the men, women and children had donned, I could not see even a single other piece of clothing. But blankets? Did they not have any blankets? How did they survive these wintry nights without blankets?

So, I asked them.

The old man's name was Nakchhedi Bhakat. Gangota by caste. He pointed inside one of the huts and said, 'Why, look at those chaffs of pulses piled up in the corner over there?'

I didn't quite understand what he was trying to say. Were those chaffs burnt to light a fire inside the huts?

Nakchhedi smiled at my ignorance.

'No, Babu. The children get into those mounds and sleep at night. Don't you see? We've stored at least five tons of chaff in each hut. We adults too cover ourselves with those chaffs when we sleep. You won't believe how nice and warm it feels inside. Much more comfortable than two blankets, one on top of the other. Not that we can afford blankets.'

Even as the old man was saying all these astonishing things to me, I saw a young woman putting her child to sleep, and when the little boy was fast asleep, his mother carried him to a tiny mound of chaff, covered him from head to toe leaving only the face exposed, and calmly walked back to her place. I watched the entire scene in stunned silence and wondered how little I knew of humankind. Had I not witnessed it with my own eyes, would I ever have believed such a bizarre means of survival? The more I thought about it, the more I realized that I was discovering my own India in a hundred different and new ways every day.

Then I saw a girl sitting on the other side of the fire and cooking something.

I asked, 'What's she cooking over there?'

Nakchhedi said, '*Ghato*.'

'What is this ghato?'

By now the girl who was busy cooking must have wondered from where had this ignorant fool of a Babu come and sat amidst us! So many questions! The man knew nothing of this world! She giggled her heart out and said, 'Don't you know ghato, Babu-ji? Boiled maize. Just like paddy is boiled to make your rice, we boil maize to get ghato.'

In a grand gesture of benevolence to my otherwise unpardonable ignorance, the girl scooped up a tiny portion of the previously described material from her pot with the help of a wooden ladle and showed it to me for my much-needed education.

'What do you have it with?'

From then on, all my questions were answered by the girl. She smiled and said, 'Salt, herbs—what else?'

'Have you cooked the herbs already?'

'I will, once I'm done with the ghato. I've picked pea-leaves from the jungle today.'

The girl seemed quite smart and unhesitant. She asked, 'Do you live in Kolkata, Babu-ji?'

'Yes.'

'Is it true that there are no trees in Kolkata? Have they really chopped down all the trees?'

'Who's told you such a thing?'

'Someone from our village, he works in the city. He had told me once. How is it, Babu-ji—your Kolkata?'

For the next few minutes, I tried my best to explain to this simple, forest-dwelling young girl what a metropolis such as Kolkata looked like. I do not know how much of it she understood, but at the end of it, she simply smiled and said, 'I feel like seeing Kolkata. But there's no one to take me there.'

I spent a few more hours with them. It was quite late by now, the night was becoming darker by the minute. Their meals had been cooked. Out came the large vessel from the hut. The aforementioned sticky, semi-solid stuff was poured in it, a few generous sprinkles of salt were thrown in, and the whole gang sat in a circle with the vessel in the centre, and began to eat.

I said, 'Will you head home once you are done here?'

Nakchhedi said, 'It'll be some time before we can get home, Babu-ji. Once we are done here, we will go to Dharampur, to reap paddy. Paddy is not grown here, but they grow it over there. Once we are done with paddy, we would set off for Munger, to reap corn. By the time we are finished over there, it would be summer; then we will be back here once again. Then we have a break for a few days. Once the monsoons are over, it will be time for maize again. After maize, it will be pulses and a second season of paddy in Dharampur and Purnia. We keep roaming around from one place to another all through the year, Babu. When there's a new crop in a new place, we go there. What would we eat otherwise?'

'Don't you have a house of your own?'

It was the girl who responded. She seemed to be in her mid-twenties, with dark and shiny skin and a shapely figure, in the prime of her youth. She also seemed quite good with conversation, and in the rustic South-Bihar dialect that she spoke, her voice sounded rather sweet too.

She said, 'Of course, we do, Babu-ji. We have everything. But we can' be at home all the time. We will go home towards the end of summer, and we'd stay till the middle of the monsoons. Then we would set off once again. That's our work, and for work we have to travel from one place to another. Moreover, there's always so much to see when we go to new places. Why, this very place of yours is about to turn into a carnival in a few days—just wait till the harvest season is over. Musicians, dancers, clowns and mimes. Have you never seen any of these here? Well, how could you? There were forests all around so far. This is perhaps the first year of harvest. Just a fortnight more. This is when everyone gets to earn their bread.'

It was cold and dark beyond the reach of the fire. Far away in the darkness, someone was beating a tin canister. My eyes fell on the rickety huts that these people lived in with their families and children, with no doors to protect them from the many perils of the nearby forest. Just the other day, a tiger had dragged a baby away from its mother's side. Who could say if it would not decide to come around to these huts? But strangely, I noticed that they did not seem bothered at all. There was no sense of fear or the anticipation of a threat looming large. They were all sitting out in the open, late into the night, chatting and cooking and happily having a hearty meal. I said, 'You people need to be a little more careful. You do know that there's a man-eating tiger roaming around, don't you? A man-eating tiger can be very cunning and dangerous. As much as you can, try and stay indoors after dark, and light a fire near the doorway. The forest is just over there, and it's quite late in the night—'

The girl said, 'We are quite used to this, Babu-ji. We get a lot of trouble from wild elephants at the place in Purnia where we go to harvest paddy every year. They come down from the hills at night and go on a mad rampage, destroying all the crop. Those forests are even more dangerous.'

The girl threw a few more dried stems of tamarisks into the fire. Then she came forward a little and said, 'A few years ago, we were living and working near the foothills of the Akhilkucha range. One night, I was cooking outside my hut, when I looked up to see four or five wild elephants coming towards me from the distance. They looked like walking hills in the dark themselves. I immediately picked up my little boy, grabbed my daughter by her hand and rushed into the hut. I hid them there and stepped out to find that the beasts had stopped a few yards away from the hut. I was shivering from head to toe, Babu-ji, I couldn't even cry for help. Elephants don't see so well, they identify us humans by our smell. The winds must have been blowing in the other direction, or whatever the reason might have been, the elephants slowly walked away. Wild buffaloes here, wild elephants over there. We are quite used to this by now.'

Seeing that it was quite late in the night, I returned to my hut.

In another fifteen days, the entire scene at Fulkiya Baihar underwent a complete change. As soon as the mustard plants were dried and their seeds plucked out, different kinds of people began coming from various places. From Purnia, Munger, Chapra and other towns, Marwari businessmen came with their sacks and their weighing scales to buy the seeds. Along with them came the coolies and the cart-drivers. Then came the sweet sellers, who set up temporary shacks and started selling delicious snacks, sweets and savouries with infectious enthusiasm. A group of people came selling many colourful and cheap wares—things such as glass utensils, dolls, cigarettes, cheap fabric and soaps.

Along with these people came the performers—dozens of them. They sang and danced, made people laugh with their buffoonery and made quite a bit of money. Even those who dressed up as Ram and Sita, or those who simply carried around a small vermillion smeared statue of Hanuman through the crowd earned a neat sum of money.

Just a year ago, riding through the desolate woods and fields of Fulkiya Baihar after dark used to be a scary proposition. And when I looked at it now, I could hardly recognize the place! Young boys and girls giggling and running around, blowing their tin trumpets and whistles. Men and women dancing and singing, people laughing and making merry. As if the whole of Fulkiya Baihar had turned into a big fat carnival all of a sudden.

Even the population had increased by a significant margin. Scores of huts and cottages came up overnight. No money was needed to build dwellings over here. There were more than enough plants and trees in the forests nearby, providing a steady supply of dried branches, twigs, leaves, barks and whatnots. Add to these the enviable physical labour of these men and women.

The tehsildar of Fulkiya came to me and said that we ought to ask these traders and performers, and whoever else had come to Fulkiya to earn an income, to pay us a tax. He said, 'You set up a makeshift cutcherry right here, Huzoor.

I'll have these people brought to you one by one, you listen to them and then decide a suitable tax amount.'

I had a chance to meet so many interesting people in the process!

I used to start in the morning and sit in the cutcherry till 10 a.m., then start at 3 p.m. and continue all the way till 6 p.m. in the evening.

The tehsildar said, 'These people wouldn't stay here for too long. Once the harvest is over and the trading had been done, they will leave. We need to make sure they pay up before they do.'

One day, on seeing a Marwari businessman buying seeds from the farmers, I got the distinct feeling that he was cheating on his weights. I asked my men to check the weights and balances of every single trader in Fulkiya. When the crackdown began, one or two traders were brought to me; they were duping the farmers and had been caught red-handed. I immediately threw them out and asked my men to see that they never returned. The farmers had toiled day and night to grow their crop, and I for one would not let them be cheated of their rightful price.

But soon I realized that it was not just the crop traders who were cheating the farmers. Various kinds of people were looking for an opportunity to fleece the poor, gullible men and women.

For instance, out here, there was not much cash transaction that took place. Instead, while buying fancy items from the hawkers, the farmers would pay in kind, mostly in mustard seeds that they had just reaped. But more often than not, they—especially the women—gave away more seeds than what their purchases were worth. They were far too simple and gullible for the shrewd city traders, and it was not too difficult for them to be smooth-talked into paying as much as four times than what they ought to have.

Even the men were not any less gullible in these matters.

All they did all day was to buy imported cigarettes, shirts and footwear. Once the money from the crops started flowing in, these men and women did not know what to do with it. They started buying flashy clothes, dazzling bangles, glass and enamel utensils and packet after packet of sweets and snacks. They spent a lot of money listening to songs and watching the dance recitals as well. Of course, there were the donations to the mock gods and fake worships too. Months after months of grinding labour, night after night of staying awake and guarding their crops from boars and buffaloes, throwing themselves face to face with poisonous snakes and blood-thirsty tigers—all to earn a handful of money, only to be happily thrown away over a period of these fifteen days.

There was one good thing about these people though—none of them drank alcohol or toddy. Drinking had never been a pastime among the Gangotas or the landless Brahmins. Some of them drank bhang, but no one really had to buy it. The forests of Labtulia and Fulkiya had plenty of cannabis, and all that one had to do was to go there and pluck off some leaves.

One day, Muneshwar Singh came to me and said that a man was breathlessly running away without paying his taxes—if I gave the word, he could be caught and presented before me.

I asked in a surprised tone, 'What do you mean running away? On foot?'

'Yes, Huzoor, faster than a horse. He must have crossed the lake and reached the edge of the jungle by now.'

I asked for the fugitive to be brought to me.

Within an hour, four–five sepoys dragged the man in.

On seeing the man standing in front of me, I was left speechless. There was no way he could have been a year less than sixty! All his hair had turned grey, there were wrinkles on the skin of his face and his hands. One look at him and I realized that the man must not have had a proper meal in ages.

I soon learnt that the man had dressed himself up as the 'naughty butter thief' and earned quite a bit of money over the last few days. He had been living in a temporary shed under Grant Sahib's banyan tree, and for several days now, the sepoys had been asking him to pay his taxes, because the harvest season was almost over and people would start leaving soon. The man had been putting it off every day, so the sepoys had given him an ultimatum. Today, the sepoys got word that the man had wrapped up all his belongings and was heading out of Fulkiya towards Purnia. When Muneshwar Singh went to pay him a visit, the man suddenly threw everything and started running.

But somehow, I had a doubt in my mind. Were the sepoys telling the truth? For instance, if by 'naughty butter thief', they meant the boyhood avatar of Lord Krishna, would a sixty-year-old man be able to pull off such a stunt? Moreover, how could this man run as fast a horse—so much so that it took the sepoys such a long time to nab him and bring him back?

But everyone present there vouched for both the facts.

I asked the man in a stern voice, 'What's gotten into you, eh? Why would you do something so silly? Don't you know that you need to pay your taxes? What's your name?'

The old man was shivering like a tiny leaf caught in a tempest. It was quite evident from his face that the sepoys had not been very kind to him.

In a trembling voice, the man informed me that his name was Dasharath.

'Where are you from?'

'I'm a landless Brahmin, Huzoor, from Munger district—Sahebpur.'

'Why were you running away?'

'I wasn't running away, Huzoor.'

'Very well then, pay your taxes.'

'I haven't earned a dime, Huzoor. How can I pay my taxes? My dance fetched me some amount of mustard seeds, I sold that to have a meal or two. I swear in the name of the Lord.'

The sepoys jumped in, 'He's lying, Huzoor, don't listen to him. He's earned a lot over the last few days. He must have hidden it all. If Huzoor permits, we'll search him right now.'

The man immediately folded his hands in fear and said, 'I'll tell you how much I have on me, Huzoor.'

The he pulled out a small purse, emptied it on my table and said, 'This is all I have, Huzoor—just thirteen annas. I don't have a family, nor do I have any friends. Who will give me money at my age? I go from one farm to another, dance for the farmers and make my living. All I have till the next harvest season are these thirteen annas—and even that is three months away. I will hardly be able to have one scanty meal a day with this – that's all. Now the sepoys are saying I have to pay eight annas in taxes. I would be left with just five annas, Huzoor. How would I survive three months on five annas?'

I said, 'What do you have in that cloth bundle of yours, show me?'

The old man untied his bundle, and out came a small tin-wrapped mirror, a crown made of cheap tinfoil—crested with a peacock father, colour to smear on his cheeks, a garland of beads, etc. Equipment and makeup to turn himself into little Krishna.

'I don't even have a proper flute, Huzoor. A long tin flute would cost me no less than eight annas. I just pretend to play this bit of stick now. The Gangotas are simple people, they are easy to fool. But back home in Munger, they will all laugh at me if I tried to pass off this stick for a flute. I wouldn't get a single penny, Huzoor.'

I said, 'Well then, you show us your dance, in lieu of your taxes.'

The man's relief was apparent from the way he slowly broke into a wide grin. And when he donned his crown, put on his makeup, picked up his 'flute' and began his dance, I was moved beyond words. That a sixty-year-old man could turn himself into a little boy with such ease and grace was beyond my imagination, and that he could make his audience laugh with every single expression of his wizened face and with every single movement of his frail-looking limbs was in itself a matter of great skill and artistic acumen. The man would sometimes furiously frown in anger at being admonished by his imaginary mother, and would smile naughtily at other times as he distributed his stolen butter among his fellow thieves. The way he puffed up his lips and cried when his mother would tie up his hands as punishment was a sight to see!

All for a few annas! Just a few annas!

I had never seen such a strange and magnificent dance in all my life. Nor had the sepoys, who till not very long ago, had not hesitated to rough up the old man, but who were now finding it difficult to suppress their giggles before Manager Babu.

When the recital came to an end, I gave the old man the applause he deserved. I said, 'I have never seen anything like this, Dasharath. You dance so well! Your taxes are pardoned, and I'm giving you these two rupees as a reward. You did really well!'

In another ten to twelve days, the trading of the crops was over, and everyone left. Only the farmers stayed back. The shops and shacks were gone, the singers, dancers and hawkers—all went looking for other sources of income. The reapers and labourers had stayed back to enjoy the entertainment, but now, even they began to leave one by one.

[2]

One day, I was out for a stroll, and while returning to my hut, I decided to pay a visit to Nakchhedi Bhakat.

Dusk was about to fall. On the western fringes of Fulkiya Baihar, the large blood red sun was about to dive behind the green lines of the forest. These sunsets, especially the ones in winter, presented such breathtakingly gorgeous sceneries, that I often made my way up to the top of the Mahalikharup Hills in the evenings to take in their beauty.

On seeing me, Nakchhedi quickly rose to his feet and struck me a salute. He said, 'Manchi, go get something for Babu-ji to sit on.'

I had seen an old woman living in Nakchhedi's hut; she must have been his wife. She often did odd jobs here and there—chopping wood, walking all the way to Bhimdastola to fetch water from the wells and more. Manchi was the girl who had told me the stories about the wild elephants. She came and lay a mat made of dried catkin stems on the floor for me to sit.

Then, she gave me the sweetest of smiles along with a perky nod of her head, and in her sweet 'chikachiki' dialect from South-Bihar, she asked me, 'Did you like the fair at the Baihar this year, Babu-ji? Didn't I tell you that there'd be singing and dancing and such colourful things to buy? Please sit; we haven't seen you in some time. We're leaving soon, you know?'

I sat on the mat right outside the door of the hut, in a way that I could see the sunset right in front of my eyes. All around me, there was a soft reddish tinge on the trees of the forest, and there was an indescribable sense of peace and quiet that had befallen the vast expanse of Baihar.

I said, 'Are you all leaving tomorrow?'

'Yes, Babu-ji'.

'Where are you headed?'

'Purnia, Babu-ji. Kishanganj.'

I must have fallen silent in my admiration of the scenery around me. Manchi said, 'Did you like the fair, Babu-ji? I had a lot of fun! There were so many singers and dancers. One day, one of my friends came and told me that there was a man sitting under the large berry tree in Jhollutola; he was playing his dholak and singing one song after another. We rushed there to see. You won't believe what a beautiful voice he had!'

I watched the innocent young girl as she went on and on describing all the wonderful things she had seen and experienced at the fair—that too with animated expressions and unbridled excitement.

Nakchhedi said in a reprimanding tone, 'That's enough now, Babu-ji lives in Kolkata, he has seen much more than any of us. Don't mind her, Babu-ji, she's far too childish for her age. It's because of her that we had to stay back all these days. She's so silly, and always blabbering away—I worry about her sometimes.'

I had never asked Nakchhedi if Manchi was related to him, but on listening to him today, I realized she must have been his daughter.

I asked, 'When are you planning to give her away in marriage?'

Nakchhedi looked shocked for a few seconds. Then he slowly said, 'I don't know what you mean, Babuji.'

'Why, won't you get your daughter married anytime soon?'

'My daughter?'

'Isn't Manchi your daughter?'

On hearing my words, the first to start giggling was young Manchi. Nakchhedi's aged wife also hid her chuckles behind her palm and stepped back into the hut.

Nakchhedi was visibly hurt. He said in a grave tone, 'She's not my daughter, Babu-ji. She's my wife—my second wife!'

Not knowing what else to say, I simply uttered an exclamation that could mean one of several things—'Oh!'

What followed were a few awkward moments of silence. I quickly began to scamper for something to say, but words failed me.

Finally, Manchi said, as if nothing had happened, 'Let me light a fire, it's getting cold.'

This winter had been particularly unforgiving. As soon as the sun set, it almost seemed like we were living somewhere in the icy heights of the Himalayas. The horizon had lit up with the red hue of the setting sun, the sky above it was blackish blue.

At a short distance from the hut, there was a bush of dried catkins. As soon as Manchi lit the bush on fire, flames as high as ten–twelve feet began to rise up to the skies. We went and sat by the fire.

Nakchhedi said, 'She's still a child, Babu-ji. Always demanding silly things. Take this year, for instance. I earned all of fifty to sixty kilos of mustard seeds this time. This wretched girl must have spent at least a third of it in buying fancy stuff from the fair. If I said 'no', she sat in the corner and cried all day. I finally had to give in.'

I thought to myself, 'You must have thought about that before marrying a girl at least a third of your own age.'

Manchi threw her arms in the air in protest, 'Why, haven't I promised you not to buy anything in the next harvest season? This time, they were selling some good stuff at dirt cheap rates, so . . . '

Nakchhedi flared up in an instant, 'Dirt cheap? Those shrewd hawkers and shopkeepers made a fool out of you, you silly woman! Dirt cheap, eh? Would you believe it, Babu-ji? She paid five kilos of mustard to buy one comb! Just one comb—can you believe it? And just the other year, in the farms of Tirashi Ratanganj . . . '

Manchi flared up too. She jumped up and said, 'Wait, Babu-ji. I'll show you what I bought. You see for yourself and tell me if it isn't cheap.'

Before I could stop her, the young girl had made a dash for the hut, and in less than a minute, had returned with a covered basket woven out of dried catkin-stems. One by one, various items from her proud purchase came out of the basket, and were carefully and lovingly laid out on the mat before me.

'Look how large this comb is, Babu-ji. Tell me if this should cost anything less than five kilos of mustard? Have you seen the colour of the thing? Isn't it simply marvellous? And look at this soap, see how nice it smells. No, no, go on, smell it! This I got for five kilos too. You tell me, Babuji, wasn't it a good bargain?'

I sighed and looked at the soap—an item of extraordinarily poor quality, that would have cost no more than an anna, or perhaps less, in any market in Kolkata. Even at the end of harvest season, five kilos of mustard would have cost at least seven and a half annas, if not more. This poor, innocent jungle-dwelling young girl knew nothing of the ways of the world; the shopkeepers in the fair had clarly taken advantage of her ignorance.'

But Manchi didn't show any signs of stopping. With great enthusiasm and excitement, she showed me her hairpins, a ring crested with a gem that was obviously fake, china dolls, an enamel dish, half a reel of red ribbon and many other things. I smiled to myself as I realized that no matter which country or which strata of society they belonged to, the wish-lists of women were roughly identical to each other, and in that sense, the feral girl Manchi was not too different from her educated, city-bred sister in any other part of the world. The propensity to collect and proudly own seemingly meaningless trinkets was God's gift to womankind, and the wrath of good old Nakchhedi—as of the most powerful or affluent nobleman in the world—was futile and meaningless in the face of such natural instincts.

But what was that one item from her priceless trove that Manchi was saving for the end? Her zeal was so infectious that by now, even I was curious to know!

Finally, with a proud smile that lit up her face in the dying twilight, she held up before me her most prized possession.

A blue and yellow garland of *hinglaaj*!

The elation on her face was a sight to behold! Unlike her urban counterparts, she had not learnt how to hide her feelings. As I stared at her singing the praises of her trivial knick-knacks, I saw more than a young girl. I saw a clean, pure and unadulterated feminine mind, something that would be rather difficult to witness in the so-called civilized society of ours.

'Isn't it beautiful?'

'Fantastic!'

'Guess how much I paid for it? I'm sure you wear this in Kolkata?'

Not just me, I knew of no one in the entire city of Kolkata who wore a garland of hinglaaj, but despite that, I knew that by any stretch of imagination, such an item could not have cost more than six annas. I said, 'I wouldn't know. How much?'

Manchi grinned and said, 'Just seventeen kilos of mustard! Isn't that a steal?'

I sighed. How could I tell her that she had been conned out of her wits? These things were bound to happen in these places. And what had happened had happened. What would be the point of getting her rebuked and chided by her already aggrieved husband? That smile on her face was far more priceless than a few annas.

I realized that I would have to be more careful in the future. I should have kept a strict watch on the rates in the fair. But I was new to these parts, I had no experience. Why, I did not even know that there would be a fair during harvest season. Lesson learnt. I would have to ensure that such things did not happen from next year onwards.

The next morning, Nakchhedi left for Purnia, with his two wives and two little children in tow. Before he left, he had come to my hut to pay his taxes. Manchi had come along with him. I noticed that she had put on the garland of hinglaaj around her neck. She smiled and said, 'We will come again, Babu-ji, this time before the monsoons, to reap the corn. Would you be here then? I make pickles of wild myrobalan every year, I will get some for you.'

I had quite liked the sweet young Manchi. When she left, I couldn't help but feel a slight pang of sadness in my heart.

CHAPTER 11

[1]

I once had a strange experience in the forest.

To the south of the Mohanpura Reserve Forest, fifteen to twenty miles from its borders, there was a vast jungle of sal and kendu leaves. One day, I heard that this jungle was being sold on auction, and the very next day, I got a cable from my headquarters carrying express instructions for me to go to the auction, bid for and secure the kendu leaf jungle.

But I was not prepared to bid for a jungle unless I had seen it with my own eyes. At the same time, the day of the auction was almost upon us. So, the day after I got the cable, I set out for the forest on horseback.

My men had started their journey with my luggage at the crack of dawn. I caught up with them on the banks of the Karo river outside Mohanpura Forest. My collector Banwarilal was with me.

Karo was all but a thin mountain stream, with hardly knee-deep water, flowing over a bed of smooth colourful pebbles. Banwarilal and I got off our horses, because their hooves could slip over the pebbles. The banks themselves were covered with fine white sand—so fine, in fact, that our feet sank in them all the way to our knees. When we reached hard ground on the other side, it was almost 11 a.m. Banwarilal said, 'I think we should cook our meals here, Huzoor, we might not find water anywhere later on.'

There were jungles on both sides of the river, not too dense though. Sal and palash, mostly, with large rocks and boulders strewn amidst them. There was no sign of habitation anywhere around.

Despite our best efforts to cook and consume a hasty lunch, it was 1 p.m. by the time we resumed our journey.

Even at sundown, when there was no sign of any end to the jungle, I began to wonder if we should stop for the day and take shelter under one of the many large trees that stood all around us. My mind went back to the two small villages that we had crossed on our way—one was called Kulpal, the other Burudi. But that was around 3 p.m. in the afternoon. Had I known then that we would not be able to ride out of the forest even by nightfall, I would have asked Banwarilal to make necessary arrangements for spending the night in one of those villages.

As the night began to grow darker, the forest too seemed to become denser and denser. In the beginning, we were able to maintain a steady pace through the trees and bushes. But now, as the trees and vines all around began to close in on us, the path ahead became narrower and narrower. The place where we were standing now was completely surrounded on all sides by massive trees, there foliage hiding the twilight sky from our views.

And how beautiful the spot was! A strange white flower had bloomed all around us in thick bunches, its pristine white now mildly tinged with the soft blue hue of the dying evening light. Banwarilal said, 'Those are the flowers of the wild *teuri*, Huzoor. Vines of a kind, the flowers bloom around this time of the year.'

Everywhere I stopped and looked, the flowers were there, and that too in large numbers—as if someone had scooped up a handful of freshly picked cotton and strewn it on the heads of the trees. Far from the eyes of the civilized man, in the middle of a dense forest, mother nature had safely guarded such breathtaking images of unknown beauty! The man from the city, the loveless man, the busy man had no right to enter these woods. Such beauties were reserved only for the wild at heart, be it man or beast.

Poor Banwarilal! He must be wondering why this Bengali babu from Kolkata was stopping his horse every other minute and staring at the forest with his mouth wide open, and how on earth could an absent-minded man such as him run the affairs of the estate. It was perhaps because of my indulgences that we had been irredeemably delayed for the night. Whatever may have been the reason, Banwarilal did not say anything to me. We decided to stop for the night under a large *asan* tree—Banwarilal, myself, and the other seven-eight men in our party.

Banwarilal said, 'These jungles are not safe. Light a large fire, and everyone stay close to it.'

My camp-chair had been set up next to the fire. I sat in it and looked up at the night sky through a gap in the foliage. All around me, there were white bunches of wild Teuris blooming in their full glory. Right next to my chair were tall blades of dry grass that had turned golden in colour. They emanated a mildly scorched smell, which mixed with the smell of the sunburnt ground and the fragrance of some unknown wildflower to resemble the distinct smell that came from the painted and decorated idols of Goddess Durga. I sank back deep into my chair and felt a strange sense of freedom—a feeling that was not possible anywhere else in the world other than the depth of these forests. Words cannot describe the joys and pleasures of such a unique and content feeling.

Suddenly, one of the porters came and informed Banwarilal that while gathering dried branches and twigs to feed the fire, he had seen something strange in the middle of the forest. The place was not safe, he said, there were bound to be ghosts and spirits watching us, and apparently, we had chosen a poor spot to pitch our tents.

Banwarilal said, 'Come Huzoor, we need to go check out what the man saw.'

We followed the porter into the jungle, and after walking for some time, the man pointed towards a certain spot and said, 'That's where it is, Huzoor. I won't go any further.'

Step by step, I walked up to the indicated spot. Rising from behind a bush of thorns and vines was a wooden pillar, and at the top of the pillar was carved a monstrous face. Horrid enough to scare the life out of the poor old man who had unexpectedly stumbled upon it in the middle of the night.

There was no doubt in my mind that it was man-made, but where on earth had this pillar come from? It looked pretty worn out, but there was no way to tell how ancient it was.

The night passed. We woke up early in the morning and reached our destination by 9 a.m.

On reaching there, we were greeted by one of the employees of the current owner of the forest land. He took us on a round of the jungle. I was busy surveying the place, when suddenly, beyond a dry ditch to my right, I saw a wooden pillar rising from behind a dense green cluster of bushes—just like the one I had seen the previous night, complete with a similar monstrous face carved on it.

I called Banwarilal and showed him the pillar. The owner's employee happened to be a local man; he said, 'There are a few of those at various places in the forest. Many years ago, this forest was under the rule of a tribal king. Those pillars were carved by the tribesmen; they marked the borders of his kingdom.'

I asked, 'How do you know all this?'

He said, 'I've been listening to the stories for several years now, Huzoor. And moreover, the descendant of the king is still alive.'

I was rather curious to hear that. I asked, 'Where does he live?'

The man pointed towards a certain direction and said, 'There is a small village towards the north of this forest. He lives there. Even today, he commands great respect among the people of this land. Ever since I came here, I have heard that his ancestors had a vast kingdom—bordered on the north by the foothills of the Himalayas, on the south by the Chota Nagpur plateau, with Munger on the west and the Kushi river on the east. Everything in this area—hills, mountains, rivers, streams, jungles—once belonged to his ancestors.'

I suddenly recalled that back at my cutchery, schoolmaster Ganori Tewari had once told me that the descendant of the aboriginal king of the region was still alive. Not only that; he had also told me that the people of the land still considered him as their king. The forest employee who had given us this remarkable information was named Buddhu Singh, and contrary to his name, he was rather smart and intelligent. He had been working here for several years now, and seemed to be quite conversant with the local history.

Buddhu Singh said, 'These tribesmen had put up a brave fight against the Mughals, Huzoor. When the Badhshah's men would try to cut through their land to enter Bengal, these people used to put up a fight with their hand-strung bows and arrows. But soon, their kingdom was taken away from them. They fell in battle, but not without a fight. A very brave race, Huzoor, but nothing's left of them anymore. Whatever little was left was lost after the Santhal Revolution of 1862. The leader of the revolution is still alive, he is the one who the tribesmen call their king now. His name is Dobru Panna Veervardi. He is very old now, and lives in abject poverty. But all the forest tribes of the region still consider him as their king. They say that the kingdom may have been lost, but the king still lives.'

I felt a strong urge to meet the king.

I ought to take some gifts along while paying the king a visit, I thought; at least, protocol demanded so. So what if he was not the king anymore, his ancestors were, and from whatever little I had heard of him so far, it was quite clear that he deserved all the respect that he received from his people.

By afternoon, I had purchased a few fruits and a couple of large hens from the nearby market. By 2 p.m., I had finished my survey; so, I called Buddhu Singh and said, 'Let's go pay the king a visit.'

Buddhu Singh did not seem too keen. He said, 'I don't think that's a good idea, Huzoor. He may be a king, but of uncivilized, barbaric forest tribes. He's not fit to speak to someone like you.'

I turned a deaf ear to his advice and set out to meet the forest king. Banwarilal and Buddhu Singh came with me.

The village that was once the capital of the erstwhile kingdom was now reduced to a habitation of twenty or so families.

The walls of the huts were built of mud, the roofs out of thatch and hay. A noteworthy feature of all the huts was that they were kept very clean and tidy. Images of snakes, lotuses, vines and such were carved on the walls. Little boys were running around in carefree frolic and the women were busy with their domestic chores. The young women were astonishingly well built and rather attractive, and despite the poverty that was apparent all around me, there was an unmistakable glow on their faces. As we passed, everyone stopped what they were doing and stared at us.

Buddhu Singh asked a woman in the local dialect, 'Is the king home?'

The woman responded by saying that she had not seen him all day, but then where else could he be. We proceeded towards the king's home.

[2]

From Buddhu Singh's expressions, it seemed to us that the place where we had come and stood in the village was a majestic grand palace. In reality, it was just an ordinary looking house. The only distinguishing feature of the house, however, was that it was surrounded on all sides by a stone wall. Right behind the village there was a hill, and it was quite apparent that the stones had been brought from there. There were several children running around in the compound; some of them were babies, crawling on all fours. They had necklaces made of beads and some sort of blue fruit-seeds hanging around their necks. A couple of them were quite good looking. A sixteen- or seventeen-year-old girl came running in response to Buddhu Singh's call, and seemed surprised, and somewhat frightened, to see us.

Buddhu Singh said, 'Is the king home?'

I asked Buddhu Singh, 'Who's the girl?'

Buddhu Singh said, 'She's the daughter of the king's grandson.'

I figured the king's enviable longevity must have deprived several generations of men, both young and old, from ascending to the throne.

The girl said, 'Come with me; he is sitting at the foot of the hills.'

As we followed the girl, I could not help but marvel at the fact that she was indeed a princess, and that for several generations, her ancestors have ruled this place. What a prestigious family she belonged to!

I asked Buddhu Singh, 'Ask the girl what her name is.'

Buddhu Singh said, 'Her name is Bhanumati.'

'Oh, how wonderful!'—I thought—'Bhanumati! Princess Bhanumati!'

The young princess had comely features. Her face had a soft, simple and lovely appeal. But not only was her attire far from being regal, it fell short of being able to maintain the decency of a civilized society as well. The hair on her head was coarse and matted, and she wore a beaded necklace around her neck. She pointed towards a large myrobalan tree from afar and said, 'There he is, sitting under that tree and grazing the cows.'

Grazing the cows!

I was shocked out of my wits! The king of the entire province, the fiery leader of the Santhal Revolution—His Royal Highness King Dobru Panna Veervardi—was grazing cows?

Before we could ask her anything, the girl walked away, and as we took a few more steps towards the tree she had indicated, we could see an old man sitting under it and smoking tobacco out of a dried leaf of sal.

Buddhu Singh said, 'Salaam, Rajasahib.'

From the way Dobru Panna responded, it seemed to me that although his hearing was intact, his eyesight must have been poor.

He said, 'Is that you, Buddhu Singh? Who's that with you?'

Buddhu Singh said, 'A Bengali babu has come to see you, Rajasahib. He's brought some gifts for you. Please accept them.'

I personally walked up to the old man and placed the hens and other items before him.

I said, 'You are the king of the land. I have come a long way to meet you.'

The large, stately build of the man was evident to the fact that King Dobru Panna must have been an exceedingly handsome man in his youth. There was a twinkle of wisdom and intelligence in his old eyes too. He seemed very pleased with my courteous gesture. He stared at me for some time and said, 'Where are you from?'

I said, 'Kolkata'.

'Oh! That's too far from here. It's a beautiful city, I'm told.'

'Have you never been there?'

'No, we are forest people, this forest is our home. The city won't suit us. Take a seat. Where did she go? Bhanumati, come here, girl!'

The young girl came running.

'Listen, this Bengali gentleman and his men are going to stay with us tonight. Go see to it that their meals and other arrangements are taken care of.'

I immediately protested, 'Oh, no, no! We can't. I just wanted to come and meet you. We can't stay—'

But Dobru Panna said, 'Out of the question, I can't let that happen. Bhanumati, take these things away, child.'

I gave Banwarilal a sign, and he carried the gifts I had brought and followed the girl all the way to the king's home. I could not refuse the old man's request; one look at his face was enough to fill my heart with the deepest reverence for him. Leader of the great Santhal Revolution, descendant of an ancient royal dynasty (so what if it was a primitive tribe), the brave Dobru Panna was inviting me into his home. Well, his wish was my command.

From everything that I had seen so far, it was quite evident that King Dobru Panna was living amidst great poverty. In fact, I was rather shocked to see him grazing his own cows. But then I remembered that countless kings and noblemen before him, and significantly more affluent than him, had been reduced to abject penury, forcing them to take up far more lowly occupations than rearing cattle, simply in order to survive.

The king himself rolled a sal leaf cigar and handed it over to me. There were no matches, but a small fire had been burning under the tree; he lit a dry leaf and held it in front of me.

I said, 'Yours is such an illustrious dynasty, it is my good fortune to have met you in person.'

Dobru Panna said, 'There's hardly anything left anymore. We are the descendants of the sun. These hills and forests, the entire region used to be our kingdom. When I was a young man, I had waged war against the Company. I am an old man now. And we lost in the war. It's all over now. There's nothing left.'

It didn't seem to me that the king was aware of anything that was happening in the world outside these hills and forests. I was about to say something in response to his laments, when suddenly, a young man walked up to us.

King Dobru said, 'My youngest grandson, Jogru Panna. His father is not here today, he has gone to pay a visit to the Queen of Lakshmipur. Listen Jogru, Babu-ji and his men will stay with us tonight. Make sure that all necessary arrangements are made.'

The strapping young man said, 'May we serve porcupine meat for you, Babu-ji?'

Then he turned towards his grandfather and said, 'I had laid some snares in the forest on the other side of the hills, went looking this morning to find a couple of porcupines trapped in them.'

The king apparently had three sons, and they in turn had eight to ten children of their own. All members of this extended family lived together in the same compound and under the same roof. Hunting and rearing cattle were their primary means of livelihood. Other than this, anyone in the region, who came to the king with appeals to settle disputes and other matters, brought the customary gifts such as milk, hens, goats and fruits.

I asked, 'Do you do some farming as well?'

In a voice laced with unmistakable pride, Dobru Panna said, 'We don't do all that in our family; we've never done that. Hunting is the most honourable profession and it has always been so. That too—hunting with a spear. If you hunt with bows and arrows, there's no valour in that. Because you can't offer that to the gods; so, that's not what the brave do. But things are different now-a-days, everyone seems to be accepting everything. My eldest son brought me a gun from Munger; I've never cared to touch it. Hunting with a spear in hand is real hunting.'

Bhanumati came and placed a shallow dish made of stone next to me.

The king said, 'Go ahead, rub some oil on your body. There's a lovely stream over there; you and your men can go take your bath there.'

Once we had taken our bath and returned, the king asked Bhanumati to take us to a room in his house. We followed her to the room, where she offered us a large tray of rice and a few freshly uprooted potatoes. Jogru had skinned a porcupine by now; he offered the meat to us. Bhanumati disappeared inside the house and returned with some milk and honey.

My cook was not with me; so, Banwarilal went about peeling the potatoes and I tried to light the earthen oven placed in the corner. But unaccustomed as I was to such endeavours, I soon realized how difficult the job was. The large pieces of wood just would not catch fire. After one or two attempts, when I failed, Bhanumati came running and dropped a dry and abandoned bird nest in the oven, making the fire light up in an instant. As soon as her job was done, she immediately went and stood by the wall. I realized that the princess was not just cheerful and intelligent, she was quite dignified at the same time.

King Dobru Panna sat at the doorway throughout, keeping a constant watch on the hospitality of his guests. After we had had our meals, he said, 'As you can see, I'm not the king that my ancestors were. I'm sorry I couldn't do more for you; I couldn't even offer you a decent room. Deep in that forest is a large hill, and on top of that hill are the ruins of my ancestral palace. I have heard from my father that many years ago, my ancestors used to live there. Those days are gone, time has worn everything out, but the idol of our family's deity has miraculously survived.'

I was rather curious about the entire thing. I said, 'Would you mind if we paid a visit to the spot?'

'What's there to mind? But there's nothing much left up there. But fine, I'll take you there. Jogru, you come with us.'

I protested, I couldn't let a ninety-two-year-old man climb up a hill, after all! But my protest was swiftly turned down. King Dobru Panna smiled and said, 'I go up there every now and then. The graves of all my ancestors are up there, you see. I pay them a visit every full-moon night. Come, I'll show you the place where they are sleeping.'

A range of hills that the locals called Dhanjhari had come in from the north-east and taken a sharp turn towards the east, and it was at this turn that there was a deep recess of sorts. Below this natural recess was a sprawling valley, and the forest that covered the slopes of the hills had continued down to the valley and run away towards the horizon. It almost seemed like a green waterfall had descended from the top of the hills and turned into a river that had submerged the entire valley in a verdant pool of water. Everywhere I looked, all I saw was green. Miles and miles of dense, dark green forest running away towards Gaya and Ramgarh. A narrow walking path through the woods took us all the way up to the top of a hill.

At a certain spot, we saw a massive boulder, and on the ground underneath the boulder, there was a hole—the kind of hole that foxes dug on the ground to hide in, or potters dug to bake their clay in. The mouth of the hole was covered by a small undergrowth of sal saplings.

King Dobru said, 'We need to get into that hole. Come with me. There's nothing to fear. Jogru, you go first.'

With my heart beating faster than a speeding horse, I entered the hole. There could be a tiger or a bear inside. Snakes were almost certain to be present.

We had to crawl on our knees for some distance before we could stand up. It was pitch dark inside, but after some time, as the eyes began to adjust to the darkness, we began to see things around us. We were standing in the middle of a large cave—at least twenty to twenty-two feet long and fifteen feet wide. On the north wall of the cave, we noticed a hole similar to the one we had come in through, and were told that it was a passage to a larger cave on the other side of that wall. Needless to say, we were not too keen on entering the second hole. The roof of the cave was not too high; a standing man could raise his hand and touch the roof. There was a foul and musty stench in the air, thanks to all the bats. Other than that, the cave also served as a nesting place for foxes, mongooses, wild cats and other creatures. Banwarilal whispered in my ears, 'I think we should go back, Huzoor. This place isn't safe.'

This, apparently, was the ancestral hill fort of Dobru Panna.

It was in fact a massive natural cave formation. In ancient times, warriors could hide out in these caves when they were outnumbered, undetected from enemies, because the mouth of the cave faced upwards—towards the top of the hill.

The king said, 'There's another secret passage to this cave, but we are not supposed to talk about it. Only members of my family know about it, and although no one lives here anymore, they guard the secret with their lives.'

Once we came out of the cave, I breathed a sigh of relief.

We resumed our climb, and after some time, reached a massive and ancient banyan tree, with hundreds of its branches spreading across almost an acre of land on top of the hill.

King Dobru Panna said, 'I request you to take off your shoes, please.'

There were several large slabs of stone arranged all around the massive trunk of the tree. The king said that this was their ancestral graveyard. Beneath each slab of stone lay a member of the royal family. I looked around in awe and wonder. At some places, the branches of the tree had come down and turned into tree trunks themselves, with their own roots finding their way deep into the ground. Some of the stones were so old that these branching offshoots had completely engulfed them, making them nearly disappear within their monstrous clutches.

King Dobru Panna said, 'This banyan tree wasn't here in the past, this place was a nice little garden of sorts. A small sapling grew into this gigantic tree over the years, killing every other tree around it. It is so old that now, the original trunk doesn't even exist anymore. It's only those offshoots that are holding it up. If we were to chop it off, you'll find dozens and dozens of gravestones underneath. You can imagine how old this graveyard is.'

I stood speechless under the giant all-encompassing tree and felt a strange sensation in my veins—one that I had not felt so far, neither when I had met the king who seemed more like an aged Santhal coolie, nor when I had met the princess who I found to be no different than any other Ho or Munda girl in the prime of her youth, and certainly not when I had been inside the fort, which was nothing but a frightening dwelling place of beings both earthly and otherwise. But on seeing this ancient mountaintop gravesite, with so many ancient members of the royalty peacefully sleeping under the cool shade of a humongous tree, my heart was filled with a wondrous, incomparable and unparalleled humbling feeling that I had never experienced before in all my life.

The gravity, the mystery and the ancientness of the spot were indescribable. The sun was about to set, the leaves of the mammoth tree over our heads were being bathed by the golden rays of the sun. Even the other peaks of the Dhanjhari and the vast expanse of wilderness in the valley beneath us were being touched by the same soft light. The rapidly elongating shadows of the approaching dusk lent a dignified and silent mystery to the royal tombs.

Not far from the city of Thebes was the Valley of the Kings—a site that had served as the burial grounds of the great Egyptian emperors and kings. Today, the site was being thronged by tourists from all over the world. In peak season, it would be impossible to find a room in one of the hundreds of hotels that had come up around the spot. The skies over the valley were no less clouded by the ancient mysteries of the past than they were by the dark smoke swirling up from the expensive cigars and pipes of tourists. But neither in the thrill of its mystery, nor in the grave dignity of its stature was this desolate burial site any less than the celebrated Valley of the Kings. History might have forgotten all about it, the wrath of time might have been unkind to its upkeep, but the hallowed grounds still preserved the remains of those who were once potent kings—uncivilized, wild, jungle-dwellers, but those who ruled their people with such great care and affection that centuries later, one of their destitute descendants was still being hailed as the monarch with the same loyalty and reverence as his great ancestors had commanded. This unassuming site had remained hidden in the hills, and will perhaps forever remain so. The tombs of these kings had neither the pomp nor the grandeur of the affluent pharaohs of Egypt, for they were not only wild in customs and manner but wild at heart as well. They never bothered to amass wealth at the cost of their people's welfare. Their culture and civilization were the same as those of the primitive man—one of enlightenment, not of greed or intolerance. With the simplicity of a man-child, they had carved out a humble home for themselves in a cave, built modest tombs for their dead and erected naïve signposts to announce their borders. Standing on top of the hill, under the shade of that massive tree that evening, I saw a rare and revealing glimpse of an ancient and venerable era that went much beyond our day-to-day comprehension—an age in comparison to which, even the Vedas and the Puranas seemed modern and contemporary.

In my mind, I saw the nomadic Aryans traversing the perilous mountain passes of the north-west, making their way like an unstoppable torrent into an ancient India hitherto ruled by primitive tribes and clans. The subsequent history of India was comprised entirely of the history of this Aryan civilization. The history of the vanquished non-Aryans was conveniently and promptly erased from human memory. Such lost and unwritten history now remained hidden in these mountain caves, in these dark forests, and within the skulls and bone-dust of crumbling skeletons buried in those graves. The conquerors had never bothered to decipher the history of the aboriginals, and thousands of years later, even today, the descendants of those primitive tribes continue to face shocking neglect, ruthless discrimination and abject poverty. And the opulent Aryans, blinded and dazzled by their arrogant pride in their own civilization, had never cared to look after these people, nor do they do so now. I myself, Banwarilal, Buddhu Singh—we were all representatives of that ruthless and vainglorious Aryan civilization. And King Dobru Panna, princess Bhanumati, and prince Jogru Panna represented the ancient, vanquished, primitive people of this beautiful land. In the dying light of the afternoon, here we were, two tribes—symbolizing two different civilizations—standing face to face with each other. In my mistaken sense of pride, in my unforgivable indifference towards their customs and culture, I had looked down upon the king as an old Santhal man, I had seen the dignified and well-mannered young princess as a Munda coolie, I had labelled the warm and zealous tour of their ancient palace as a perilous journey into a damp and filthy foxhole. Was this not a great tragedy of history in itself? One that had played out on the top of this hill in the middle of this forest in the dying light of the setting sun?

Before the royal gravesite could be completely enveloped in darkness, we made our way back to the valley.

On the way down, I saw a tall slab of stone erected in the middle of the jungle. It was smeared with vermilion, and surrounded by several marigold and mirabilis plants that had been evidently planted by human hands. There was another much larger and taller stone standing right in front of the first one—this one was covered in vermilion too. We learnt that this was a holy site, and that from ancient times, the stones were worshiped as idols of the deity of the royal family. In the past, there used to be human sacrifices here. Now, hens and pigeons were offered as sacrifice from time to time.

I asked, 'Which god is this?'

King Dobru said, 'Tyandbaro, the god of the wild buffaloes.'

I remembered Gonu Mahato's fascinating story, the one he had told us the previous winter.

King Dobru said, 'Tyandbaro watches over us. Had it not been for him, hunters and poachers would have killed every single buffalo in the forest for their hides and horns. But Tyandbaro protects them. Every time a herd is about to be hunted or trapped, he appears out of thin air—a number of people have seen this with their own eyes.'

Had I been a regular member of the urban-centric civilized society, I would perhaps not have lent any credence to the existence of this forest deity. But standing there, surrounded by hills and forests on all sides, I began to ask myself a question that I would never have asked under any other circumstances—what if Tyandbaro really did exist? What if the legend was true?

Several years later, when I had returned to Kolkata, I had once seen, in the scorching heat of the afternoon sun, a pair of buffaloes being ruthlessly whipped by the driver of an overladen cart in the streets of Burrabazar. On seeing the poor animals suffer, I had thought to myself, 'Oh Tyandbaro, I wish these were the forests of Chota Nagpur and Madhya Pradesh; I wish you would come and free these mute animals from their plight. Oh, how I wish you would come! But no, these were the civilized streets of the civilized city of Kolkata. A glorious marvel of the Aryan civilization! Here, even a watchful and caring deity such as you were as helpless as the vanquished King Dobru Panna.'

I had to catch a bus from Naowada to Gaya, so I set out soon after dusk. Banwarilal returned to the camp with my horse. Before I left, I had met princess Bhanumati one last time. She was waiting for me at the palace doors with a bowl of buffalo milk in her hands.

CHAPTER 12

[1]

One day, Raju Pandey sent word to the cutcherry that wild boars had been wreaking havoc in his china grass farm every night, and that thanks to a couple of full-grown tuskers among them, all he could do was to beat a tin cannister to make some noise when the beasts came. The cutcherry had to do something about this, or else his entire crop would be damaged.

On hearing this, I personally went to the spot with a gun that very evening. Raju's hut and farm were right in the middle of the dense forests of the Narha Baihar. Habitation was scant and farms were few, so the nuisance caused by wild animals were relatively more frequent.

Raju was working in his farm. On seeing me, he dropped everything and came running. He took the reins of my horse and tied it to the trunk of a myrobalan tree nearby.

I said, 'How come I don't see you these days, Raju? Don't you come to the cutcherry anymore?'

Raju's hut was surrounded on all sides by dense jungles of tall grass and catkins, with a kendu or myrobalan tree raising their heads from here and there. I wonder how he stayed in the middle of these desolate woods! Not a soul to talk to, at the end of a hard day's labour. Strange man!

Raju said, 'I just don't find the time, Huzoor. I'm having a tough time guarding the crop anyway. Moreover, I have the buffaloes to look after.'

I was about to ask why rearing three buffaloes and tending to a farm as small as a couple of acres took up all his time, when Raju himself rattled off such a detailed list of his day-to-day activities, that it seemed quite natural to me that the man had found no time for social visits at all. Working in the farm, taking his buffaloes out for grazing, milking them, making butter, daily prayers and ceremonies, chanting the Ramayana, cooking his meals—even hearing all about it seemed overwhelming to me. That was not all, it seemed, the man had to stay up all night and beat a tin cannister to try and keep the beasts at bay.

I said, 'When do the boars come?'

'They don't come at a fixed time, Huzoor. But only after nightfall, though. Just wait a bit longer, they'll come in large numbers.'

But there was something else that was driving my curiosity even more than the boars; how could a man live in a place like this all by himself? So, I asked Raju.

He said, 'I'm used to it by now, Huzoor. I have been living by myself for a long time. I don't face any problems at all; in fact, I quite like it. I work hard all day, and when night falls, I sing a bhajan, or chant the name of the Lord. It's a nice and comfortable little life I have here.'

Raju, Gonu Mahato and Jaypal—there were more people like them living in various parts of the forest, all by themselves. Through their eyes, I could see a world that was unfamiliar to the rest of the world.

I was aware of a certain worldly addiction of Raju though—the man was very fond of tea. Knowing that he would not have the luxury of drinking tea in the middle of this forest, I had taken some along with me. I said, 'Raju, would you like to brew up some good old tea? I've brought some for you, and here's some sugar.'

Visibly overjoyed, Raju took water in a massive pot and put it on his earthen oven. The tea was ready, but other than a small bronze bowl, Raju had no other utensil. Raju offered me tea in the same bowl, and himself sat down with the humongous pot to enjoy the refreshing beverage.

Although Raju could read and write in Hindi, he knew very little of the world outside this forest. He had heard of this city named Kolkata, but he had no idea where it was. His knowledge of Bombay or Delhi was no more than his knowledge of the moon. As for towns, he had been to Purnia, that too many years ago, and just for a few days.

I asked, 'Have you ever seen a motorcar, Raju?'

'No, Huzoor. I have heard that it runs on the road by itself, without being pulled by a cow or a horse. It lets out a lot of smoke, it seems. Apparently, there are quite a few of them in Purnia these days. I've not been to the city in a long time now, it costs a lot of money to go, and I can't afford it.'

I asked Raju if he wanted to visit Kolkata, assuring him at the same time that he would not have to spend anything and that I would pay for his trip.

Raju said, 'The city is an obnoxious place, Huzoor. Full of thieves, cons and thugs. People say it's inauspicious to go to the city. Every single man is trying to cheat you. Someone from my village had been to the city once, to visit a doctor, there was something wrong with his foot. The doctor cut his foot open and said, how much will you pay me? So he said, I'll pay you ten rupees. On hearing this, the doctor cut his foot open a bit more and said, now tell me, how much will you pay? He said, I'll pay you five more, Doctor Sahib, please don't cut my foot anymore. The doctor said, that's not enough, and started cutting more. The poor man began to cry, but the more he wept, the more the doctor chopped off his foot with a knife. Finally, he ended up cutting off the entire foot, Huzoor! Oh, what a ghastly affair, I shudder to think of it!'

Trying my best to suppress a chuckle, I remembered this was the same Raju who had once seen a rainbow in the sky and told me, 'You see that rainbow, Huzoor? It rises from the mounds that termites make. Trust me, I've seen it with my own eyes.'

In the courtyard outside Raju's hut, there was a large and tall asan tree. We were sitting beneath it and drinking our tea. In every direction I looked, there were dense forests—kendu, gooseberry, flowering vines of *bahera* and other plants. The fragrance of bahera flowers seemed to have sweetened the evening breeze. What a delightful experience it was—relishing a strong cup of tea in such a beautiful location! I tried to remember when was the last time I had sat amidst such wondrous natural surroundings to savour a cup of tea, that too in the company of a man as simple in thought and action as Raju Pandey. But I could not. It was an experience as uniquely pleasant as it was strange.

I said, 'Tell me something, Raju. Why don't you ask your wife to come and stay with you here? Then you wouldn't have to live alone, and she can help you with the cooking.'

Raju said, 'Oh, she's long gone, Huzoor. It's been seventeen or eighteen years since she passed away. Ever since then, I can't seem to be able to stay at home.'

That a man like Raju could have witnessed something remotely similar to a romance in his life was beyond my imagination, but from whatever he said next, I realized that there was no other term that could have been a more fitting description of what he had experienced with his wife.

Raju's wife's name was Sarju. When Raju was eighteen years old and Sarju was fourteen, he had been in the tutelage of her father for a few days, back at Shyamlaltola, in North Dharampur district. Apparently, the girl's father, who ran a small school of his own, used to teach him grammar.

I asked Raju, 'How long were you in that school?'

'Not very long, Babu-ji, just over a year. But I didn't write my exams. It was there that the two of us met for the first time, and . . . gradually . . .'

Out of respect for me, Raju finished off his sentence with a short cough.

I encouraged him to carry on, 'And then?'

'But Huzoor, her father was my teacher. How could I say such a thing to him? And then one day, in the month of October, on the day of the Chhatt festival, Sarju put on a lovely yellow sari and went to the river with her friends to take a dip. So, I . . .'

Another polite cough. Raju was silent again.

I egged him on once again, 'Go on, tell me, don't be shy—'

'Well, I wanted to meet her, so I was hiding behind a tree. Of late, I wasn't getting much of a chance to see her—I had heard that her father was trying to strike an alliance for her marriage as well. When the group of girls went singing by the tree—as you know, Huzoor, on the day of the Chhatt, girls go singing all the way to the river to take a holy dip—so, when the girls went past me, Sarju saw me hiding behind the tree. She gave me a smile, and I smiled back. I gave her a signal with my hand, asking her to deliberately fall behind, so that she could drop off the procession. She shook her head and gestured—not now, while coming back.'

A half-blushing-half-proud smile of teenage love slowly spread across the face of the fifty-two-year-old Raju Pandey, and the pensive gaze of a distant dream appeared in his bleary eyes—as if they were searching for the fourteen-year-old girl who had evoked a hitherto unknown sensation of joy and bliss in his juvenile mind many years ago. As if it was in her pursuit that this lonesome man was living in the middle of this dense and desolate forest. As if he lived here, hoping against hope that someday, she would come, and he would have the good fortune of her company again.

I was quite enjoying his story. So I said eagerly, 'What happened then?'

'Well, when she was on her way back, she deliberately lagged behind the rest of her gang. And then we met. I said, I can't take this anymore, Sarju. I don't get to see you, nor can I concentrate on my studies. What's the point of suffering like this? I'm thinking of going away, forever. Sarju began to weep. She said, "Why don't you speak to my father?" On seeing her tears, Huzoor, something happened within me. I did what I never thought I would be able to do. I gathered all my courage one day and spoke to my teacher. We belonged to the same cast; so, there were no objections to our marriage. And then one day, we were man and wife!'

It was a simple tale of ordinary romance—one that I would not have cared for had I listened to it in the din and busy clamour of city life, and one that I would have certainly dismissed as a mushy anecdote of rustic courtship under any other circumstances. But on listening to the same story in the idle and unhurried ambiance of the evening woods, I savoured every moment, every single emotion associated with it. That a detailed description of something so simple, so commonplace and so mundane as a man and a woman falling in love with each other and crossing several hurdles to end up in each other's arms could be so mysterious, so enchanting and so heart-warming—I would never have known, had I not heard Raju Pandey's fascinating love story that evening.

By the time we had finished our tea, the crescent moon had risen in the night sky, and the treetops were being washed in the soft and silvery moonlight.

I picked up my gun and said, 'Come Raju, let's go and take a look at those boars.'

There was a large indigo tree on one side of the farm. Raju pointed towards it and said, 'We need to climb that tree, Huzoor. I have built a machan at the top this morning.'

I found myself in a bit of a spot, for I had not climbed a tree in a long time, that too in the middle of the night. But Raju encouraged me and said, 'It's quite simple, Huzoor. I've made some bamboo rungs too, you will have no trouble at all.'

I handed over my rifle to Raju, and with some amount of difficulty, managed to climb up to the top and sat on the machan. Behind me, the fifty-two-year-old Raju climbed the tree with enviable ease and grace, joining me soon on my perch. The two of us sat side by side, my gun in my hand and our eyes fixed on the ground below.

As the hours passed, the light of the moon grew brighter. There was an alluring charm in the silvery haze that had spread all around us by now. We were perched high up on a tree, looking down upon the breeze-swept ground. A fascinating experience in itself!

After some time, a pack of foxes began to yelp from within the surrounding jungle. And moments later, I saw a large lump of darkness rush out of the woods and enter Raju's farm.

Raju said, 'There it is, Huzoor!'

I pointed my gun at the animal, but as it came nearer, we saw in the moonlight that it was not a boar, but a nilgai.

I had no intention of killing a nilgai; so, I asked Raju to shoo it away. The animal made a swift exit and I fired a shot in the sky to scare it away.

A couple of hours passed. Wild roosters began to crow from within the southside jungle. I had hoped to kill one of the full-grown tuskers, but we did not even catch a glimpse of the small ones. I realized I had made a mistake by firing the blank.

Raju said, 'No use waiting anymore, Huzoor. Let's go down, I'll make some dinner for you.'

I said, 'Oh, I can't stay. It's hardly ten in the night. I need to get back to the cutcherry. I'll have to head out early morning, there's some work pending at the survey camp.'

'Please don't leave without having dinner, Huzoor.'

'I wish I could stay, Raju. But it wouldn't be safe riding through the forests of Narha Baihar after hours. I must go now; please don't mind.'

I mounted my horse and said, 'I hope you wouldn't mind if I came here once in a while to have a cup of tea with you?'

Raju said, 'Please don't say that, Huzoor. It will be my honour. I know you brought the tea and the sugar along, because I love drinking tea. You are too kind, Huzoor. It will be my absolute pleasure to have you here again. Please come whenever you feel like.'

I looked at Raju one last time that night and realized that for a man of his age, he was quite good looking, and that many years ago, the scholarly father of his teenage bride had taken a rather wise decision by giving his daughter's hand in marriage to his bright young pupil.

The night was dark, because the moon had set by now. I was riding through the woods by myself. There was no light anywhere, nor any sound. There was absolute silence everywhere, as if I had been banished from Earth to some distant lifeless planet. The Scorpius had risen in the dark sky over the horizon and countless other stars were twinkling over my head. Beneath this bejewelled firmament was the vast and silent expanse of the Labtulia forest. In the faint light of the stars, I could see the tips of the wild catkins swaying in the mild breeze. Somewhere in the distance, a pack of foxes announced the hour. Farther away, the dark outline of the Mohanpura Forest Reserve was etched in the horizon. There was no other sound, except for the constant chittering sound of some unknown insect. On listening very carefully, I could hear the almost unnoticeable sound of a few other insects too. What a bewitching romance I witnessed in my free life! What unfathomable joys the close proximity to nature had brought me! But most of all, what a strange sense of mystery that the forest was enveloped in! I could not really say what that mystery was. What I did know was that I had never felt the same sensation ever since I had returned to the city.

As if it was during these nights, surrounded by constellations and galaxies, the gods in the skies were dazed in the intoxicating dreams of creation—an imagination that would lead them to create countless worlds in the future, along with countless images of beauty and countless new forms of life. Only the soul who spent his days in the leisurely and languid pursuit of knowledge and truth, only he whose life was filled with the humility of the behemoths and the pride of the tiniest creatures that roamed the universe, who refused to remain constrained by the spans of a lifetime and whose yearning to travel far and wide gave him the wisdom to ignore his insignificant moments of earthly joy and sorrow—only such a soul was able to see the mysterious image of these gods.

Those who had laid down their lives in their repeated attempts to scale the Everest had perhaps been able to witness this image of the creator. Standing on the sandy beaches of the Azores Islands, when Columbus had looked at the logs of wood floating ashore and tried to decipher the secret message that the distant continent beyond the vast ocean had sent him, it was in that precise moment that the great explorer must have realized the mysteries of God's creation. And those who sat at home, smoked tobacco all day, gossiped about the neighbour's daughter and took their frustration out on their barbers and their washermen—such undeserving people could never hope to witness that solemn glimpse of the creator of this universe.

[2]

There was a survey being conducted in the hills and forests on the north banks of the Michhi River. I had been camping there for a week or so. I would have to stay for at least a couple of weeks more.

The spot where we had camped was very far from our estate, somewhere near the kingdom of Dobru Panna. Of course, it was no longer his kingdom anymore; so, one could say that the place was close to King Dobru Panna's home.

A lovely place! It was a valley—wide open on one side, narrow and shut in on the other, hill ranges spread out from the east to the west, and right in the middle of it all was this horseshoe shaped valley—rugged and covered in dense jungles, with small and large boulders strewn everywhere, amidst thorny bushes and large deciduous trees. A number of mountainous streams had descended down the hills from the north and flown away through the open mouth of the valley. The banks of these streams were covered in deep, almost impenetrable jungles, and having lived here over the last few days, I had come to know that these jungles were frequented by tigers. So far, I had seen deer and heard the crows of wild roosters in the early morn. I had even heard the call of jackals, but had neither seen nor heard a tiger yet.

On the eastern façade of the hills was a massive cave. Right at the mouth of the cave was a large banyan tree; its leaves rustled in the breeze, night and day. On the walls of this cave were several carvings and inscriptions; perhaps, they had been drawings or images of some kind in the primitive past, but were quite faint and indecipherable now. I often stepped inside the cave and looked around, marvelling at all the joyous celebrations, all the peals of laughter and wails of grief, the ups and downs of survival and stories of savage tyranny and gentle love that these walls must have witnessed in the distant past.

Just a few yards from the mouth of the cave, by the banks of the stream lived a family of forest-dwellers. A couple of shanties—one large, one small—with branches and twigs for walls, and leaves for roof. In a plain, open area outside the huts lay a small oven for cooking, built with stones and rocks brought from the forest. The huts themselves stood in the shade of a large almond tree. The courtyard was perpetually covered in a soft carpet of almond leaves that had fallen off the tree.

There were two girls in the family—one was sixteen-seventeen years old and the other was fourteen or so. They had a dark complexion, comely faces and slightly chubby figures. Every morning, I saw them take their buffaloes out for grazing in the hills, and by the time I returned to my tent for my evening cup of tea, I saw them pass by on their way home.

On one such evening, the older of the two girls stopped at a little distance from the tent and sent her younger sister to me. The girl came running to me and said, 'Babuji, salaam. Do you have a beedi?'

'You smoke?'

'I don't smoke, my sister does. Will you give us one? Please?'

'I don't have a beedi, I have a cigar. But I won't give it to you, because it's too strong, you won't be able to smoke it.'

The girl ran away.

Later that evening, I walked up to their huts. The head of the family seemed rather surprised to see me. He greeted me courteously and welcomed me to his home. I saw the two girls sitting by the oven and having a meal of ghato or boiled maize for dinner. No ingredients other than a bit of salt.

Their mother was busy boiling something over the kiln. A couple of babies were running around playfully.

The man of the family seemed to be in his fifties. Strong, sturdy build. On being asked, he said that he had come from the Siuni district and was living here on these hills for a year or so now, thanks mainly to the abundance of grass and fresh drinking water. Moreover, there was a particular kind of bamboo that was found in these jungles—one could use them to make rattan baskets and trays. They were also used to make headcovers, the kind that farmers wore to protect themselves from the heat of the sun or from heavy torrential rains as they worked in the open fields. Apparently, all these fetched a neat amount of money in the fair of the Akhilkucha village.

I asked, 'How long do you plan to stay here?'

'As long as our heart desires, Babu-ji. We usually don't stay at one place for more than a year, but we have taken to a liking to this place. It's beautiful out here, and this place has another major advantage. The woods up there are full of custard apples. My daughters used to bring back a basketful of custard apples every time they went up the hills with the buffaloes. For two whole months, we have had only custard apples twice a day. Ask them, if you don't believe me.'

Her mouth still full, the older girl beamed in excitement and said, 'Oh! There's a spot up there on that hill over there to the east; there are so many custard apple trees there! Hundreds of ripe fruits, fallen on the ground, split open. No one to claim them. We pick them up and bring them home, one basket at a time.'

Suddenly, someone walked out of the dense woods, stood in front of the huts and called out, 'Sitaram, Sitaram! Can I have some fire?'

The head of the family replied, 'Please come, Baba-ji. Please come.'

It was an old sadhu, with matted hair and dreadlocks covering his head and most of his face. The sadhu had seen me by now, and seemed at a loss of words. In fact, he seemed somewhat frightened too. With some amount of hesitation in his manner, he stood in one corner.

I said, – 'Namashkar, Baba-ji.'

The sadhu did raise his hand in blessing, but he still seemed quite nervous.

In a bid to calm him down, I said in a soft voice, 'Where do you live, Baba-ji?'

The response came from the host instead. He said, 'Baba-ji lives deep within the forest, over there, right at the point where the two hills meet. He has been here for quite some time.'

The aged sadhu had sat down in one corner. I turned towards him and asked, 'How long have you been living here?'

The sadhu seemed to have gathered some courage by now. He said, 'Must have been sixteen years at least, Babu Sahib.'

'You stay here all by yourself? Aren't you afraid of the tigers in the jungle?'

'Who else is going to stay with me, Babu Sahib? I take the name of the Lord. Can't afford to be afraid, at my age.'

I observed the man for some time and said, 'You must be around seventy years old, right?'

The sadhu smiled and said, 'No, Babu Sahib. I'm well over ninety. I used to live in a jungle near Gaya; lived there for ten years. And then, one day, those jungles were sold, and they started chopping down all the trees one by one. So, I had to run away from there. I can't live amidst people.'

'There's a cave here. Why don't you live in it?'

'Not just one, Babu Sahib, there are several caves here. And the place where I currently live may not be a cave exactly, but it's somewhat like a cave. As in, I have a roof over my head, and walls on three sides.'

'How do you make a living? Do you beg for alms?'

'I don't step out of my home, Babu Sahib. The Lord takes care of my food. Some days, I boil green shoots of bamboo and have them. There's a kind of root found in the jungle, which tastes somewhat like red potatoes and is very sweet. Some days, I have those. I also have ripe gooseberries and custard apples. Gooseberries, in particular—I have a lot of those. If you have gooseberries every day, year after year, you won't get weaker with age. You can remain young in both body and spirit. People from the village down below sometimes come up to pay me a visit. When they come, they bring milk and grist and other items.'

'Have you ever come face to face with a tiger or a bear in the jungle?'

'No, never. But I have seen a scary python-like snake in the forest once—it was lying still deep within the woods, and I almost stumbled upon it. Its body was thick and dark, looked just like the trunk of a tree. There were red and green diamond-like marks on its skin. Its eyes were burning like the fire in that kiln. I'm sure it is still in the jungle somewhere. That day, I had seen it lying quietly by the stream, perhaps waiting for a deer to pass by. It must be hiding in some cave right now. Well, I must be going, Babu Sahib. It's quite late in the night.'

The sadhu took a burning piece of ember and walked away into the darkness. I heard that he came here once in a while to ask for fire, and when he came, he often stayed back for some chitchat.

The moon was rising, and a strange silence seemed to be hanging over the sylvan valley. Other than the steady burble of the mountain stream, and the occasional crowing of a wild rooster from deep within the forest, there was no other sound.

I made my way back to my tent. On the way, I had stopped for a few unhurried moments under a large simul tree to admire the hundreds of fireflies glowing in the dark, flying in circles—up and down and sideways—etching thousands of dazzling luminous geometric figures on the dark background of the forest.

[3]

It was here at the survey site that the poet Venkateshwar Prasad first came to see me. A tall, slim figure—clad in a dark serge coat and a shabby dhoti, a head full of rough, unkempt hair—the man seemed to be well into his forties.

I realized he had perhaps come looking for a job. I said, 'How can I help you?'

He said, 'I've come to see you, Babu-ji (I noticed he did not address me as 'Huzoor'). My name is Venkateshwar Prasad. I am originally from Bihar Sharif, in Patna district. I now live in Chakmakitola, around three miles from here.'

'I see. So, what do you want here?'

'I'll tell you, Babu-ji, with your kind permission. I hope I'm not wasting your time?'

By then, I was almost certain that the man would ask for a job. But by not addressing me as 'Huzoor', he had earned both my respect and my attention. I said, 'Come and have a seat. It must have been a long and exhausting walk for you.'

I also noticed that the man's Hindi was very refined. I myself did not speak in such a refined manner. I had been living amidst rustic farmers, sepoys and local villagers for several years, and in doing so, I had picked up some of their tongue, mixed it with idioms from Bengali and created a strange hotchpotch dialect of my own. Let alone speaking, I had never even heard such elegant and polished Hindi ever before. So, choosing my words carefully, I said, 'Tell me, how can I help you?'

He said, 'I've come to recite some of my poetry to you.'

I was rather shocked to hear this. I understood that the man was a poet, but why come all the way into this dense jungle up the hill to recite his poetry to me?

I said, 'You are a poet? I'm happy to know that, and I'd be glad to listen to your poetry. But how did you know I was here?'

'Well, as I said, I live around three or so miles from here, on the other side of those hills. Everyone in my village has been saying that a Bengali gentleman has come from Kolkata and was living here in these woods for a few days. I knew that erudite people such as you would understand the true value of knowledge. The bard has said—

> *The learned values the words of the poet*
> *The budding pupil learns from his wisdom*
> *But to one who has no knowledge nor the will to learn*
> *Poetry is but the grass beneath one's feet*

Venkateshwar Prasad recited his first poem to me. A lengthy piece involving a ticket checker, booking clerk, station master, guard and many other people working in some remote and imaginary railway station. There were questions in my mind about the quality of the poem, but I must also say that with my limited knowledge of the poet's sophisticated language, I understood very little of it. So perhaps, I would not be a good judge of the man's skills. Every now and then, I uttered a word or two of encouragement and praise, just out of courtesy.

This went on for a long time. Venkateshwar Prasad showed no signs of stopping, let alone bidding farewell to me and walking back the same way he came.

Almost two hours later, he paused to catch his breath, flashed a smile and said, 'What do you think, Babu-ji?'

I said, 'Excellent! I have never heard such poetry before. Why don't you send your poems to any magazine?'

Venkateshwar made a sad face and said, 'Everyone in my village says I'm mad, Babu-ji. Do you really think there is anyone living in this godforsaken place who can understand poetry? Today, I am honoured to recite to you—that too to my heart's content. Only a man like you could understand the true merit of my poetry. I had been wanting to meet you ever since I had heard about you.'

That day, when he left, I thought I had seen the last of him. But the very next evening, he returned to the camp and started pleading with me to come pay a visit to his humble home. Unable to decline his ardent pleas, I set off with him— on foot, nonetheless—for his home in Chakmakitola.

Although the sun had not set yet, it was quite late in the evening when we reached our destination. Before me, there lay vast fields of wheat and maize, and the slanting shadows of the northern hills had fallen on them. The place seemed so quiet and peaceful! A flock of egrets flew over the fields and perched themselves on top of a thorny bamboo grove. A bunch of rustic boys and girls were dipping their hands in the mountain stream in a bid to catch tiny fishes.

In the village, the huts and houses seemed to be cramped together, their roofs touching each other. Most of the houses did not seem to have a courtyard inside. Venkateshwar took me to a mid-sized house with a thatched roof. The sitting room was right on the side of the road, and I took my seat on the wooden stool that was offered to me. I saw the poet's wife soon after; she personally came and placed a generous portion of dahi vada and fried corn in one corner of the same stool I was sitting on, but without uttering a single word. Not that she was in a veil or something similar though. She must have been in her mid-twenties, had a pleasant dark complexion, a calm and soothing disposition, and although I would not describe her as good-looking, it was also true that she had a rather agreeable and cordial presence. There was something very graceful and elegant about her.

There was something else that I noticed that day—the health of the poet's wife. Ever since I had come to the forests, I had found the general health of the women in the region to be a hundred times better than that of an average woman back in Bengal. They were not fat; rather, they were quite stockily built, muscular and had well-toned figures. The poet's wife was no different.

After some time, the lady brought me a bowl full of curd made from buffalo milk and went behind the door. She rattled the chain of the door to draw her husband's attention, and Venkateshwar went and spoke to her. Upon his return, he smiled and said to me, 'My wife says we've made a new friend today, so we must test your friendship. She's mixed a lot of chilli-powder in that curd. She says you must have it all at one go.'

I smiled and said, 'Well, in that case, I must say that friendship is all about sharing and caring. So, I propose that all three of us shall have this curd. Please, I insist, do come and join me.'

I heard the woman of the house laughing from behind the door. But I was not one to let go; on my insistence, all three of us shared the curd.

After some time, she went back to the interior of the house and returned with a plate of sweetmeats. Then she herself said in a soft, playful voice, 'Ask Babu-ji to have these homemade sweets; it will give his throat some relief from all the burning.'

I could not help but marvel at her soothing voice and immaculate diction!

In all these years, I had become an admirer of the local dialect, which was a heavily accented form of Hindi that I myself did not speak. This form of Hindi was not to be found in books, and was only used in the spoken form. Rooted, grounded, and sweetened by the rustic tongue of local women, this dialect had essences of all the natural beauty that marked its milieu. It reminded one of the hills, jungles, farms and open fields that surrounded it, it painted a unique picture of the sunset and carried the whispers of the swans as they flew by. I must confess that I found myself drawn to this beautiful dialect.

I turned to the poet and said, 'Would you please recite a couple of your poems?'

Venkateshwar Prasad's face beamed with the joy of having found an admirer. He had composed a rural ballad, a love story of sorts, and he narrated it to me. On the bank of a small canal, there used to live a young man. While he used to sit and guard his farm of maize, a young girl used to come to the other bank to fill her pot with water. The boy was captivated by the striking beauty of the girl; he used to avoid eye contact with her and sing a song to his goats or whistle a tune. Once in a while, their eyes would meet and the girl would blush. Every day, the boy would vow to tell the girl that he loved her, but when the time would come, he would fear rejection and remain silent. Days and weeks passed, as did months and years. Seasons came and seasons went. But his untold secrets and unspoken words remained buried in his heart. And then one day, the girl did not come. Nor did she come the next day, or the week after. Where had the girl gone? Why would she not come to see him anymore? Every day, the young man would sit on the bank of the canal and wait for the love of his life. And every evening, he would have to come away sad and dejected. Several months passed by, but just like that, the girl was gone from the young man's life. Finally, the heartbroken lover was forced to leave the place and go far away to take up a job. Several years passed by, but even after all this time, he had not been able to forget the pretty little lass he had met on the banks of the canal.

As I stared at the blue hills in the distance and listened to the tragic tale of unfulfilled love, I wondered if the poem itself was autobiographical in nature. Had Venkateswar Prasad himself had such a lovelorn experience? His wife's name was Rukma—I knew because he had dedicated a poem to her, and had recited the poem to me back at my camp.

CHAPTER 13

[1]

After almost three months, the survey work came to an end, and I was to return to my estate.

I was a long way from the estate, twenty-two miles to be precise. It was the same route that I had taken to visit the spring fair a few years ago, and I came across the same forests of sal and palash, the free undulating rocky fields and the high and low hills on my way back. A couple of hours into my journey, I noticed a faint outline on the distant horizon— the Mohanpura Reserve Forest.

I had not had a chance to witness this familiar sight in the last three months. Having spent all these years in this place, I had developed such a deep bond with Labtulia and Narha Baihar, that every time I had to leave them behind and stay away for a few days, it seemed to me that I had left home and was living in an alien land. After three long months, as I was on my way back to the cutchery, my heart danced at the very sight of the Mohanpura Forest in the distance, although I knew that the borders of Labtulia were still a good seven-eight miles away.

On the base of a small hill, a vast expanse of land had been cleared to sow seeds of Kusum flowers. These would be used to extract oil. Now that the flowers had bloomed, several men and women were busy plucking them.

I was riding by the edge of the farm, when suddenly, someone called out to me, 'Babu-ji, O Babu-ji—Babu-ji—'

I looked around to find Manchi, the girl from the previous year, waving at me. I was pleasantly surprised, and as I stopped my horse, Manchi came running with a sickle in her hand. She said, 'As soon as I had seen the horse in the distance, I knew it was you. Where had you gone, Babu-ji?'

Manchi looked just the same as I had seen her last year. In fact, she seemed to have put on a bit of weight. Thanks to the pollen from the petals of the Kusum flower, her hands and clothes had turned red.

I said, 'I had some work to do in the Baharaburu Hills, had to stay there for a few months. I'm going home now. What are you doing here?'

'We are plucking Kusum flowers, Babu-ji. It's quite late, you must have been riding for a long time. Why don't you take a break? Look, our *khupri* is just over there.'

My repeated protests went completely unheeded. Manchi dropped everything and led me to her hut. Her husband Nakchhedi Bhakat came running from the farm when he heard that I had come.

Nakchhedi Bhakat's first wife was in the hut; she was busy cooking. She too was delighted to see me.

But Manchi seemed the most excited. She quickly made a mat of maize hay for me to sit on. Then she offered me a tiny bowl of Mahua oil and said – 'There's a nice little pond to the south of this village, please take a dip in it. Come, I'll show you where it is. The water is cool and refreshing.'

I said – 'I won't take a bath in those waters, Manchi. All the villagers use those waters to wash their utensils and clothes. Are you drinking the same water? In that case, I'm afraid I can't drink this water. In fact, I think I should make my way home now.'

Manchi and her husband looked at each other's faces. I realized that my suspicion was not unfounded and that they too were drinking the water from the pond. Where else would they find water in the middle of the forest? They had no other choice.

Manchi was visibly crestfallen, and when I saw her helpless expression, I myself felt sorry for her. These were simple people; not even once had they imagined that it could be unwise or unsafe to consume this unhygienic and polluted water. If I were to decline their hospitality and leave on the pretext of the quality of water they were offering me, I would be hurting the honest sentiments of these poor people.

I said, 'Fine, I'll drink this water, but only after you've boiled it well. And I think I'll skip the bathing today.'

Manchi said, 'Oh no, Babu-ji. I'll boil an entire tin drum full of water for you. You take your bath. Please sit, I'll arrange everything for you.'

Manchi fetched the water and began preparations for a meal. She said, 'I can't offer you the food that I've cooked with my own hands, obviously. But here, I've made all the arrangements, please come and cook yourself a nice meal.'

'Of course, you can! I'll have anything you cook.'

'No, Babu-ji. We are lower caste people; you shouldn't eat anything cooked by us. I can't commit such a grave sacrilege.'

'Don't worry. I'm telling you, it's alright. Trust me.'

After several assurances, Manchi sat down to cook. The dishes themselves were nothing special—just a few impossibly thick handmade rotis and a curry made from wild fruits of *dhundhul* or sponge gourd. Nakchhedi Bhakat had fetched a pot of buffalo milk from somewhere.

While she was cooking, Manchi gave me a detailed narration about all the places she had been to and all the things she had been doing in the past few months, including the story of a kid goat that she had tamed and taken a great deal of liking to and how, one inauspicious day, she had lost it in the woods. I had no other option, but to sit there and listen to her stories all along.

She said, 'Babu-ji, do you know about the hot water spring in the estate of Kankowada? Have you been there?'

I had to admit that although I had heard about it, I had never had a chance to visit the place itself.

Manchi said, 'You know Babu-ji, they didn't let me take a dip in the spring over there. They beat me black and blue when I tried to.'

Manchi's husband said, 'What a riot, Babu-ji! The priests over there are inhuman beasts, the lot of them.'

I said, 'What happened exactly?'

Manchi turned to her husband and said, 'Yes, yes, tell everything to Babu-ji. He lives in Kolkata. When he writes about them, those rogues will be put in their right place.'

Nakchhedi said, 'The spring is called the Suraj Kund, Babu-ji. It's a holy place, supposedly. Travellers and pilgrims take their baths there. We were reaping legumes near the hills of Amlatoli, when one day, we learnt that it was a full moon night. So Manchi stopped her work in the fields and went to take a dip. I had a fever that day; so, I decided not to go. My first wife, Tulsi, didn't want to go either; she is not very religious, you see? So Manchi was about to get into the water when the priests stopped her and said, hey you, what do you think you are doing? She said, I want to take a bath. They asked, what caste do you belong to? She said, Gangota. Then they said, we don't allow Gangotas to take a bath in these waters, these are holy waters, get out of here. But you know how she is, Babu-ji. She said, this is a mountain spring, anyone can take a bath here. Why, look at all those people bathing over there! Are they all Brahmins and Kshatriyas? Having said these words, she tried to get into the waters, but two men came running, dragged her out of the water, punched and thrashed her mercilessly and threw her out. She came home crying that day.'

'What happened after that?'

'What could happen, Babu-ji? We are poor Gangotas; we travel from place to place; we reap the crops for rich landlords. Who would listen to our complaints?'

I said, 'Don't you worry, Manchi. I will take you to Sita Kund in Munger, that's a bigger spring, and very nice and clear water.'

Manchi said excitedly, 'Alright, Babu-ji! But will you please write about those men who beat me? You Bengali Babu-jis have a lot of power in your pens. If you write about what they did, that will teach them a lesson.'

I said, 'I most definitely will.'

After this, Manchi fed me the meal she had cooked with great affection and care. I spent a lovely afternoon amidst these simple, warm-hearted people.

When I took their leave, I asked them to come to Labtulia Baihar in the next reaping season, and was assured that they would certainly come.

As I was leaving, Manchi waved at me with a radiant smile, and as I waved back at her, I couldn't help but marvel at her warmth, her beauty, her uncomplicated nature and her generous hospitality. She may have been poor, but in the middle of the forest, she looked just like the deity of the jungle—full of life and free spirit.

Today, after several years, I fulfil the promise I had made to a wild jungle-dwelling young girl. A girl who had an infinite amount faith in the pen of a Bengali gentleman she had befriended over an evening meal. I do not know if by writing about the injustice she had faced, I would be of any use to her after all these years, nor do I know where she is and in what condition, or if she is even alive. But I had given her my word, and I have honoured it.

[2]

The monsoons had arrived. Dark clouds had spread across the skies, and if you stood anywhere in Labtulia or Narha Baihar, under Grant Sahib's banyan tree, for instance, you could see that a fresh green carpet of newly sprouted catkins had covered the ground all around you.

One day, I received a letter from King Dobru Panna, inviting me to celebrate the Jhulan festival with him. I decided to go. Raju and Matuknath insisted on coming with me; so, I decided to take them along too. Since they were to travel on foot, they started early in the morning.

At around half past one in the afternoon, I crossed the Michhi River. The rest of my men took another hour to cross, and once they had done so, I left them to take some much-needed rest and gave free rein to my horse through the fields.

The western skies were overcast, and soon, it began to rain heavily.

Oh, what a magnificent sight of the rains I witnessed in the middle of the wilderness that day! The grey of the clouds was a stark contrast to the blue of the distant hills in the horizon. Grave lumps of cloud were showing threatening streaks of lightning within them. In gracious welcome of the rains, dozens of peacocks had spread their feathers, dancing in joy on the branches of simul and kendu by the side of the road. Drenched to their very bones, rustic urchins were giggling and trying to catch fishes with their handmade traps in the tiny mountain brooks that had now become mighty streams. Pale boulders were getting wet and turning jet black in colour and sitting atop them was a lone buffalo-herder, rolling tobacco in dried sal leaves and smoking his cigar without a care in the world. A serene, silent land—jungle after jungle, wilderness after wilderness, streams, hilly hamlets, the ground covered in red earth and strewn with pebbles, a flowering piyal here and a blooming *kadam* there.

Just before dusk, I reached King Dobru Panna's palace.

The room that I had stayed in the last time had been cleaned, dusted and prepared for my arrival. The walls had been smeared with fragrant mud from the hills, and lotuses, trees and peacocks had been painted on them. The sal-wood pillars of the room had been festooned with flowers and vines. My bedding had not arrived yet; I had reached ahead of the rest of the traveling party, but I did not face any trouble at all. A new mat had been laid in one corner of the room, and a couple of clean white pillows were brought in after I arrived.

After some time, Bhanumati came in with a large brass tray of fruits along with a pot of boiled milk, with another girl of roughly her age following right behind with offerings of betel leaves, betel nuts and a number of spices.

Bhanumati was wearing a purple sari that reached up to her knees, with a garland of red and green Hinglaj flowers around her neck and a couple of spider lilies adorning the thick bun of hair on her head. While from her physical appearance, one could see that she was clearly in the prime of her youth, even the most casual glance at her eyes would reveal her childlike innocence.

I said, 'How are you, Bhanumati?'

Bhanumati did not know how to offer a namaskar, she simply smiled innocently and said, 'I'm fine, Babu-ji. How are you?'

'I'm fine too.'

'Please have something to eat. You must be hungry after riding all day.'

Having said this, she did not wait for me to respond. She simply knelt down on the ground next to me, picked up a piece of ripe papaya and placed it on my palm.

I was pleasantly surprised by her free, unhesitant manner. To someone from Bengal, this unrestrained, open attitude of a sixteen-year-old girl towards a relative stranger would come as somewhat of a shock. I realized that even in my urban sensibilities, my Bengali mentality towards girls and women were unnecessarily complicated and narrow, and that it did not allow me to be open with them—neither in action nor in thought. The women of this region, be it Bhanumati, or Manchi, or Venkateshwar Prasad's wife Rukma—were as free and open as the terrain itself. Perhaps, the forest had had some sort of influence on them, which led them to be frank and liberated in both body and spirit, without having to succumb to the meaningless urban traditions of ill-defined feminine courtesy and social taboo. The vast forest and the lofty hills had given them the power to love and be loved as freely and as generously as nature itself.

Bhanumati, for instance, was still sitting right next to me and feeding me literally with her own hands. Just as one human being would feed another. For the first time in my life, I had witnessed the close and innocent proximity of a young woman, and felt the joy of her fond affection. Had this simple act of warmth and tenderness been carried out in the city, the primitive woman that dwelt in the mind and spirit of young Bhanumati would have been crushed under the burden of orthodoxy and prejudice that we see on a daily basis but choose to ignore.

Bhanumati had perhaps come to realize that the Bengali gentleman she was feeding so fondly was her family's well-wisher, someone who would not harm them in any way, but would stand with them if needed. The affection I received from her that day, therefore, was the same that I would have received from a member of my own family.

Several years have passed since that day, but for some reason, the memory of a childlike and affectionate young princess feeding me with her own hands, with no guile, no hesitation and no complication in her mind, was still bright and dazzling in my mind. This seemingly simple and trivial little gift of so-called unrefined and primitive barbarianism was far more valuable to me than all the riches and treasures of urban civilization.

King Dobru had been busy with the preparations of the festival since morning. He now came and sat in my room.

After the usual exchange of greetings, I asked, 'Do you celebrate the Jhulan festival here every year?'

King Dobru said, 'Celebrating the Jhulan has been a long-standing custom in our family. All our kith and kin are coming from far-flung places. A hundred kilos of rice will be cooked in this house tomorrow.'

Matuknath had come with great hopes, he had perhaps expected that the 'King' would shower an erudite Brahmin like him with riches. Now that he was here, he seemed quite crestfallen. Even his school was in better condition than this palace.

Raju could not supress his feelings either, once we were alone, he blurted out, 'What king, Huzoor? He's just a Santhal chief! Even I own more buffaloes than he does.'

It was rather amusing to see that he had already carried out such an extensive investigation into the King's possessions and financial affairs. Cattle—as I had come to know by now—was the chief index of prosperity among the people of this region. Whoever had the greatest number of cattle was considered the most affluent.

Late at night, when the silvery moonlight and the trees of the orchard had cast a mesh of shadow and light on the vast courtyard of what was once indeed a palace, I heard a strange song in the chorus of all the women of the royal household. The following night would bring the full moon of the Jhulan—a festival in which Lord Krishna and his consort Radha would be praised through music and dance as they sat in each other's arms on a *jhulan* or a swing. A night before that auspicious day, newly-arrived female relatives and the princess's close girlfriends were busy rehearsing their recitals.

As I continued to listen to the songs and the sound of the madals, I must have fallen asleep sometime in the early hours of the morning.

[3]

They may have been sceptical of the King's prosperity, but the next day, Matuknath, Raju and even Muneshwar Singh were absolutely fascinated on seeing the celebrations at the Jhulan festival.

I woke up in the morning to find that at least thirty to forty girls of Bhanumati's age had come from near and far villages and gathered at the palace to take part in the festivities. One good thing I noticed was that unlike in other such celebrations, none of these girls had consumed any mahua toddy. When I said as much to King Dobru, he smiled and said in a voice clearly laced with pride, 'The girls in my family have not taken to drinking. And not just the girls, as long as I am around, no one would dare to drink in front of my family.'

In the afternoon, Matuknath came and whispered into my ears, 'This King is definitely poorer than me, Huzoor. All that he has given us for cooking our meals are thick red rice, a ripe pumpkin and a few wild dhundhuls. Now what do I do, tell me? There are so many of us, what do I cook for everyone?'

I had not seen Bhanumati all morning. When I had sat down for my meal, she came in with a bowl of milk.

I said, 'I liked that song you and your friends were singing last night.'

She smiled and said, 'I didn't know you knew our language.'

I said, 'Of course, I do! I have been in this region for so many years now.'

'I hope you are coming to the festival this evening?'

'Yes, that's what I am here for. How far would I have to walk?'

Bhanumati pointed in the direction of the Dhanjhari hills and asked, 'You've been to those hills, haven't you? You must have seen our temple up there?'

Meanwhile, a group of girls, roughly the same age as Bhanumati, had gathered at the doorway, whispering into each other's ears, and curiously observing a Bengali babu having his meal.

Bhanumati turned towards them and said, 'What do you think you all are doing over here? Go, get out of here, the lot of you!'

One of the girls seemed relatively more fearless than the others, she stepped forward and said, 'Hope you're not feeding those raw berries to Babu-ji on the day of the Jhulan?'

Although I myself could not decipher the meaning hidden in what had seemed to be a simple question to me, the rest of the girls laughed out in loud unison and started falling over each other in bouts of convulsive laughter.

I asked Bhanumati, 'Why are they laughing like that?'

Bhanumati replied in a shy voice, 'I don't know! You have to ask them.'

Meanwhile, another girl brought a red starfruit sprinkled with chilli flakes and said, 'Here's a spicy pickle for you, Babu-ji. Bhanumati is only feeding you sweets, we can't let that happen.'

Everyone laughed out once again. The entire room seemed to have lit up, thanks to the innocent and guileless smiles of so many teenage girls.

Just before dusk, a group of young boys and girls started walking towards the hills, and we followed behind them. What a beautiful procession it was! To the east, beyond the borders of Nowada-Lakshmipura stood the Dhanjhari hills, and through the jungles at the foothills of the Dhanjhari ran the Michhi river, flowing from south to north. High above the jungles that covered the top of the hills, the full moon was rising in the night sky. On one side, there was a green valley spread out till as far as my eyes could see, on the other were the hills of Dhanjhari themselves. After walking for a mile or so, we reached the base of the hills. And after climbing for some time, we saw a plateau of sorts—a flat, open area on the side of the hill. Right at the centre of this open space stood an ancient piyal tree—its trunk naturally adorned with pretty flowers and thick veins. King Dobru said, 'This is a very old tree; ever since I was a little boy, I have been seeing girls dancing under this tree on the night of the Jhulan.'

We sat on a palm-leaf mat on one side, and in the middle of that moonlight-washed jungle, almost thirty smiling young girls began dancing around the piyal tree. Along with them, a group of strapping young boys began to dance while playing the madal all the while. I saw Bhanumati dancing right at the front of the group of girls. All the girls had garlands adorning the buns of hair on their head, and flowers adorning their arms, necks and wrists.

This went on late into the night. Once in a while, when the group got tired, they would sit down and rest. But soon, the singing and dancing would resume, as would the sound of the madals echoing in the hills. The moonlight, the beat of the madals, the rain-washed hills, the valley down below, and amidst all these, the enchanting dance of a group of shapely, dark-skinned, pretty young girls—it all seemed like a beautiful painting that some unknown artist had created on his canvas, or like the euphonic tune of a joyous melody that came floating in the air and filled the listener's heart with glee. As I stared ahead, I could see the mythical Solanki princess and her friends dancing to their heart's content right before my eyes. I could see the young goatherd Bappaditya stumbling upon them and watching them surreptitiously, till he is caught and discovered by the princess's girlfriends— who, in an innocent rush of joy and excitement, dressed the poor goatherd up as Krishna and the princess as his consort Radha and made them swing to the sound of music all night, before giving them to each other in a mock marriage.

> *Oh, the joys, the joys of this night—*
> *The blue moon sways on the swing of light!*

As the beat of the madals began to intoxicate me, my mind went far—way far—back into the history of this ancient land. India, in the stone ages, shrouded in myth and mystery, its age-old primitive culture had come alive in front of my eyes in the form of a dance of the daughters of the hills and the sons of the forest. Thousands of years ago, in hundreds of jungles and hills such as the ones I was sitting in right now, had there not been young girls like Bhanumati and her friends? Had they not danced around a tree on a full moon night, swaying to the drum-beats of their male companions? Their playful smiles and peals of laughter had not faded away altogether, and even after hundreds of years, perhaps they were still hiding in the hills of Dhanjhari and the jungles that covered them—looking upon their descendants and smiling in contentment, knowing that despite everything that had tried to erase their memories from history, there were still some people who cared for them and kept their spirits alive.

It was quite late into the night by now, the moon had disappeared behind the forests towards the west. We made our way back down from the hills. We were lucky that the skies were not overcast tonight, but the moist air of the night had turned quite chilly. As I returned to the palace and sat down for my dinner, Bhanumati came in with a bowl of milk and a few sweets.

I said, 'You and your friends danced so well!'

She smiled shyly and said, 'You must be joking, Babu-ji. You are from Kolkata; why would anyone from the city want to see our dance?'

The next day, Bhanumati and her grandfather King Dobru Panna refused to let me take their leave. But I simply had to, for I had several important affairs of the estate to attend to. When I was leaving, Bhanumati walked up to me and said, 'Babu-ji, will you get me a mirror from Kolkata? I had a mirror a long time ago, but it's broken now, and I can't use it anymore.'

A sixteen-year-old beautiful and charming teenage girl did not have a mirror! What on earth were mirrors for, then? In less than a week, I asked my men to get a nice hand-held mirror from Purnia and had it sent to Bhanumati.

CHAPTER 14

[1]

A few months passed by; it was the middle of February. I was returning to the cutcherry through the forests of Labtulia. As I was riding through, I heard the sound of laughter and a few words spoken in Bengali, presumably from the direction of the lake. I stopped my horse and listened carefully. Yes, indeed. There were feminine voices too. Curious to see who these people were, I turned my horse around and proceeded towards the lake. On reaching the banks, I saw a group of nine–ten Bengali gentlemen sitting on a mat by the catkin bushes and chatting away. Five or six teenage girls were busy cooking nearby, and a bunch of seven–eight boys and girls were running around playing. I was staring at the scene and wondering where on earth had so many people come from, and what were they doing in the middle of this dense forest, when suddenly, everyone's eyes turned towards me and one of them said, 'Now, who the hell is this bugger?'

I got off my horse and walked towards them. I said, 'You gentlemen seem to be Bengalis? Where are you from?'

The men were extremely embarrassed, they said, 'Oh, you are a Bengali too? Oh, er . . . please don't mind . . . er . . . we didn't . . .'

I said, 'Not at all. But where are you from? And what are you doing here?'

As it turned out, the elderly gentleman in the group was a retired deputy magistrate, a Ray Bahadur. The rest of the group comprised of his sons, daughters, nephews, nieces, grand-children, sons-in-law and their friends. Apparently, the Ray Bahadur had read a book back in Kolkata, from which he had learnt that the jungles of Purnia district provided excellent opportunities for game hunting. So, he had come to live with his brother in Purnia for a few days, hoping to do a bit of hunting. From there, he and the rest of the gang took the 10 a.m. train in the morning to reach Kataria. They then hired a boat to take them down the Kushi river and came to this jungle for a picnic, because they had heard that the woods in these parts were full of unparalleled natural beauty. Once the picnic was over, they would walk four miles to reach the Kushi river next to the Mohanpura Forest Reserve and take the boat back to Kataria tonight.

I was truly amazed at this rather ambitious and perilous plan. All that they seemed to have with them was a double barrel shotgun. Armed with this puny weapon, they had come all the way into this dense jungle for a picnic? Along with their families, nonetheless? I admired their courage, no doubt, but at the same time, I felt that at least the old and wise Ray Bahadur ought to have shown a bit more prudence in the matter. Even the local forest-dwellers stayed away from the Mohanpura Forest Reserve after dusk. There were tigers in those forests, and wild boars and snakes were regularly seen. This was no place for a picnic, certainly not with children.

The Ray Bahadur refused to let me go without a cup of tea. I had to sit with them and face a barrage of questions. How long had I lived in the forest? What was my business here? Was I a timber trader? After narrating my entire history to them, I invited them to spend the night at my cutcherry. But they did not agree, stating that it was absolutely imperative for them to get back to Purnia by midnight. Or else the other members of the family would begin to worry.

In the short time that I spent with these people that day, I failed to understand why they had come for a picnic here in the middle of the woods. Ten metres from where they were, there were rows after rows of beautiful flowers that had bloomed, now that spring was here. But not once did I find them so much as looking at those flowers, let alone admiring them. Nor did they seem to show any interest whatsoever in the enjoying the unhindered views of the Labtulia terrain, the hues of the sun setting over the hills beyond the lake, or the sweet chirping of the birds all around. All that they seemed to be busy doing was shouting and yelling, singing at the top of their voices, running around, cooking food. Among the girls, two were in college, apparently, and the others were still in school. One of the boys was a student at the medical college in the city, the others were in various schools and colleges too. But none of them seemed to have any appreciation for nature and its many wondrous gifts. They had, in fact, come here to hunt—as if the rabbits, the deer and the birds had all eagerly queued up by the side of the road, waiting for these people to come and oblige them by taking their lives.

In all my life, I had never met anyone who was so deprived of even the slightest trace of imagination as were the girls in the party. They were running around, gathering woods to light a fire for the cooking, blabbering incessantly—not even once did they look around to see what an ethereal spot they were sitting in and cooking their hotchpotch!

One of the girls said, 'Lots of pebbles here—will come in handy to strike the tin-cutter!'

Another said, 'Oh, what a godforsaken place! I spent the whole of yesterday looking for some good rice in town. Not a single shop had a decent grain of rice. How am I supposed to cook pulao for everyone, eh?'

I sighed and wondered if these girls knew that within a few yards from where they were sitting and engaging in meaningless gossip, fairies danced in the moonlight late in the night.

Then came the stories about the movies. They had seen one as recently as last night, it seemed, in Purnia itself. It was an atrocious headache-inducing affair, apparently. Soon, comparisons with the cinema of Kolkata started creeping into the discussion. I realized these people had nothing better to do with their lives than to engage in meaningless chatter.

At around 5 p.m. in the evening, the entire party left, leaving dozens of empty tins of jam and condensed milk in the middle of the verdant forests of Labtulia.

[2]

By the end of spring, all the wheat in Labtulia had ripened. Last year, most of the land in our estate had been used to grow mustard. This time around, it was wheat that seemed to be of primary interest to the farmers. Which was also why the reaping season had come earlier, in the beginning of April.

Strangely enough, the reapers seemed to know all this beforehand, and had preponed their arrival in Labtulia from winter to summer this year, building huts and khupris by the side of the jungle or in the middle of the open fields and living in them with their families. Almost two thousand acres of crops were to be reaped, so the number of reapers were no less than three–four thousand. Word came that more were on the way.

I set out on my horse at dawn and returned only by dusk. So many new people all around, among them were thieves, thugs, drunks and addicts—I had to keep an eye on everyone, or else nasty incidents could happen at any time—there being no sign of a police outpost within miles of the estate.

One day, I saw two boys and a girl sitting by the side of the road and weeping their hearts out.

I got off my horse and asked them, 'What's the matter with you all?'

The gist of what they said in response was this: these boys and the girl were not from around here, they had come from the village of Nandalal Ojha. They were siblings, and had come to see the fair of the reaping season. They had arrived here this morning, and the elder brother had almost immediately started gambling. The game itself involved putting a stick upright at a distance and asking a player to throw a rope at it without tying a lasso. If the player could tie the rope around the stick before pulling it back, he was paid four paise to every paise he bet on the game.

The elder brother had ten annas with him, upon losing all of which, he had turned towards his younger brother's

eight, and finally, his little sister's four. Having failed to tie
a knot around the stick even once, the lad had lost all their
money and now the three siblings had no means to get back
home, let alone see the fair or buy anything to eat.

Having consoled them, I asked them to take me to the
spot where the gambling had taken place. At first, they could
not even recall the place where the bets were being placed.
After some time though, they pointed in the direction of a
myrobalan tree in the distance and said that the swindler
had set up his game under it. I looked at the tree, there was
not a soul to be seen in its vicinity. Sepoy Roop Singh's
brother was with me, he said, 'Such swindlers don't stay at
any one place for long, Huzoor. He must have scooted a
long time ago.'

Towards the evening, the swindler had been caught.
The man had set up his impossible puzzle in another village
a couple of miles away; my men went and caught him red-
handed. The boys and their sister confirmed that this was
indeed the man who had conned them.

The man refused to pay back at first, arguing that he
had not taken any money by force, and that the boy had
voluntarily placed his bets and lost all his money. Not only
did he finally have to cough up all the money that the three
siblings had lost, I also asked my men to hand the crook over
to the police.

The man fell at my feet. I said, 'Where are you from?'

'Ballia district, Babu-ji.'

'Why do you do this? How many people have you cheated
this way?'

'I'm a poor man, Huzoor. Please spare me this time, all I
earn are two to three rupees over as many days.'

'Which means you earn more than what these poor people do.'

'No, Huzoor. Such days are rare, I end up earning a meagre thirty or forty rupees in a year, at best.'

I let the man go that day, but only on the condition that he was not to be seen in my estate ever again.

I was both surprised and worried on not seeing Manchi among the reapers this time. She had said over and over again that she would come to Labtulia when the wheat would ripen. But the reaping season had come and gone, and there was no sign of her.

I asked around among the labourers, but no one could tell me anything about her. There was no other estate as large as ours in the vicinity, except perhaps for the Diwara estate near Ismailpur, south of the Kushi river. But why would she go there, so far away, when the wages were the same?

Finally, towards the end of the fair, I heard of Manchi from a Gangota labourer. He knew Manchi and her husband Nakchhedi Bhakat, having worked with them on several occasions. It was from this man that I learnt that Manchi and her husband had been seen reaping crop in the government estate of Akbarpur. That was the last anyone had seen of them.

By the middle of June, the harvest season had ended, when out of the blue, I was surprised to see Nakchhedi Bhakat on the courtyard of the main cutcherry one day. Nakchhedi fell at my feet and began to weep bitterly. This made me even more surprised. I asked, 'What's the matter, Nakchhedi? Why didn't you come to the harvest this year? How is Manchi? Where is she?'

The summary of what Nakchhedi said was this: he had no knowledge of Manchi's whereabouts anymore. While they were working in the government estate, Manchi had left them behind and run away. A desperate search had yielded no result.

I was shocked and stupefied to learn of this unexpected and tragic bit of news. I also realized that I had no sympathy for the old Nakchhedi, and that all my worries were for the safety and wellbeing of that young and wild girl. Where had she gone? Who could have led her on and taken her away? What dreadful circumstances must she be living in right now? I recalled how she had a fascination for cheap knick-knacks. It would not have been too difficult for someone to beguile her with the promise of shiny trinkets.

I asked, 'Where is her son?'

'The boy is no more, Huzoor. He died of smallpox last winter.'

I was utterly saddened to hear this. The loss of her child must have driven the poor girl insane, and she must have wandered away in shock and grief. After a moment's silence, I asked, 'Where is Tulsi?'

'She is with me. Please give me some land, Huzoor. The two of us are too old to make a living out of harvesting other people's crop. Manchi was very active; she used to do most of the work. Now that she is gone, we just can't seem to make ends meet anymore.'

That evening, I went to Tulsi's hut to find her sitting with her children and picking seeds out of China grass. On seeing me, she began to weep. I realized that Manchi's disappearance had left her as sad and distressed as her husband, if not more. She said, 'It's that old fool's fault, Huzoor—all of it. When those government people came to the fields for vaccination, he bribed them with four annas and sent them away. Didn't let anyone take the vaccines. He said, if we take those vaccines, we will have smallpox. You won't believe me, Huzoor, within three days, Manchi's boy died of small-pox. That poor girl was shell-shocked. She wouldn't eat, she wouldn't drink—all she did all day was sit in the corner and cry.'

'And then?'

'Then, Huzoor, the government people threw us out of the estate. They said, your boy has succumbed to smallpox, we won't let you live here. There was this young Rajput fellow, he had his eyes on Manchi. The day we left the estate, that very night, Manchi disappeared. I had seen that Rajput fellow loitering around the hut that morning. I know it was him, Huzoor, he must have been the culprit. Of late, Manchi had been talking about Kolkata a lot. I knew something was about to happen.'

I too recalled how Manchi had expressed her desire to visit Kolkata to me on several occasions. The cunning Rajput fellow must have guiled her away with the promise of taking her to the city.

I knew that in such cases, most of the girls of this region ended up working as coolies in the tea gardens of Assam. Did the spirited but ever so gullible Manchi also have such a cruel outcome written in her destiny?

I was particularly furious with the old Nakchhedi Bhakat. It was all his fault. Why did he have to marry such a young girl at his age? And when the government-sanctioned inoculators had come to help them, why had he foolishly sent them away? If I indeed were to give him any land, it would be out of sympathy for his aged wife Tulsi and her children, and not for him.

And so I did. I had received instructions from the headquarters directing me to lease out the land in Narha Baihar. Nakchhedi Bhakat became my first lessee in the region.

But the entire expanse of Narha Baihar was covered with dense forests. There were hardly a few local people who had started clearing out the jungle and building their huts there. Quite naturally, Nakchhedi was quite hesitant to accept my offer in the beginning. He said, 'I have heard there are tigers in those jungles, Huzoor. I have my children to protect.'

Without mincing my words, I told him quite clearly that if he did not like the land, he was free to leave. Left with no choice, Nakchhedi was forced to start a new life in Narha Baihar.

[3]

Ever since Nakchhedi had started living on his new land, I had never been to his hut. But the other day, at dusk, as I was making my way back to the cutcherry through Narha Baihar, I noticed two huts adjacent to each other. One of them had a lamp burning inside it.

I was not aware that this was where Nakchhedi lived. On hearing the sound of my horse's hooves, an old woman stepped out of the hut—it was Tulsi.

'So this is where you live? Where is Nakchhedi?'

Tulsi seemed to be at a loss of words, perhaps on seeing me all of a sudden. She quickly rolled out a rough mat made of hay and said, 'Please come and rest a bit, Huzoor. He has gone to Labtulia, to buy oil and salt from the shop. My elder son has gone with him.'

'And you are here in the middle of this forest all by yourself?'

'I've got used to all that, Babu-ji. We are poor people; we can't afford to be afraid. And staying alone is written in my destiny! As long as Manchi was around, I never had to fear anything. You very well know how spirited she was, Babu-ji!'

I noticed how the old woman had nothing but sororal fondness for her husband's second wife. I also realized that she knew that I would love to hear about young Manchi.

Tulsi's daughter Suratiya said, 'Babu-ji, I'm trying to tame a nilgai fawn—would you like to see it? The other day, just after sunset, it had lost its way and was standing and trembling in the woods behind the hut; so Chhania and I brought it home. It has been with us since then. A gentle little kid.'

I said, 'What does it eat?'

Suratiya said, 'Only China seed husk and tender leaves. I pick green kendu leaves from the woods and bring it to her; she seems to like it very much.'

Tulsi said, 'Don't just stand there and talk, girl. Bring it to Babu-ji.'

Suratiya pranced out with the agility of a doe and moments later, her shrill girlish voice rung out from behind the hut, 'Oh no, Chhania! Where is the baby? There—there it is! Grab it, grab it by its legs.'

In a matter of minutes, having rolled around on the ground for some time and successfully foiled the misguided and rather dangerous attempt of the fawn to escape into the forest, the two sisters entered the hut once again, out of breath this time, but smiling and holding their prized pet close to their hearts.

To help me in my examination of the fine animal, Tulsi lit a piece of wood and held it up. Suratiya said, 'Isn't she pretty, Babuji? A bear had come to eat her last night. You see that mahua tree out there? That's the one the bear had climbed to get to those mahua flowers—it was quite late in the night—my father, my mother, everyone else was fast asleep. I was awake in my bed, I could hear its grunts and footsteps outside. And then it came and stood behind our hut, just over there. I grabbed my nilgai close to my chest and lay down quietly, holding my breath. She had sensed the bear too, and was frightened; so I had to cover her mouth to stop her from bleating. I stayed up the whole night, even after the bear was gone.'

'Weren't you scared, Suratiya?'

'Scared? No, of course not! I don't get scared so easily. When I go to the forest to gather wood, I see so many bears. I'm not scared of anything.'

Suratiya held her head high and uttered her words with pride.

The hut was surrounded on all sides by kendu trees; their large, thick trunks rising up to the skies resembled the chimneys of a factory. Even in daytime, the place looked scary, like some deep and remote corner of the Redwood jungles of California. Now that it was dark, there were foxes yelping and bats screeching all around, fireflies glowing in the bushes. How a lone woman could live in the middle of this forest with her children, I would never understand. But in all the years that I had spent here, if there was one thing that I had learnt about the forest was that it never harmed anyone who sought shelter in it. The forest was mysterious, it was all-knowing, but most of all, it was kind and benevolent.

After a few more minutes of chatting, I asked, 'Has Manchi taken all her things with her?'

Suratiya said, 'No, she left everything behind. Even that favourite box of hers. Wait, I'll show it to you.'

The box was fetched and opened in front of me. A comb, a small mirror, a couple of beaded garlands, a cheap green handkerchief—just like the doll-box of a little girl. But I could not see the hinglaj garland I had seen the last time, the one she had bought from the fair.

Oh, where had the poor girl gone? Leaving her family and her prized possessions behind? The rest of her family had finally taken some land and settled down, but Manchi still remained a vagabond, wandering from place to place, perhaps wretched and destitute.

When I was mounting my horse, Suratiya bid me farewell and said, 'Please come again, Babu-ji. I have woven a new bird trap, and tamed a *dahuk* or waterhen, and a *gurguri* bird or a wallcreeper, too. When they call out, other birds from the forest come and fall in the trap. I will show you the next time you come.'

Riding through the dense jungles of Narha Baihar at night was a chilling and hair-raising experience. To my left was a small mountain stream, which I could not see. I could only hear the soft murmur of the flowing water. A heady concoction of sweet fragrance had filled the night air—must have been from all those unnamed wild flowers blooming everywhere. The night was so dark at times that I could not even see the mane of my horse. But soon after, the stars would come out and I would get a faint impression of the woods I was in.

The forests of Narha Baihar was home to hundreds of species of birds, animals, plants, vines and trees. Nature had showered this land with priceless treasures. The Saraswati Kundi was towards the north of the Narha Baihar. Old maps from historical surveys revealed that the Saraswati Kundi was once part of the Kushi river. The ancient ravine that the river flowed through had now turned into a dense rich forest.

Where there once flowed a mighty river
Now lay only the sandy silt of time

I stared at the indescribable beauty of nature that lay all around me. But at the same time, my heart sank as I remembered that there was a dark fate awaiting the forests of Narha Baihar. I was so deeply in love with these forests, and yet it had to be my hands that they would have to be destroyed by. Within the next two years, this entire land would have to be leased out, and every inch of this forest would be cut down, chopped, burnt and cleared to make room for human habitation. Slums after slums would pop up their ugly heads in this beautiful land. Nature's own handiwork, centuries in making, would be destroyed in an instant—gone forever, never to return.

And what would we get in return? Rows after rows of hideous shanties, filthy drains, cowsheds, farms of corn and maize, stacks of hay, tattered charpoys, flags and emblems of gods and deities, uninviting bushes of cactus, enough tobacco to cover the whole region in smog, not to forget the unstoppable episodes of cholera and smallpox. I bowed my head in shame and asked for forgiveness from the ancient forest.

I did keep my promise to Suratiya though—a few days later, I went back to watch her trap birds.

With a couple of cages in their hands, Suratiya and Chaniya took me to the open fields outside the forests of Narha Baihar.

The evening was upon us. Casting long shadows of the trees on the ground, the sun was setting behind the hills. The two girls stopped under a simul tree and put their cages down on the ground. One of the cages had a dahuk in it, the other had a gurguri. Both birds had been tamed and taught to attract the attention of other wild birds flying around in the jungle. The dahuk started calling out.

The gurguri, however, was silent at first. Suratiya let out a sweet whistle, snapped her fingers a couple of times and said in a singsong voice, 'Come on now, sister, sing for me. Sing for me . . . '

The gurguri immediately called out—'Gurrrr-gurrr-gurrrr . . . '

At that moment, it seemed to me that the rest of the world had suddenly fallen silent, and that there was no sound in the universe other than the sweet calls of these two winged creatures. There we stood, in the vast open field, surrounded by hills on three sides and by the dense forest on the fourth, under a sky that was rapidly changing its colour, under stars that had begun to appear one by one on the canopy over our heads. Under a nearby tree, where a bunch of pretty yellow Dudhli flowers had bloomed on the grass, Suratiya set up her trap – a wooden cage of sorts. She hid the dahuk and gurguriya cages beneath this trap and said to me—'Come Babuji, we will go and hide behind those bushes over there. The birds won't come if they see us.'

For a long time, we sat behind a few saplings of sal and simul, crouching to stay out of sight. The Dahuk would stop from time to time, but the Gurguri kept on calling incessantly—'Gurrrrr-gurrrr-gurrrrr . . . '

I shut my eyes and listened to the sweet unearthly call! After some time, I said—'Suratiya, will you sell that Gurguriya to me? I will pay you whatever you want.'

Suratiya said—'Quiet, quiet, Babuji! Listen! Do you hear that?'

I raised my ears and listened. After a few moments of silence, another sound came floating from beyond the northern borders of the field, from the edge of the forest— 'Gurrr-rrr-rrrrrr . . .'

I shivered in the excitement of the moment. The wild bird had answered the call of its caged companion.

Gradually, as the minutes passed by, the call seemed to draw closer and closer to us.

For a long time, there were two distinct calls, the interval between them diminishing rapidly. Finally, a time came when the two calls seemed to merge with each other and become one. And then, suddenly, it was all back to just one call—I recognized it as that of the bird in Suratiya's cage.

Suratiya and Chaniya made a dash for the cage, a bird had fallen in the trap. I ran after them too.

The bird's legs had been caught in the wood, it was flapping around in the cage. The instant it had realized that it was in a trap, it had stopped singing. I could not believe my eyes, what a strange thing I had seen that evening!

Suratiya gently clasped her palms around the trapped bird and brought it out of the cage. She said, 'Did you see how we caught it, Babu-ji?'

I asked, 'What do you do with these birds?'

She said—'My father sells them in the market of Tirashi-Ratanganj. One Gurguri sells for two paise, a Dahuk sells for seven paise.'

I said—'Sell me that Gurguri, I'll buy it from you.'

Suratiya happily gave me the bird that evening. But no matter how much I insisted, I could not make her take any money for it.

[4]

In the month of October, I received a letter carrying the news of King Dobru Panna's demise. The letter also said that the royal family was in dire financial straits. I was requested to pay a visit, if possible. The letter had been sent by Jogru Panna, Bhanumati's uncle.

I set out at once and reached Chakmakitola a little before dusk. The late king's eldest son and grandson were there to receive me. Apparently, King Dobru Panna had suffered a nasty fall while he was out grazing his cows, and had injured his knee in the process. It was this injury that had finally claimed his life.

The vultures had begun circling around the palace. The local moneylender, for instance, had come as soon as he had heard the news of the king's death, and had promptly taken possession of all the cattle—flatly refusing to hand them back if his loan was not paid back along with the accrued interest. There were problems at the palace too. The new king was to be formally coronated the next day, but there was no money for the ceremony. Moreover, without the cattle, the royal family would have to starve to death. The dairy from the cows and the buffaloes was the primary source of income for the family.

I asked the moneylender to come and see me. His name was Birbal Singh. The man did come, but I soon realized that he was a crook of the first order. He simply did not want to listen to anything that I had to say to him. All he wanted was his money, and he wanted it right then.

Bhanumati broke down in front of me. She was very fond of her great-grandfather. The king was like a protective shelter to all of her family, she said, and now that he was gone, all the trouble had started brewing. Despite all my consolations, the poor girl just would not stop crying. She said—'Come, Babuji. I will take you to his grave. I don't like it here anymore, all I want is to sit by his grave and weep.'

I assured her that I would come with her, but that I needed to find a solution to the moneylender problem first. But despite my best attempts, the fiery Rajput stuck to his demands. The only grace he showed us was to leave the cattle in the royal shed for the time being, but with strict instructions not to draw even a drop of milk from them under any circumstances. It was only after a couple of months later that a solution to the repayment of his loan could be found, but more of that later.

I found Bhanumati standing all by herself outside the palace. On seeing me, she said—'It's about to get dark soon, we won't be able to go after some time. Let's go now.'

The fact that she saw no problem in going up the hill at dusk with only me for company revealed that she now thought of me as a close family friend and a well-wisher. The simplicity of this girl from the hills touched my heart that day.

The veil of twilight had descended upon that verdant valley.

Bhanumati was walking too fast, almost like a frightened doe. I called out to her and said—'Listen, Bhanumati. Let's go a little slow, shall we? Oh, and is there a *shiuli* plant anywhere nearby?'

Bhanumati probably knew the plant I was referring to by an entirely different name, so I was unable to explain it to her. As we were climbing up the hill, I could see clearly up to a great distance. The blue Dhanjhari hills seemed to embrace the valley and the headless kingdom of the recently departed Dobru Panna with the consoling love of a parent. There was a steady breeze blowing over the sprawling valley.

Bhanumati was walking ahead of me, she stopped and turned around to ask—'Are you having trouble climbing, Babuji?'

'No, not at all. Just go a little slow, that's all.'

After some time, she said—'I will now have no one to look after me, Babuji.'

The words were uttered in between breathless gasps and whimpers. Although I felt for her, I was rather amused by her childish behaviour at the same time. It was her old great-grandfather who had passed away, after all—not a parent, nor a sibling, nor a grandparent or an uncle or aunt or a cousin. All of these people were very much alive and they cared for her too. But then, Bhanumati was a woman after all, and a young one at that. It was not unusual for her to try and draw the attention and empathy of a man, nor to want to be consoled at a moment such as this.

Bhanumati said—'Oh, you will come from time to time, won't you Babuji? You will take care of us, won't you? Promise me you won't forget?'

I said—'Why would I forget? I will surely come once in a while.'

Bhanumati puffed her lips in a mock huff and said—'I know you will forget. As soon as you go back to the city, you will forget about this land, about us . . . about me . . . '

I said in a soft, affectionate voice—'Why, didn't I send you the mirror? Did I forget?'

Bhanumati's face brightened up in an instant. She said—'Oh, what a pretty mirror that was! You're right, I had forgotten to tell you about it!'

When we reached the graveyard and stood by King Dobru's grave, the place seemed to be waiting in silence for the crescent moon to rise and rid the solemn site of the rapidly approaching darkness of the evening.

I asked Bhanumati to pick some flowers from the jungle so that I could strew them on the king's grave. This custom was unknown to the people of this land, so Bhanumati seemed quite excited and happy to do it. I found a wild shiuli plant in one corner and directed Bhanumati to it. She picked a handful of pristine white shiulis, and the two of us strew the flowers on King Dobru Panna's grave.

And at exactly that moment, a flock of white egrets fluttered their wings and flew away from the top of the ancient banyan tree towards the valley—almost as if the souls of all the oppressed and forgotten ancestors of Bhanumati had expressed their gratitude on being set free. Perhaps for the first time, a descendant of the Aryans had paid his respects to the grave of a primitive and barbarian tribal king.

CHAPTER 15

[1]

There was this one time when I had no other option but to seek financial help from moneylender Dhaotal Sahu. That year, despite the unexpectedly poor earnings of the estate, we fell short of registering the mandated minimum revenue of ten thousand rupees. My tehsildar Banwarilal advised me to make up for the shortfall by lending money from Dhaotal Sahu, adding that he would never say no to me. Dhaotal Sahu was not one of my lessees, he lived in the government-controlled estates. I had never had any business with him, so I was not so sure if he would be willing to lend me as much as three thousand rupees simply on the basis of personal guarantee.

But such was the need of the hour. One day, with Banwarilal for company, I paid a secret visit to Dhaotal Sahu's home. The secrecy was important, because I did not want the rest of the cutcherry to know that I was having to borrow money to plug the gap in our revenues.

Dhaotal Sahu lived in a filthy and congested slum in Pausadiya. There were a few charpoys placed in the courtyard of a large mud hut. Dhaotal Sahu was busy fixing a wicket fence around a small tract of land in one corner of the yard, upon which he had grown some tobacco plants. On seeing us approach, he dropped everything and came running. He was visibly nervous on seeing me, and for several minutes, we found him running around, looking for a chair or a stool that would, in his eyes at least, befit my stature. He kept mumbling all the while, 'Dear God! I . . . I wasn't expecting you to pay this poor man's humble home a visit, Huzoor. Please come, please come, where will you sit? Would you mind sitting here? Or . . . here perhaps? Please come, Tehsildar Babu.'

I did not see any servants around. Dhaotal Sahu had a plump grandson named Ramlakhiya living with him, the boy started running in and out of the house, attending to us. From the look of the house and its furnishings, there was no way to know that a millionaire resided in it.

Ramlakhiya took the saddle off my horse's back and tied him under the shade of a tree. Then he ran in to fetch water, so that we could wash our feet. Dhaotal Sahu himself began fanning me with a handmade palm-leaf fan. One of his granddaughters ran inside to fetch tobacco for me. I was quite embarrassed with all the attention; so, I said, 'You don't have to do all this, Sahu-ji, and there's no need for tobacco. I'm carrying my own cigars with me.'

In spite of all the traditional hospitality that I had received, I was hesitating to tell the man the real purpose of my visit. How could I possibly say such a thing?

Dhaotal Sahu said, 'You must have come to hunt for birds, Huzoor?'

'No, in fact, I have come to see you, Sahu-ji.'

'To see me? About what, Huzoor?'

'Our estate's annual revenue has fallen short of the target this year. I would have to borrow around three and a half thousand rupees to make up for it. I was wondering if I could borrow the money from you.'

It took me some effort to say the words, but then the job had to be done, so there was no point beating around the bush.

Dhaotal Sahu did not take a second to respond, 'Well, there's nothing to worry about. This is a simple matter, and if I might say so, there was no need for you to take all the trouble to come all the way here for such a trivial matter. All you had to do was to send a note to me through Tehsildar Babu, and I would have taken care of everything.'

Now I would have to tell him the truth—that I would have to borrow the entire money in my own name, for I did not have the power of attorney to borrow money on behalf of the estate. Would Dhaotal Sahu be willing to lend such a large amount of money to a stranger like me? I had no personal property to offer him as mortgage. With some amount of hesitation, I explained the matter to him.

'Sahu-ji, the situation is such that the papers would have to be in my name, not in the name of the estate.'

Dhaotal Sahu seemed quite taken aback, 'Papers? What papers, Huzoor? You have personally come all the way to my home, to borrow a little bit of money, just because there has been a small shortfall in the revenues of the estate. You needn't have come, I tell you, you could have just sent word, your wish is my command, Huzoor. And there's absolutely no need for any papers. It will be my honour to offer the money to you, and when the estate's earnings go up, you can send the money back to me. That's all there is to it.'

I said, 'I'm giving you a hand-note, I'm carrying the ticket with me. Or alternatively, I can sign in your books.'

Dhaotal Sahu folded his hands and said, 'Please do not embarrass me Huzoor, there is no need for any of this. Please forgive this poor servant of yours, and spare me the sin of doing such things. I am giving you the money, you don't have to sign anywhere.'

For the next few minutes Dhaotal Sahu turned a deaf ear to all my requests in the matter. He stepped inside to fetch a bundle of notes, handed it over to me with great reverence and then said, 'But Huzoor, I have a small request.'

'Sure, what is it?'

'I can't let you go just like that. I'll ask them to get the freshly-washed pots and pans out for you, please cook your meal, and have your lunch here.'

Once again, all my protests were tenaciously turned down. Finally, I turned to Banwarilal and said, 'Will you be able to cook? I don't think I can manage.'

Banwarilal said, 'That won't do, Huzoor, you will have to do the cooking. In these remote areas, if people come to know that you have had a meal cooked by my hands, they will never talk to me ever again. Don't worry, I will tell you how to do it.'

Dhaotal Sahu's granddaughter brought out a large pan from inside the house. During the cooking, she and her grandfather kept guiding me, offering me various tips and pieces of advice.

When her grandfather had stepped inside for a while, the young girl said, 'You see my grandfather, Babu-ji? One day, we'll be on the streets because of that man. He goes around lending money to everyone, doesn't charge any interest, doesn't get proper paperwork done, doesn't ask for mortgages. Naturally, no one pays him back anymore.

He trusts everyone, and everyone takes advantage of him, cheats him of his dues. There have been instances when he has gone to people's homes to lend them money, would you believe it?'

There was another villager sitting there and listening to us talk. He now said, 'When we are in trouble, we know that Sahu-ji is there for us. He has never sent anyone away from his doorsteps, Babu-ji. He is an old-fashioned man, such an affluent moneylender, but he has never been within the vicinity of the courts all his life. He says those places are not for a man like me. He is scared of the courts and lawyers. Truly, the man has a heart of gold.'

It took me six months to repay the money that I had borrowed from Dhaotal Sahu that day. In all these months, Dhaotal Sahu had not set foot within the borders of our estate in Ismailpur, not even once, lest I think that he was rushing me to pay him back. The very definition of a gentleman!

[2]

I had not had a chance to pay a visit to Rakhal Babu's home for over a year now, after the harvest fair was over, I decided to go there. Rakhal Babu's wife, whom I had started calling 'Didi' or sister by now, was very happy to see me. She, in turn, referred to me as a brother or 'Dada'. She said, 'Why don't you come to see us anymore, Dada? I can't tell you what it means to see a familiar face from back home in this place. And moreover, in our current condition—'

Having said this much, her voice choked, and she began to weep silently.

I looked around. The signs of poverty were still there, but this time, there seemed to be some order in the affairs of the family. Rakhal Babu's eldest son had started working as a tin-maker in a small workshop at home. Although his income was meagre, but at least the family were getting by.

I told Rakhal Babu's wife, 'Why don't you send your younger son to your brother's place in Kashi? Let him go to a school over there.'

She said, 'He is not my brother, Dada. I wrote to him several times when my husband passed away. After the third letter, he sent me ten rupees. I have never heard from him ever again in the last one and a half years. No, Dada. My son will find a way to make his living here, just as his brother has. Let him work in the fields, let him rear buffaloes. But I will not send my son to live with such a man.'

I was to return to the cutcherry right then, but Didi did not let me. I was told that I would have to stay back for lunch. Apparently, she would make a special dish for me.

I had no other choice but to accept. Mixing ghee and sugar with the grist of corn, Didi made some delicious sweetmeats. This was served with a sweet porridge of cornflour. Her hospitality did not seem to have been affected by her indigence.

She said, 'I had kept some corn aside for you, from after the monsoons. I know you like corn.'

I said, 'Where did you get corn? Did you buy them?'

'No, I got them from the farms. Once the harvest is over, there are always some cobs lying around on the ground, the farmers forget to pick them up, or simply don't notice. So, I go and pick these cobs up from the ground once they are gone.'

I was surprised to hear this. I said, 'You go to farms to pick up corn cobs?'

'Yes, late at night; no one would come to know that way. And not just me, several other girls and women from the village go there to pick up cobs, and so, I go with them. I used to get a basketful of cobs each day, at least. This September, I must have got as many as ten baskets of cobs, if not more.'

Despite the tinge of pride in her voice, I felt very sad for her. These kinds of activities were usually done by poor Gangota girls. The Kshatriya and Rajput girls of the region would never do something like this, no matter how poor they were. I was very saddened to see that a Bengali woman was having to stoop so low and resort to such petty acts of thievery just to keep her family from starving. Her poverty and the company of the people around her had slowly begun to lead her to the dark path. I could not say anything to her that day, for my intention was not to shame her or embarrass her. But I did realize that it was just a matter of time before she would totally transform herself into a poor Gangota labourer.

Far from the railway station, in the most remote and rural habitations of the region, I knew of a few other Bengali households who were in the same situation, more or less. In these families, one of the toughest tasks was to find a suitable groom for their daughters. I knew a Bengali Brahmin family, for instance, who lived in a remote village in South Bihar. Their financial condition was very poor and there were three daughters in the family—the eldest one being twenty-one or twenty-two years old, the middle one, twenty and the youngest one, seventeen. None of them were married, nor were there any chances of them getting married anytime soon. Finding another Bengali family in this province, that too a Brahmin one, with a man of marriageable age was virtually impossible.

The twenty-two-year-old girl was quite pretty, but she did not speak a word of Bengali. By looks and appearance, by manners, she was no different from a local rural girl.

Even her name was Dhruba, a common Bihari name.

Her father had come to this village many years ago, with the intention of practising homeopathy. When that did not work, he leased some land and started farming. When he passed away, his eldest son took the reins of the family. But despite his best efforts, he could not make arrangements for the marriage of his sisters. In particular, he could not afford the dowry for them.

Dhruba was just as wild and free-spirited as Kapalkundala. She used to address me as 'Bhaiya' or brother. She was strongly built and was not only adept at doing all the chores of the household, but most of the work that men would do in the fields too. Her elder brother had apparently gone on to say that for the right groom, he would even agree to offer all three of his sisters in marriage to the same man. Even the three girls did not seem to have any problem with this.

One day, I had asked the middle sister Jaba, 'Don't you ever want to go to Bengal?'

Jaba had responded in fluent local dialect, 'No Bhaiya, the water over there is too soft for my liking.'

I had heard that even Dhruba was quite keen on getting married. It seemed that she herself had told her friends and family that the man who would marry her would never have to hire anyone to tend to his cattle and that she herself was quite capable of chaffing as much as six kilograms of wheat and making grist out of them—all in less than an hour.

Even after all these years, the poor, unfortunate Bengali girl must still be tending to her brother's cattle, carrying bundles of crop from one farm to another, or busy in some form of labour or the other. Why would any man want to bring a girl like her home as his wife amidst fanfare and celebration and that too without having received any dowry for his 'extreme generosity'?

Even today, when dusk fell over the calm and serene open fields, the luckless Dhruba was perhaps still carrying a bundle of woods from the forest and walking wearily down a narrow path in the hills through the dense jungles. She had not found the love of a soulmate that she so keenly desired. No man had ever come to accept her as his wife. As I sat in my cutcherry and shut my eyes, sometimes, I could see her face, still smiling, still as spirited as ever. Just as I could see the frightened face of Rakhal Babu's widow, as she hid like a thief in the darkness, waiting for the right opportunity to steal a handful of corn cobs from someone else's farm, just so she could ensure that her sons had a hearty meal.

[3]

On the way back from Bhanumati's place, I witnessed the first rains of the monsoon that year. It rained day and night, the sky was overcast with dense kohl-coloured clouds; the horizon beyond Narha and Fulkiya Baihar looked faint, the Mahalikharup hills had disappeared from view and the tip of the treeline in Mohanpura Forest Reserve would sometimes reveal itself in the haze only to hide behind the relentless showers moments later. The Kushi towards the east and the Karo towards the south had flooded, apparently.

Miles after miles of catkin and tamarisk bushes were getting drenched in the rain. Sitting on a chair in the veranda of my office, I could see a lone friendless dove sitting for hours on end in the catkin bushes in front of me and getting drenched to its bones in the rain.

On some days, it would be virtually impossible for me to stay indoors. I would don a raincoat and set out on horseback.

Oh, how free I felt! How unstoppable and vivacious were the joys of simply being alive! The incomparably beautiful ocean of green that I found myself in the midst of! Green made greener by the monsoons. From the fringes of the Narha Baihar all the way to the faint and distant edges of the Mohanpura Forest, all I could see was this ocean of green, the rain pouring down upon it in torrents, the winds creating waves on its surface, and I, the solo mariner navigating these green swells and surges, speeding through them in ecstatic exuberance in search of some imaginary port of call.

I used to brave the rains and ride through the open fields in this manner quite often. Sometimes, I would enter the woods of the Saraswati Kundi and find that this secret treasure trove of nature had been blessed with even more riches that were unimaginably bountiful and graciously plentiful, thanks to the joint and caring efforts of Jugalprasad and Mother Nature herself. Dozens of new varieties of wildflowers had bloomed, several never-seen-before vines had branched out from one treetop to another. Staring at these wondrous beauties, I could say with certainty that there were very few places in all of India that were as pretty and full of natural beauty than the jungles of Saraswati Kundi. The monsoons had brought with them a carnival of red campions, the lakeshore had been completely covered by them. The waters of the lake were covered with large white aquatic watercrofts, with a distinct tinge of blue on them. Just the other day, Jugalprasad had planted a new kind of vine in the woods; it had begun to grow now. Jugalprasad worked as an accountant in the Azmabad cutcherry no doubt, but his heart and mind always seemed to wander in these heavenly gardens.

It would get dark soon. The foxes had begun to yelp. Thanks to the dark clouds hanging overhead, dusk would fall sooner than expected. I would turn my horse around and head back to the cutcherry.

As I rode through the vast open fields of Baihar, I would imagine a benevolent divinity looking down on me. These clouds, this dusk, these forests, these foxes singing in chorus, these flowers floating on the waters of the Saraswati Kundi, Manchi, Raju Pandey, Bhanumati, the hills of Mahalikharup, the family of the poor forest-dwellers living by the mountain spring, the sky, the horizon—everything was part of an elaborate plan that the divine being had devised eons ago. Everything I saw around me, and everything else that I did not were all buried like a seed somewhere deep in his thoughts. And it was through his blessings that this evening was being drenched in the merciful shower of his infinite grace and affection. This incessant downpour was the evidence of his compassion; this unbridled joy I felt in my heart was nothing but his words being whispered in my ears—words which echoed within the minds of men and women and made them conscious of their very being. There was no reason to fear this benevolent god. His love and kindness was much vaster than the vastness of the Fulkiya Baihar or of the overcast sky. The weaker you were, the poorer you were, the more the divine grace he showered you with, the more he stood by you, the more he protected you.

The image of the divine presence that I would see with the eyes of my mind was not merely that of a venerable and wise old judge. Nor was it that of a revered and timeless philosopher who was aware of all the secrets of life and death. As I stared at the free and moonlit expanse of the Narha or Fulkiya Baihar, or at the blood-tinged clouds that hovered over the distant hills, it often seemed to me that the wondrous divinity also manifested the self into such emotions as love and romance, as beauty and poetry, as art and contemplation. The Divine showered us with infinite love, created all the admirable feats of nature with the deft touches of an artisan, and willingly gave oneself to lovers who needed hope and love more than anything else. And yet, when required, the Divine would present oneself as the one truly potent scientist, as the greatest visionary of all, and created millions of stars and planets and nebulae—all in the blink of an eye.

[4]

One day, in the middle of the heavy rains, Dhaturia came to the Ismailpur cutcherry.

I was delighted to see him after so many days.

'How are you, Dhaturia?'

Putting his small bundle of possessions on the ground, he joined his hands to offer me a namaskar. Then he said, 'I came to show you my dance, Babu-ji. These last few days have been tough, no one has agreed to pay me for a recital. So, I thought, let me go to the cutcherry; they will surely want to see me dance. I have learnt a few new ones too, Babu-ji.'

I noticed how pale and thin Dhaturia looked. I felt bad for the poor boy.

I said, 'Would you like to have some food first, Dhaturia?'

Dhaturia hung his head and gave a slight nod, accompanied by a shy smile.

I called my cook and asked him to bring some food for the boy. There was no rice in the kitchen right then, so milk and *chira* or flattened rice were brought. Seeing Dhaturia gobble the food up, I realized he had not had anything to eat for the last two or three days.

In the evening, Dhaturia danced for us. In the middle of the forest, several people had gathered around the courtyard of the cutcherry to see Dhaturia dance. There have been significant improvements to the lad's skills since the last time I had seen him perform. I realized, once again, that the boy had what it takes to be a true artist—a hunger for perfection and the perseverance required to achieve it. I gave him a little money, and the people of the cutcherry too put some money together for him, although I knew that all of it put together would not last him too long.

The next morning, Dhaturia came to see me before he left.

'When would you go to Kolkata next, Babu-ji?'

'Why, what's the matter?'

'Would you take me along? Remember I had told you . . . ?'

'Where are you off to at this hour? Have your lunch here before you go.'

'No, Babu-ji. There's a wedding in Jhollutola; the daughter of a Brahmin gentleman is getting married today. I will try my luck there. Perhaps, they will agree to see me dance. It's a good sixteen miles walk from here. If I don't start now, I won't be able to reach before evening.'

Somehow, I just could not bring myself around to let Dhaturia leave. I said, 'If I were to give you some land in the cutcherry, would you be able to live here? Do a bit of farming, grow some vegetables and stay here with us.'

Matuknath Pundit also seemed to have taken a liking to the boy. He was quite keen on enrolling Dhaturia into his school. He said, 'Yes, Huzoor. Ask him to stay. I will make him a master in grammar in less than two years.'

Dhaturia said, 'You are like my elder brother, Babu-ji. I look up to you, and you have always been kind to me. But will I be able to do farming? I have never done it before and I know nothing about it. I really enjoy dancing and I don't know if I would like to do anything else for a living.'

'Very well then, you can continue to dance from time to time. No one is asking you to do only farming.'

Dhaturia seemed quite happy to hear this. He said, 'I will do as you say, Babu-ji. You know very well what your words mean to me. Let me come back from Jhollutola, and then I will stay here with you, in your shelter.'

Matuknath said, 'And that will be a good time to put you in my school as well, what do you say? You can work all day and learn from me at night. You shouldn't remain illiterate all your life, young man. A few rules of grammar and a bit of poetry—such things can take you a long way in life.'

After this, Dhaturia sat down and explained a few things to us about the art of dance, but I could not understand most of it. He spoke about the fine differences between the nuances of the Ho-Ho dance of Purnia and a seemingly identical dance that had originated from the Dharampur region. He also explained the meaning of a new hand gesture that he had himself invented.

He said, 'Babu-ji, have you seen the girls from Ballia district dance during the Chhat festival? There is a similarity

between that and the Chakkarbazi dance. What are the
dances back in your place like, Babu-ji?'

I told him about the 'butter thief' dance that I had seen in
last year's harvest fair. Dhaturia smiled and said, 'Oh, that's
nothing, Babu-ji. That's a simple dance—from the villages of
Munger. All it does is to make the ignorant Gangotas happy.
There's nothing much in it.'

I said, 'Do you know that dance? Why don't you
show me?'

Once again, Dhaturia turned out to be quite
knowledgeable and skilled in his art. He gave a remarkable
performance of the 'butter thief' dance in the courtyard of the
cutcherry. The same expressions of childish anger, the same
gestures of distributing the stolen butter among his imaginary
friends—everything. And it seemed to suit him better because
he was indeed a boy.'

After some time, Dhaturia set off on his journey once
again. Before he left, he said, 'You have been nothing but
kind to me, Babu-ji, and I owe you everything. If you would
only take me to Kolkata. The people there would love to see
my dance.'

That was the last I saw of Dhaturia.

A couple of months later, not too far from the Kataria
station on the BNW railway line, a young boy's corpse was
discovered on the tracks. Several people identified it as the
body of the dancing boy Dhaturia. Was it an accident? Or
had Dhaturia taken his own life? If he had, then what made
him do it? I did not have answers to any of these questions.

Of all the men, women and children that I had come in
contact with during my stay in the forest, Dhaturia stood
out like a shining exception. The sweet, benevolent, lively,

greedless, malice-free, ever-smiling, ever-excited and true artist that I had seen in that boy was rare to find anywhere else, be it the wilds or the so-called civilization of the cities.

[5]

Three more years passed by.

The entire jungle estates of Narha Baihar and Labtulia had to be leased out. The region was now completely bereft of any forestation whatsoever. The cruel hands of man took no more than a day to destroy what nature had created and nurtured for hundreds of years. Now, there were no more hidden streams beside which night fairies could be seen dancing and frolicking about and no bamboo groves amidst which the kind and benevolent deity Tyandbaro could stand firm and resolute for the safety of the wild buffaloes.

No one referred to the Narha Baihar by that name anymore. Labtulia had been reduced to a slum. As far as one could see, only huts and houses stood side by side in a congested mess, their roofs touching each other. Whatever little open space was left, the slum dwellers had turned them into crop farms. Even the tiniest sections of the farms were cordoned off by cactus fences. The vast, open and free plains of Labtulia had been chopped, sliced and sectioned by the greed and fear of humankind.

Only one spot had managed to survive in its full glory— the forestland on the shores of the Saraswati Kundi.

For the sake of my job, and in serving the interests of my employer, I had leased out almost all the land in the estate, but I had not been able to bring myself to let the virgin forests of Saraswati Kundi—with its hundreds of varieties of flowers, plants, trees and vines, all carefully nurtured by the hands of Jugalprasad—fall into the hands of those who would not appreciate its value. Dozens of farmers kept coming to me with requests to lease the forest. They had even offered to pay lease and taxes at rates significantly higher than usual, because the land itself was quite fertile, and thanks to the proximity to a water body, the problem of irrigation could be easily resolved. Despite several such pleas, I had remained firm on my decision and said no to everyone.

But how long could I hold out this way? I had been receiving letters from the headquarters more frequently than ever, asking why I was delaying the leasing out of the forests of Saraswati Kundi. So far, I had somehow managed to hide behind some excuse or the other, but I also knew that the time would soon come when no amount of evasion would work anymore. Humans are inherently greedy. For a cob of corn or a handful of china seeds, one would not hesitate to ravage even the garden of Eden.

The people of this place, in particular, had no appreciation for natural beauty at all. All that they knew was how to glut like beasts and live in their own worlds. Had this been any other country, laws would have been passed to safeguard and preserve such forests from the evil eyes of land sharks and make them accessible to those who truly cared for nature—just like there is the Yosemite National Park in California, the Kruger National Park in South Africa or the Albert National Park in the Belgian Congo. Our landlords and fiefs could not care less for landscape, nor for flora and fauna that were to be protected and treasured. All they cared about was money—money in the form of taxes and leases.

In the midst of such blind men, I often wondered how a man like Jugalprasad could have been born. It was because of him and his efforts that I had still not been able to part with the forests of Sarswati Kundi. Although I did not know for how long I would be able to hold out against the pressures mounting on me from all quarters.

In any case, my work over here was almost about to come to an end.

It had been three long years since I had been to Bengal. Every now and then, I felt a strong urge to go, as if the whole of Bengal was my home. A home where there was some imaginary lady waiting for me with the twinkle of eager anticipation in her eyes. This place was nowhere as beautiful as it used to be in the past anymore, there were only slums and huts and farms—all crude and devoid of a woman's touch.

One night, for no apparent reason, I felt a sudden and strange sensation of joy and longing deep in my heart. It was a full moon night; so, without wasting a minute, I put the saddle on my horse's back and set out for the jungles of Saraswati Kundi, for that was all that was left in the name of forests in this estate.

There it was! The moonlight reflecting on the water of the lake. And not just reflecting, it almost seemed like the ripples on the surface of the water were breaking down the moonlight into millions of glass shards—all glittering in the dark. Quiet, serene, silent stood the trees of the forest, surrounding the lake on three sides. A flock of red geese were frolicking in the water. The sweet smell of shefali was wafting about in the air, for although this was the middle of summer, the shefali flowers bloomed yearlong in this forest.

I rode around on the shores of the lake for hours, soaking in the sights, sounds, smell and touch of the last remaining sanctum of nature in the region. Lotuses had bloomed in the water of the lake. Closer to the shore, watercrofts and Jugalprasad's spider lilies had formed a floating raft of sorts. I stared at all this and sighed. I was going home after so many years. Home, where I would be able to speak to people in my own tongue and eat food cooked by my loved ones, where I would be able to watch a film or a play every week, where I would be able to meet all my old friends after such a long time.

Gradually, the feeling of joy and longing began to surge within me. The time was right and so was the place. The eagerness of returning home, the moonlit night, the sparkling waters of the lake, the sweet smell of hundreds of flowers all around me, the diagonal canter of my beloved horse, the cool wind on my face. All in all, it seemed like a dream! Oh, a dream, indeed! The deep intoxication of joy! As if I was a wild and young god by myself, racing ahead through the barriers of time, with nothing or no one to stop me. As if being a wanderer was my destiny, my good fortune, the one true sign of my victory and a kind blessing bestowed upon me by some benevolent deity.

Perhaps, I will never return to this spot ever again. Who knew if I will live long enough to return? Farewell, Saraswati Kundi! Farewell, O trees of the shore! Farewell, my beloved moonlit forest! When I stand in the middle of the crowded streets of Kolkata, I will think of you. The rustling of your leaves, the whispers of your breeze, the gentle lapping of your waters on the shore, the innocent call of your doves and the cackling of geese swimming in your waters—all these will ring in my ears like the gentle strum on the strings of an invisible sitar. Farewell, Saraswati Kundi!

On my way back, a mile or so from the lake, I chanced upon a few huts built on what was once a forested land. There were people living here now, and this place had been named *Naya Labtulia* or New Labtulia—just like New South Wales or New York. The family that had settled here must have fetched a number of branches and logs from the forests of Saraswati Kundi (for there were no large trees anywhere else in the vicinity) and erected a few huts. In the courtyard of the huts were a broken bottle of oil, either coconut or rancid mustard, a few wicker baskets, a couple of pots and pans made of brass, a few sickles and spades and amidst all these, a naked dark-skinned baby was crawling around, and an equally dark-skinned, portly woman was sitting and watching the baby without saying a word. This was what the household comprised of. And not just Labtulia, this was the same portrait of human possessions for as far as Ismailpur and Narha Baihar. I wonder where these people came from. They did not have a land or house that they could call their own, nor did they seem to have any love or longing for their kin or neighbours, or any urge whatsoever of returning to their own village. They wandered from place to place. They had settled here for now, but would soon move to the sandy shores of Munger or the Terai plains in the foothills of the Jayanti Hills. They moved anywhere they wanted to, and built a home for themselves.

On following and investigating a familiar voice, I saw Raju Pandey sitting inside one of the huts and explaining the meaning of a religious sloka to the inhabitants. On seeing him, I got off my horseback and was warmly welcomed inside. Raju said that he had come to administer an Ayurvedic medicine to one of the members of the family who had been taken ill. As a fee, the head of the family had paid him a handful of barley and eight paise. Raju Pandey was so happy with this clearly meagre compensation for his services that he had forgotten all about getting back home and had promptly sat down to discuss religion and philosophy with the family.

He said, 'Please have a seat, Babu-ji. We need to settle an argument, once and for all. Tell me, do you think there is a place where the world ends? I have been trying to tell these people that just like there is no end to the sky, similarly, there is no end to the earth either. Isn't that right, Babu-ji?'

Never in my wildest imagination had I expected to come face to face with a scientific matter of such great significance while out for a ride in the forest in the middle of the night.

I had always known Raju Pandey to be a thinker. He could sit and spend hours analyzing critical scientific and philosophical theories in his head. And as for the solution to such theories, I had always known him to offer explanations that were fundamentally original in thought. For instance, rainbows sprouted from termite hills. Or that the stars were nothing but the spies of the devil, sent to keep an eye on the ever-increasing human population on earth, so on and so forth.

On explaining whatever little I knew about our planet to Raju, he argued, if what I had claimed was indeed true, then why did the sun always rise in the east and set in the west, which ocean did it rise from at dawn and which ocean did it drown in at the end of the day—had the scientists of the world been able to throw some light on that? On hearing Raju use the expression 'throw some light', the

Gangota family stared at him with great admiration, and then gave me a look of sympathy, as if to express their genuine concern about how I would be able to hold up in the face of such vast erudition.

I said, 'That's not what happens Raju, the sun doesn't go anywhere, it remains stationary in one place. It only looks like it is moving.'

For the longest period of time, Raju kept staring at me with a surprised look on his face, even as giggles and sneers began to arise from various parts of the room. I sat there and realized why Galileo had been thrown behind the bars all those years ago.

After some time, Raju said, 'You are telling me that the Sun God does not wake up in the hills of the east in the morning, and does not dive into the ocean of the west at the end of the day?'

I said, 'No.'

'They have printed this in these books of yours? The ones written in English?'

'Yes.'

I had heard that knowledge gave courage and confidence to a man. The calm and innocent Raju, who had never raised his voice against anyone, now said in a stern and assertive voice, 'That's as good a lie as I have ever heard, Babu-ji. It's a proven fact that the Sun God rises from a specific cave in the eastern hills. There is a sadhu in Munger who had once walked hundreds of miles, all the way to the eastern borders and reached that cave. Of course, he could not go inside, because the mouth of the cave was covered with a slab of stone. But he did see the Sun God's chariot parked outside. He saw it with his own eyes; it was glittering, because it was made of mica. You and I won't be able to look at it, Babu-ji! But this sadhu was a great man. Not only did he see the chariot, he even managed to chip off a bit of mica from its wheels. A large glittering piece—this big—my cousin Kamtaprasad has seen it with his own eyes.'

Having said this much, Raju relaxed in his seat, smiled a little and passed a proud and sweeping glance across the room, only to find everyone staring at him with absolute awe and wonder.

I realized that in the face of such indisputable and irrefutable evidence to the sun's resting place in the eastern hills, it would perhaps be in my own best interest to resist from saying anything more to the contrary that night.

CHAPTER 16

[1]

One day, I told Jugalprasad, 'Let's go look for new plants in the hills of Mahalikharup.'

Jugalprasad said with great enthusiasm, 'There's a particular variety of vines that are found in the jungles of those hills; they aren't found anywhere else. The locals call it the *cheehadh* vines. We'll look for those.'

Our path ran through the new slums of Narha Baihar. By now, people had settled in, and even the neighbourhoods had been named, mostly after the names of the local chiefs of the area—Jhollutola, Roopdastola, Begumtola and others. The sound of maize being ground in the mortars was echoing in the air. Smoke was billowing out of mud houses. Naked children were rolling around in the dirt and dust.

The northern borders of Narha Baihar were still covered in dense forests. But there was not even a square inch of jungle left in Labtulia Baihar. About three-fourths of the jungles of Narha Baihar had disappeared too, leaving only about a thousand acres of land in the north. Jugalprasad was naturally quite upset about this.

He said, 'These Gangotas ruined it all, Huzoor. These people never stick to a spot, they keep moving around from place to place. Such a beautiful forest, and they had to come and ruin it.'

I said, 'They can't be blamed, Jugalprasad. The landlords are paying revenues to the government, it is only natural that they would want to make some money out of their land. It is the landlords who have leased the land to these subjects, I don't think we can blame the poor Gangotas for what happened.'

'Please don't give away the Saraswati Kundi, Huzoor. It's taken me years to collect all the plants and vines and grow that forest.'

'It's not up to me, Jugal. I've been trying to hold out against the wishes of my employers so far, but I don't know how long I can continue to do that. The land is fertile over there, and people have been eyeing those woods for some time.'

A couple of my sepoys had accompanied us. Having no clue as to what we were talking about, they vehemently shook their heads and assured us that there was nothing to worry about, after a good crop in the forthcoming harvest season, not even a tiny bit of the forest in Saraswati Kundi would remain. Needless to say, such assurances darkened our spirits even more.

The hills of Mahalikharup were almost nine miles away. They were faintly visible from the windows of my office. By the time we reached the foothills, it was already ten in the morning.

What a bright and beautiful morning it was! I wondered why the sky looked so blue on some days. Even the sunlight looked so different. The dark blue sky seemed to intoxicate my senses. The green leaves looked near transparent when the rays of the sun fell on them. Thanks to the deforestation in the Narha Baihar and Labtulia, hundreds and thousands of birds had come and taken refuge in these hills—their incessant chirping never sounded so sweet before!

The woods were dense in the hills. The last remaining jungles brought a sense of relief and made my spirit free of all constraints. I could sit anywhere I want, lie down, fall asleep and laze around in the cool shade of piyal and other trees. The vast desolate forest would soothe my nerves and lull me to a serene slumber.

We had started our ascent—large trees towered above our heads, their branches blocking the sunlight from reaching us—numerous streams and mountain brooks were flowing down the side of the hills. The leaves of myrobalan, kadam, segun and other trees were rustling in the breeze. A couple of peacocks called out from somewhere within the forest.

I said, 'Jugalprasad, where are the cheehadh vines that you had told me about?'

We found the vines after several more minutes of climbing. The leaves resembled those of lotus, the vines themselves were thick and heavy, so much so that they had to rely on other plants and trees to support their own weight. The fruits looked like flat beans, but were wider—some as wide and stiff as the famed slippers of Cuttack. The fruits contained round pebble-shaped seeds. We boiled a few seeds and tried eating them; they tasted just like potatoes.

We had come a long way above the base of the hills. In the distance—far from where we were—was the Mohanpura Reserve Forest. Towards the south—over there, was our estate. Beyond that were the faint shimmering outline of the jungles of the Saraswati Kundi. On the other side was the remaining quarter of what used to be the jungles of Narha Baihar, and to the east was the Kushi river flowing along the borders of the Mohanpura Forest Reserve. It was a very picturesque scenery.

'Look, Huzoor! Look at that peacock!'

A massive peacock was perched on the branches of a nearby tree. A sepoy raised his gun to shoot the bird, I sternly forbade him to do that.

Jugalprasad said, 'There's an ancient cave here in the hills somewhere, Huzoor. I've been looking for it ever since I've come here. There are strange drawings on the walls, no one knows who made those drawings.'

Perhaps some prehistoric ancestor of man had etched those drawings on the walls of the cave. Millions of years of history, joys, sorrows, rage, love, envy, greed, kindness and friendship—all represented in one brief moment of creativity, when time stood still.

This was an opportunity that I was simply not willing to forego, so we pushed on through the jungle looking for the cave. And we did find the cave, but it was too dark inside, so we could not gather the courage required to step inside. Even if we were to enter the cave, we would not be able to see anything. We would have to return some other day, better prepared. There were bound to be venomous snakes inside, and I was not willing to put my future to jeopardy in the pursuit of a glimpse of the ancient past.

I turned towards Jugalprasad and said, 'Why don't you plant a few new varieties of plants and trees here? No one will ever cut down the jungles in the hills. Labtulia is gone; Saraswati Kundi could follow too . . . .'

Jugalprasad said, 'You're right, Huzoor. I hadn't thought of that. But you are too busy these days; so, I shall have to do this all by myself.'

'I'll come from time to time and see how you are progressing. You go ahead and start.'

Mahalikharup was not just one hill, it comprised of a range of hills of varying heights. Some were less than two thousand feet high, and were considered as one of the lower branches of the Himalayan Range, although the actual Himalayas and the jungles of the Terai were more than a hundred miles away from here. Standing on the hills of the Mahalikharup and staring towards the plains below, I got the distinct feeling that I was looking at what was once a vast ocean—an ancient time when the future seeds of humankind lay submerged in the depths of a massive prehistoric body of water. The furious waves of this ocean would lash away at the sides of the hills and leave signs and impressions of a time that was now long forgotten.

Jugalprasad showed me at least eight to ten new varieties of plants, flowers and vines in the hills. None of these were available in the forests of the plains. The jungles here looked different and even the trees and plants looked strange.

The sun was about to set. The strange scent of an unknown wildflower had reached me quite some time ago, but as the sun began to slant towards the western horizon, the scent began to grow in intensity. Doves, hill parrots, hortits etc. began to settle down on the branches of the trees and discuss the adventures of the day with each other in a steady chitter.

Had there been no threat of tigers, and had my companions not succumbed to such fears, I would have liked to stay back after dusk to witness the nocturnal splendour of the hilltop jungles. But that was not to be.

Muneshwar Singh said, 'There are more tigers in these hills than there are in the Mohanpura Forest Reserve. Even the woodcutters and fruit-pickers make their way back down before dark. And no one dares to climb these hills alone, not even in the middle of the day. There are tigers, of course, and cobras are abundant too. Don't you see how dense the forest is?'

Hence, we had no other choice but to begin our descent. As I was climbing down, my attention was constantly being drawn to the leaves of the trees overlooking the steep ravine by my side. For between those leaves, I could see Venus and Jupiter twinkling in the twilight sky.

[2]

One day, as I was passing by the hut of one of the new settlers, I saw Ganori Tewari sitting in the courtyard of the house and eating a lump of grist off a sal leaf.

'How are you, Huzoor?'

'I'm fine. When did you arrive? And where were you all these days? Are these people related to you?'

'No, Huzoor. I was simply passing by, and it was almost noon; so I felt hungry. I am a Brahmin; so these people invited me in for a meal. I didn't know them, but now I do.'

The man of the house stepped forward and folded his hands to offer me a namaskar, 'Please come, Huzoor. Please take a seat.'

'No, I'm fine, thank you. How long have you been here?'

'It's been two months since I've leased the land, Huzoor. But I still haven't been able to till it yet.'

A little girl came running from within the house and dropped a few green chillies on Ganori Tewari's plate. Tewari was having grist of pulses, with salt and chillies. How such a massive lump of grist would find its way into the tiny stomach of as lanky a man as him—I found difficult to comprehend. Ganori was a vagabond in the truest sense of the term. There was a shabby bundle of cloth and a ragged quilt placed next to him—I realized these were the sole worldly belongings of the man. I told him, 'I'm busy right now. Come and see me at the cutcherry in the evening.'

Later that evening, Ganori arrived at the cutcherry.

I said, 'Where have you been all these days?'

'I was in a village in the Munger district, Huzoor. I've been moving around a lot, been to quite a few villages, in fact.'

'What did you do in all these days?'

'I used to run schools and teach young boys.'

'So, none of the schools lasted for long?'

'Not more than two to three months, Huzoor. None of the boys pay the fees.'

'Have you found yourself a wife? How old are you?'

'I can't feed myself, Huzoor. How can I marry? I am thirty-four now.'

I realized Ganori was in a bit of trouble. I also remembered how he had once come to the cutcherry uninvited, just to have a meal of rice. Perhaps, he had not had rice for several months now. He must have been wandering from village to village, eating grist and such in Gangota households.

I said, 'Stay back tonight, Ganori. Kontu Mishra cooks for me, he will prepare a meal for you. I hope you don't have a problem with that?'

Ganori was visibly delighted to hear this. He flashed a smile and said, 'Kontu belongs to the same class of Brahmin as me, Huzoor. I have had food cooked by him in the past too. There's no problem at all.'

Then he said, 'Huzoor, now that you've broached the subject of marriage, I should probably tell you what happened. Last year, after the monsoons, I started a school in a village. There was a Brahmin family in the village—same class of Brahmins as us. I used to live with them in their house. I was all set to marry the daughter of the family, everything was fixed, so much so that I even bought myself a nice little waistcoat from Munger town—when all of a sudden, the neighbours started whispering, saying all kinds of things against me. They said—he is a penniless school-master, he doesn't have a house of his own, doesn't have food to eat, don't give your daughter in marriage to him. Before I knew it, the wedding was called off. So, I decided to leave the village.'

'Had you met the girl? Was she good looking?'

'Of course, I met her, Huzoor! She was beautiful! But then when I thought about it, I realized what they did was quite natural, after all. I don't have anything, why would they want to give their daughter in marriage to someone like me?'

I realized Ganori Tewari was quite hurt at the wedding being called off. Perhaps, he had taken a liking to the girl.

After that, he spent several hours sitting and chatting with me. On listening to his story, I learnt how little he had received from life. He had had to wander from one village to another, all for a fistful of grains to fill his stomach. But even that was not to be. He had lived a half-fed, half-alive existence for the better part of his life, mostly depending on the mercy of people.

He said, 'So, I figured I'd go back to Labtulia and try my luck there. I'd heard that the jungles of Labtulia are all gone, and hundreds of new settlers have come to live here. I am planning to start a school here. So, I came. I think my luck will finally turn. What do you think, Huzoor?'

I made up my mind right then—that I would start a school in Labtulia and put Ganori in charge of it. So many young boys and girls had come with their parents and elders to live in Labtulia. They were all my subjects, so it was my responsibility to look after their education.

[3]

It was a beautiful full-moon night. Jugalprasad and Raju Pandey came down for a chat. A few hutments had sprung up at a little distance from the cutcherry—a man from that slum had come down too. It had been only thee days that he had come and settled here from Chhapra district.

The man was telling us about his life, about all the places that he had been to and lived in along with his wife and son, all the homes that he had had to set up, all the huts that he had had to build—on the banks of rivers and in the middle of the forest. Three years here, five years there. He had apparently lived on the banks of the Kushi river for over ten years at a stretch. But in all these years, he had not been able to bring about any improvement in his situation. This time, he had come to try his fortune in Labtulia.

The life of a wanderer was a strange one. From my conversations with these people, I had learnt that they were completely free of all bindings. Nothing tied them down to a place. They did not belong to any social structure whatsoever, nor did they feel any affection for their own home. They had no problem setting up a new home under the blue sky, in the middle of a valley or on the sandy and desolate beaches of a river.

Their outlook towards love, loss, life and death fascinated me. But what struck me as most curious was this man's unflinching faith that he would, some day, be able to turn his luck around.

How he hoped to do so by cultivating merely five acres of land in a godforsaken place such as Labtulia was not only difficult, but impossible for me to try to understand.

The man's age had crossed fifty. His name was Balabhadra Sengai, he was a Kolowar peasant by caste, more commonly known in these parts as a Kolu. Even at this age, his enthusiasm was indefatigable.

I asked, 'Where did you use to live before you came here, Balabhadra?'

'In Munger district, Huzoor, on the banks of a river. I lived there for two years. But last year, I had a bad crop, couldn't use even a single cob of corn. So, we left the place and started looking for a way to improve things. That's what life is about, after all, Huzoor—improving things. Progress and prosperity! Now the Lord has brought us to Huzoor's shelter, let's see what is in store for us.'

Raju Pandey said, 'When I first came to Labtulia, I had six buffaloes. Now I have ten. Labtulia is a good place, there are more than enough opportunities here.'

Balabhadra said, 'Help me buy a pair of buffaloes, Pandey-ji. After this year's crop, I will have to buy buffaloes. There's no better way to prosper in life.'

Ganori was listening to the conversation all this while. He said, 'That's true. Even I want to buy a pair of buffaloes. If only I could . . .'

The hills of Mahalikharup and even those of the distant Dhanjhari looked like a faint outline in the full-moon light. There was a slight nip in the air; so, a small fire had been lit before us. On one side sat Raju Pandey and Jugalprasad and on the other sat Balabhadra and a few new subjects.

Sitting near the fire and listening to their conversation, I was wondering how strange their notion of prosperity was! Their needs were simple—from six buffaloes to ten, from ten to twelve. Sitting under a star-studded sky and witnessing the moonlit hills in the distance, I marvelled at the human mind, and its varied aspirations.

Jugalprasad was the only one to abstain from such financial discussions, though. He had come into this world with a different set of ambitions altogether. Cows, buffaloes, land and such other matters found no place in his thoughts.

After some time, he said, 'Have you seen the *hansa* vines I had planted in the eastern jungles of Saraswati Kundi, Huzoor? They have become this thick by now. Even the spider lilies have bloomed in large numbers by the water this year. What do you say? Shall we go for a stroll there in the moonlight?'

I felt sad for Jugalprasad and his genuine love for the forest land of Saraswati Kundi, especially when I knew that I would not be able to save it for too long.

Meanwhile, Matuknath Pandit came and joined us. His school had over fifteen students by now. Lady Luck had finally smiled at him. Last year, he had received so many sacks

of wheat and maize from the families of his students that he
had had to erect a small granary in the courtyard of his school.

Matuknath Pandit was a live example of the fact that
perseverance was always followed by prosperity. And
thanks to prosperity, Matuknath's entire personality had
changed. The same sepoys and clerks of my cutcherry who
used to brand him as a madman now spoke to him with
respect and looked at him with admiration. The number of
students in his school seemed to be growing too. Whereas
no one cared about Jugalprasad or Ganori Tewari. On
the other hand, Raju Pandey had managed to earn quite
a bit of respect from the new settlers. One could often see
him running around from one household to another with
his bag of medicinal roots and barks, checking the pulse
of a sick boy here or treating an old man there. But Raju
Pandey had a big problem. He never quite understood the
importance of money. He seemed perfectly happy to be
treated with respect. Even a hearty chat with the family of
his patient delighted him to no end, and he considered it
compensation enough for his efforts.

[4]

Within the next three to four months, hundreds of settlers
had come and occupied the land from the foothills of the
Mahalikharup hills all the way up to Labtulia, and even the
northern borders of Narha Baihar. The land had already been
leased out and some people had started cultivation as well—
but human habitation was still scarce till some time ago. But
this year, people came by the droves and began to settle down.

So many different kinds of people and their families! One family was seen arriving with a sickly pony—the poor animal's back laden with beddings, utensils, piles of wood, idols of gods and deities, earthen ovens and other whatnots. Another came with their children riding on buffaloes, along with brass utensils, broken lanterns and even charpoys piled on the backs of the beasts. Some other families were reported to carry their belongings—including their children—on their own backs and walking for miles to reach their destination.

Among these people were men and women from all castes—from amicable and pious Brahmins to Gangotas and Dosads. I asked Jugalprasad, 'How come there are so many people coming to settle here? Didn't they have houses of their own all this while?'

Jugalprasad was visibly depressed. He said, 'This is how people are over here, Huzoor. They have heard that land was being distributed here at low costs; so, they have all flocked here. If things work out for them, they will continue to stay. Or else, they will pack up and leave again.'

'Don't they have any allegiance to their own homes? The ones that their ancestors built for them?'

'No, Babu-ji. Their primary occupation is to lease fresh land for cultivation and make money out of them. They don't care where they live. As long as they get a good crop and the rent is low, they will stay.'

'And after that?'

'After that, they will try to look for fresh land and low rents once again. As soon as they find one, they will pack their bags and set out once again—lock, stock and barrel. That's what these people have been doing all their lives.'

[5]

The other day, I had gone for a land survey under Grant Sahib's banyan tree, the tindal named Asrafi was busy with his measurements, I was sitting on my horse and watching him work, when I suddenly saw Kunta walking towards the village.

I had not seen Kunta for quite some time. I told Asrafi, 'I don't see much of Kunta these days, does she still live here?'

Asrafi said, 'Why, haven't you heard, Babu-ji? She wasn't here for a long time.'

'How come?'

'Rashbehari Singh had taken her home one day. He told her, your late husband was like a brother to me—come and stay in my home.'

'I see.'

'She lived there for a few months, but as you can see from her appearance, her situation did not improve at all. In fact, Rashbehari Singh had been saying some really nasty things to her, and apparently, he even tried to abuse her. So, a month or so ago, she ran away from there and has been living here since. Apparently Rashbehari Singh held a dagger to her throat, to which she said, go ahead kill me, you can take my life, but you will never take my honour.'

'Where does she live now?'

'A Gangota family in Jhollutola has given her shelter. They have a tiny hut next to their cowshed, she lives there.'

'How does she manage? Doesn't she have two–three children to take care of?'

'She begs for alms. Sometimes, she goes from farm to farm picking up whatever crop has been thrown away or left behind, does odd jobs here and there too. She is a good girl, Babu-ji. She may be the daughter of a courtesan, but she has her own values and principles. She has never been known to do anything bad or dishonourable.'

The survey work came to an end. A subject from Ballia district had leased this land, he would be coming tomorrow to build his house. And that would bring a dismal end to the glory of Grant Sahib's banyan tree too.

The top of the Mahalikharup hills had begun to turn golden. A flock of cranes flew towards the Saraswati Kundi. The sun was about to set. Dusk would fall soon after.

I had a sudden moment of epiphany.

All this land would be gone, not a tiny fraction of it would remain. This vast expanse of Labtulia and Narha Baihar— all of it would disappear. Droves of strangers had come and gobbled up all the land. But the people who had been living in these forests forever, people who did not have the means, or the good fortune – would they be deprived and driven out of their homes just because they did not have the money to pay their lease? These people with whom I had spent so many years, those I had loved and cared for, those who had been nothing but nice to me—could I not do anything for them?

I told Asrafi, 'Asrafi, will it be possible for you to bring Kunta to the cutcherry tomorrow morning? I would like to have a word with her.'

'Certainly, Huzoor. Whenever you say.'

At exactly 9 a.m. next morning, Asrafi brought Kunta to my office in the cutcherry.

I said, 'How are you, Kunta?'

Kunta folded her hands in greeting and said, 'I am fine, Huzoor.'

'And your children?'

'They are fine too, thanks to Huzoor's grace and kindness.'

'How old is your eldest son, Kunta?'

'He has just turned eight, Huzoor.'

'Does he know how to rear buffaloes in the field?'

'Who would trust such a young boy with their buffaloes, Huzoor?'

Despite all the misfortunes that she had had to go through, I noticed Kunta was still quite beautiful. She had a comely appearance—made more honourable by an unmistakable sense of pride, courage and chastity.

This was the same teenage girl, daughter of a famous courtesan in Kashi, lovestruck, starry-eyed, with the flame of hope and love still burning in her heart. No amount of misfortune, no evil eye cast upon her had been able to extinguish that flame. No wonder she had lived a life of penury and misery, no wonder she was reduced to the wretched destitute that stood before me now. Love had brought Kunta to this land, and she had never compromised on love. She had upheld the sanctity of love.

I said, 'Would you like to take some land, Kunta?'

For several moments, it seemed to me that Kunta had not quite heard what I had said. After some time, she muttered, 'Land, Huzoor?'

'Yes, land. A new lot is being distributed right now.'

Kunta was silent for some time, lost in some faraway thought. Then she said, 'There was a time when we ourselves had acres of land. One by one, everything was lost. I don't have anything to give you in return for your kindness anymore, Huzoor.'

'Why, won't you be able to pay the necessary advance against the land?'

'I go from farm to farm in the dead of the night, picking cobs of corn and pulses, Huzoor. Like a thief! A thief is what I have been reduced to! Hiding from everyone's sight, lurking in the dark. When dawn breaks, I barely manage to collect half a basket of corn. That's all I feed my children. I myself go hungry most of the days. How will I pay you any money?'

Kunta choked up and lowered her head. Tears began to drop from her eyes. Asrafi quickly stepped out of the room. I had known him for some time now. He was a young man, with a soft heart.

I said, 'Fine, Kunta. What if I told you that you don't have to pay me any advance?'

Kunta looked up at me with tears and surprise in her eyes.

Asrafi immediately stepped back into the room and waved his hands in front of Kunta in excitement, 'Huzoor is giving you land, just like that, you don't have to pay anything. Do you understand?'

I asked Asrafi, 'If she is given some land, how will she plow it, Asrafi?'

Asrafi said, 'Oh, that will not be a problem, Huzoor. There are so many Gangota farmers out there, someone or the other will give her a couple of plows, I'm sure. I will take care of that, Huzoor.'

'Very well then, how much land do you think would be enough for her?'

Asrafi said, 'Since Huzoor is being so kind to her, I see no reason why she should not have a large tract of land. Perhaps, five acres or so will be good for her.'

I turned towards Kunta and asked her, 'If I were to give you five acres of land without asking for any advance, will you be able to grow a good crop and pay back the lease to the estate? Of course, you don't have to pay any lease for the first two years. But from the third year, you will be expected to pay the lease.'

Kunta kept looking back and forth at our faces, wondering if we had brought her into the cutcherry to play yet another cruel joke on her. For the longest period of time, she could not say anything at all. Then, she somehow managed to utter a few words, 'Land! Five acres of land!'

Asrafi once again turned to her and said, 'Yes, Huzoor is giving you five acres of land. You don't have to pay anything for the first two years. Then, from the third year, you pay your taxes. Is that alright with you?'

Kunta stared blankly at my face for some time and then said, 'Huzoor is very kind, I . . . '— and then she suddenly burst into tears.

I gestured to Asrafi and he escorted Kunta out of my office.

CHAPTER 17

[1]

After dusk, the new settlements of Labtulia were a pretty sight to see. The moonlight would seem faint, thanks to the fog. Vast expanses of agricultural land. Two or three lamps shimmering in the dark in various slums. Thousands of people, hundreds of families had come to our estate looking for means to sustain themselves. Forests had been cut down and cleared out and farming had begun. I did not know the names of all the slums, nor did I seem to know anyone anymore. I had spoken to a few of them and realized that their ways of life were no less alien and mysterious to me than those mute shanties standing here and there like ghosts in the foggy moonlit night.

Take their food habits, for instance. There were three primary food crops that were grown in our estate throughout the year—maize in autumn, pulses in winter and wheat in summer. Maize was grown in relatively smaller quantities because there was not enough land suitable for its growth. Pulses and wheat were abundant, although the output of wheat was less than half of that of pulses. Naturally, the staple food in these regions was the grist of pulses.

Paddy was not grown at all. The land was simply not suitable for the cultivation of paddy. And this was not just true for our estate, there was no paddy to be found in the entire region—not even in the government estates. Which is why rice was rarely available here, and was considered a delicacy. Some of the more affluent connoisseurs with uncompromisable culinary habits did manage to trade pulses for paddy, but the number of such exceptional people could be counted on one's fingertips.

Coming to housing, in all of the five thousand acres of land on which huts and shanties had sprung up, almost all the houses had wild catkins for roofs, and catkin stems for walls. Some of the settlers had applied a layer of wet mud on them, others had not. Bamboo trees were a rarity in the region; so, jungle trees, especially the branches of kendu and piyal, had been sliced to build the pillars of the houses.

Most of them were Hindus, but I did not know why or how they had chosen Lord Hanuman as their deity, from among the three hundred and thirty million gods and goddesses that were available to their collective knowledge and belief. Without exception, there would have to be a flag of Hanuman fluttering in the wind in the middle of every single slum. This flag was worshipped, prayed to, and smeared with vermillion during every festival. Ram and Sita did have some following, but their humble servant seemed to have outshone their divinity by a long margin. Deities such as Vishnu, Shiva, Durga and Kali were hardly worshipped, if at all. I certainly had not seen anyone praying to them in my estate.

In fact, I did know one devout follower of Shiva. His name was Drona Mahato, he belonged to the Gangota caste. Several years ago, someone or the other had apparently

brought a large block of stone from somewhere and placed
it under the flag of Hanuman in the cutcherry. The sepoys
would offer it water some time, or smear red vermillion on it
from time to time. But more often than not, no one seemed
to pay particular attention to the stone, and it stood neglected
most of the time.

Over the last couple of months or so, a new slum had
come up not too far from the cutcherry—Drona Mahato
had come and settled there. He must have been no less than
seventy or seventy-five years old, at least. He was a man from
the older times, which was why his name was Drona. Had he
belonged to the newer generation, his name would have been
something like Doman, Lodhai or Maharaj.

Anyway, the aged Drona happened to notice the stone on
one of his visits to the cutcherry. The next morning, he began
what was to become a daily ritual of walking all the way to the
Kalbalia river to take a dip in the waters and then fetching the
river water all the way back to the cutcherry to give the block
of stone a fond and caring bath. Having taken his time to
gently wash the stone from top to bottom, the old man would
pay his respects and then head home.

I had once asked Drona, 'The Kalbalia is more than
fourteen miles away. Why do you walk all the way to the
river every morning? Why don't you get water from the pond
instead?'

Drona had said, 'Nothing satisfies Lord Mahadev more
than water collected from the rapids, Babu-ji. It is a great
honour for me that I have been chosen to give him a bath
every day.'

God created humankind, and humankind created God.
Word of Drona Mahato's pious act of devotion soon began

to spread far and wide like wild fire. Every other day, one or two people began to come from nearby villages to pay their respects to the block of stone. A certain variety of fragrant grass grew in this region, in which the leaves and the stem let out a delightful scent. The more the grass dried, the more intense the fragrance became. Someone brought a few blades of grass from the fields and planted them around the idol of Shiva. One day, Matuknath Pandit came to me and complained, 'Babu-ji, how come so many Gangotas are coming every day and pouring water on Lord Shiva's head? Should they be allowed to do this?'

I said, 'As far as I can see, it was because of one of those Gangotas that everyone came to know about the idol, Panditji. Why, you yourself have been around for so many years, how come I haven't seen you pour a pot of water on the idol even once?'

Furious at my response, Matuknath said, 'That's not an idol of the Lord, Babu-ji. It's just a piece of rock, that's all.'

'Well, if that is so, then why are you so worried about people pouring water on it?'

From that day onwards, Drona Mahato became the chartered priest of the Shivalinga in the courtyard of the cutcherry.

Chhat was a big festival in the region in autumn. Girls from all the villages wore yellow saris and walked together in a procession towards the Kalbalia river. There were festivities throughout the day. In the evening, anyone walking by the villages were bound to find their mouths watering, thanks to the aroma wafting in the air from all the sweetmeats being made. Boys and girls sang, laughed and danced to their heart's content late into the night. It was difficult to believe that this was the same place where, till merely a few years ago, all one could hear in the night were the footsteps of nilgais, the laughing of the hyenas and the coughing of the tiger (those who are experienced will know that while coughing, the tiger makes a sound which is identical to the one we humans do).

I had been invited to Jhollutola on the evening of the Chhat festival. This was just one of the fifteen invitations that I and my staff at the cutcherry had received that year.

My first stop was at the residence of Jhollu Mahato, the chief of Jhollutola. As I had said before, the villages in the region were named after the names of their chiefs.

I noticed that there was still some bit of forested land existing behind Jhollu Mahato's house. He welcomed me and offered me a seat under a tattered canopy that had been set up in the courtyard. The respected elders of the village were all present there—dressed in spotless white dhotis and waistcoats. They sat in front of me, on a grass-weaved mat laid on the ground.

I said, 'I'm sorry, but I'll have to decline any food. I have to go to several other places tonight.'

Jhollu said, 'We can't let you go without having some sweets. The women have put in a lot of effort into making the sweets, more so when they heard that you would be coming.'

What could I do? With the accountant Goshtha Babu and Raju Pandey as company, I sat down on the mat. Then came the sweets—made of wheat and jaggery, and served on sal leaves. Each sweet was as big and as hard as a one-inch thick brick. I picked one up to inspect it, and soon reached the conclusion that let alone eating it, if I were to throw it at one of the several gentlemen who sat there staring at me with their mouths open, it would cause some serious injury, if not cause instant death. There were beautiful designs on each of the sweets though—of flowers, vines and leaves—which had rendered their harsh texture even more cruel and unbearable.

Despite all the efforts that the womenfolk had put into preparing them, I simply could not bring myself up to eating the sweets. Having taken a single bite, I had come to realize that there was no taste in them at all, least of all sweetness. I reckoned the Gangota womenfolk were not skilled in the culinary arts at all. Raju Pandey, on the other hand, gobbled up as many as five of those unquestionably inedible sweets right before my eyes in no time, before putting a check on his zeal and refraining from asking for more, perhaps because I was staring at him in shock and surprise.

From Jhollutola, I went to Lodhaitola. Then to Parbattola, Bheemdastola, Asrafitola and Laxmaniatola. Everywhere I went, there were singing and dancing. None of these people would be sleeping tonight. There would be joyous laughter and merrymaking throughout the night.

One thing was undeniably true, though. Everywhere I went, I found that the womenfolk had taken great care to summon their best cooking skills in order to prepare sweets for me. When I sat down to eat, these women were seen stealing curious glances at the Bengali Babu from the city from behind the curtains and around the corners. And while I was most grateful to them for their gracious hospitality, I simply could not bring myself up to praise their sweets. In some places, I had to encounter sweets even worse than the ones that had been served to me in Jhollutola. Being the kind man that he was, Raju Pandey refused to let the efforts of the ladies go to waste. After a while, I stopped counting the number of those rock-like sweets that he had consumed. And not just him, many of the other Gangota invitees seemed to have no problem biting into those monstrous sweets and gulping down as many as twenty to thirty at a time. It was an incredible sight, and it had to be seen to be believed.

I went to Chhaniya and Suratiya's place too, in Narha Baihar.

On seeing me from a distance, Suratiya ran up to me.

'How come you are so late, Babu-ji? My mother and I have been waiting for you since dusk; we've made some delicious sweets for you. We were wondering what was taking you so long. Please come.'

Nakchhedi welcomed us in warmly.

When the sweets came, I told Suratiya, 'Tell your mother to take these away, I won't be able to eat them.'

Suratiya seemed surprised. She said, 'But there are just a few here, Babu-ji. Won't you eat these at least? My mother has cooked them especially for you, she has put milk and raisins in them. My father had travelled all the way to Bheemdastola to get good quality wheat for the sweets, just because you were coming. Oh, please have some, won't you?'

I realized my mistake. These were poor people, what I found as inedible was manna from heaven for them. These young boys and girls waited throughout the year for these very sweets. I should not have declined what they were offering to me. Just to make them happy, I desperately had a couple.

Then I said, 'It's delicious. But I am stuffed, Suratiya—we have had to keep several invitations throughout the evening. I would come back some other day and have more of these.'

On our way back, I noticed a small bundle in Raju Pandey's hand. From the way he was carrying it, it was obvious that it was quite heavy. But he looked quite happy.

On seeing me staring at his bundle, he grinned and said, 'What could I do, Huzoor? Everywhere I went, they wanted me to pack some sweets. And, these won't turn bad, they'll last for days. I wouldn't have to cook for a week.'

The next morning, Kunta came to the cutcherry and placed a brass plate in front of me with some amount of hesitation. The plate was covered with a clean white cloth.

I asked, 'What is this, Kunta?'

Kunta replied in a shy voice, 'Just a few sweets for the festival, Babu-ji. I had come twice last night, but you weren't in.'

I said, 'Yes, I had to keep a number of invitations in the estate. I returned quite late last night. Thank you for bringing me these sweets.'

I removed the cloth from over the plate and found a few sweets, a tiny heap of sugar, a couple of bananas, a skinned coconut and an orange.

I said, 'This looks delicious!'

Kunta hesitated for a moment and said in a soft voice, 'Please have everything, Babu-ji, I've made the sweets specially for you. My only regret is that I couldn't serve them hot.'

'That's not a problem at all, please don't worry. I will have all of them. They look really nice.'

Kunta folded her hands in gratitude, bowed her head and walked out of the room.

[2]

One day, sepoy Muneshwar Singh came to me and said, 'Huzoor, there's a man lying on a tattered piece of cloth under a tree in the forest. People are not letting him enter the village; they are pelting stones at him. Shall I bring him to you?'

I was quite surprised to hear this. Dusk was about to fall, soon it would be completely dark, and although it was not too cold, we were in the month of October already: there would be a lot of dew after dark and the late nights will bring the chill. Under such circumstances, why was a man lying on the ground in the forest? And why were the villagers throwing stones at him?

I went out with Muneshwar Singh to investigate. On the other side of Grant Sahib's banyan tree (named thus after the British surveyor Mr Grant, who had pitched tent under the tree while on a survey trip in the forest estate of Labtulia), under an arjun tree in the middle of the woods lay a man on the already moist ground. It was too dark to see the spot clearly; so, I said, 'Who's over there? Where are you from? Come out in the open.'

The man almost crawled out from behind the bushes on all fours. He was in his fifties and seemed too frail to stand up straight. He was trembling in fear and wore shabby and tattered clothes. For a long time, he kept peeping out from behind the bushes and staring at us, with the same look on his face as a feeble prey would have, with a predator hot on its pursuit.

It was only when he crawled out of the dark that we noticed the deep wounds on his left hand and his left leg. It was perhaps because of those wounds that he was unable to stand up.

Muneshwar Singh said, 'Huzoor, it's because of those wounds that the villagers were trying to chase him away. They refused to give him water to drink and pelted stones at him.'

I said, 'What's your name? Where are you from?'

The man was shocked speechless. There was terror and helplessness in his eyes. Moreover, he had seen the stick wielding Muneshwar Singh standing behind me. Perhaps, he had assumed that I had problems with his taking shelter in the forest too, and had come with a sepoy to chase him out.

He muttered in a trembling voice, 'My name? My name is Giridharilal, Huzoor. I am from Teentanga.'

And then, in a tragically pleading voice he uttered a few more words, 'Water . . . some water . . . please . . . '

I had recognized the man by now. This was the same Giridharilal that I had met in the spring fair, in the tent of Brahma Mahato. The same shy and polite look on his face was still there, but now, it was mixed with an expression of terror too.

I immediately turned to Muneshwar Singh and said, 'Go back to the cutcherry and come back with a few men as soon as you can, bring a charpoy too.'

Muneshwar Singh left to obey my orders.

I said, 'What has happened to you, Giridharilal? I know you. Don't you recognize me? We had met in Brahma Mahato's tent during the spring fair a few years ago, remember? You don't have to worry, there's nothing to fear. Tell me what happened to you?'

Giridharilal began to cry bitterly. Showing me his arm and leg, he said, 'I cut myself while working, Huzoor, and these wounds just don't seem to heal. I have done everything that everyone has advised me to do, but the wounds seem to be spreading. Then, after a few months, people began to say, you have leprosy. They don't let me enter the village. I somehow manage to beg for food. I don't have any shelter to spend my nights; so I entered the forest and—'

'But how come you're here—so far from home?'

All the talking and weeping had left Giridharilal out of breath. He took a moment to catch his breath and said, 'I was on my way to the hospital in Purnia, Huzoor. If I don't go to the hospital, these wounds will kill me.'

For a second or two, I was stunned, and I could not help but wonder at the indomitable human will to survive! Purnia was more than forty miles from where Giridharilal lived. On the way was the Mohanpur Forest Reserve, full of tigers and other wild animals. With numb and wounded limbs, almost crawling on all fours, this man was dragging himself along, hoping to cross jungles, hills, rivers and ravines to reach a hospital!

The charpoy arrived. I asked the sepoys to take Giridharilal to a hut that had been lying vacant and unused near the compound of the cutcherry. On seeing a leper, the sepoys had put in a mild protest, but when I explained everything to them, they promptly sprang into action.

Giridharilal had not eaten in days. After drinking some hot milk, he seemed to feel a little better.

In the evening, I went to his hut to find him fast asleep.

The next morning, I summoned the local medicine specialist, Raju Pandey, who sat by Giridharilal's bed with a grave face checking his pulse. I said, 'Look Raju, tell me frankly if this is something that you can handle, or if I should send him to Purnia?'

Raju frowned and replied in a hurt tone, 'Thanks to Huzoor's blessings, I have been doing this for several years now. Give me fifteen days. This man's wounds will completely heal in less than fifteen days.'

I made the mistake of listening to Raju Pandey. Not because of his incompetency, no. Thanks to his roots and barks, the wounds began to heal in five–six days. But trouble was, no one wanted to take care of Giridharilal, no one wanted to apply medicine on his wounds or even wash the glass that he drank water from.

Moreover, he came down with fever—high fever.

With my options quickly running out, I decided to call Kunta. When she came, I explained everything to her and said, 'You get me a Gangota woman from the villages. I will pay her whatever money she asks for. If this man is not looked after, he is going to die.'

Without thinking twice, Kunta said, 'I will take care of him, Babu-ji. And you don't have to pay me anything.'

Kunta was a Rajput woman. How would she look after an ailing lower caste Gangota man? I figured she had not quite heard me right.

I said, 'You will have to wash his utensils, feed him, clean him up and wash his soiled clothes. He is completely confined to his bed. How will you do all this?'

Kunta said, 'You must be thinking about my caste, Babu-ji? But tell me, how did the people of my caste, my own people behave with me? What have they done for me, when I needed their help? No, Babu-ji. I don't belong to any caste. And you have always been nothing but kind to me. I will do anything you say. I will take care of this man and nurse him back to health. You don't need to speak to anyone else.'

Thanks to Raju Pandey's medicines and Kunta's tireless care, Giridharilal got back up on his feet within a month. I tried to offer Kunta some money, but she refused to take any. I knew she had started addressing Giridharilal as 'Baba' by now. She said, 'How can a daughter take money for looking after her father? I don't want to earn the wrath of the all-seeing God, Babu-ji.'

Of all the good deeds that I have done in my life, perhaps the chief among them was to give some land to Giridhari and help him start a new life in Labtulia.

I had been to his hut once. By then, he had been able to till his two acres of land and grow a reasonable amount of wheat. I also noticed that he had planted some lemon trees around his hut.

'What would you do with all these lemons, Giridharilal?'

'Those lemons will make a fine sherbet, Huzoor. I can't afford sugar, so I'm going to mix a bit of jaggery with the lemon juice and oh, what a delicious sherbet they would make!'

Giridharilal's calm, simple and humility-laced face lit up brightly with hope and joy.

'Good, fat lemons they'll turn out to be. I take care of them every day, you see. It had been a long-standing dream of mine—that if I could have a piece of land of my own someday, then I would plant a row of stout lemon trees. I love drinking sherbet, Huzoor, I always have. Oh, how everyone used to insult me and throw me out when I went to their homes, asking for a lemon. I have my own lemon trees now. I will drink my own sherbet. No one can insult me anymore.'

CHAPTER 18

[1]

It was time to leave this place now. I felt a strong urge to meet Bhanumati one last time. With its lovely forests and its moonlit nights, the Dhanjhari mountains had secured a special place in my heart.

I decided to take Jugalprasad along.

Jugalprasad had mounted Tehsildar Sajjan Singh's horse, but just after we had crossed the border of our estate, he said, 'This horse won't do, Huzoor. As soon as it picks up a gallop inside the jungle, it will stumble and fall, and I'll lose my legs too. I will go back and get another one.'

I assured him that nothing of that sort would happen. Sajjan Singh was a seasoned rider, he had ridden to Purnia a number of times on this very horse to attend our court hearings. The path to Purnia was far more treacherous, and Jugalprasad as aware of that.

Soon, we had crossed the Karo river.

And then, forest after forest! Lush, lovely, desolate forests! As I have said before, these forests were not too dense. Saplings of kendu and sal, trees of palash and mahua, shrubs of berries—all stood scattered here and there. The soil on the undulating ground was red in colour and strewn with stones, rocks and pebbles. Every now and then, we could see footprints of wild elephants on the ground. There was no sign of any human habitation whatsoever.

I felt a sense of relief on having left the congested and ugly slums of Labtulia behind. Other than the Saraswati Kundi, these were the only remaining forests in the province now.

By noon, we had crossed those two villages in the jungle—Burudi and Kulpal. After that, the scattered woods lay behind us, and the dense forests began. We rode on. It was the end of November, so the air was cool, crisp and pleasant.

Far away on the horizon, the Dhanjhari mountains now emerged.

We reached the cutcherry by dusk. This was the cutcherry of the kendu jungle that our estate had bought in the auctions. A manager had now been stationed here.

The man was a Muslim, named Abdul Wahid, he came from the Shahabad district. Not only did he give us a warm welcome, he insisted on our staying back for the night. He said, 'It's good that you reached before nightfall, Babu-ji. The forests are full of tigers.'

Night had fallen. The leaves of large trees all around us were rustling in the breeze. I was planning to sit on the veranda of the cutcherry, but after what the manager said, I decided to play it safe and sit inside next to an open window instead.

Suddenly, a strange animal called out from deep within the jungle. I asked Jugal, 'What was that?'

Jugal said, 'That's nothing, Huzoor, just a *hural*.'

I knew that the locals referred to a wolf by that name. Later that night, I heard a hyena's laugh a couple of times.

Curdled my blood, to be honest. It sounded just like a patient of asthma wheezing and coughing, followed by bouts of hysterical laughter.

The next day, we set off early in the morning, and reached the late king Dobru Panna's capital, Chakmakitola, by 9 a.m. Bhanumati seemed overjoyed by my unexpected arrival. She was finding it difficult to contain her excitement.

'I was thinking about you yesterday, Babu-ji. Why hadn't you come all these days?'

Bhanumati was looking a bit taller than I had expected and perhaps, a bit slimmer as well. Her face still looked as pretty as ever though.

'You'll take a bath in the stream, won't yout? Shall I get the mahua oil or the *karua* oil for you? The stream had been fed well in the monsoons this year, you'll see!'

I had noticed that in matters of cleanliness and personal hygiene, Bhanumati was quite different from the average Santhal girl. Her simple and elegant attire and make-up set her apart from other girls of her age and distinguished her as the child of a royal family.

The room that I was sitting in was surrounded by large trees of Asan and Arjun. A bunch of wild green parrots were sitting on the branches of the trees and chittering away. The winters were just around the corner; so, despite the sun having risen high up in the sky, the air was still cold. Less than half a mile ahead of me lay the Dhanjhari mountain range. A narrow path meandered down from the top of the hill all the way to the backyard of the king's palace. And far away towards the east, like blue lumps of cloud, I could see the hills of the Gaya district.

How I wish I could take a lease of the kendu forest, build a hut next to one of the mountain streams and live here in the middle of this valley of green bliss! Labtulia was gone forever, but Bhanumati's kingdom would perhaps be spared by the evil eyes of greed and pelf. The land over here was full of murrum and pyrite, so growing a crop was difficult here. Had it been an ideal spot for cultivation, this place would have vanished before my eyes too. But then again, if it were to be found some day that the ground here was rich in copper, matters could get worse.

I shut my eyes and shuddered in my imaginings. I saw smoke billowing from the chimney of a copper factory. Trolley lines, miles after miles of workers' slums, foul-smelling open drains carrying sewage water, mountains of coal ash from engines and turbines—shops, tea stalls, cheap theatres screening dubious films (only three annas for the matinee show, please take your seats latest by noon), country shops selling local hooch, tailoring shops, Homeo Pharmacy (patients of poor means treated here absolutely free of cost) and the quintessential Hindu Hotel. The factory's siren just blared the 3 p.m. hoot. Out came Bhanumati with a basket of coal on her head, walking towards the congested and crowded market in order to earn her daily living, 'Who wants my cooooaaaallll? Good coal, good coal, lights easily, burns longer. Four paise for a basket of cooooaaalllll.'

I opened my eyes to find Bhanumati standing in front of me with a shallow bowl of oil. Other members of her family came and greeted me warmly. Bhanumati's uncle, the young Jogru was walking towards the house, with his eyes focused on the branch of a tree that he was busy sharpening with a knife. As soon as he looked up and saw me, he greeted me with a warm smile. I liked the young man, there was something very sweet and elegant about him.

I said, 'So, Jogru, how's the hunting coming along?'

Jogru smiled and said, 'I'll bring something for you today, Babu-ji. What would you prefer—porcupine, or pigeon or jungle-fowl?'

After taking a refreshing bath in the stream, I returned to the palace. Bhanumati brought me her own mirror (the one I had got for her from Purnia) and a wooden comb.

After a hearty meal, I was resting in my room, when Bhanumati came to me and said, 'Come, Babu-ji, we'll go up the hill. You love going up there, don't you?'

Jugalprasad was fast asleep. When he woke up, we set out for the climb. We as in—Jugalprasad, myself, Bhanumati and another young girl—Bhanumati's twelve-year-old cousin, the daughter of Jogru Panna's elder brother.

After hiking for half a mile, we reached the base of the hill. Having climbed through the forest for some time, a most agreeable smell began to intoxicate me. I was wondering what the source of such a pleasant fragrance could be, when I looked around to realize that after all these days, and much to my surprise and delight that there were a number of *chhatim* trees in the forest. This tree had clusters of seven leaves, and now that winter was approaching, thick bunches of white flowers had bloomed amidst those leaves. The smell was coming from the flowers.

It was not one or two chhatim trees that I saw—entire jungles of only chhatim trees, all in full bloom. Chhatims and *keli kadamba*—this was different from the usual *kadamba* flower trees. Keli kadamba was a different species of flowerless trees, with beautiful zigzag branches and large leaves that looked like the leaves of segun.

In that cool November afternoon, standing in the middle of a forest of ivory white fragrant flowers, I looked at the shapely young Bhanumati and wondered if she herself was a dark-skinned and breathtakingly beautiful deity of the forest. This land, these forests, the banks of the Micchi river, the valley of the Karo river, the Dhanjhari hills on one side, the Naowada hills on the other—her ancestors had ruled them all. She came from a powerful lineage, a revered line of royal blood, but was now reduced to a neglected Santhal girl, thanks to years of humiliation and exploitation by those who had vanquished her forefathers and left her in abject poverty. Every time I saw Bhanumati, that unwritten episode of the history of India played out in my mind like a great tragedy.

As I stood there, soaking the atmosphere of the place in, I knew that this lovely afternoon was to join the ranks of some of the most favourite memories that I would cherish for the rest of my life.

Bhanumati said, 'Come, don't you want to go up all the way?'

I said, 'How lovely the flowers smell! Shall we sit here for some time? The sun would disappear behind those hills soon.'

Flashing her sweetest smile, Bhanumati said, 'Whatever you wish, Babu-ji. Let's sit here if you want to. But won't you offer flowers to the graves? Ever since you taught me last time, I go up the hill every day to offer flowers to my ancestors' graves. There's no dearth of flowers here, as you can see!'

Far away in the valley below, the Michhi river meandered like a serpent through the woods, flowing towards the north. After some time, the sun set behind the distant hills towards Nowada. As soon as it did, I felt the chill in the air, and the fragrance of the flowers grew stronger. Darkness began to descend rapidly in the valley, and towards the mountains.

Bhanumati picked a few chhatim flowers and put them on the bun of her hair. Then we began to climb again. Each of us had a chhatim twig in our hands. We climbed all the way up to the top of the hill. I had reached the ancient banyan tree and the royal graveyard beneath it. Large boulders were strewn all around us. Bhanumati and her cousin Nichhni strew flowers on King Dobru Panna's grave, Jugalprasad and I did the same.

Bhanumati was a simple girl. She was visibly excited and genuinely happy. She said, 'Let's stay here for a while, Babu-ji. I feel so happy!'

And in my mind, I was thinking, 'This is the end. I will never be able to come here again. I will never be able to see these sights, or hear these sounds, or smell these soul-soothing aromas ever again. This was my final farewell to these hills, these rivers, these valleys, these ancient graves, these forests, these trees and plants and vines and flowers, and to Bhanumati as well. After six long years of living in the middle of the forest, I was now supposed to return home to Kolkata, but as the day of my departure came near, I felt as if I was leaving my heart, my mind and my soul behind in these forests.

For a moment, I wondered if I should tell Bhanumati that I was leaving forever, and that I would never return. I felt a strong urge to know what she would have to say to that. But then I asked myself—what would I gain by breaking the heart of a simple forest girl? Why ruin the moment that she was enjoying so much?

With the coming of the evening, another fragrance reached my nostrils. There were scores of shiuli flowers in the jungles all around. As the evening became cooler, the sweet smell of the shiuli flowers was spreading magic in the air. The chhatim trees were down below, it was quite a bit of climb downhill to reach those trees. Meanwhile, fireflies had begun to glow in the dark. The fresh, cool air lent a calm, soothing sensation to my mind. Anyone who filled his lungs with this air everyday was bound to live a long and healthy life.

I did not feel like coming down. But the forest was full of wild animals, and it would get dark soon. Moreover, Bhanumati was with me. Jugalprasad was too busy looking for new species of plants and flowers to notice the beauty of the sunset or of the valley down below. The man was crazy alright, but perhaps this world needed more of such crazy people.

It is said that Noorjahan had had *chinar* trees brought from Persia and planted them in Kashmir. Noorjahan was not there to see it anymore, but the whole of Kashmir was full of beautiful chinar trees now. Someday, Jugalprasad would pass into the great beyond, but even after a hundred years from that day, as the waters of the Saraswati Kundi would gently lap the shore, the moist evening air would still be rife with the sweet smell of spider lilies. Or perhaps in some bushes deep within the forest, hundreds of swan-like flowers would sway in the breeze and turn the woods into a heavenly garden of exhilarating beauty. So, what if Jugalprasad was not there to see it! So what if no one knew that it was an insane man named Jugalprasad who had planted all those trees, vines and flowers?

Bhanumati said, 'Look to your left, Babu-ji. That's the Tyandbaro tree, remember?'

I had not seen the tree at first, there was no moon in the sky tonight. But in the faint light of the stars, I now saw the tree of the kind and ever-protecting deity of wild buffaloes in the forest.

We had climbed down quite a bit, and reached the chhatim forest. The sweet smell was stronger than ever. I realized I was feeling a little heady.

I told Bhanumati, 'I want to sit here for some time.'

After spending a few meditative moments in the forest, as I was making my way down the hill, only one thought was resonating in my mind, 'Labtulia was gone forever, and so was Narha Baihar. But the hills of Mahalikharup and Dhanjhari still remained. Perhaps, a day would come when the people of the country would crave to see a forest. But all they would be able to see would be factories, chimneys, cars, roads, houses and buildings. Perhaps then, people would realize the value of the forest. Perhaps then, they would understand what the forest meant. And perhaps then, they would come running to the forest, much like they go on a pilgrimage to visit a holy place. Till that day, till such time when man realizes what he has done, let this forest remain just the way I had seen it tonight.'

[2]

Later that night, Jogru Panna and his elder brother apprised me of the current financial situation of the family. They had not been able to repay the moneylender's debt yet. In fact, they had had to borrow more money to buy a pair of buffaloes, for there was no other option. A trader from Gaya used to come and buy ghee from them, but even he had not been coming for the last three to four months. Almost twenty kilos of ghee were lying in one corner of the house, but there was no one to buy it from them.

Bhanumati came and sat at a little distance from us. Jugalprasad was a tea-addict, I knew he had brought his own tea and sugar with him. But perhaps out of shyness, he was hesitating to ask for hot water. I said, 'Can we get some hot water for a few cups of tea, Bhanumati?'

Princess Bhanumati had never made tea in all her life, nor did she know what it meant or looked like. There was no custom of drinking tea in these regions. On being explained what needed to be done, she fetched boiling water in an earthen pot. Her sister brought a few bowls made of stone. We offered tea to Bhanumati, but she politely declined. After some amount of initial hesitation, Jogru Panna took a couple of cautious sips, and then proceeded to finish the entire bowl of tea. He ended up asking for more.

After tea, everyone went back to work, but Bhanumati stayed behind. She said, 'I hope you'd be staying with us for a few days, Babu-ji. You've come after so many days this time. I won't let you leave tomorrow. In fact, I have an idea. Let's go see the Jhati Waterfall tomorrow. Lot of dangerous forests all around it, full of wild elephants. Lot of peacocks too. It's a fascinating place! There's nothing quite like it anywhere else in the world!'

I was quite amused by her simple, innocent words, and wanting to know what he thought of the 'world', I decided to probe her a bit more on the subject.

'Have you ever been to a city, Bhanumati?'

'No, Babu-ji.'

'But do you know the names of any cities?'

'Gaya, Munger, Patna.'

'Haven't you heard of Kolkata?'

'Yes, I have, Babu-ji.'

'Do you know where it is?'

'No, Babu-ji. I don't know that.'

'Do you know the name of the country we live in?'

'Why, yes, of course. We live in Gaya.'

'Have you heard of the country called India?'

Bhanumati shook her head and told me that she had never heard of India, and that she had never left Chakmakitola and gone anywhere. She even asked me where India was, and how far was it from Chakmakitola.

After some time, she said, 'My great grandfather had brought a buffalo home, it used to give plenty of milk twice a day. Things were different back then, Babu-ji, we weren't as poor as we are now. Had you come then, you could have had some lovely cream. My great grandfather used to make it himself. It was so sweet and delicious! These days, we don't get much milk from the buffaloes. In fact, no one seems to care about us anymore.'

After a few moments, she swung her arm around and said, 'Do you know, Babu-ji? Everything you see around you was our kingdom, many years ago. The whole wide world, in fact—all ours. The Gors and Santhals you see in the forest— they don't belong to the same caste as ours. We are the royal family. They are our subjects, they consider us their rulers.'

I did not know how to respond to her. Her regal pride seemed rather inapt when juxtaposed against the fact that her family was so deep in debt that even their cattle were being seized by the village moneylender.

I said, 'Yes, Bhanumati, I am aware of your glorious—'

'Yes, and then one day, a tiger took that buffalo of ours. The one that my great grandfather had brought.'

'I see. But how?'

'He had taken the buffalo out for grazing under the hill. That's where the tiger attacked.'

I said, 'Have you ever seen a tiger?'

Bhanumati raised her dark eyebrows and said, 'Oh, of course I have! Come to Chakmakitola in the winters, Babu-ji, you'll see what I mean. We can't even let our cattle roam free in the courtyard of the house then, they get dragged away by tigers—that too in the middle of the day!'

And then she suddenly called out, 'Nichhni, Nichhni, come here . . . quick!'

When her sister came and stood beside her, Bhanumati said, 'Nichhni, tell Babu-ji what the tigers used to do in our yard all of last winter? And how Jogru uncle had set a trap, but they avoided falling into it?'

Before the little girl could say anything, Bhanumati suddenly said, 'Oh, I'd almost forgotten! Will you please read me a letter? Someone had sent a letter from somewhere, but there's no one here who knows how to read, so it's been lying around. Go Nichhni, go get the letter. And ask Jogru uncle to come here.'

Nichhni was unable to locate the said letter; so, Bhanumati herself went looking for it and brought it back to be deciphered by me.

I said, 'When did this arrive?'

Bhanumati said, 'Must have been six-seven months now, Babu-ji. None of us can read, so we had kept it aside. We thought when Babu-ji would come, he will read it for us. Go Nichhni, go and call everyone. Tell them that Babu-ji will read the letter now.'

I held the six-seven-month-old unread missive against the light of the fire from Jugalprasad's earthen oven, while a roomful of people sat around me, waiting with bated breath. The letter was written in Hindi, and was addressed to King Dobru Panna. A trader from Patna had inquired of the King if there was any kendu leaf jungles around, and if there were, at what rate they were being leased out.

This letter was in no way related to this family, because they did not own any forest land in the region. And why just in the region, they did not own any land anywhere, for that matter. How was a city trader—who might have heard the name of King Dobru Panna—expected to know this tragic fact? Had he known the circumstances in which the former royal family now spent their days, he would not have wasted his money on paper and postage.

Jugalprasad was sitting at a little distance, cooking a meal for us. The fire from his earthen oven had illuminated a section of the veranda. The other half was being washed by moonlight, although the moon was still new. Its thin crescent had come out from behind the Dhanjhari hills just now and was visible over the treetops. In its light, I could clearly see another crescent before my eyes – that of the mountain range that lay beyond the valley. The playful sound of Chakmakitola's children was ringing in the air. What a beautiful night I was spending in these remote village! Even Bhanumati's silly stories seemed so lovely! I was suddenly reminded of my chat with Balabhadra on progress and prosperity.

What does man want, really? Prosperity or happiness? Of what use was mindless prosperity, if there was no sign of happiness in one's life? I myself knew of several people who had been immensely successful in their lives, but all at the cost of peace and happiness. They had everything they could ever want, which is precisely why they did not feel like enjoying anything anymore. Nothing seemed to give them joy. To them their own lives seemed monotonous, grey and meaningless. The window to their heart and soul had been long shut, so much so that no pleasure, no joy, no delight seemed to be able to make their way into their hearts and make them happy anymore.

Oh, if I could stay back here! If I could marry Bhanumati and start a new life with her. She, the simple, forest girl, would sit in this room by that fire and chatter away with those silly childish stories of hers. And I would sit and listen to her. To her, and to the calls of the hurals, the calls of the wild roosters, the trumpets of the wild elephants, the laughing of the hyenas. Bhanumati may be dark skinned, but there were very few girls back home in Bengal who were as pretty and as attractive as her. Not to forget that simple, spirited and uncomplicated mind of hers. A mind full of kindness, compassion and love.

I may be dreaming, but what a beautiful dream it was! Who wanted prosperity? I certainly did not. I would be glad to leave all the prosperity in the world to the likes of Balabhadra and Rashbehari Singh.

Jugalprasad asked me if he could serve my dinner. Bhanumati's family was impeccable in their hospitality. Vegetables were rare to come by in this region, but Jogru had still managed to find potatoes and brinjals for me. Fine pulses, bird meat, home-made ghee of the highest quality, rich fatty milk—they had given me more than I could ask for. And to top it all, Jugalprasad was a skilled cook.

I had asked Bhanumati, Jogru, Nichhni and others in the family to dine with me that night. Because none of them were used to this kind of food. I wanted them to sit with me and have their meal, but they refused to touch their food before I had finished my meal.

The next day, as I was about to leave, Bhanumati did something completely unexpected. She suddenly grabbed my hand and said, 'I won't let you go today, Babu-ji.'

I kept staring at her face for a long time and felt a deep sense of loss.

Thanks to her repeated pleas, I could not leave in the morning. After a hearty lunch in the afternoon, I bid them farewell. For the last time.

Once again, I found myself in the fond embrace of the forest. As I gently rode along, it seemed to me that Bhanumati was standing by the side of the path. Bhanumati! Not the girl, but the woman. I had never seen this image of hers, never witnessed this forlorn and wistful look in her eyes. She stood waiting in anticipation of her lover, looking at the path that he had traversed to disappear deep within the jungle. Perhaps he had gone up the hill to hunt, and would return soon. I shut my eyes and blessed her pure, honest soul with all my heart. Amidst a thousand fireflies glowing on the slopes of the Dhanjhari hills, amidst the sweet smell of Chhatim flowers that set the dew-wet evening air on fire, and amidst the sweet chitter of hundreds of birds all around, may her secret meeting with the man of her dreams bring her all the joys and bliss of life that she deserved.

Within a week of my return to the estate, I bid farewell to everyone and left Labtulia forever.

As I was leaving, Raju Pandey, Ganori Tewari, Jugalprasad, Asrafi tindal and many others walked alongside my palanquin all the way to the new settlement of Maharajtola. Matuknath

Pandit kept chanting his Sanskrit slokas all along, finally blessing me with health and happiness. Raju said, 'Labtulia will become barren after you are gone, Huzoor.'

It may be relevant to state here that in this region, the word 'barren' was used in a very wide context. For instance, if someone was munching fried corn, and was hating its taste, he might say, 'This corn is so barren'. I do not know in what context the word was said to me that day.

There was a girl who had been standing in the courtyard of the cutcherry all morning. As I sat in my palanquin, I noticed that she was weeping bitterly. It was Kunta.

Giving a new lease of life to the helpless Kunta was one of the very few good deeds of my life as a manager of the estate. Among my several regrets was the fact that I could not do anything for the unfortunate forest girl Manchi. Lord knew where she was, and in what condition. If she would have been here today, I would have ensured that she had enough to take care of herself.

As I was crossing the borders of Narha Baihar, I saw Nakchhedi's hut, and I remembered Manchi's face more than ever. Suratiya was standing outside the hut, on seeing my palanquin, she came running. Chhaniya followed behind her.

'Where are you going, Babu-ji?'

'Bhagalpur. Where is your father?'

'Jhollutola. He's gone to get some seeds for the maize. When will you be back?'

'I won't be back.'

'Come now, I know that's not true! You're just pulling my leg, aren't you?'

When I had crossed the borders of Narha Baihar, I peeped out of the palanquin and looked back one last time.

Hundreds of huts and shanties, scores of villages, people conversing with each other, trading in the markets, little boys and girls playing and shouting, cows and buffaloes, barns and carts. It was I who had chopped off miles after miles of dense forests to set up this busy and overcrowded human habitat over the last six-seven years. Just the day before, this was exactly what everyone was talking about, 'What you have done is amazing and extremely commendable, Babu-ji! You have completely changed the face of Narha and Labtulia.'

Those were the words that hurt me the most right now.

Indeed! I had completely changed the face of Narha and Labtulia!

As I looked at the Mahalikharup Hills and the Mohanpura Forest Reserve in the distant horizon, I felt an aching sense of emptiness within me, and I bowed my head.

May the ancient gods of the forest forgive me all my sins. Farewell!

[3]

This was all a long time ago—almost fifteen–sixteen years had passed by since then.

I was sitting under a chestnut tree and thinking about those good old days.

The sun was leaning towards the western horizon now.

Not a day went by when my heart did not pine for the forests of Narha and Labtulia—the irredeemable, irreplaceable bounty of nature that had disappeared off the face of the earth all because of me. Every now and then, from a misty, forgotten past, the jungles of Saraswati Kundi and Mahalikharup Hills waved out to me and called my name in a faint whisper. And I often wondered how they all were these days—those beautiful, innocent people I had met back in the forest? Had Kunta finally been able to find some happiness in her life? Suratiya must have grown up by now! Did Matuknath still teach in his school these days? Did Bhanumati still go up the hills of Dhanjhari to strew shiuli flowers over her ancestors' graves? Rakhal Babu's wife, Dhruba, Giridharilal—who knows in what condition they were in after all these years?

And I often thought of Manchi. Had she found her penitence and gone back to her husband? Or was she still plucking tea leaves in the hills of Assam?

So many years had passed by. If only I could see their faces once again.

~ ~ ~